tasha found herself facing Mario.

'You danced w... ...d.

'...ever be m...

'...l you ask...

'No,' he said. 'I'm ... to ask you.'

But ...he spoke his arm went around her waist in a ...p too firm for her to resist, even if she had wa...d to.

On... before they had danced together. One night in ...nice, when they had been having supper at an ...door café in St Mark's Square, a band had sta...d to play and before she'd known it she'd be... waltzing in his arms.

'Is ...is all right?' he'd whispered.

'I'... et you know later,' she had teased.

It ...d lasted only a few minutes, and she had pro...ised herself that one day she would dance ...him again. But the next day they had broken ...and it had never happened again. Until now.

It was unnerving to feel his arms about her, his hand on her waist, holding her close. Her heart was beating softly but fervently. She glanced at him, trying to know if he felt the same. Would he invite her to dance with...

79 697 423 5

...nced with everyone else', he observed...

...be any turn?'

...you ask me...

...no. I'm not going to ask you...

...spoke up in worst among her wrist...
...to turn for her to rest, even if she had...

On... decorous... and danced together. One night
in... When they had been having supper at
...door-cum in St. Mark's square, a band had
...to play and before she'd known it she'd
...hurling in his arms.

...'all right', he'd whispered.

...you know how', she had teased.

...lasted only a few minutes, and she had
reminded herself that one day she would dance
...him again. But the next day they had broken
...it and never happened again. Until now.

...tune-vibes, to feel his arms about her, his
...head on her waist, pulling her close. Her heart
was beating wildly, fearfully. She glanced at
...trying to... he felt the same. Would he
invite her to dance with him again?

REUNITED WITH HER ITALIAN EX

BY
LUCY GORDON

Published in Great Britain 2015
by Mills & Boon, an imprint of Harlequin (UK) Limited,
Eton House, 18-24 Paradise Road, Richmond, Surrey, TW9 1SR

© 2015 Lucy Gordon

ISBN: 978-0-263-25117-3

23-0315

Harlequin (UK) Limited's policy is to use papers that are natural, renewable and recyclable products and made from wood grown in sustainable forests. The logging and manufacturing processes conform to the legal environmental regulations of the country of origin.

Printed and bound in Spain
by CPI, Barcelona

Lucy Gordon cut her writing teeth on magazine journalism, interviewing many of the world's most interesting men. She's had many unusual experiences, which have often provided the background for her books. Once, while staying in Venice, she met a Venetian who proposed in two days and they've been married ever since. Naturally this has affected her writing, in which romantic Italian men tend to feature strongly. Two of her books have won a Romance Writers of America RITA® Award. You can visit her website at lucy-gordon.com.

PROLOGUE

VENICE, THE MOST romantic city in the world.

That was what people said, and Natasha was becoming convinced that it was true. Where else could she have met the man of her dreams within hours of arriving, and known so soon that she was his and he simply must become hers?

Sitting in a café by a small canal, she looked out at the sun glittering on the water. Nearby she could see a gondola containing a young man and woman, wrapped in each other's arms.

Just like us, she thought, recalling her first gondola ride in the arms of the man who had changed the world in moments.

Mario Ferrone, young, handsome, with dancing eyes and a rich chuckle that seemed to encompass the world. She'd met Mario just after she'd arrived in Venice on a well-earned holiday. He'd insisted on showing her the city. As his brother owned the hotel where she was staying, she'd briefly thought this a professional service, but that idea soon changed. There was an instant attraction between them, and nothing had ever seemed more wonderful than the time they spent together.

Until then, there had been little in her life that could

be called romance. She was slim, pretty, humorous, with no difficulty attracting admirers. But where men were concerned she had an instinctive defensiveness.

It went back to her childhood, when her father had abandoned his wife and ten-year-old daughter for another woman. Until that moment Natasha's life had been happy. Her father had seemed to adore her as she adored him. But suddenly he was gone, never to get in touch again.

Never trust a man, her mother had told her. *They'll always let you down.*

She'd been content to heed the warning until Mario came into her life and everything turned upside down.

Her own reactions confused her. Her heart was drawn to Mario as never before to any other man. Sometimes her mother's voice echoed in her mind.

No man can be trusted, Natasha. Remember that.

But Natasha felt certain that Mario was different to all other men—more honest, more trustworthy, more faithfully loving.

Last night he'd kissed her with even greater fervour than before, murmuring, 'Tomorrow I want to…' Then he'd stopped, seeming confused.

'Yes?' she'd whispered. 'What do you want?'

'I can't tell you now…but tomorrow everything will be different. Goodnight, *mi amore*.'

Now here she was in the café where they often met, waiting for him to appear and transform her world yet again.

She almost ached with the yearning to know what he'd meant by 'everything will be different'. Was he going to propose marriage? Surely he must.

Oh, please hurry, she thought. How could Mario keep her on tenterhooks when it mattered so much?

Suddenly, she heard his voice call, 'Natasha!' Looking up, she saw him walking by the canal, waving to her from a distance.

'Sorry I'm late,' he said, joining her at the table. 'I got held up.'

She had a strange feeling that he was on edge.

'Is everything all right?' she asked.

'It will be, very soon,' he said.

His eyes never left her and every moment her conviction grew that tonight they were going to take the next step—whatever it might be.

He took her hand. 'There's something I've been trying to tell you for days but—'

'Trying? Is it so hard to tell me?'

'It could be.' His eyes met hers. 'Some things just aren't easy to say.'

Her heart was beating with anticipation and excitement. She knew what he was going to say, and she longed to hear it.

'That depends how much you want to say them,' she whispered, leaning close so that her breath brushed his face. 'Perhaps you don't really want to say this.'

'Oh, yes, you don't know how much it matters.'

But I do know, she thought happily. He was going to tell her how much she meant to him. In a moment her life would be transformed.

She took his hand in hers, sending him a silent message about her willingness to draw closer to him.

'Go on,' she whispered.

He hesitated and she regarded him, puzzled. Was it really so hard for him to reach out to her?

'Natasha—I want to tell you—'

'Yes—yes—tell me.'

'I'm not good at this—'

'You don't need to be good at it,' she urged, tightening her clasp on his hand. 'Just say it—'

'Well—'

'Traitor!'

The screamed word stunned them both. Natasha looked up to see a woman standing by the table, glaring at them. She was in her thirties, voluptuous, and would have been beautiful but for the look of livid hatred she cast on Mario.

'Traitor!' she screamed. *'Liar! Deceiver!'*

Mario's face was tense and pale as Natasha had never seen it before. He rose and confronted the woman, speaking angrily in Italian and pointing for her to leave. She screamed back at him in English. Then turned to Natasha.

'It's about time you knew what he is really like. One woman isn't enough for him.'

She raved on until Mario drew her into a corner, arguing with her vigorously. Natasha could no longer hear the words but there was no mistaking the intensity between them. The dark-haired woman's rage grew with every moment.

'He's a liar and a cheat,' she screamed in perfect English.

'Mario,' Natasha said, 'who is this woman? Do you really know her?'

'Oh, yes, he knows me,' the woman spat. 'You wouldn't believe how well he knows me.'

'Tania, that's enough,' Mario said, white-faced. 'I told you—'

'Oh, yes, you told me. Traitor! Traitor! *Traditore!*'

For a moment Natasha was tempted to thrust herself between them and tell Mario what she thought of him in no uncertain terms. But then her impetuous temper flared even higher, driving her to a course of action even more fierce and desperate. While they were still absorbed in their furious encounter, she fled.

She ran every step of the way to the hotel, then up to her room, pausing at the desk to demand her bill. Nothing mattered but to get away from here before Mario returned. It had all been a deception. She'd believed in him because she'd wanted to believe, and she should have known better. Now she was paying the price.

'You were right,' she muttered to her mother's ghost. 'They're all the same.'

The ghost was too tactful to say *I told you so*, but she was there in Natasha's consciousness as she finished packing, paid her bill and fled.

She took a boat taxi across the water to the mainland, and from there she switched to a motor taxi.

'Airport,' she told the driver tensely.

Oh, Mario, she thought as the car roared away. *Traitor. Traditore.*

CHAPTER ONE

Two years later...

'I'M SORRY, NATASHA, but the answer's no, and that's final. You just have to accept it.'

Natasha's face was distorted by anger as she clutched the phone.

'Don't tell me what I have to do,' she snapped into the receiver. 'You said you were eager for anything I wrote—'

'That was a long time ago. Things have changed. I can't buy any more of your work. Those are my orders.'

Natasha took a shuddering breath as yet another rejection slammed into her.

'But you're the editor,' she protested. 'Surely it's you who gives the orders.'

'The magazine's owner tells us what to do and that's final. You're out. Finished. Goodbye.'

The editor hung up, leaving Natasha staring at the phone in fury and anguish.

'Another one?' asked a female voice behind her. 'That's the sixth editor who's suddenly turned against you after buying your work for ages.'

Natasha turned to her friend Helen, who was also her flatmate.

'I can't believe it,' she groaned. 'It's like there's a spider at the centre of a web controlling them all, telling them to freeze me out.'

'But there is. Surely you know that. The spider's name is Elroy Jenson.'

It's true, Natasha thought reluctantly. Jenson owned a huge media empire that until recently had provided her with a good living. But he'd taken a fancy to her and pursued her relentlessly, ignoring her pleas to be left alone. Finally he'd gone too far, forcing her to slap his face hard enough to make him yell. One of his employees had seen them and spread the story.

'Everyone knows you made him look a fool,' Helen said sympathetically. 'So now he's your enemy. It's a pity about that quick temper of yours, Natasha. You had every right to be angry but…well…'

'But I should have paused before I clobbered him. I should have been calm and controlled and thought about the future. Hah!'

'Yes, I know it sounds ironic, but look at the price you've paid.'

'Yes,' Natasha said with a heavy sigh.

As a freelance journalist her success had been dazzling. Magazines and newspapers clamoured for her sassy, insightful articles.

Until now.

'How can one man have so much power?' she groaned.

'Perhaps you need to go abroad for a while,' Helen suggested. 'Until Jenson forgets all about you.'

'That would be difficult—'

'It needn't be. The agency found me a job in Italy, doing publicity. It would mean going out there for a while.

I was about to call them and say they'd have to find someone else, but why don't you go instead?'

'But I can't just… That's a mad idea.'

'Sometimes madness is the best way. It could be just what you need now.'

'But I don't speak Italian.'

'You don't have to. It's an international thing, promoting the city all over the world.'

'It's not Venice, is it?' Natasha asked, suddenly tense.

'No, don't worry. I know you wouldn't want to go to Venice. It's Verona, the city of *Romeo and Juliet*. Some of that story is real, and tourists love to see Juliet's balcony and other places where different scenes are set. So a group of luxury hotel owners have clubbed together to create some publicity for the place. Of course, I know you're not exactly a fan of romance—'

'It doesn't bother me,' Natasha said quickly. 'I'm not going into retreat just because one man— Well, anyway—'

'Fine. So why don't you take this job?'

'But how can I? It's yours.'

'I really wish you would. I accepted it impulsively because I'd had a row with my boyfriend. I thought we were finished, but we've made up and it would really suit me if you went instead of me.'

'But if they're expecting you—'

'I've been dealing with the agency. I'll put you in touch with them and sing your praises. Natasha, you can't let your life be ruled by a man you haven't seen for two years. Especially when he was a cheating rogue. Your words, not mine.'

'Yes,' she murmured. 'I said that. And I meant it.'

'Then go. Put Mario behind you and put Elroy behind you, too. Seize your chance for a fresh start.'

Natasha took a deep breath. 'All right,' she said. 'I'll do it.'

'Fine. Now, let's get started.'

Helen logged on to her computer and contacted the agency. Moments later, Natasha was reading an email, written in efficient English, offering her the assignment and giving her instructions:

You will be dealing with Giorgio Marcelli. The hotel owners employ him to handle publicity. He looks forward to welcoming you to Verona.

'You see, it's a no-brainer,' Helen said. 'I'll leave you to have a think.'

She departed.

Left alone, Natasha stared out of the window, trying to decide what to do. Despite what Helen said, it wasn't easy to make up her mind.

'Not Venice,' she had asserted and Helen had reassured her, because she knew that nothing would persuade Natasha ever to go back to that beautiful romantic city where her heart had been broken.

Natasha thought back to herself as a very young woman, haunted by her mother's warnings never to trust a man. She had pursued a successful career, devoting her time to her writing, avoiding emotional relationships. Of course she could flirt and enjoy male company. But never for very long. Eventually distrust would make her back away from any man who attracted her.

She'd been glad of it, sure that caution would protect her from suffering her mother's fate. On that she had been resolved.

Until she'd met Mario.

He had affected her as no other man ever had. Together they had walked the streets of Venice, drifting by the canals. In one tiny alley he'd drawn her into the shadows for their first kiss. Despite her attempts to obliterate the memory, it still lived in her now.

Her whole body had responded to him, coming alive in ways she had never dreamed of before. She could sense the same in him, although every instinct told her that he was an experienced lover. Wherever they went, women had thrown admiring glances at him and regarded Natasha with envy. She'd guessed they were thinking how lucky she was to be sharing his bed. That day had never come, although several times Natasha had been on the verge of giving in to temptation.

As the day of her departure neared, Mario had begged her to stay with him a little longer. Blissfully happy, she had agreed.

Even now, two years later, remembering that happiness was the most painful thing of all, despite her frantic attempts to banish it from her memory, her heart, her life.

She imagined his face when he'd returned to the table and found her gone.

Vanished into thin air, she thought. *As far as he's concerned I no longer exist, and he no longer exists to me.*

In fact, the man she'd believed him to be had never existed. That was what she had to face.

Bitterly, she replayed the scene. She'd been so sure that he was about to declare his feelings, but when he'd said, 'There's something I've been trying to tell you for days,' he'd actually been planning to dump her.

He'd probably spent the afternoon with Tania, perhaps in her bed.

She thought he was being unfaithful to her with me.

In fact he was being unfaithful to both of us. That's the kind of man he is.

After fleeing from Venice, Natasha had done everything she could to disappear for ever, changing her email address and phone number.

But one email from him had just managed to get through before the old address was cut off:

Where did you vanish to? What happened? Are you all right?

Yes, she thought defiantly. *I'm all right. I got rid of the only person who could hurt me. And nobody is ever going to do that to me again.*

She'd never replied to Mario, merely instructing the server to block his emails. Then she'd moved in with Helen. If he came to her old flat he would find the door locked against him as firmly as her heart was locked against him.

At night she would lie awake, dismayed by the violence of her response. He had touched her emotions with an intensity that warned her to escape while there was still time. That way lay the only safety.

Oh, Mario, she thought. *Traitor. Traditore.*

Since then she'd devoted herself to work, making such an impression that she came to the attention of Elroy Jenson. The media magnate had propositioned her, certain that a mere freelance journalist would never refuse him. When she did refuse he couldn't believe it, persisting until she was forced to slap his face and bring her successful career to a sudden end.

After that, her life had been on a downward spiral. Her

income had collapsed. Now she could barely afford the small rent she paid on the room she rented from Helen.

The time had come for firm action. And if that meant leaping into the unknown, she would do it. The unknown had its attractions, and suddenly she was ready for anything.

She exchanged brisk emails with Giorgio, the publicity manager. He informed her that she would be staying at the Dimitri Hotel and a driver would meet her at the airport. Two days later she embarked on the journey that might lead to a triumphant new life, or a disaster. Either way, she was venturing into the unknown.

During the flight to Verona she kept her mind firmly concentrated on work. *Romeo and Juliet* was a story that had long touched the world: two young people who fell in love despite the enmity of their families. In the end, they chose to die rather than live without each other.

Legend said that Shakespeare's play was based on real events. The lovers had really lived and died. It would be her job to immerse herself in the story and entice the world to join her.

The driver was at the airport, holding up a placard bearing the words 'Dimitri Hotel'. He greeted her with relief, and ushered her into the car for the three-mile journey to Verona.

'The hotel is in the centre of town,' he said. 'Right next to the river.'

Verona was an ancient, beautiful city. Delighted, she gazed out of the window, enchanted by the hints of another, mysterious age. At last they drew up outside a large elaborate building.

'Here we are. Dimitri Hotel,' the driver said.

As she entered the elegant lobby, a man came forward.

He was in his sixties, heavily built, with a plump, smiling face. He greeted her in English.

'The agency told me there had been a change of plan,' he said. 'Apparently the original candidate couldn't make it, but they say you have excellent credentials.'

'Thank you. I'm an experienced journalist. I hope I can live up to your expectations.'

'I'm sure you will. I'm very glad you're here. I promised the President the lady would be here for him tonight and it's never good to disappoint him.'

He gave a comical shudder which made Natasha ask, 'Is he a difficult man? Scary?'

'Sometimes. Mostly he's very determined. People don't cross him if they can help it. He only bought this hotel just under two years ago and set about changing everything practically the first day. There's been a massive redecoration, and the staff has been reorganised to suit him. Everything has to be done his way. Nobody argues.'

'You called him the President.'

'President of the *Comunità*. It was his idea that a group of hotel owners of Verona, the *Comunità*, should all work together. They thought it would be an easy-going organisation but he said it needed leadership. The others just did as he suggested and named him President.

'A while back one of the other owners thought of challenging him for the top job, but he was "persuaded" not to. Nobody knows how, but neither was anyone surprised.

'When he gives his orders we jump to attention, especially me, because he could fire me any time he likes. I'm only telling you so that you'll take care not to offend him.

'We'll dine with him tonight and tomorrow you will meet all the *Comunità* members. They're looking forward to having you spread the word about our lovely city.'

'But isn't the word already out? Surely *Romeo and Juliet* is the most famous love story in the world?'

'True, but we need to make people realise how they can become involved. Now, I'll show you to your room.'

On their way up they passed two men having a noisy argument. One was clearly in command, yelling, *'Capisci? Capisci?'* so fiercely that the other backed off.

'What does that word mean?' Natasha asked curiously. 'It really scared the other guy.'

'It means "Do you understand?"' Giorgio laughed. 'It's really just a way of saying "You'll do as I say. *Get it?*"'

'It sounds useful.'

'It can be, if you're trying to make it clear who's in charge.' He grinned. 'I've had it said to me a few times. Here's your room.'

Like the rest of the place, her room was elegant and luxurious. A huge window looked out over the river, where the sun shone on the water. The atmosphere seemed peaceful and she took a deep contented breath.

When she'd unpacked she took a shower and began work on her appearance. For this meeting she was going to look her best.

She was attractive so not too much effort was required. Her blue eyes were large and expressive. Her blonde hair had just a touch of red that showed in some lights but not in others.

Natasha pinned her hair high on her head, suggesting businesslike severity. Usually, she preferred to let it flow, curved and luscious about her shoulders in a more relaxed way.

But not tonight, she mused, studying herself in the mirror. *Tonight I'm a businesswoman, here to earn a living.*

She fixed her hair firmly away from her face until she felt it conveyed the serious message she intended. Giorgio had warned her that the owner was a man to be reckoned with, but she could deal with that. She'd meet him on his own ground, a woman to be reckoned with.

'I did the right thing in coming here,' she whispered. 'Everything's going to be fine.'

In Venice, a city where most of the roads were water, motor cars could only come as far as Piazzale Roma, the car park on the edge of town. In the glowing heat of a sunny day, Mario Ferrone went to collect his car, accompanied by his brother Damiano.

'It sounds like your hotel is doing really well,' Damiano said. 'You've got a great future ahead of you.'

'I think I just might have,' Mario said, grinning.

'No doubt,' Damiano said cheerfully. 'After all, look who taught you.'

This was a reference to Damiano's successful career as the owner of several hotels. Mario had learned the trade working in many of them and had finally become ambitious for his own establishment.

'That's right, I learned from the best,' Mario said. 'And having a place in Verona is a help. Several of us hoteliers have got together to promote the *Romeo and Juliet* angle.'

'The city of lovers,' Damiano said wryly. 'That should suit you. You'd hardly believe some of the tales I've heard about you.'

'Not recently,' Mario said quickly.

'No, you've settled down these last couple of years, but before that I remember you gave a whole new meaning to the term "bad boy".'

'Most of us do before we find the right woman,' Mario pointed out.

'True. I wasn't a saint before I met Sally. But you haven't met your "Sally", so what made you suddenly become virtuous?'

'Virtuous? Me? No need to insult me.'

Damiano grinned. 'So is it just a smokescreen?'

'No. I really have changed, not necessarily for the better.'

'Don't say that. You're much improved—quieter, more serious, more grown-up...'

'More suspicious and demanding, nastier sometimes,' Mario said quietly.

'Hey, why do you put yourself down?'

'Perhaps because I know myself better than anyone else does. I'm not the nice guy I used to be—if I ever was.'

'So what made it happen?'

Mario clapped him on the shoulder. 'Don't ask me. It's a long story, and one that—well, that I don't care to think of too often. Let's leave it. I'd better be going. Giorgio has hired a journalist he says will be brilliant at promoting the *Romeo and Juliet* angle. I'm meeting her for dinner when I get back tonight.'

'Best of luck. Goodbye, brother.'

They embraced each other. Damiano stood back, waving as Mario turned out of the car park and across the causeway that led to the mainland.

From Venice to Verona was nearly seventy-five miles. During the journey Mario reflected wryly on his brother's words. Damiano didn't know that one of the turning points in Mario's life had been Damiano's marriage to Sally, four years earlier. Mario had been strongly attracted to Sally, something he'd had to fight. He'd fought it by working in Damiano's hotels in Rome, Florence, Milan, only rarely returning to Venice.

Until then his life had been free and easy. He was young, charming and handsome, with no trouble attracting women. He'd had many girlfriends. Too many, he now realised.

He'd returned to Venice for the birth of his brother's son and found, to his relief, that Sally no longer attracted him, except as a sister. He'd settled into a life of work and pleasure.

Then had come the other great turning point in his life, when he'd met the one woman who could make a difference, drive away the loneliness and give his existence meaning.

Fantasy dictated that she should feel the same and throw herself into his arms. The bitter reality was that she had walked out on him, slamming the door in his face, condemning him to a bleak isolation that was all the worse because he had glimpsed a glorious future, and come so close to embracing it.

Buying the hotel two years ago had been a lucky chance. The owner was eager to sell and accepted a discounted price, and now Mario felt that he was headed for success and independence. If he did nothing else in his life he would triumph in this, he vowed to himself. With that hope to guide him he could banish the pain and bleakness of the last two years.

At last he reached the hotel. Giorgio came to the entrance to greet him.

'It's all set up,' he said.

'Has the lady arrived?'

'Yes, an hour ago. She's not who I was expecting. The

agency made a last-minute change, but she seems serious and professional.'

'I can't wait to meet her.' As they walked across the elegant lobby, Mario looked around him at the place he was
beginning to regard as his kingdom. 'You know, I have
the best possible feeling about this,' he said. 'We're on the
right road, and we're going to reach a great destination.'

'One where the money is,' Giorgio supplied with a
grin.

'Of course, but that's not the only thing. Somehow,
everything is beginning to feel right.'

'That's the spirit. Get settled in and then I'll introduce
you to... Mario? Mario, is something wrong?'

But Mario didn't hear him. His attention had been
drawn to the great staircase that led to the next floor. He
was staring at it like a man stunned. A young woman
was walking down the stairs. She moved slowly, pausing
to look at the paintings on the wall, so that at first she
didn't seem to notice Mario standing by the bottom step.

When her eyes came to rest on Mario she stopped suddenly, as if unable to believe her eyes.

A terrible stillness came over Natasha as she looked down
the staircase, trying to understand what was happening.
It was impossible that Mario should be standing there,
staring up at her with a thunderstruck expression.

Impossible.

And yet it was true. He was there, looking like a man
who'd seen a nightmare come to life.

She tried to move but the stillness enveloped her. Now
he was climbing the stairs slowly, as though unwilling
to approach her too quickly or come too close. When he
spoke it was uneasily.

'I believe…we've met before.'

A dozen answers clamoured in her head, but at last she heard herself say, 'No, never.'

That took him off-guard, she could see. While he struggled for a reply, Giorgio's voice reached them from the bottom of the stairs.

'Aha! I see you two are getting acquainted.' Waving cheerfully, he climbed up to join them.

'Natasha, let me introduce Mario Ferrone, the owner of the hotel and President of the *Comunità*. Mario, this is Natasha Bates, the lady who's going to tell the world about Verona.'

Mario inclined his head formally. '*Buongiorno, signorina.* It's a pleasure to meet you.'

'How do you do?' she said, nodding towards him.

'Let's go and eat,' Giorgio said, 'and we can have a good talk.'

Downstairs, a table was laid for them in a private room overlooking the river. Giorgio led Natasha to the chair nearest the window and drew it out for her.

A waiter hurried in, eager to serve the hotel's owner. His manner was respectful and she was reminded of Giorgio's words:

'When he gives his orders we all jump to attention…'

She'd known him as a cheeky playboy, always ready to laugh and use his charm. It was hard to see the man he'd been then as the stern authoritarian that Giorgio described now. But his face had changed, growing slightly thinner, firmer, more intense. Even his smile had something reserved about it.

Turning her eyes to him briefly, she caught him glancing at her and realised that he was studying her too. What did he see? Had she also changed, becoming older, sterner, less relaxed? Probably. Perhaps she should be glad, for it would make her stronger. And she was going to need strength now.

Giorgio claimed her attention, filling her wine glass, smiling at her with an air of deferential admiration. He had probably been handsome in his youth, and still had the air of a practised flirt.

'How much were you told about this job?' he asked her.

'Only that some Verona hotel owners had got together to promote the city's connection with *Romeo and Juliet*,' Natasha said.

'That's right. It's already well promoted by the council, which works hard to bring tourists here. But the hotel owners wanted to enjoy a bit more of the spotlight, so they formed the Comunità di Verona Ospitalità so that they could make the most of being in the town that saw the greatest love story in the world.

'Shakespeare didn't invent *Romeo and Juliet*. There really were two families called Montague and Capulet, and they did have children who fell in love, and died. It happened in the early fourteenth century. In the next two hundred years the story was told and retold, until finally Shakespeare based his play on the legend. Tourists come here to see "Juliet's balcony" and imagine the balcony scene happening there.'

'Which it didn't,' Mario observed drily. 'The house belonged to a family called Capello, but the council added the balcony less than a hundred years ago.'

'But if everyone knows that—' Natasha mused.

'They know it but they ignore it,' Giorgio said cheerfully. 'People are often tempted to believe only what they want to.'

'How true,' Natasha murmured. 'That's why we're all so easily taken in.'

She didn't look directly at Mario as she said these words, but she had a sense that he was watching her with an air of tension that matched her own.

'And that's what we can make use of,' Giorgio said. 'Juliet's balcony, Juliet's tomb, where Romeo killed himself because he couldn't bear life without her, and where she killed herself for the same reason. Is it true? It is if we want it to be.'

'Oh, yes,' Natasha mused. 'True if we want it to be—until one day we have to face the fact that it isn't true, however much we want it.'

'But that's show business,' Giorgio said. 'Creating a fantasy that makes people happy.'

'And what more could we want than that?' Mario asked.

He raised his glass and drank from it, seemingly oblivious to her. But the next moment he said, 'Tell us something about yourself, *signorina*.'

She turned her head, meeting his eyes directly. 'What did you say?'

'I said I'd like to know about you. I'm sure there is much you could tell us. What are your family obligations? Are you free to live in Verona for several weeks, or is there someone at home who will be missing you?'

'I suppose there must be,' Giorgio said. He assumed a chivalrous air. 'This is a lovely lady. She must have crowds of men following her.'

'That doesn't mean that I let them catch up,' Natasha teased.

'Some women are very good at keeping out of sight,' Mario said.

'Of course,' Giorgio agreed. 'That's the secret. Let them chase after you, but don't let any of them get close enough to know what you're thinking and feeling.' He kissed her hand gallantly. '*Signorina*, I can see you're an expert in keeping your admirers wondering.'

'But just what are they wondering?' Mario asked. 'Will any of them arrive here to assert his "rights"?'

'What rights?' Giorgio demanded. 'She's not married.'

'That's irrelevant,' Mario observed. 'You have only to study *Romeo and Juliet* to see that men and women make that decision within a few moments of meeting. And nobody dares get in their way.'

'When people fear betrayal they can get violent,' Giorgio agreed.

Natasha nodded. 'And if they know for sure that they've been betrayed, there's no knowing how far they'll go to make someone sorry,' she mused, letting her glance rest on Mario.

She was glad to see that he understood the silent message. Before her eyes he flinched and averted his gaze. When he spoke again it was in a voice so defiantly businesslike that it told its own story.

'So we can expect a jealous lover to follow you out here?' he said curtly.

She faced him, reading the chilly hostility in his eyes, answering it with her own.

'On the contrary. You can be certain that nothing will make me leave before my work is finished,' she said calmly. 'Unlike some people, I'm honest about my intentions. I don't make promises and break them.'

'That's not exactly what I asked.'

No, she thought. *You asked whether I'd had the nerve to replace you with another man.*

She gave him her most confident smile, as though his questions merely amused her.

'Let me assure you that I am free,' she said. 'No man tells me what to do, and if anyone tried—' she leaned closer to him '—I would make him regret that he ever knew me.' She added significantly, 'I'm good at that.'

'I believe you,' he said.

Giorgio glanced at them curiously. 'Hey, do you two already know each other?'

'No,' Natasha said quickly, before Mario could speak.

'Really? I feel like I'm watching a fencing match.'

'It's more fun that way,' she said lightly. 'Go on telling me about Verona. Unless, of course, Signor Ferrone has decided he doesn't wish to employ me. In which case I'll just pack up and go. Shall I?'

She made as if to rise but Mario's hand detained her.

'No need for that,' he said harshly. 'Let's get on with the job.'

'Yes, that's the only thing that matters,' she said, falling back into the chair.

For a moment he kept his hand on her arm. 'So we are agreed? You will stay?'

'I will stay.'

CHAPTER TWO

MARIO RELEASED HER. 'As long as we understand each other.'

Natasha drew a tense breath as the bitter irony of those words swept over her. They had never understood each other. Nor could they ever, except on the lines of mutual defensiveness and mistrust.

She turned to Giorgio, assuming her most business-like tone.

'So it's time I consulted with the Publicity Manager. Tell me, what are my instructions?'

'We must go on a trip around Verona,' he said, 'study-ing all the significant places. Especially the balcony. These days you can even get married in Juliet's house. And afterwards the bride and groom always come out onto the balcony for the photographs.'

'Useful,' she said, taking out her notebook and be-ginning to write. 'The balcony scene is the most famous part of the story.'

'Yes, people love to imagine Juliet standing there, yearning for her lover, saying, "Romeo, Romeo, where art thou Romeo?"'

'She doesn't say "where",' Natasha objected. 'She says "Wherefore". It means "Why?" She's saying "Why did you have to be Romeo, a Montague, and my enemy?" In Shakespeare's time, if you wanted to know why someone had behaved in a certain way, you'd say—' she assumed a dramatic attitude '"—Wherefore did thou do this, varlet?"'

'Varlet?' Giorgio queried.

'It means rascal. You'd say it to someone who'd behaved disgustingly.'

Giorgio gave a crack of laughter. 'I must remember that. Rascal—*briccone*.'

'Or *traditore*,' Natasha observed lightly.

'Aha! So you know some Italian words?' Giorgio said eagerly.

'One or two,' she said with a fair assumption of indifference.

'I'd give a lot to know how you learned that particular one,' he said cheekily.

'You'll just have to wonder,' she chuckled.

Mario wasn't looking at her. He seemed completely occupied with his wine.

A man appeared in the doorway, signalling to Giorgio.

'I've got to leave you for a moment,' he said. 'But I'll be back.' He laid a hand on Natasha's shoulder. 'Don't go away. I have a very good feeling about this.'

'So have I,' she said. 'I'll be right here.'

When Giorgio had gone, Mario refilled her wine glass.

'Be cautious about Giorgio,' he said. 'He turns on the charm as part of his trade.'

'But of course,' she said cheerfully. 'It's a form of show business. No harm in that.'

'As long as you're not taken in.'

'I'm not. These days, nothing and nobody manages to deceive me.'

He raised his glass to her in an ironic salute.

'This is quite a coincidence,' he said. 'I wonder which of us is more shocked.'

'We'll never know.'

'Just now you were very determined to say we didn't know each other.'

'Would you have said differently?' she asked, watching him.

'No, but I doubt I'd have said it so fast or emphatically. You denied knowing me as though your life depended on it.'

'But we didn't know each other. Once we believed we did but we were both wrong. You thought I was easy to fool or you wouldn't have wasted your time on me. You never reckoned on Tania turning up and showing me what you were really like.'

'I admit I once had a relationship with Tania, but it was over.'

'Was it? I don't think she believed that. She still felt you were hers. That's why she felt so betrayed when she saw us. No, it was me you were planning to leave. That's why you kept hinting about something you wanted to tell me. You said it wasn't easy, but then it's never easy to dump someone, is it?'

He turned very pale. 'Isn't it? You dumped me without any trouble.'

'Dumping you was the easiest thing I'd ever done, but that's because you gave me cause.'

'But the way you did it—vanishing so that I could never find you. Can you imagine what I went through? It was like searching for a ghost. I nearly went mad because you denied me any chance to explain—'

'Explain what? That you were fooling around with

both of us? If you'd been the man I thought you— Well, let's leave it there. You weren't that man and you never could be. It's best if we remain strangers now.'

'*Remain?*' he echoed sharply. But then his voice changed to wry, slightly bitter acceptance. 'Yes, we always were strangers, weren't we?'

'Always were, always will be. That's a very good business arrangement.'

'And you're a businesswoman?'

'Exactly. It's what I choose to be. *Capisci?*'

He nodded. '*Capisco*. I understand.'

'From now on, it's all business. The past didn't happen. It was an illusion.'

'An illusion—yes. I guessed that when you vanished into thin air. And now you've reappeared just as suddenly.'

'Another illusion. I'm not really here.'

'So if I look away you'll vanish again?'

'Perhaps that's what I ought to do.'

'No,' he said with a hint of suppressed violence. '*No!* Not again. You could never understand how I— Don't even think of it. *Capisci?*'

'*Capisco*. I understand very well.'

'Promise me that you won't leave.'

'All right.'

'On your word of honour.'

'Look—'

'Say it. Let me know that I can trust you this time at least.'

'Trust me *this time*? As though I was the one who deceived— You've got a nerve.'

'He's coming back,' Mario said hurriedly, glancing to where Giorgio had appeared. 'Smile.'

She tried to look at ease but it was hard, and as soon as Giorgio reached the table she rose.

'I'm going to bed,' she said. 'It's been a long day for me, with the flight.'

'You're right; get some rest,' Mario said. 'We'll all meet here tomorrow morning at nine.'

They shook hands and she departed at once.

Giorgio watched her go, then eyed Mario wryly.

'What's going on with you two?' he queried. 'You're on edge with each other. For a moment I really thought there'd been something between you.'

'Not a thing,' Mario assured him. 'And there never could be.'

'Pity. Romeo and Juliet were "star-crossed lovers". It could have been interesting to have them promoted by another pair of star-crossed lovers. After all, if a couple is meant for each other but just can't get it together—well, it's not in their hands, is it? They just have to enjoy it while they can, but then accept that fate is against them.'

'Isn't that giving in too easily?'

'It's what Romeo and Juliet had to accept.'

'And then they died.'

'They died physically, but it doesn't usually happen that way. Sometimes people just die inside.'

'Yes,' Mario murmured. 'That's true.'

'I'll call the other members of the group and fix a meeting. They'll just love her. We've found the right person. Don't you agree?'

Mario nodded and spoke in an iron voice. 'The right person. Not a doubt of it. I must be going. My work has piled up while I've been away.'

He departed fast, urgently needing to get away from Giorgio's sharp eyes that saw too much for comfort.

Upstairs, he headed for his bedroom, but paused before entering. The room allocated to Natasha was just across the corridor and he went to stand outside, looking at her door, wondering what was happening behind it.

The evening had torn his nerves to shreds. The woman he'd met had been as unlike the sweet, charming girl he remembered as steel was unlike cream. His heart told him it was impossible that they should be the same person, but his brain groaned and said it was true.

This was the heartless creature who had vanished without giving him a chance to defend himself, leaving him to hunt frantically for weeks until he'd realised that it was hopeless. And her manner towards him had left no doubt that she was enjoying her triumph.

A sensible man would have sent her away at once. Instead, he'd prevented her leaving, driven by instincts he didn't understand, nor want to face.

From behind her door came only silence. He moved closer, raising his hand to knock, then dropping it again. This wasn't the right moment.

Instead of going into his room, he turned away again and went downstairs into the garden, hoping some time in the night air would clear the confusion in his mind. But also doubting that anything would ever be clear again.

Natasha paced her room restlessly. After such a day she should have been ready to collapse into sleep, but her nerves were tense and she feared to lie awake all night, thinking the very thoughts she wanted to avoid.

Mario had blamed her for disappearing without giving him a chance to defend himself, and in so doing he'd touched a nerve.

Perhaps I should have let him say something, she thought. *Why didn't I?*

Because I'm my mother's daughter, said another voice in her mind. *And I can't help living by the lessons she taught me. Never trust a man. Don't believe his explanation because it'll be lies and you'll only suffer more. In fact, don't let him explain at all. Never, never give him a second chance.*

She'd fled Mario because she feared to listen to what he might have to say. Thinking the worst of him felt safer. That was the sad truth.

But now, meeting him again and getting a sense of his torment, she felt uneasy about her own actions.

'No,' she said. 'No, I'm not going down that road. What's done is done. It's over.'

In the last year she'd often suffered from insomnia and had resorted to some herbal sleeping pills. She took them out now, considering.

'I'm not lying awake fretting over him. This is war.'

She swallowed two pills but, instead of going to bed, she went outside for a few minutes. The tall window opened onto a balcony where she could stand and look down on a narrow strip of garden. There were flowers, a few trees and beyond them the Adige River, glowing in the evening light. Now it was easy to slip into the balcony scene and become Juliet, yearning over the man who'd captured her heart before she knew who he was. When she'd realised that she'd fallen in love with an enemy, it was too late.

'Too late,' she murmured. 'The last thing I wanted was to meet him again. I came here to start a new life. *Mario, Mario, wherefore art thou, Mario?* But it had to be you, didn't it? When I'm looking forward to meeting new people, you have to pop up. *Wherefore did thou do this, varlet?'*

In her agitation she said the words aloud. Alarmed at herself, she retreated through the window, shutting it firmly.

Outside, all was quiet. Darkness was falling, and there was nobody to notice Mario standing, alone and silent, beneath the trees. He had come straight into the garden after leaving Natasha's door, wondering if some light from her room would reassure him. What he had seen stunned and confused him. Her whispered words seemed to float down, reaching him so softly that he couldn't be sure he'd actually heard them.

To believe what he longed to believe was something he refused to do. That way lay danger, disillusion—the things he'd promised himself to avoid in future. So he backed into the shadows, his eyes fixed on her window until the light went out and his world was full of darkness.

Promptly at nine o'clock the next morning Mario appeared at the breakfast table, frowning as he saw only Giorgio there.

'Where is she?' he demanded. 'I told her nine o'clock.'

'Have a heart,' Giorgio begged. 'It's only a few minutes after nine. She's not a machine, just a lovely lady.'

'She is an employee being paid a high salary, for which I expect punctuality and obedience to my wishes. Kindly call her room.'

'I've been calling it for half an hour,' Giorgio admitted. 'But there's no reply. Perhaps she doesn't want to talk to us.'

Or perhaps she can't, said a voice in Mario's mind.

He remembered the woman she had been the evening before, bright, completely at ease, ready to challenge him every moment.

Yet there had been something else, he realised. Beneath her confident manner he'd sensed something different—troubled, uneasy. Their meeting had taken them both by surprise. His own turmoil had startled and shaken him, making him struggle not to let her suspect his weakness, the more so because she had seemed free of any weakness.

But then he'd seen a new look in her eyes, a flash of vulnerability that matched his own. It had vanished at once, but for a brief moment he'd known that she was as alarmed as he was.

He remembered how he'd stood under her balcony last night, watching her, sensing again that she was haunted, but resisting the impulse to reach out to her. Her disappearance now hinted at new trouble. If he went to her room, what would he find? The confident Natasha, laughing at his discomfiture? Or the frail Natasha who couldn't cope?

Abruptly he took out his mobile phone, called her room and listened as the bell rang and rang, with no reply.

'If it was anyone else you'd think they'd vanished without paying the bill,' Giorgio observed. 'But we're not charging her for that room, so she's got no reason to vanish.'

'That's right,' Mario said grimly. 'No reason at all.'

'I'll go and knock on her door.'

'No, stay here. I'll see what's happened.'

Swiftly, he went to his office and opened a cupboard that contained the hotel's replacement keys. Trying to stay calm despite his growing worry, Mario took the one that belonged to Natasha's room and went upstairs. After only a moment's hesitation, he opened her door.

At once he saw her, lying in bed, so still and silent that alarm rose in him. He rushed towards the bed and leaned down to her, close enough to see that she was breathing.

His relief was so great that he grasped the chest of drawers to stop himself falling. Every instinct of self-preservation warned him to get out quickly, before he was discovered. But he couldn't make himself leave her. Instead he dropped onto one knee, gazing at her closely. She lay without moving, her lovely hair splayed out on the pillow, her face soft and almost smiling.

How he had once dreamed of this, of awakening to find her beside him, sleeping gently, full of happiness at the pleasure they had shared.

He leaned a little closer, until he could feel her breath on his face. He knew he was taking a mad risk. A wise man would leave now, but he wasn't a wise man. He was a man torn by conflicting desires.

Then she moved, turning so that the bedclothes slipped away from her, revealing that she was naked. Mario drew a sharp breath.

How often in the past had he longed to see her this way? He had planned and schemed to draw her tenderly closer! The night of their disaster had been meant to end like this, lying together in his bed, with him discovering her hidden beauty. But then a calamity had descended on him and wrecked his life. How bitter was the irony that he should see her lovely nakedness now.

She moved again, reaching out in his direction, so that he had to jerk away quickly. She began to whisper in her sleep, but he couldn't make out the words. Only escape would save him. He rose, backed off quickly and managed to make it to the door before her eyes opened. Once outside, he leaned against the wall, his chest heaving, his brain whirling.

At last he moved away, back to the real world, where he was a man in command. And that, he vowed, was where he would stay.

Giorgio looked up as Mario approached. 'No luck finding her?'

Mario shrugged. 'I didn't bother looking very far. Try calling her again.'

Giorgio dialled the number, listening with a resigned face.

'Looks like she still isn't—no, wait! Natasha, is that you? Thank goodness! Where have you been? *What?* Don't you know the time? All right, I'll tell Mario. But hurry.' He shut off the phone. 'She says she overslept.'

Mario shrugged. 'Perhaps the flight tired her yesterday.'

Giorgio gave a rich chuckle. 'My guess is that she was entertaining someone last night. I know she'd only just arrived, but a girl as lovely as that can entertain anyone whenever she wants. I saw men looking at her as she came down those stairs. Did you expect such a beauty?'

'I didn't know what to expect,' Mario said in a toneless voice.

'Nor me. I never hoped she'd be so young and lovely. Let's make the best of it. Juliet come to life. Oh, yes, finding her was a real stroke of luck.'

A stroke of luck. The words clamoured in Mario's brain, adding more bitterness to what he was already suffering. He didn't believe that a man had been in Natasha's room last night, but the sight of her naked had devastated him. He could almost believe she'd done it on purpose to taunt him, but the sweet, enchanting Natasha he'd known would never do that.

But was she that Natasha any more?

Had she ever been?

'I just know what she's doing right this minute,' Giorgio said with relish. 'She's turning to the man next to her in the bed, saying, "You've got to go quickly so that nobody finds you here." Perhaps we should have someone watch her door to see who comes out.'

'That's enough,' Mario growled.

'With a girl as stunning as that, nothing is ever enough. Don't pretend you don't know what I mean. You were fizzing from the moment you saw her.'

'Drop it,' Mario growled.

'All right, you don't want to admit she had that effect on you. After all, you're the boss. Don't let her guess she's got you where she wants you—even if she has.'

I said drop it.

'Steady there. Don't get mad at me. I was only thinking that if there's an attraction between you, we can make use of it.'

'And you're mistaken. There's no attraction between us.'

'Pity. That could have been fun.'

Slowly, Natasha felt life returning to her as she ended the call from Giorgio.

'Nine-fifteen!' she gasped in horror. 'I was supposed to be downstairs at nine. Oh, I should never have taken those sleeping pills.'

The pills had plunged her into a deep slumber, which she'd needed to silence her desperate thoughts of Mario.

But at the end he'd invaded her sleep, his face close to hers, regarding her with an almost fierce intensity. But he wasn't there. It had been a dream.

'I just can't get away from him,' she whispered. 'Will I ever?'

She showered in cold water, relishing the feeling of coming back to life. Dressing was a simple matter of putting on tailored trousers and a smart blazer and fixing her hair back tightly. Then she was ready to go.

She found Giorgio and Mario downstairs at the table.

'I'm so sorry,' she said. 'I didn't mean to be late but I was more tired than I realised.'

'That's understandable,' Giorgio said gallantly.

Mario threw him a cynical look but said nothing.

'Where's that waiter?' Giorgio asked, frowning. 'I'll find him and he can bring you breakfast.'

He vanished.

'I'm glad Giorgio's gone,' she said. 'It gives us a chance to talk honestly. Last night you stopped me getting out of my chair, and told me to stay. But is that really what you want? Wouldn't you be better off without me?'

'If I thought that I'd have said so,' he retorted.

'But think of it, day after day, trying not to get annoyed with each other, pretending to like each other. Surely you don't want that? I'm giving you the chance to get rid of me, Mario.'

'What about you? Do you want to make a run for it?'

'I can cope.'

'But you think I can't. Thanks for the vote of confidence. We're business professionals and on that basis it can work.'

'You're right,' she said. 'Shake.'

'Shake.' He took her extended hand. 'Perhaps I should

warn you that Giorgio has some rather fancy ideas about you. He thinks you had a lover in your room last night and that's why you overslept.'

'*What?* I'd taken some herbal pills to get to sleep after a strenuous day. A lover? I'd only been here five minutes.'

'Giorgio sees you as the kind of woman who can attract men as fast as that.'

'Cheek!'

'In his eyes it's a compliment.'

She scowled for a moment, then laughed. 'I guess I'll learn to put up with him.'

Giorgio reappeared with her breakfast.

'Eat up and we'll get to work,' he said. 'I'll get you a map of Verona.'

'I've got one,' she said, drawing it from her bag. 'I bought it at the airport so that I would be ready. The more you plan, the simpler life is.'

'True,' Mario murmured, 'but there are some things that can never be planned.'

'And you can't always anticipate what they might be,' she agreed. 'You can try, but—' She shrugged.

'But they always take you by surprise,' he murmured.

'Not always. Just sometimes. It's best to be ready.'

Giorgio looked from one to the other as if his alarm bells had sounded again.

'It's time we were making plans,' he said. 'I've called the others in the group, and they're dying to meet you. We're all invited to dinner tonight at the Albergo Splendido.' He beamed at Natasha. 'It'll be your big night.'

'Then I'd better prepare for it,' she said. 'I'll look around Verona today so that I can sound knowledgeable at the dinner. Otherwise they'll think I'm an amateur.'

'Good thinking,' Giorgio said. 'I'll escort you, and we'll have a great time.'

'Now, here—' Natasha pointed to a street on the map '—this is the Via Capello, where I can visit Juliet's house. I'd like to go there first, then the house where the Montagues lived. Finally, I'd like to see the tomb. Then I can work out my plans.'

'We'll leave as soon as you've finished breakfast,' Mario told her.

CHAPTER THREE

THE CHAUFFEUR-DRIVEN CAR was waiting for them, and soon they were on their way around the city.

Natasha already knew a good deal about Verona, having read about it on the plane. It was an old city, much of which went back to Roman times, two thousand years ago. Several places survived from that era, including a huge arena where gladiators had once slain their victims, but now was used for musical performances.

The streets were lined with historic buildings, many hinting at mystery and romance, all seeming to come from a more intriguing and beautiful age. She kept her eyes fixed on them as they drove through the town, trying to absorb its atmosphere.

'We're just turning into the Via Capello,' Mario said. 'We'll reach Juliet's house at any moment.'

A few minutes later the car dropped them at the entrance to a short tunnel. They joined the crowd walking through to the courtyard at the far end, where the balcony loomed overhead. Natasha regarded it with shining eyes.

'It's lovely,' she said. 'Of course I know it was put up less than a hundred years ago, but it looks right. It fits the house so perfectly that you can almost see Juliet standing there.'

'She's actually over there,' Giorgio said, pointing at a figure standing a little ahead, beneath and to the side of the balcony. It was a bronze statue of a young woman.

'Juliet,' she breathed.

As she watched, a woman walked up to the statue and brushed her hand against its breast. She was followed by another woman, and another, then a man.

'It's a tradition,' Mario explained. 'Everyone does it in the hope that it will bring them good luck. That's why that part of her is shining, because it's touched so often. People like to make contact with Juliet because they see her as a woman who knows more about love than anyone in the world.'

'Perhaps that's true,' Natasha murmured. 'But she knows tragedy as well as love.'

Intrigued, she went to stand before the statue. Juliet's head was turned slightly to the side, gazing into the distance as though only in another world could she find what she sought.

Natasha watched as a woman touched Juliet, closed her eyes and murmured something. At last her eyes opened and she stepped back with a smile, evidently feeling that she had received an answer.

If only it was that simple, Natasha thought. *If Juliet really could give me advice I'd ask her about the way my head is whirling, about how I'm feeling, and how I ought to be feeling. But she can't help me because she doesn't exist. She never really did, not the way people believe in her. That kind of love is just an illusion.*

She turned away to find Mario waiting. He moved closer, leaving Giorgio at a distance, and speaking quietly.

'Were you consulting Juliet?' he asked, raising an eyebrow.

'No,' she said. 'She's a fantasy. Nothing more.'

'How very prosaic.'

'I am prosaic, and I'm glad. It's useful.'

'But if you're going to promote the romantic fantasy, shouldn't you believe in it?'

She surveyed him with her head on one side and a faint ironic smile on her face.

'Not at all,' she said. 'It isn't necessary to believe something to persuade other people that it's true.'

'I wonder if you're right.'

A flash of anger made her say quickly, 'You know I'm right. We all know it at heart.'

'So—' he hesitated '—you're telling me that you've toughened up?'

'By a mile. So beware.'

'No need to tell me that.'

'So I've got you worried already? Good.'

For a wild moment he was tempted to tell her of the confused reactions that had rioted in him when he first saw her on the stairs. There had been an incredible moment of pleasure that the sight of her had always brought him, and which even now remained. But it had collided with a sense of alarm, as though a warning bell had sounded, letting him know that she would bring fear and darkness into his life.

But he suppressed the impulse to speak. How satisfied she would be to know that she could still throw him into confusion.

'Don't tell me I'm the only one who's toughened up,' she challenged him. 'Haven't you?'

'No doubt of it. It's called survival.'

She nodded. 'Right. As long as we both understand that, there's no problem.'

For them there would always be a problem. But there was no need of words.

'Now, I have a job to do,' she said briskly.

'Yes, let's look around further.'

Suddenly there was a cry from the far side of the courtyard.

'Buongiorno, amici!'

'Amadore!' Giorgio exclaimed, extending his hand in welcome.

The three men exchanged greetings in Italian, until Giorgio said, *'Signorina*, this is Amadore Finucci, a fellow member of the *Comunità*. Amadore, this is the Signorina Natasha Bates, who doesn't speak Italian.'

'Then it will be my pleasure to speak English,' Amadore said, seizing her hand.

She gave a polite response and he carried her hand to his mouth.

'Miss Bates,' he said.

'Please, call me Natasha.'

'Thank you—Natasha. When did you arrive?'

'Yesterday,' Giorgio said. 'Your father has invited us to dine at your hotel tonight.'

'Yes, he told me. I must leave now, but I look forward to seeing you this evening.'

He departed. Natasha eyed Mario curiously, puzzled to find him frowning.

'You're not pleased about this invitation?'

'That's because his hotel is one of the most luxurious in town,' Giorgio said. 'Mario's jealous.'

'I'm not jealous,' Mario said firmly. 'I admit I envy him having a bottomless pit of money to spend on the place.'

'His ballroom has to be seen to be believed,' Giorgio told her.

'Ballroom,' she echoed. 'Romeo and Juliet met in a ballroom.' She turned to Mario. 'Does your hotel have a ballroom?'

'No. None of the other hotels do.'

'Then that gives me an idea. Can we return to the hotel now? I need to get to work.'

'Aren't we going on to Romeo's house?' Giorgio asked.

'I'll do that tomorrow. Today, I have urgent things to do.

'Could you please provide me with a list of every member of the *Comunità*, and their hotels? Then I can check their locations and assess their requirements.'

'I'll see to it as soon as we arrive.'

As they walked back to the car, Giorgio murmured to Mario, 'A woman who knows her own mind. Perhaps we should beware.'

'There's no perhaps about it,' Mario replied grimly.

On the way back to the hotel Natasha took out her notebook and wrote in it swiftly and fiercely. Ideas were coming to her in cascades and she needed to capture them fast. This was the part of any project that she liked best. So absorbed did she become that she was unaware of the journey, and looked up suddenly when the car stopped.

'We're here,' Mario said. He'd been watching her silently.

'I need something to eat,' Giorgio declared. 'Suppose we meet downstairs in half an hour, for a feast?'

'Not me, thank you,' Natasha said. 'Perhaps you could send something up to my room?'

'But we could all celebrate together,' Giorgio protested.

'We can celebrate when I've made a success of this job. Let's hope that happens.'

'It'll happen,' Giorgio said. 'You're going to be just fantastic, isn't she, Mario?'

'No doubt of it,' he said bleakly.

'You're very kind, both of you. Now, excuse me, gentlemen.'

Giving them both a polite smile, she headed for the lift.

Upstairs, she plunged into work, making more notes about the morning before things went out of her head. She was so immersed in her work that at first she didn't hear the knock on the door. It had to be repeated louder to capture her attention.

'Sorry,' she said, pulling it open, 'I got so—' She checked herself at the sight of Mario standing there with a trolley of food.

'Your meal, *signorina*,' he said.

She stared at the sight of the food. Someone had taken a lot of trouble preparing this meal, which Mario laid out for her with care.

'Giorgio told the kitchen to produce their best, to make sure you stay with us,' he said. 'So you have chicory risotto, followed by tiramisù, with Prosecco.'

Her favourite wine. How many times had he ordered it for her in Venice? And he had remembered.

'It's delicious,' she said politely as she ate.

'I'll tell Giorgio you approve. And I brought you this,' he said, handing her a large file.

It was the information she'd requested about the *Comunità*—hotels, owners, background information.

'That man I met today seems to come from the biggest and best,' she said, flicking through it. 'The Albergo Splendido.'

'It was a palace once. You'll like it. You're making a considerable impression, you know.'

'Amadore certainly seemed to think so.'

'Just don't take him too seriously. He flirts with every woman on the planet.'

She gave a brief laugh. 'You warned me about Giorgio; now you're warning me about Amadore. But you don't need to. I can recognise when a man is role-playing. He puts on a performance as the "romantic Italian" because he thinks an Englishwoman is bound to be fooled. I don't mind. He's charming. But don't expect me to fall for it.'

'I suppose I should have known you'd say that,' Mario growled. 'I wonder if you ever fall for anything.'

'Not these days. Never again.'

'And you think that's admirable?'

'I think it's safe.'

'And safety matters more than anything else? Never mind who you hurt.'

She turned on him, her quick temper rising. 'Who *I* hurt? Did I really hear you say that? After what you did?'

'I didn't do what you thought I did, and I could have explained. But you vanished without giving me a chance to defend myself.'

'What was there to defend? I know what I saw.'

'Natasha, why won't you realise that you misunderstood what you saw? Yes, I'd been having an affair with Tania. I'm not a saint. I've never pretended to be. But it was only a casual relationship and I'd started to feel that it must end. Things had changed in my life. I'd met you and nothing looked the same. I had to face the fact that I wanted you, not her.

'So that day I met Tania and told her we couldn't be together any more. But I couldn't make her believe it. When I left her she followed me, and that was how she found us together.

'I went after her, trying to explain that I was sorry to hurt her, but she screamed at me and ran off. I came back to our table, hoping I could make you understand. But you were gone. I tried your phone but you'd turned it off. I went to the hotel but you'd left just a few minutes earlier. Over the next few days I tried your phone, your email, your apartment, but you'd shut off every way of contacting you. It was like you'd ceased to exist.'

'Exactly. I *had* ceased to exist. The girl I was then—naive, slightly stupid, ready to be fooled—vanished into nothing. But now there's another woman in her place—suspicious, awkward, ready to give as good as she gets. She exists. She's me. She's rather hard. You won't like her. Be wise. Get rid of her.'

His face was suddenly tense. 'I think not. I prefer to keep her around and make her face up to what she did.'

'Is that why you got me back here?'

'What do you mean by that?'

'I don't believe it's coincidence that we just happened to meet again.'

He paled. 'You think I manipulated this situation?'

'You could have.'

'And I'm telling you I didn't. How dare you? Perhaps I should accuse *you* of manipulation. Did you persuade your friend to let you take her place?'

'No way. I had no idea you'd be here until I saw you on the stairs.'

'Nor I. Let's get this clear, Natasha. I didn't trick you into coming here. I didn't want to see you again, not after the way you behaved.'

'The way *I*—?'

'You left me feeling as though I was hanging off the edge of a cliff.'

'I know that feeling,' she said softly, with anger in her voice.

'All right. For the moment we have to accept things as they are. We're enemies but we need to be allies as far as this job's concerned. Our fight is still on, but it's a fair fight.'

'Is it? I wonder if your idea of a fair fight is the same as mine.'

'I guess we'll find that out.'

A beep from her mobile phone interrupted him. Answering it, she found a text:

You didn't have to run away. We can sort this out.

There was no name, but there didn't need to be. This wasn't the first text that Elroy Jenson had sent her since he'd shut her out of his media empire. Clearly he'd expected her to cave in and come crawling back.

She had to make him stop doing this.

Swiftly, she texted back:

Forget me, as I've forgotten you.

His reply came at once:

If that were true you wouldn't have run away. Come home. I can do a lot for you.

She groaned, wondering how much more of this she could take. She'd thought that by coming to Italy she could put Jenson behind her.

'What's the matter?' Mario asked. 'Who has upset you?'

'It's nothing,' she said quickly. 'I'm fine.'

'I don't think so. Perhaps you should change your mobile number. Doing that works well because then the guy can't reach you. But of course you know that. Here—'

Before she could stop him he'd seized the phone from her hand and was reading the text.

'Just tell him to— What does he mean, run away?'

'I've been running away from him for months. He's Elroy Jenson, the man who owns a great media empire. It stretches all over the world—England, America, Europe—'

'Yes—' Mario broke in '—I've heard of him. Some of his papers are in this country. Not a man you'd want to antagonise.'

'I used to make a good living writing for his newspapers and magazines, but then he decided that he fancied me. I didn't fancy him but he wouldn't take no for an answer. He kept pestering me until I slapped his face. Unfortunately, some of his employees saw it and the word got out. Since then none of his editors will buy articles from me.'

'And he keeps sending you these messages? Why don't you just change your mobile phone number?'

'I have. Several times. But he always manages to get the new one. He's a powerful man and his tentacles stretch far.'

'Bastardo!'

'If that means what I think it does, then yes. Now I can't earn a living in England and he's coming after me.'

'Thinking you'll turn to him for the money? And he'd like that—knowing that you'd only given in to him out of need?'

'He'd enjoy it. He's that kind of man. But he's going

to be disappointed. I'll do anything rather than what he wants.'

'Anything? Including taking a job with a man you hate?'

'Even that. This job's a lucky break for me. It gets me out of England.'

'But you have to put up with me.'

'Stop being melodramatic. You're not so bad. I can manage. We've put the past behind us.'

He smiled wryly, trying to come to terms with her words. 'You're not so bad' implied a casual acceptance that should have been a relief but felt more like an insult.

'Yes, we've put it all behind us,' he agreed. 'And now we can concentrate on business, which is what we're here for. You need to make a living and I need to repay the bank loans I had to take out to buy this place.'

'That must be a heavy burden,' she said.

'It is. Damiano wanted to help me by lending me some money, and standing guarantor for the bank loan. But I wouldn't let him do either. This is my hotel, and mine alone.'

'I remember meeting Damiano in Venice. And his wife. They were very nice to me.'

'They both liked you a lot.'

In fact both Sally and Damiano had nudged him, saying, 'She's the one, Mario. Go on, make sure of her.'

And when things went wrong they had united again to call him 'The biggest idiot of all time'. It was a remark that still stung him.

'Why wouldn't you let him help you?' she asked.

'I just prefer to control my own life,' he said in a voice that was suddenly hard.

A tantalising memory flickered through her mind:

Mario, two years ago, young, carefree and easy-going. Somehow he had changed into this grimly self-sufficient man who mistrusted the world.

'I prefer it too,' she said. 'You feel safer, like wearing a suit of armour. But is that always a good thing to wear?'

'That depends on who challenges you,' he said.

His eyes, fixed on her, left her in no doubt of his message. Her presence was a challenge, one that he would fight off ruthlessly.

'But you wouldn't need a suit of armour against your older brother,' she said. 'Helping you is surely what older brothers are for?'

'Possibly, but I needed to stop being the younger brother, leaning on him. I told him I could do it alone, so I've got to prove that's true. I simply mustn't fail.'

'And I mustn't fail either,' she said, 'so in future we're going to concentrate on being practical. Please leave me now, and when I've finished my research I'll see you and Giorgio at supper.'

'Good luck with the work,' he said, and departed.

He went quickly to his office and went online. A few minutes' research told him all he needed to know about Elroy Jenson: his creation of a media empire, his money, his far-reaching power.

But it was the man's looks that amazed him. He'd expected a slobbering, middle-aged monster, a man no woman could want to be with unless she was after his money. But Jenson was well built, even handsome, with a riotous head of curly hair. A woman lucky enough to have captured his attention would have every reason to flaunt her triumph.

But not Natasha.

No man impresses her, he thought. *She decides what she wants, and woe betide him if he can't live up to it.*

He glanced at himself in the mirror.

'But could any man live up to it?' he murmured.

Researching the Albergo Splendido, Natasha could easily believe that it had started life as a palace. It was seven hundred years old and magnificently built.

To dine there meant dressing in style. Luckily she'd brought with her a black satin figure-hugging dress that managed to be both decorous and elegant.

Giorgio nodded approval. 'Lovely. You'll make their heads spin. Let's go.'

As they walked to the car Mario said, 'Aren't you making too much of her appearance? Surely it's her efficiency we need to promote?'

'Efficiency alone isn't enough. She's got that extra "something" special, and it's going to make all the difference.'

'I'll take your word for it,' Mario said coldly.

At the hotel Amadore was waiting for them. 'Everyone's here,' he said. 'They're longing to meet you.'

He led her into a room filled with tables at which sat crowds of men and women, who broke into applause at the sight of her.

There could be no doubt that she was the star of the evening. Amadore introduced her to each guest, one by one, giving the name of the person and of their hotel.

'Ah, yes,' she said to one elderly man. 'That's the place where—'

He listened, open-mouthed, as she revealed her in-depth research. She did the same thing with several of the other hotel owners and was rewarded by looks of admiration.

'You see what I mean?' Giorgio murmured to Mario. 'A brilliant lady, clever and hard-working. We've struck gold.'

Mario didn't reply.

When she'd met all the guests she sat down at the head table for the meal, which turned out to be a glorious banquet, adorned with the finest wines.

'Mmm, lovely,' she said, sipping from her glass.

'Everyone thinks of Verona as the site of the love story,' Giorgio told her. 'But it's also surrounded by vineyards. Most of the hotel owners have some sort of investment in vineyards.'

'The wine you're drinking now was produced in my own vineyard,' Amadore said.

'It's delicious,' she said, sipping again.

'Thank you, *signorina*.'

They clinked glasses.

Soon she saw that everyone was looking at her expectantly.

'They're waiting for your speech,' Mario murmured.

'But I can only speak English,' she protested. 'Will they understand?'

'Hotel owners tend to speak English because your country sends us many tourists.'

Mario got to his feet.

'My friends,' he said, 'it has been our pleasure tonight to meet the lady we've employed to promote us to the world. Now let us hear her plans.'

There was applause as Natasha rose. For a few moments she was nervous but the warm, friendly atmosphere enveloped her and she began to enjoy herself as she laid out the ideas that had been forming in her mind.

'Every hotel has something to connect it to the story,' she said. 'Some are near Juliet's house, some near Romeo's house, some are near the tomb.'

'Some of us aren't so lucky,' a man called. 'Our hotels aren't near anywhere significant.'

'Don't be so sure,' she said. 'Remember the scene where Romeo's friend Mercutio is stabbed to death by Juliet's kinsman? That happens outdoors in the street. But which street? Nobody knows for sure, but perhaps some of your hotels are nearby.'

Natasha looked out at her audience, smiling and nodding appreciatively as she spoke. She was fulfilling all their highest expectations. Applause rang in her ears.

CHAPTER FOUR

'NOW FOR THE next stage,' Natasha said. 'I'll want to talk to you all individually, and then I'm going to write my first piece explaining how "Romeo and Juliet" are still alive in Verona if people know how to find them. We'll invite them to come here, and stay in your hotels. By that time I'll have produced several more texts.'

'But who will publish these?' called a voice from the floor.

'Anyone she sends it to,' Giorgio called back. 'This lady is a very notable journalist with many connections. She gets published everywhere.'

More applause, but Natasha held up her hand for silence.

'We're not going to take chances,' she said. 'This "article" will actually be an advertisement. We buy a double-page spread and insert our own text and pictures. That way we can be sure of being read. What matters is to get things done the way we want. Of course it will be costly. Advertisements have to be paid for, and perhaps some of you won't want to accept that expense. Let's take a vote. Hands up anyone who's against the idea.'

Not a single hand was raised.

'We'll do it your way,' called a voice.

There were cheers and applause, which went on until they were interrupted by the sound of music.

'That's coming from the ballroom,' Amadore told her. 'Our guests like to dance in the evening.'

'A ballroom is wonderful,' she said. 'The Capulets gave a ball for Juliet and Paris, the man they wanted her to marry, which Romeo gatecrashed to see another girl that he was in love with. Instead he met Juliet and they fell in love within a few minutes. Without that ball it might never have happened.'

'Then come and have a look,' Amadore said eagerly.

Everyone crowded after them as he led her along a short corridor, throwing open a double door at the end, revealing a huge, beautiful room where couples were whirling.

'Perfect,' she murmured.

Amadore took her hand. 'Dance with me.'

Smiling, she let him draw her into his arms and guide her onto the floor. He was an excellent dancer and she responded gladly. When the music stopped another man stepped in to claim her, then another.

At last she found herself facing Mario.

'You've danced with everyone else,' he observed. 'Will it ever be my turn?'

'Not until you ask me.'

'No,' he said. 'I'm not going to ask you.'

But as he spoke his arm went around her waist in a grip too firm for her to resist, even if she had wanted to.

They had danced together once before. One night in Venice, when they had been having supper at an outdoor café in St Mark's Square, a band had started to play and before she knew it she was waltzing in his arms.

'Is this all right?' he'd whispered.

'I'll let you know later,' she had teased.

It had lasted only a few minutes, and she had promised herself that one day she would dance with him again. But the next day they had broken up, and it had never happened again. Until now.

It was unnerving to feel his arms around her, his hand on her waist, holding her close. Her heart was beating softly but fervently. She glanced at him, trying to know if he felt the same. Would he invite her to dance with him again?

But before he could speak they became aware of a middle-aged man on the edge of the crowd, trying to attract their attention.

'Ah, there's Francesco,' Mario said. 'I hoped he'd be here. He owns one of the biggest hotels, and I always like to have him on my side. Let's go and say hello.'

Francesco beamed, greeting Natasha with an embrace.

'It's a pleasure to meet you,' he said warmly. 'Now, let me introduce my daughter, Laura.'

The young woman with him was in her mid-twenties with a beautiful face and an air of confidence that came from being always in demand.

'How have you done?' she said carefully to Natasha.

'No,' her father interrupted her. 'Not like that, *cara*. The English say "How do you do?" not "How have you done?"'

'How do you do?' Laura echoed, smiling. 'Is that right?'

'That is perfect,' her father said.

He spoke proudly and Natasha knew a slight twinge of sadness as a memory came back to her from long ago. She had heard that pride before, in her own father's voice, in her childhood, before he'd abandoned her without a backward glance.

But this was no time to be brooding over the past. She thrust the memory aside, returning Laura's greeting with the appearance of warmth.

Then Laura turned her attention to Mario, saying, 'And how do you do?'

'There's no need for such formality,' Mario said, shaking her hand. 'We already know each other.'

'Indeed we do,' Laura said, glancing at Natasha as she spoke.

Natasha returned her look with interest. She had the feeling that Laura was sizing her up as possible competition.

Then Amadore appeared beside them. 'Do I get another dance?' he asked.

'Of course.' Natasha let the charming hotel owner enfold her in his arms and twirl her gently across the floor.

Out of the corner of her eye she could just see Mario gliding past with Laura, who seemed to be trying to dance as close to him as possible.

'There the women go again,' Amadore said, 'parading themselves to get his attention.'

'Do you mean Signor Ferrone?' Natasha asked.

'Oh, yes. He's a lucky man. Every female makes eyes at him, and the rumour is that he can have any woman he wants.'

So nothing had changed, she thought, remembering how women's eyes had followed Mario during their time together. How they had envied her, being with him. How little they had known how he could make a woman suffer.

'Look at that,' Amadore said, still regarding Mario with envy. 'The way she's pressed up against him is almost indecent.'

Natasha managed to chuckle. 'Oh, come on. A man's entitled to enjoy himself if he can.'

'That's very generous of you. Most women don't take such a relaxed view.'

'I can afford to be relaxed. My life is arranged just the way I want it.'

'You're luckier than most of us then.'

Mario, just a few feet away, glanced at them only briefly before swinging Laura away to the far side of the ballroom. There, he found more female attention to distract him from sights he didn't want to see and thoughts he didn't want to think.

But it lasted only a short time. When he next looked at Natasha she was sitting down scribbling in her notebook. Two men were sitting beside her, while another two looked over her shoulders. As the music came to an end he began to approach her, but Amadore detained him.

'Lovely lady,' he said. 'Every man is interested. Luckily she's not interested in them.'

'She told you that?'

'We were watching Laura making a play for you. I disapproved but she said you were entitled to enjoy yourself. I complimented her on her relaxed attitude and she said she could afford to be relaxed as her life was arranged the way she wanted it.'

'She probably just said that to shut you up.'

'Maybe. But it wouldn't surprise me if back home she has a trail of eager pursuers.'

'You could be right,' Mario growled.

He could see that Natasha had finished making notes, and was rising to move away. He got to her quickly.

'Still working?' he said.

'I've had an idea. I need to talk to everyone again.'

'Then let's return to the dining room.' He offered her his arm, saying, 'You've done well tonight. The contract will be ready soon.'

'Contract?'

'For you to sign. The whole *Comunità* is determined to secure your professional services. Are you willing to stay with us?'

'Yes,' she said softly. 'I'm willing.'

When they were gathered in the dining room again she addressed everyone. 'I think we should take some photographs of Romeo and Juliet. They say a picture's worth a thousand words, and we can send ours all over the world. We'll need to hire actors, then we'll photograph them on the balcony, in the tomb, anywhere that seems atmospheric.'

'We can't pose them on the official balcony,' Mario said. 'There are always tourists there. But this hotel has a balcony that will do.'

It was agreed that they would all meet again when the arrangements were made. Now all Mario wanted was to get away. Nothing had prepared him for being so close to her for hours, and he needed to be alone.

'Sleep well,' he told her as he escorted her to a chauffeur-driven car. 'You've worked hard today and there'll be more tomorrow.' He opened the car door. 'I'll see you tomorrow morning. Goodnight.'

He walked away.

Back in her room, Natasha undressed and went to bed. It had been a successful evening and she should have felt triumphant. Perhaps she would have done if Mario had returned with her, and been here to share her sense of achievement. But he had left her alone while he spent the night somewhere else.

Images of Laura danced through her mind, pursued by Amadore's voice saying '…he can have any woman he wants.'

She tried to shut the thoughts down. She and Mario were no longer part of each other's lives, and she cared nothing where he was now, or who he was with.

She lay down and managed to sleep. When she awoke she could hear a noise in the corridor outside, as though someone was turning a key in a lock. She rose and opened her door just in time to see Mario's door closing.

It was six in the morning.

She half expected him to be late for breakfast but he was there before her, calm, collected and ready for work.

'You were right about hiring actors,' he said. 'We'll have a file of pictures soon. In the meantime I've been making some notes of my own—'

But before she could look at them her phone beeped with another text.

'Is he hounding you again?' Mario demanded.

'No, it's not him,' she said, looking at the screen. Then she drew in her breath sharply. 'Oh, no—no! *Please, no!*'

'What is it?'

'Nothing,' she said sharply.

'Don't tell me it's nothing when it affects you like that. Let me see.'

Without asking her permission, he took the phone from her.

'What's this?' he demanded, reading, *'Sorry, your cheque bounced.'*

'How dare you?' she said furiously, snatching the phone back.

'Who's hounding you for money? Is it him?'

'No, it's my friend Helen, and she's not hounding me. She's been letting me stay in her flat and she got me this job. Before I left I gave her a cheque for my share of expenses. I owe her so much and I've repaid her like this. I didn't mean to. I thought there was just enough in the bank.'

'Right, we'd better get your contract sorted at once. Wait for me here.'

As he left she sat there, deep in gloom. Shame pervaded her and for a moment she wished she could do what Mario had accused her of, and vanish into thin air.

After a few minutes Giorgio appeared.

'The boss says I'm to give you the contract to sign,' he told her. 'Let's go into his office.'

In the office he laid out papers before her. 'Just sign at the bottom.'

She picked up the pen, then paused. 'Wait, are you sure this contract is right?'

'The boss says it is.'

'But I know what the agency offered me—the money was far less.'

'The fee has been changed. The boss says you're worth more.'

Her head was spinning. The new amount was much larger than the one she had been quoted before.

'You need to give me your bank details so that some money can be paid to you today,' Giorgio said.

Dazed, she gave him the necessary information and signed the contract at the bottom of the last page.

'And you must put your initials on the other pages,'

Giorgio told her. 'He wants to make very sure that you're ours and nobody else's. He knows good value when he sees it. Ah, here he is.'

Mario had come into the room, and stood watching as Natasha finished signing. Glancing over the papers, he nodded and handed them to Giorgio, who left the room.

'I hadn't expected so much,' she said. 'You didn't have to do that. But thank you.'

'You have nothing to thank me for, *signorina*,' he said firmly. 'You're vital to this project and I've taken the necessary steps to make sure the *Comunità* keeps your services.'

She nodded, replying in the same formal voice, 'You can be sure that I will remain loyal to the *Comunità, signore*.'

'Excellent,' he said. 'Then we understand each other.'

'I'm sure we do.'

Oh, yes, she thought. They understood each other perfectly, but in ways that could never be expressed in words. He'd moved swiftly to save her from disaster, but in such a way that there was no fear of them growing closer. They were *signore* and *signorina*, and nothing else.

Not long after, she accessed her bank account on the Internet and found that a large sum of money had already been deposited, enabling her to pay her debt to Helen. That was a relief and she was able to enjoy an hour wandering the streets, absorbing the feel of the city.

When she returned she found that the photographs had arrived. Giorgio and Mario were going through them, studying the pictures of young models, seeking one with the perfect combination of beauty and innocence. She joined in and after a while she discovered exactly what she wanted.

Finding Romeo was harder. He had to be handsome, with splendid legs, since Romeo would be wearing tights. At last she found what she wanted.

'Perfect,' Mario said, studying the picture. 'Good-looking and vulnerable.'

'Vulnerable?' Giorgio queried. 'He's one of literature's great heroes.'

'He also fell for everything that was said to him,' Mario observed wryly. 'Not one of the world's great minds.'

'That's what happens to people in love,' Natasha said. 'They set their minds aside and believe what they want to believe.'

'And soon learn their mistake. All right, let's hire these two.'

Giorgio got straight onto the phone, made the contact and arranged for the two young people to appear in a couple of days.

'Paolo and Lucia,' he said. 'They'll be here ready to start on Thursday morning.'

'That's fine,' Natasha said. 'It gives me some more time to work on my ideas.'

The next two days were abuzz with action. Some of the time was spent visiting Romeo's house, and twice Natasha was invited to dine with other members of the *Comunità*. Mario accompanied her on these trips, but did not sit next to her at the dinner table.

She thought she understood. Having tied her down with the contract, both legally and financially, Mario preferred to keep a certain distance between them.

But the money in her bank account was a big relief. There was no doubt that in Mario she'd made a good professional association. She must cling to that thought.

By day they were absorbed in preparing for the photo shoot. Giorgio hired a photographer experienced in taking dramatic pictures. He also found a theatrical costumier.

'She'll join us tomorrow with a big variety of costumes,' he told Natasha. 'Our models can try several until we find the right ones.'

'Juliet will need something exotic for the ballroom,' Natasha said. 'Then an elegant dress for the wedding scene, and a very simple one for the tomb. Right, I'm going to bed. It's going to be a busy day tomorrow.'

'Does anyone know where Mario is?' Giorgio enquired.

'He left an hour ago,' Natasha said. 'He must be busy.'

On the way upstairs she wondered if Mario was in his room, or had he gone to be with the same person he'd probably visited the other night?

Passing his door, she couldn't help pausing to hear if any sound was coming from inside. She blamed herself for yielding to the temptation, but she couldn't help it.

Then she heard his voice. He was on the telephone, speaking Italian in a warm, laughing tone.

'Non è importante. Non è importante.'

She didn't need to know the language to understand what he was saying: 'It's not important'. Mario was reassuring somebody that what was happening now didn't matter to him.

She hurried into her room and locked the door, wishing she'd resisted temptation and vowing to be stronger next time.

Next morning Lisa, the costumier, arrived early. She was a tall businesslike woman who spoke perfect English and went through Natasha's requirements with no trouble.

'Let's hope Romeo is handsome and has a good figure,' she said briskly.

'He looked good in the photo I saw, but I haven't met him yet,' Natasha admitted.

'That's a pity. To be suitable he must be sexy. We need the women to sigh over him and say, "I want some of that".'

'But he'll only be a picture,' Natasha protested. 'We're selling the town, not Romeo himself.'

Lisa chuckled. 'You think that, do you?'

Natasha gave a wry smile. 'Well, it's what I need to believe. But I guess you're right.'

'Share the joke, ladies,' Giorgio called from nearby, where he was talking with Mario.

'You wouldn't understand it,' Lisa told him. 'We're laughing at men, and men never realise how funny they are.'

'That's very true,' Natasha said. 'And if you try to explain they still don't understand.'

Mario gave her an odd glance which she returned with an air of teasing confidence. She felt a certain cheeky pleasure in having disconcerted him. The day had started well. Whatever happened now, she felt she could cope.

They all set out for the Splendido, where everyone was waiting, eager to begin. The next hour was spent going through a variety of garments.

'I like this one,' Natasha said, holding up a long white ballgown. It was simple and elegant, perfect for a girl making her debut in society. 'Juliet can wear this at the ball.'

Giorgio looked impatiently at his watch.

'They should be here by now. What's happened to them?'

He snatched up his phone and dialled. Almost as soon as he was through, an expression of outrage overtook him.

'*Sì? Che cosa? Cosa vuol dire che non posso venire? Oh, dolore bene!*'

He hung up.

'What's happened?' Mario demanded.

'They're not coming. There's been a mix-up with the dates. They thought the shoot was next week.'

'Oh, no, what are we going to do?' Natasha cried. 'It's all set up for today.'

'There's only one thing we can do,' Giorgio said. 'Find another Romeo and Juliet.'

'But we haven't got time to search,' she protested.

'We don't have to search. We've got the duo we need right here.' He threw out his arms towards her and Mario. 'Romeo and Juliet.'

She stared. 'You can't possibly be serious.'

'I'm perfectly serious. You're beautiful enough to be Juliet, and Mario can just about get by as Romeo.'

'It won't work,' Mario growled. 'As though I could—'

'It's got to work,' Giorgio said. 'You're the only two who can do it in the time available. We've got to start right now, otherwise all our plans are in a mess. Come along, you two. Be professional.'

'He's right,' Mario growled. 'We have no choice.'

'Go next door and get changed,' Amadore said. 'Natasha, a maid will come with you.'

She looked around wildly. Surely there must be some other way. But there was no other way. Only this could save her plans for the success she simply had to have.

The maid appeared and took her to the room assigned as Juliet's dressing room. The dress fitted perfectly onto her slender, delicate figure. But her hair didn't seem right, pulled tightly back.

'I think Juliet would wear it hung loose,' she said.

The maid nodded, and got skilfully to work. Natasha watched, only half believing, as the self she knew disappeared and naive, vulnerable Juliet took her place. The merest touch of make-up heightened the impression, and she was ready to go.

As she entered the ballroom heads turned. Giorgio made a clapping movement and Amadore whistled.

She noticed neither of them. Her attention had been seized by the man standing a little further off. Mario had transformed into Romeo, wearing a dark blue doublet and tights. It would need a fine figure to get away with such a revealing costume, but Mario was tall, splendidly built and handsome enough to steal the spotlight.

Suddenly a memory came flooding back to her. Two years ago, during their precious short time together in Venice, they had spent a day on the beach. Her first sight of him, half naked in swimming trunks, had had a stunning effect on her, making her intensely aware that her own swimwear was a bikini, leaving much of her body uncovered.

Oh, yes, she'd thought as she enjoyed the sight of his long, strong legs as he raced across the beach. *Oh, yes!*

After that everything had changed. They spent the day chasing each other, bathing in the sea or stretched out on the sand, and with every moment she wanted him more. She'd feasted her eyes on his smooth, muscular body, seizing every chance to lean closer to him, cherishing the brief moments when her flesh brushed against his.

It had been her first experience of fierce desire and it revealed her to herself in a new light. In the past she had flirted, laughed, teased, but never before had she wanted a man with such fervour. When their eyes met she believed she saw the same intensity in him, and promised herself that soon he would carry her to a new world.

That night they'd parted with only a kiss. She had told herself he was biding his time, waiting for her to be ready to move on.

Three days later they had parted for ever.

Shaking off the memory, she began to walk towards Mario, tense for the moment when she would see his reaction to her. Would the past return to haunt him too? What would she see in his eyes?

At last Mario looked up, saw her and nodded.

'Splendid,' he said. 'Giorgio chose Juliet well.'

His tone was polite but nothing more, and his eyes were blank.

'And you look fine as well, Signor Ferrone,' she said, striving to match him for blandness.

'Well, like Giorgio said, I'll "just about get by".'

'Everybody ready?' Amadore called. 'This way.'

He indicated an archway at the far end of the ballroom. Mario offered Natasha his arm and she took it, saying, 'Thank you, *signore*.'

He leaned closer to her, murmuring, 'Don't call me *signore*. My name is Mario. If you address me formally people will think something is wrong between us.'

'And we mustn't let them think that,' she agreed. 'Shall we go?'

CHAPTER FIVE

THERE WAS A cheer when they came into the ballroom. Lisa nodded, as though to say that Romeo's looks met her high standards.

The photographer studied them with approval and said he would start with portrait shots.

'First I'll take you separately, then together. Juliet, you first.'

'Juliet? I'm Natasha,' she said lightly.

'No, today you are Juliet.'

'He's right,' Giorgio said. 'You don't pretend to be Juliet. You *are* Juliet. You can go back to being Natasha tomorrow.'

'If I want to,' she said, entering into the spirit. 'Natasha might be too boring.'

'That's the spirit,' Giorgio said with a grin.

She turned this way and that, smiled, looked sad, smiled again.

'Now throw your arms out,' Giorgio said. 'Imagine you're looking at someone who's the great happiness of your life.'

She did so, reaching towards the camera with a yearning look.

Mario, watching from the sidelines, turned his head

to avoid seeing that expression on her face. He remembered it too well from the past, and couldn't bear to be reminded of it now that the past was over.

Then he too had to pose for portrait shots.

'This way, that way,' the photographer called. 'Turn your head a little. Good. Now the two of you together.'

The first shot was a formal pose, with Juliet standing just in front of Romeo, his hands on her shoulders.

'Now turn and look into each other's eyes. Keep hold of each other but lean back a little so that I can see both of your faces.'

They obeyed, studying each other seriously, then smiling according to instructions.

'I think Romeo should frown a little,' Lisa called. 'And he should try to look sexy so that we know why Juliet fell for him.'

Mario scowled, annoyed at the comment and even more exasperated by the fact that Natasha collapsed with laughter.

'Don't worry,' she called. 'I can pretend if I have to.'

'And perhaps Juliet had to,' Giorgio said cheerfully. 'Maybe she didn't really fancy Romeo at all. She was pursuing her own agenda. *That's it!* Romeo, that grim look is perfect. Keep it up.'

'Yes, keep it up,' she chuckled. 'Just think how I'm going to thump you later.'

'Juliet, that smile is wonderful,' the photographer called. 'It says a lot about the kind of marriage they would have had if they'd lived. One where he got worked up and she laughed at him. I'm beginning to think nobody ever really understands this pair.'

'No,' she murmured so that only Mario could hear. 'Nobody really understands.'

'He's talking nonsense,' Mario growled.

'He's grandstanding to make us play our parts,' she said. 'It's his job. So we have to do ours.'

'Juliet,' Giorgio called, 'reach up and brush his hair forward a little, around his face.' She did so, hearing the camera click madly.

'That's it—now again—and again—gently—Juliet's longing to caress his face, and this is her chance.'

Natasha told herself that she was merely obeying orders, but she couldn't hide the truth from herself. She wanted to do this—wanted to touch his face, his body, his heart. Even through the lightness of her caress she felt the tremor that went through Mario, despite his attempt to suppress it. She could sense his reaction because it mirrored her own.

But could he suspect the feelings that were going through her at being so close to him? Suddenly, his face had softened. The grim look she saw on it so often faded, leaving a faint echo of the young, gentle man she had loved. His eyes were fixed on her intently but that might be no more than playing his part. If only she could tell.

'Right, that's it,' came Giorgio's voice. 'Now for the balcony scene. Come this way.'

The balcony at the back of the Splendido was decorated much like the one at Juliet's house, and had the advantage of being several feet lower so that Romeo and Juliet could be closer to each other. Mario stood below, reaching up, while Natasha leaned down to touch his hand while the camera clicked away.

'Perfect,' Giorgio cried at last. 'You two are doing a great job. It's wonderful how well you work together.'

They said what was necessary and followed him back

to the ballroom, where another selection of garments was laid out for them.

'Romeo believes that Juliet is dead,' Giorgio said. 'So he comes to the crypt where her body lies. He finds her there, says his farewells and takes his own life. Then she wakes, finds him dead, and she too chooses death. We'll shoot this scene in the cellar.'

With the maid's help, Natasha donned a plain gown and they all went down to the hotel's cellar, where a stone bench had been prepared for her to lie on.

'Ow!' she said, stretching out on it. 'That stone's really hard.'

'Is it really painful?' Mario asked her quietly.

'No, I'll be all right.'

'Let me put something under your head.'

'No, that would spoil it. But thank you.'

He still looked worried but let it drop.

'Walk up to her body,' Giorgio said. 'Look into her face as though you can't believe it's true. Good. Just like that.'

Lying there with her eyes closed, Natasha yearned to open them and see Mario's expression, to meet his eyes. But she must resist temptation and be content with the feel of his breath on her face.

'Lay your head on her breast,' Giorgio instructed.

The next moment she felt him lying against her and gave a slight gasp.

'Now kiss her,' Giorgio said,

She braced herself for the moment his mouth touched hers. It was the faintest possible sensation but she told herself to endure it.

'Again,' Giorgio said. 'Remember, you've lost the only woman in life that you could ever care about.'

Mario kissed her again before laying his head once more on her breast. At last Giorgio called out that the scene was over.

'Now for the big one,' he said. 'The moment when they meet.'

In the ballroom Natasha donned the glamorous gown and watched while the maid worked on her hair. When everything was ready Giorgio guided 'Romeo and Juliet' into position.

'It's during the ball. Juliet is standing there, watching everyone, particularly Paris, the man her parents want her to marry. But then she sees Romeo watching her. Their eyes meet.'

Mario turned his head so that he gazed at Natasha. She gazed back.

'He advances towards her,' Giorgio continued. 'That's right, Mario, a little nearer. He takes her hand, and asks forgiveness for touching her because he says he isn't worthy. But she says he is.'

Now Natasha's hand was clasped in Mario's. He was close to her, watching her intently.

'And Romeo dares to steal a kiss,' Giorgio said triumphantly. 'Go on. Let's catch that on camera.'

Gently Mario dropped his head, laying his lips on hers.

'Good,' Giorgio said. 'But I wonder if we should do it again. Natasha, it might be more effective if you put your arm around him.'

'It's too soon for that,' she said quickly. 'She doesn't yet know how she feels.'

'Nor does he,' Mario said. 'How would Romeo kiss her at this point? Would it be like this?' He laid his lips briefly over Natasha's. 'He might do it respectfully because however much he desires her he fears to offend her.

Or is he a shameless character who simply takes what he wants, like this?'

His arm went around her waist, drawing her against him, while his mouth covered hers firmly and purposefully.

She was stunned. The brief, light kiss he'd given her a few moments ago hadn't prepared her for this. Instinctively, her hands moved to touch him, but she snatched them back, unsure whether she would embrace him or push him away. She understood nothing except the disturbing pleasure of his lips on hers, and the maddening instinct to slap his face.

For two years she'd wanted to be in his arms, dreamed of it while mentally rejecting it in her rage at his betrayal. Now the sweetness of holding him again struggled with fury at his assumption that he could do as he liked and she would have to accept it.

But she could not repulse him. Whatever common sense might dictate, she must appear to react to him blissfully and chance what the future might bring. She let herself press against him, eager to feel his response, and then—

'All right, Giorgio?' Mario cried, standing back. 'Is that what you want?'

Natasha froze, barely able to believe what had happened. It seemed that the feelings that had pervaded her had been hers alone. Had he felt anything beyond the need to get the photographs right? Fury simmered inside her.

'That's fine,' Giorgio said. 'Do it just like that, for the camera.'

Then Mario's hands were on her again, drawing her nearer so that he could lay his lips on hers and hold her against him, unmoving. She could feel the warmth of his mouth, of his whole body, and her own responded to the sensation whether she wanted it to or not. Her anger flared further.

Somewhere in the background she could hear the sound of a camera, clicking again and again until at last Giorgio called, 'All right, that's it. Well done, you two. Now let's think about the next scene.'

'I need a little fresh air first,' Natasha said, quickly slipping out of the nearest door into a corridor.

She ran until she reached a corner behind which she could hide. She must escape Mario lest he suspect that she'd just discovered the power he still had over her.

But when she looked around she found him facing her.

'Did you follow me?' she demanded.

'I thought that was what you meant me to do. Don't you have something you want to say to me?'

'Oh, yes, I have a thousand things,' she said furiously. 'You've got a nerve, doing what you did back there.'

'Kissing you, you mean? But you owed it to me. When we parted you never kissed me goodbye.'

'I never thumped the living daylights out of you either, which I was surely tempted to.'

He seemed to consider this. 'So you think I deserve to have you slap my face? Very well. Do your worst.'

'What are you saying?'

'Go ahead. Slap me if it will make you feel better.'

He jutted his chin out a little and stood waiting.

'Stop talking nonsense,' she snapped.

'I mean it. You can do what you like and I promise not to retaliate.'

'This is all a big joke to you, isn't it?'

He shook his head. 'My sense of humour died the

day you left. In the weeks I spent trying to find you I buried it deep underground. So what now? Aren't you going to hit me?'

'Certainly not. It would be unprofessional. I might leave marks on your face that would spoil the next photographs. The matter is closed.'

He saluted. 'Yes, ma'am. Whatever you say, ma'am.'

'Oh, stop it—stop it! Stop trying to make a fool of me, of yourself, of both of us.'

Suddenly, his manner changed. The wry irony died and a bleakness came into his eyes. 'You silly woman,' he said quietly. 'Don't you realise that we all have our own way of coping.'

'And that's your way? Well, this is my way.'

Without warning, the swift temper she'd vowed to control swept over her, driving her to do something she knew was madness. She seized his head in her hands, drew it down and covered his mouth with her own. At once she could feel his hands on her and sensed the same confusion as she had felt herself—to deny the kiss or indulge it joyfully?

But he was going to indulge it. That was her decision, and she would give him no choice. She slightly softened the pressure of her mouth so that the kiss could become a caress, her lips moving over his in a way she had once known delighted him. She sensed his response in his tension, the sudden tightening of his arms about her.

Now she was ready to taunt him further. The pressure of her mouth intensified, and his breath came faster as his excitement grew. His lips parted as he explored her more deeply. He was no longer merely receiving her kiss but returning it in full, seeking to take command but not succeeding. The command was hers, and she would keep it whether he liked it or not. Her spirit soared. She was winning.

He drew back a little. 'Natasha—'

'Take warning, Mario. Two can play this game. You won't defy me again. If you do I'll make you sorry.'

She felt him tense, saw his eyes full of disbelief as he understood her meaning. Then it was all over. 'You had to do that, didn't you?' he rasped. 'You had to tease me— make me think—but it wasn't a kiss. It was revenge.'

'Revenge can be very sweet,' she said, pushing him away. 'That's one of the things I learned from you. Did you think you were going to get away with what you did back there? You just had to show me that you were the boss, and how I felt didn't count.'

He shook his head. 'You won't believe this,' he said in a hard voice, 'but I kissed you because I wanted to. I'm ashamed of that now because it seems so stupid to imagine that you had any kindly feelings left. But, idiot that I was, I thought some part of you might still be the old Natasha, the sweet-natured girl I loved and wanted to be with.

'But you warned me about that, didn't you? You told me that Natasha was dead. I couldn't believe it, but I believe it now. You did this to get your own back by reminding me of what I've lost.'

'You lost it because you didn't want it,' she said.

'Keep telling yourself that,' he said quietly. 'In the end you may come to believe it. In those days I wanted you more than I've ever wanted any woman. And I could have told you that if you hadn't vanished when you did. You landed us in this desert, not me. You did it by losing your temper and acting without thinking anything through. We didn't have to end up here. We could have been married by now, and expecting our first child. Instead—well, look at us.'

'Stop it! *Stop it!*' she screamed, turning away from him with her hands over her ears.

'Yes, the truth can be very painful, can't it? I could have devoted my life to loving you. Instead, I've come so close to hating you that it scares me.'

'Well, at least that's getting the truth out into the open. You hate me.'

'I didn't say that. I said I came close to hating you. I've never been able to take the final step, but I have a feeling that will come soon.'

She made no reply. The unexpected glimpse he'd given her of his own feelings had set off an aching misery inside her. He didn't hate her, but he would if he could. She wanted to scream and bang her head against the wall.

She turned away but he pulled her around to face him.

'You won't let me tell you my side of it and I think I know why,' he raged. 'Because you're a coward, Natasha. You're afraid to know the truth. If you had to face the terrible thing you did, you couldn't bear it. Everything could have been so different for us if you hadn't condemned me so quickly.'

She didn't reply. Something inside her choked the words back before they could escape.

'If you knew how I planned that day,' Mario said. 'I'd told you that I had something important to say to you. I was going to ask you not to go home, to stay with me, become my love.

'My relationship with Tania was never serious. She was a very experienced woman who surrounded herself with various male "friends". I knew I wasn't the only man in her life but it didn't trouble me because I wasn't in love with her and she wasn't in love with me.

'But when I met you, things changed. Suddenly I no longer wanted "a bit of fun". I wanted something serious and I wanted it with you. Nobody else. Just you. So I met up with Tania and I told her that we couldn't see each other any more.

'She was angry, but I thought she understood. Then it happened. She descended on us; you disappeared. If you could have seen what I went through trying to find you, how deep in despair I was—well, I guess you'd have enjoyed it.'

'I wouldn't have believed it,' she retorted. 'You? In despair, when you played the field so easily?'

'I'd done with playing the field. That life was all over for me. And if I could have explained that—made you understand... But what's the use? You only believe what you want to believe.'

She stared at him, trying to take in his incredible words. It was as though she'd become two people—one recoiling from him, one reaching out, longing to know more.

'Are you two there?' Giorgio's voice came along the corridor.

'We're here,' Mario called back.

'Ah, good.' Giorgio appeared around the corner. 'Time to get changed back into normal clothes. No more photographs today, but we're going to see Romeo's house.'

Natasha escaped to the dressing room and rid herself of the costume. It was a relief to don modern clothes and become herself again. Juliet could be banished, at least for a while.

The longer the better, she thought, staring into the

mirror and brushing her hair fiercely so that it fell down over her shoulders. It looked like spun gold in the afternoon sunlight. Once Mario had made a joke about it; 'my dangerous blonde bombshell' he'd said in a teasing voice.

'I'm not dangerous,' she'd protested.

'You can be when you act on instinct. Some of your instincts could scare a man.'

'Do I scare you?' she'd teased.

'You could if I scared easily.'

Today he'd told her frankly that her headstrong temper had done much to part them.

Suppose I'd stayed to listen to his 'explanations', she thought. *Should I have done that? Should I have trusted him? No! No!'*

She scraped her hair back as tight as it would go. When she was satisfied with her appearance she went down to join them.

Romeo's house was just a few minutes away from Juliet's and could only be seen from the outside.

'It looks like a fortress,' she said, 'with those battlements.'

'A lot of buildings were created like that in those days,' Giorgio said. 'Half of the city was almost permanently at war with the other half, hence the fight between the Capulets and Montagues.'

'Buongiorno!'

A cry from a few feet away made them turn to see a man hailing them. He seemed to be in his forties, tall and strongly built, and Natasha recognised him as a member of the *Comunità* that she had met on the first evening.

'You should have told me you were coming,' he said, giving her a hug.

'I wasn't sure until the last minute,' Mario said.

'Come and have coffee with me. My hotel is just around the corner.'

As they walked there Giorgio dropped his voice to say to Natasha, 'Mario would have avoided this meeting if he could. That's Riccardo, the rival who tried to challenge him for the presidency of the *Comunità*. He's very wealthy, owns more vineyards than any of the others, and likes giving orders just as much as Mario does.'

'You said Mario got him to back off.'

'Yes. Not sure how, but the rumours say some of Riccardo's business dealings wouldn't bear inspection.'

'You mean Mario threatened him?'

'I doubt if it was a blatant threat. That isn't Mario's way. He'll just make a remark that only one man will understand—and fear. Riccardo dropped his challenge very suddenly. Mario isn't a man you tangle with, not if you've got any sense.'

Riccardo's premises were lavish and decorative, even more so than the Dimitri Hotel. Wherever Natasha looked she could see that money had been spent without restraint. It might well appear that Riccardo was a man who could challenge Mario, but after only a few minutes seeing them together Natasha sensed that this could never happen.

Riccardo was afraid of Mario. That was the incredible truth. And Mario was content to have it be so. The young man who had once enjoyed getting his own way by charm now used power to bend people to his will.

He had blamed her for disappearing, leaving him to search frantically until finally he had accepted despair. She had resisted the accusation, but now it troubled her more than she could face. This man scared other people, but admitted that she scared him.

She fell into earnest conversation with Riccardo.

'I want to see the rest of Verona,' she said. 'It's not just about *Romeo and Juliet*. There's more to life than romance.'

'No doubt about that,' Mario agreed.

They clinked glasses.

'Right,' Natasha said. 'I've done my preliminary work. Now I'm going to shut myself away for a while to get everything written. I'll see you in a few days, gentlemen.'

'So we're no longer needed?' Giorgio asked comically. 'You're dismissing us just like that? Ah, it's a hard world.'

'That's how it is,' Mario said, reflecting Giorgio's theatrical manner. 'A woman dismisses a man when she no longer needs him. We just have to accept it.'

They all laughed.

'If I'm not required for a while I'll go back to Venice for a few days,' Mario said. 'Sally, my sister-in-law, is about to give birth again. She had a hard time with her last baby so I think Damiano might appreciate having me around for a few days. I'll stay in touch—*signorina*, Giorgio will take care of you.'

'Thank you. If I have Giorgio, what more could I possibly want?'

Mario left that afternoon, bidding her a polite goodbye in front of everyone else, adding, 'Giorgio can contact me if need be. Goodbye, everyone.'

He fled.

CHAPTER SIX

IT WAS A relief for Natasha to spend the next few days without Mario. She needed time to come to terms with what he'd told her.

If you knew how I planned that day... I was going to ask you not to go home, to stay with me, become my love.

She tried to block out the memory, but it haunted her. Mario vowed he'd broken with Tania because he loved her and was preparing to tell her.

We didn't have to end up here. We could have been married by now, and expecting our first child. Instead— well, look at us.

She tried not to hear the terrible words echoing in her mind. Mario had accused her of believing only what she wanted to believe. And perhaps he was right. If he was telling the truth it meant that she had created the disaster almost single-handed.

To escape that unbearable thought, she submerged herself in work, studying not just Verona itself but its surroundings. It stood in the Veneto, the northern region of Italy that was best known for the city of Venice.

'That's why we speak Venetian here,' Giorgio told her.

'Venetian? Venice has its own language?'

'Certainly, and it's spoken throughout the Veneto. People speak Italian as well, and English is very common because of all the tourists. But you need to know about the Venetian language to really understand this area.'

'And that's what I want to do,' she said, scribbling furiously.

The next day the photographer delivered the pictures of 'Romeo and Juliet' and she studied them closely.

Mario's face fascinated her. When they had met a few days ago, she'd thought he looked older, harsher, more tense. But in these pictures he had changed again, becoming more like the young man she remembered. She thought she could see a softening in his expression as he looked at Juliet, a glow in his eyes which the camera had caught wonderfully.

She had seen that glow before, two years ago. *He must be a very good actor*, she thought. *But I suppose I knew that.*

She spent some time wandering Verona alone, drinking in the atmosphere with nobody to distract her. She found a street she thought might be the place where Juliet's cousin Tybalt killed Romeo's friend, Mercutio. Just a little further on was where Romeo could have caught up with Tybalt and stabbed him in revenge.

Nearby were two *Comunità* hotels, where she was welcomed eagerly. She looked them over, and jotted down notes in readiness for the next despatch.

There were a dozen places to visit, but she had no energy to explore further today. She had coped with the emotional strains of the last few days, but they had taken their toll. Now she was tired and her head ached a little, so she set off back to the Dimitri Hotel.

It was a relief to get back there, order a coffee and sit in the hotel café. She closed her eyes, unaware that a man was watching her a few yards away, taking in every detail about her: her air of despondency, her appearance of being apart from the world, her loneliness.

Suddenly she looked up and saw him.

'Mario!'

'Hello, Natasha.' He went to sit beside her.

'You're back from Venice then?'

'Yes, I arrived ten minutes ago.'

'Is everything all right with your family?'

'Yes, Sally came through it well and now I've got a niece.'

'Congratulations.'

'Thank you. How are things with you? You look very tired.'

'I've had a busy day, but a very satisfying one.'

'Did anyone go with you, to make sure you didn't get lost?'

'Hey, there's no need to insult me.'

'What?'

'I'm not some silly girl who gets lost every time she's in an unfamiliar street.'

'Sorry, ma'am.'

'I could have asked Giorgio to escort me, but I refused. I can manage.'

He had no doubt of her real meaning. She'd needed time alone, free of the tension that was always there between them. He understood because he felt the same.

'You work too hard,' he said. 'You always did. I remember once before, when we first met in Venice, you said you'd been working so hard that you were exhausted. I took you for a ride in a gondola, and you fell asleep.'

He said it with a smile but she recalled that he hadn't been amused at the time. He was used to taking girls for gondola rides, but not used to them nodding off in his company.

'You took me back to the hotel and said goodnight very firmly,' she recalled, smiling. 'You felt insulted at my behaviour. I always wondered what you did for the rest of the evening, but I expect you found someone else who managed to stay awake.'

'I can't remember,' he said firmly.

'Very tactful.'

They both laughed. He couldn't tell her that he'd spent the rest of that evening alone, brooding about her seeming indifference to his attentions. She had intrigued him, and he'd sought her out early next day.

'That was always the way with you,' he reflected now. 'There, yet not there, keeping me wondering.'

'I didn't do it on purpose,' she said. 'You thought I was being a deliberate tease, but I wasn't. I was wondering too.'

And that had been her attraction for him, he realised. Where other girls were often willing, sometimes too willing, Natasha had always been just out of reach. It had driven him crazy but it had kept him in pursuit of her. Until finally she had vanished, leaving him devastated.

How much had she really felt for him? To this day he didn't know, and he doubted he ever would.

But one thing was certain. She was no longer the tense, nervy creature of a few days ago. The woman who had forced a kiss on him as revenge for his kissing her had simply vanished. Now she was relaxed, in command, humorous, alluring.

'I hear that you've been working hard,' he said. 'You've been contacting the other hotel owners to get information, and showing them what you planned to write so that they could approve it. They're very impressed. My stock has risen considerably since I performed the brilliant act of securing your services.' He gave a theatrical flourish. 'Only a genius like myself could have discovered you.'

'But you didn't discover me. It was Giorgio.'

'Hush. We don't say that.' He grinned. 'And neither does Giorgio if he knows what's good for him.'

'I see. The boss gives his orders and we all jump to obey.'

'Some do. I doubt I'll ever see the day when you jump to obey.'

'But you pay my wages,' she reminded him. 'Surely I have no choice but to obey you?'

'All right, all right. You've had your joke.'

'It's not a joke. You're my employer. I know it's Giorgio who directs me, but you're the authority. If you told him to fire me, he'd have to do so.'

'There's no danger of that.'

'Actually, there's something I've been meaning to say to you.'

'What is it?' he asked with a sense of foreboding, for her tone implied a serious matter. 'Go on, tell me. How bad is it?'

'It's not bad at all. I want to say thank you.'

'Thank you? For what?' he asked, sounding nervous.

'For changing my contract so that I'm making more money. I couldn't believe it when Giorgio showed me the new one and said you'd told him to increase it.'

'But you've already thanked me,' he said. 'You did so a few minutes afterwards. I told you then that it was essential to secure your professional services.'

'Yes, you told me that, but you knew how bad my financial problems were. You could have secured me without raising the money. I think there may have been a little kindness involved too.'

He gave a slight smile. 'Kindness? Me? I'm a businessman. I don't do kindness.'

'I think you do. I can remember things in Venice—that little girl who lost her dog, and you found it for her.'

'I was only trying to impress you.'

'And you succeeded. You don't like people to know about your kind and caring streak but it's there.'

'That's practically an insult.'

'Then you'll have to put up with me insulting you,' she said.

'I think I can just about manage that.'

'The thing is—that quarrel we had the other day, when we'd finished having the pictures taken… It just flared up but I wish it hadn't.'

'So do I. I said things I didn't mean.'

'You said I was afraid to face the truth, that everything could have been different if I'd listened to you. I think you meant that and I don't blame you.'

'But do you believe what I told you—about Tania, how I'd already broken with her?'

'Please—please don't,' she gasped. 'It's in the past. It doesn't matter now.'

'Meaning that you still don't believe me.'

'I don't know,' she said in anguish. 'There are so many things battling each other in my mind—'

'I know the feeling,' he said wryly.

'But it doesn't matter.'

'Natasha, how can it not matter? You always prided yourself on being logical, but if you think what happened between us didn't matter you're talking nonsense.'

'I didn't mean that. It mattered then, but not now. The world has moved on. We've moved on.'

'Ah, yes,' he said quietly. 'We've moved on.'

'And I think we were never meant to be together. Something was always fated to go wrong.'

'Now you sound like Giorgio.'

'What do you mean?'

'Just before you arrived, he and I were talking about Romeo and Juliet being "star-crossed lovers". Sometimes a couple is meant for each other but just can't get it together. They just have to accept that fate is against them.'

'Yes,' she said thoughtfully. 'You could say that fate was against us. My problem was that you had more women in your life than you could count. Or that I could count.'

'And mine was that you don't trust any man. I've always wondered why. Was there some other guy who walked out and broke your heart?'

'In a way, yes, but it's not how you think. The man who walked out was my father.'

She fell silent until he said, 'Tell me about him.'

'I loved him, and he loved me, so I thought. And then he just vanished. I never heard from him again. We seemed to be so close but he just wiped me and my mother out of existence.'

As you did with me, Mario thought, but was too tactful to say.

'My mother was so bitter. She told me a million times that no man could ever be trusted, but she didn't need to say it. I felt it for myself.'

'So when we knew each other you were always reminding yourself that no man could be trusted—especially me.'

'No, not especially you. You mattered more than anyone else but—'

'But you instinctively thought I was no different from the rest of them. Except perhaps a bit worse.'

'No, no—it wasn't like that.'

'From where I'm sitting it was exactly like that.'

'And so you've come close to hating me,' she sighed. 'Perhaps I can't blame you.'

'Please, Natasha, forget I said that. I was in a temper. I wanted to hurt you because I resented the way you'd just shown your power over me. The way you kissed me made a point I didn't want to admit.'

'A point?' Her heart was beating fast.

'You showed me that I'm not the strong, independent fellow I like to believe I am. So I hit back with the worst thing I could think of. I didn't mean it and I'm not proud of it. Do you think you can forgive me?'

'That depends.'

'On what?' he asked cautiously.

'On whether *you* can forgive *me*.'

'There's nothing to forgive.'

'Really? What about the way you say I—?'

'Stop there,' he said quickly. 'Whatever I may have said, I take it back. It's over. It's done with. Let us be friends.'

She considered a moment before smiling and saying wistfully, 'That would be nice.'

'It's settled then.'

'Shake?' She held out her hand, but he fended her off.

'No. We shook hands the first night as professional associates. But now we're friends—and friends don't shake hands. They don't need to.' He leaned over and kissed her cheek. 'That's what friends do. And they buy each other coffee.'

'Good. Waiter!'

'No, I meant that I'd buy you a coffee.'

'Stop giving me orders. I'm buying and that's that.'

'Yes, ma'am. Anything you say, ma'am.'

'Mind you, you'll have to do the talking.'

He nodded, gave the waiter the order in Italian, then watched as she paid.

'Have you explored anywhere recently?' he asked.

'I've looked around a bit, but there's still one big place I've set my heart on visiting and that's Juliet's tomb.

'Now it's a museum,' she said. 'It seems to attract as many tourists as the balcony, so I must go there and plan the next article.'

'There's a *Comunità* hotel nearby,' Mario said. 'The Albergo Martinez. You met the owner the other night. We could dine there tonight and hear anything they have to say. Let me call him.'

He took out his phone, made a call and started talking in Italian. While she was waiting, her own mobile phone beeped. Her heart beat hard with horror when she read the text message.

After a few minutes Mario hung up, saying, 'He's expecting us in a couple of hours.'

He stopped suddenly, frowning as he saw her staring into space, full of tension.

'What is it?' he asked. 'What happened?'

'Nothing.'

'No, something's the matter. What is it?'

'No—no—I'm all right. I'd like to go to my room.'

She got up and walked quickly away. Frowning, he followed her, hurrying until he caught up and could take a firm hold of her hand. She didn't resist but neither did she respond, and he had a feeling that she had taken refuge in another world, from which he was excluded.

He accompanied her as far as her door, noting that she still looked pale and tense.

'I'll collect you in an hour,' he said.

'I'll be ready.'

Once inside, she undressed and got into the shower. There was a kind of relief in being doused with water, as though it could wash away the shock that had overtaken her.

The text on her mobile phone had been from Elroy Jenson:

You won't get away from me.

He's driving me crazy, she told herself. *And that's what he wants*.

She wondered why she hadn't told Mario what had troubled her. It should have been easy since she had already told him about Elroy, and he would have been a valuable ally. But something in her was reluctant to reveal more vulnerability. Especially to Mario.

When she had showered she put on a neat dark blue dress, suitable for a polite gathering. For several minutes she teased her hair, trying to decide whether to be seductive or businesslike. As so often with Mario, her mind was filled with conflicting thoughts.

Their conversation had been fraught with double meanings. He'd said, *I wanted to hurt you because I resented the way you'd just shown your power over me*.

But he'd implied the power of a bully, not of a woman. They had made a truce, but the battle was far from over.

When he'd pressed her to say that she believed him now she had been unable to say what he wanted to hear. She longed to believe him, but she couldn't quite make herself take the final step.

But why should it matter whether I believe him or not? she mused. *That's all over. What matters is that we can manage to be friends.*

Nico was watching for their arrival at the Albergo Martinez and came to meet them with hands outstretched. Natasha recognised him from their meeting the first night.

Over supper he described the tomb.

'Juliet was buried in the church of San Francesco al Corso, a monastery,' he explained.

'Yes, it was Friar Laurence, a monk, who married them,' Natasha recalled. 'On their wedding day they went to his cell and he took them to the church to marry them.'

'True. And when Juliet died—or at least she'd drunk the potion and seemed dead—she was taken to the monastery to be buried. These days the monastery has become a museum. You can go to the crypt and see the sarcophagus that legend says was hers.

'The museum also hosts weddings. Many people choose to become united for life in the place where Romeo and Juliet were united in eternity. Of course, if they are seeking a hotel not too far away—'

'They'll be glad to discover yours,' she said in her most professional manner. 'I shall make sure that they do.'

'*Eccellente!* Mario, you've made a fine discovery in this talented lady. Don't let her go, whatever you do.'

'Don't worry; I won't,' he said with a cheerful nod.

'Now, let us go in to supper.'

Supper was served at a large table where many people were already sitting. As they sat down Natasha became aware of something she had seen many times before. From every direction women were casting admiring glances at Mario. It had been there from the beginning, two years ago. It was still there.

And why not? she thought. *He's got the looks to make it happen. And it doesn't bother me any more.*

She soon discovered that the man sitting next to her was an ideal choice. His name was Tonio and he was an academic, specialising in English history. As history had always been one of her interests, she was soon deep in conversation with him, intrigued by his prejudiced arguments.

'You're all wrong about Richard III,' she told him. 'Shakespeare depicted him as a monster but he wasn't really—'

'You English!' he exclaimed. 'You can never believe that any of your monarchs were evil.'

'On the contrary, the evil ones are the most fun. But Richard's evil reputation is mostly a kind of show business.'

'I've studied the evidence and I tell you—'

Heads close together, they stayed absorbed in their argument, with the rest of the table regarding them with amused fascination. All except Mario, who was looking displeased, which surprised Natasha when she happened to glance up. The luscious beauty beside him was paying him fervent attention that a man might be expected to enjoy. But he seemed to be tolerating rather than encouraging her.

'I see Bianca's got her claws into a new man,' said Tonio, sounding amused.

'You speak as though it happens often.'

'With Bianca it does. She likes to cast her net wide.'

'It doesn't look as though he's fallen under her spell.'

'Not now, but give him a little time.'

Bianca was clearly a practised flirt, convinced that any man was hers for the asking. When she patted Mario's face, giggling, he smiled back politely before returning his gaze to Natasha.

'You need to look at it like this,' Tonio said, returning to their discussion. 'King Richard couldn't possibly—'

She plunged back into the argument, enjoying herself for the next half hour, until somebody put on some music and people began to dance. Suddenly Mario appeared by her chair.

'Dance with me,' he said.

'Wouldn't you rather dance with Bianca?'

'No.' He grasped her hand, drew her to her feet and onto the floor.

'I thought you were having a lovely time.' She laughed as they twirled.

'Did you really?' he demanded ironically.

'Being hunted down by a woman who'd gladly have given you anything you wanted.'

'Which would be fine if there was anything I did want from her. But I don't.'

'That wouldn't stop some men. They'd just take anything that's going.'

'I was like that once, when I was young and stupid. I grew up in the end, but by then it was too late.'

He said the last words with a wry look. The next moment the temptress glided past them. She was dancing with another man, but even so she gave Mario a glance that made him tighten his grasp on Natasha.

'Rescue me,' he growled.

'How?'

'Anyhow.'

'All right. Here goes. Aaaargh!'

With a theatrical sigh, she drooped against his chest.

'Oh, how my head aches,' she declared. 'I really must go home.'

'I'll take you,' he said.

Turning to their host, he explained that it was necessary to take Natasha away at once.

'She isn't feeling well,' he said. 'She must go to bed.'

From somewhere came the sound of choking laughter. Mario ignored it and picked Natasha up to carry her from the room. He didn't set her down until they reached the car.

'Thank you,' he said as they drove away.

'No problem. I'm really glad to leave because I need some sleep. Of course, if you want to go back and spend time with Bianca—'

'If that's your idea of a joke, it's not funny,' he said in an edgy voice.

'Sorry, I couldn't resist it.'

'Perhaps you should try to resist it. I'm just a sitting duck as far as you're concerned.'

'All right, I apologise.'

'It was getting very difficult in there.'

'You know what they're all thinking now, don't you?' she chuckled.

'Yes, they think that when we get home we're going to— Well, you can imagine.'

'Yes, I can imagine.'

'And I'm sorry. But that woman was getting embarrassing.'

'Don't tell me you're afraid of her. You? A man who's afraid of nothing.'

'You'd be surprised at some of the things I'm afraid of,' he said. 'Once you were one of them. Now you're beginning to feel like the best friend I have.'

'Good. Then we have nothing left to worry about…'

CHAPTER SEVEN

NEXT MORNING THEY drove to the monastery museum and went down into the crypt, where several other tourists had already gathered, looking at a large marble sarcophagus.

It was open at the top, revealing that it was empty now, but legend said that this was where Juliet had lain after taking the drug that made her appear lifeless. Here, Romeo had come to find her and, believing her dead, had taken his own life, minutes before she awoke. Finding him dead, she had taken her own life.

'I just don't understand it,' said an elderly man, staring into the sarcophagus. 'How could two people so young take their own lives?'

'Maybe they didn't,' said one of his companions. 'Maybe that's an invention of the story.'

'No,' Natasha said. 'It's part of the story because it was inevitable. It's what you do if life has lost all meaning.'

'And that can happen at any age,' Mario said at once.

'No,' the old man said. 'They could have got over each other and found other lovers.'

'But they didn't believe that,' Mario pointed out.

'Youngsters never do,' the man said loftily. 'But when they get older they find out that nothing ever really matters that much. Love comes and goes and comes again. It's ridiculous to believe anyone discovers the full meaning of their life as young as that.'

'No,' Mario said. 'It's ridiculous to believe that such a discovery happens to a timetable. It happens when it's ready to happen. Not before and not after.'

The old man looked at him with interest. 'You sound like an expert, sir.'

'I guess we're all experts, one way or another,' Mario said.

There were some murmurs of agreement from the little crowd as they turned away, following their tourist guide to another part of the museum.

Now that they were alone, Mario watched as Natasha looked into the sarcophagus.

'They married and had one sweet night together,' she murmured. 'But when they finally lay together it was here.'

'They lie together and they always will,' Mario said.

She turned a smiling face on him. 'You know what you've done, don't you?'

'What have I done?'

'Given me a wonderful idea that I can develop for the piece I'm writing. "They lie together and they always will." Thank you.'

He made an ironic gesture. 'Glad to be of use.'

'Would you mind leaving me alone here for a while? I just want to—' She looked around her, taking a deep breath, her arms extended.

She just wanted to absorb a romantic atmosphere without being troubled by his presence, he thought. A dreary inconvenience. That was how she saw him now.

True, she had kissed him, but in anger, not in love or

desire. And hell would freeze over before he let her suspect the depth of her triumph.

He stepped aside to a place in the shadows. From here he saw her stare down again into the tomb, reaching out into the empty space inside. What did she see in that space? Romeo, lying there, waiting for her to join him? Or Romeo and Juliet, sleeping eternally, clasped in each other's arms, held against each other's hearts?

Whatever it was, she had not invited him to be with her, because in her heart she was certain that he had left the dream behind long ago. If he had ever believed in it.

If only there was some magic spell that could enable her to look into his heart and see the truth he had carried there ever since their first meeting. Might she then look at him with eyes as fervent and glowing as she had done once, long, long ago?

He stayed watching her for a while, expecting that any moment she would move away. But she seemed transfixed, and at last he went to her.

'Are you all right?' he asked. 'You seem almost troubled.'

'No, I'm not troubled. It's just the atmosphere here, and what this tomb represents.'

'Surely it just represents death?'

'No, there's more. Finality, fulfilment, completion. They were young; they could have gone on and had lives that would have seemed satisfying. But each meant more to the other than life itself. You put it perfectly when you said people can discover what really matters while they're still young, and then they lie together for ever. This—' she looked around at the walls of the tomb '—this says everything.'

'I think we should go now,' he said. Her fascination with the place was making him uneasy.

'Yes, I've done all I need to do here. I'll spend this evening working on it. Then I'll do a new article and send it around the *Comunità*, so they can tell me what they think. I'm sure their suggestions will be useful.'

'I see you've got all the boxes ticked.'

'I hope so. That's what you're paying me for. Shall we go? We're finished here, aren't we?'

'Oh, yes,' he agreed. 'We're finished here.'

No more was said on the way back to the hotel.

Once there, Natasha hurried up to her room to get to work. She had supper served to her there and did not go downstairs all evening. She needed to be alone to think about the day. Mario's observations at the tomb had left her wondering. The old man had said he sounded like an expert about love. Mario had replied, *We're all experts, one way or another.*

One way or another. Love might be a joy or a betrayal. Which had he meant?

But I don't need to ask that, she thought. *He feels betrayed, just as I do. But how is that possible? Can we have both betrayed each other?*

He'd accused her of refusing to listen to him because she feared the truth, feared to confront her own part in their break-up. She had denied it, but could there possibly be a grain of truth in it?

Surely not, she thought. It couldn't have turned out any differently. Could it?

She had felt her own pain so intensely, but now she was confronted by his pain and it was a bewildering experience.

We'll never understand each other, she thought. *I mustn't hope for too much. Or do I mean fear too much?*

She gave herself a mental shake.

That's enough. I'm here to work and when I've finished my job I'll leave, whatever he says or does.

But the next day everything changed.

In the morning she went exploring again, wandering Verona on foot until, in the afternoon, she reached Juliet's house. There, she looked around the courtyard, meaning to go inside and see the museum.

But something drew her to Juliet's statue, still standing as it had been before, gazing into the distance.

If only, she thought, she could indulge the fantasy of asking Juliet's advice, and imagining an answer. It might help sort out the confusion in her head and her heart.

She didn't know how Mario felt, or how she herself felt. When he had kissed her she'd wanted him so much that it scared her. So she had punished him with a kiss designed to show him what he'd lost. But she too had been reminded of what she'd lost.

Into her mind came Mario's face, looking as he had at the start of the photo shoot. His expression had been— she struggled for the words—cautious, perhaps a little nervous.

She had blamed him for kissing her, thinking him too confident and self-satisfied. But did she blame him too much? Had he been uneasy, secretly wanting the kiss but unsure of himself?

I know how that feels, she brooded. *In my heart I wanted him to kiss me. Perhaps that's why I was so angry when he did.*

She sighed and turned away. Then she stopped, tense.

Mario was standing there, watching her.

'I happened to see you in the street,' he said, 'so I took the liberty of following you. Have you been inside the house?'

'No, I was about to go in.'

'Let's go in together.'

Inside, they looked briefly around the sixteenth-century furniture, absorbing the perfect atmosphere for the legend. Then they climbed the stairs and stepped out onto the balcony.

A young couple was already there, wrapped in each other's arms.

'Sorry,' the girl said, moving aside. 'We just had to come and see it again. We're getting married here next week and all the pictures will be taken out on the balcony.'

'How lovely,' Natasha said. 'The perfect place.'

'We thought so.' They kissed and slipped away into the building.

How lucky they were, she thought, to be so sure of each other, of life, of the future.

Now the light was fading, and there were few visitors. It was easy to imagine herself as Juliet, standing there looking into the night sky, unaware that Romeo was down below, watching her.

'I wonder what it was like for her,' she mused, 'to stand here, dreaming of him, then finally realising he was there, seeing him watching her, not knowing that their love was fated.'

Before he could answer, there was a shrill from her mobile phone. But she ignored it.

'Aren't you going to answer that?' Mario asked.

'No, it can wait,' she said in a tense voice. 'I didn't mean to bring it with me. I don't want to be distracted.'

The phone shrilled again.

'Answer it,' Mario said. 'Get rid of them.'

Reluctantly, she pulled out the phone and answered.

'At last,' said the voice she dreaded.

'You again,' she snapped. 'Stop pestering me.'

'Stop telling me what to do,' said Jenson's voice. 'If I want to call you I shall. Who do you think you are to give me orders?'

'Who do I think I am? I'm the woman who told you to go and jump in the lake. I'm the woman who wants nothing to do with a man as disgusting as you. You should have realised that by now.'

From the other end of the line came a crack of laughter.

'No, you're the one who should have woken up to reality, you stupid tart. You don't know what I could do to you—'

'I think I do. You've made it brutally clear.'

'That was just the start. You don't know how sorry I can make you, but you're going to find out. I know something about you, Natasha, and by the time I've finished you're going to wish you'd treated me with more respect.'

Before she could reply, the phone was wrenched from her hand by Mario.

'Jenson,' he snapped. 'Go to hell. Leave her alone or I'll make you sorry.'

A bellow of ugly laughter reached him down the line.

'Not as sorry as you'll be if you're involved with Natasha,' Jenson bawled. 'She's made herself my enemy, and if you side with her you'll be my enemy too. I have a way with enemies.'

With a swift movement Mario severed the connection. 'Jenson's still pestering you?'

'Yes, he won't stop.' She was shaking.

'All right, let's deal with this,' Mario said. He put his arms around her firmly, protectively. 'Come on, we're going back to the hotel.'

Still holding her, he led her back to his car. She almost collapsed into the seat beside him and sat with her head in her hands during the drive. To his relief, there was almost nobody in the hotel lobby and he was able to take her upstairs quickly. As soon as the door closed behind them he clasped her once more in his arms.

'It's all right,' he said fiercely. 'There's nothing to be scared of. You're safe here. Jenson is in the past.'

'No, he's not,' she groaned. 'As long as he can reach me he's not in the past. Changing my number is useless. He always finds out my new one. That's how powerful he is. I'm scared. He haunts me. When I get a text or a call from him it's as though he's actually there. He's already ruined my career, and I can't be rid of him.'

'You're wrong,' Mario said. 'He hasn't ruined your career, and he isn't going to because I'm not going to let him.'

She took some deep breaths, managing to calm down a little. Mario touched her chin, lifting it so that he could see her face. For a moment he was tempted to give her a gentle kiss, by way of comfort. But, instead, he took her to the bed, still holding her as she sat down, then drawing her head against him again.

'Thank goodness you were there,' she said. 'I couldn't have coped alone.'

'I know you couldn't,' he said morosely. 'That's why I grabbed your phone in a way you must have thought rather rude. If something threatens me I like to know how serious it is.'

'But he's not threatening you.'

'Anything that threatens you threatens me. I told you—I'll deal with it.'

'Thank you.' She clung to him. 'It's lucky it was only a phone call. If he'd turned up in person I think I'd have done something violent, perhaps strangled him.' She made a wry face. 'You're right in what you've always said about my nasty temper.'

'I've never said it was a nasty temper,' he disclaimed at once. 'It's a quick temper. Act first, think later.'

'By which time it's too late to think,' she sighed.

He didn't reply, merely tightened his arms about her.

'It's been a curse all my life,' she said. 'My mother used to say I'd come to a bad end. According to her, I got my temper from my father, and I never heard her say a good word about him.'

'You mentioned him the other day. Didn't they split up?'

'He left her when I was only ten. Just walked out and vanished. It broke my heart. Until then I'd had a wonderful relationship with my father. I was the apple of his eye. But he left my mother for another woman and I never heard from him again.'

'Never? Are you sure your mother didn't keep you apart?'

'No, he didn't write or call. I used to watch the mail arrive and there was never anything from him. I tried telephoning him but he'd changed his number.'

He didn't reply. She waited for him to remind her how she'd done the same thing, but he only hugged her closer.

'You should put all that behind you,' he murmured.

'The past is gone, but you must make sure it *is* the past. Don't let it haunt your life, or it will control you.'

'You sound as though you really know,' she said.

'In a way I do. At one time I owed so much to Damiano that the need to get free and grow up became the most important thing in my life.'

'Grow up?'

'I took a long time to get to that stage.'

That was true, she thought, remembering him two years ago. Now he was so much stronger and more serious that he was almost a different man.

'"Haunt your life",' she murmured. 'My mother never got over him abandoning us. She told me again and again that you could never trust a man.'

'And her words have stayed with you always,' he said softly.

'Not just her words. It was also the way he cut me out of his life, after I'd seemed to mean so much to him. I'd believed in his love, but it meant nothing.'

Mario uttered a soft curse. 'I wish I had him here so that I could sock him in the jaw,' he said. 'But don't let your father—or Elroy Jenson—destroy your life, Natasha. Banish them into the past, turn your back and become the person you really are.'

'Too late,' she sighed.

'It's never too late if it's what you really want.'

She would have given anything to see his face as he uttered those words, but her head was pressed against his shoulder.

'Never too late,' she echoed, resting against him. A feeling of sleepy contentment was overtaking her, and she could have happily stayed like this for ever.

Mario sensed the moment when she began to doze.

He tightened his arms about her, laying his lips against her hair, feeling an unfamiliar warmth go through him. He wanted to hold her close, but not in the hope of making love with her, only to keep her safe.

It was a feeling he'd never known before. When they had first met she had seemed strong, full of confidence, able to challenge the world and emerge victorious.

He found his mind drifting back to his own past. Since the day he'd first begun flirting with girlfriends he had never been attracted by commitment. His girlfriends had all been strong, independent, fancying him but not needing him.

Immature, he thought now wryly. *Boy, was I immature.*

Four years earlier he'd met Sally, the woman who had married his brother, Damiano. His feelings for her had grown so deep that he'd fled their home in Venice for safety's sake.

Later, he'd felt safe enough to return occasionally. His interest in the hotel business had grown. Damiano had been an excellent teacher and Mario's talent had flourished until he could manage to buy and run his own hotel. But he'd remained a playboy, dancing from girl to girl, never choosing anyone who might seriously need him.

Now he realised how much things had changed. Natasha's sadness had touched his heart. She was alone and vulnerable, and the knowledge affected him strongly. The torment he'd endured when she'd deserted him had begun to fade, overwhelmed by her need. She needed a friend to be strong for her, and something told him that he should be that person because without him she had nobody. He tightened his arms, trying to send her a silent message of reassurance. Her breathing was steady and, although he couldn't see her face, he guessed she was still dozing.

Probably just as well that they couldn't talk, he thought. Words could be a trap, especially for a man like himself, with little verbal skill. He preferred to be judged by his actions rather than his words.

Since the day she'd arrived he knew he'd been clumsy, confused. The feeling had been increased by the suspicion that she enjoyed confusing him. He'd fought back, making matters worse, he now realised. But now he knew that his own feelings didn't matter. He only wanted her to feel safe.

He eased her down onto the bed. Her head drooped to one side and her eyes were closed, as though she'd slipped away from him into another world. And yet she was still with him.

And she always would be, he resolved. He'd lost her once. He couldn't bear to lose her again. He knew he had to keep her, but for the moment he must be silent about his decision. They had far to travel before things could be said openly between them.

Moving carefully, he lay down beside her, still holding her so that her head rested against him. For a while she was still, but then her arm moved, drifting slowly across his chest as though seeking him, his help and comfort.

For a moment he thought that she might awaken and he could say some of the things in his heart. But then she grew still again, and he knew she'd slipped back into another world. One where he did not exist, he realised. Did he exist for her at all?

He looked closely into her face, hoping to read in it

some hint of an answer, but she was fast asleep. Their time would come, but for now he knew he must be patient. He closed his eyes.

In the early morning light Natasha opened her eyes to find herself in a strange world, one where her head rested against Mario and his arms enfolded her protectively.

At once she knew it was a dream. It could be nothing else.

'All right?' asked his gentle voice. 'Are you awake at last?'

'Am I—what—what am I—?'

Mario saw the dismay come into her eyes as she realised that she was lying in his arms.

'You've had a good night's sleep,' he said. 'So have I.'

'What happened? How did we—?'

'How did we end up lying together? You got a call from Jenson and it scared you. You were so upset that it seemed best not to leave you alone, so I came in here and stayed with you. But don't worry. I was just being a friend. I haven't done anything I shouldn't.'

She knew at once that it was true. Her flesh was calm and rested in a way that wouldn't have been true if he'd touched her sexually. He had merely held her gently, comfortingly in his arms, thinking only of her welfare.

'Truly,' he said. 'Stop worrying.'

'I'm not worried. I'm just glad you're here.'

'Glad?' he echoed. 'Really glad?'

'Of course. How could I not be? You said you'd keep me safe and you did. Oh, if I could only tell you how good that feels.'

'If that's what you want, that's all that matters,' he said.

Her eyes glowed and he became tense. Desire was

growing in him. He wanted to kiss her smiling mouth, caress her warm body, feel her come to new life in his arms. But he had just reassured her that he had no such temptations, and her reaction left no doubt that this was what she wanted to hear.

He wanted her, but she didn't want him in the same way. That was what he had to accept. It was all he could do for her.

She stirred in his arms and he loosened his hold, thinking she was trying to move away from him. But she turned more towards him, closing her eyes again, sliding an arm around his body and murmuring, *'Mmm!'* as though she had discovered blissful contentment.

And that was what he brought her, he reflected. It was a kind of happiness, and better than the anguish of their first encounter, days ago.

'But there could be more,' he whispered softly into her ear.

'Mmm?'

'If we're patient, there could be more between us, surely? We could take it slowly, and then—maybe—'

'Maybe what?' she murmured.

'I know we still have things to put behind us, and it won't be easy. You didn't treat me kindly, vanishing like that, but, after the way your father behaved, I guess you don't trust any of us. And I hurt you but I didn't mean to. If only you could bring yourself to believe me about that. But you will. One day I just know you will, and then everything will be wonderful.'

'Mmm.'

He gave a gentle laugh. 'I wonder what "Mmm" actually means.'

She met his eyes. 'If I knew—I'd tell you.'

'No, you wouldn't. You enjoy keeping me guessing. All right. I'll play your game because the prize we could win is worth everything.'

'Yes,' she whispered. 'But will we win it?'

'Who knows?' he said. 'We *will* know. We must. But not just yet. Something will happen. It will make everything clear—soon—soon.'

'I guess you understand more than I do. You'll tell me when the time comes—whenever that is.'

She smiled at him in a way that filled him with hope.

CHAPTER EIGHT

'I'LL LEAVE YOU now so you can get some more sleep,' Mario said. 'See you in the morning.'

He fled from the room, downstairs and out into the garden. It was just becoming light and he went to the river, where he could lean over the wall and stare into the water, brooding.

It felt wonderful to have achieved a brief emotional contact with her, but he wondered how completely she understood him. He'd spoken of his hopes for the future, but were they any more than fantasies? She had said that something would happen. But when? How long must they wait to be sure?

He looked back at the building, where he could identify her room from the faint light that still glowed inside. As he watched, the floor-length window opened and she came out onto the balcony.

He backed away into the shadows so that she wouldn't see him, but she didn't even look down. She stood motionless, her eyes turned up to the heavens as though she could find the answer to a mystery in that distant place.

Watching her on the balcony, he thought that this must have been how it was for Romeo, seeing his beloved standing there above him.

On the night she'd arrived he'd gone to stand beneath her window, looking up, longing to see her. And there she had been, reaching out into the night, her body full of anguish, speaking words he had strained to hear. Then she'd gone inside again, leaving him standing alone in the darkness, struggling to come to terms with his conflicting feelings.

Now, here he was again, watching Natasha from a distance, condemned perhaps to be always at a distance, unable to voice his emotions openly.

Romeo's words came into his head. *It is my lady, Oh, it is my love! Oh, that she knew she were!*

'Yes,' he murmured. 'It is my love. Oh, that she knew she were.'

She does know, argued a voice in his head. *You've made it very clear.*

But does she want to know? queried another voice. *Is she ready to accept?*

Her voice was still there in his mind, asking if they would win the prize. That alarmed him, as it meant she could envisage a future apart. The way ahead was still strewn with doubts and problems, and who knew what the answers would be? Or if there would be any answers?

Romeo had reached out from beneath Juliet's balcony, letting her know he was there, telling her of his feelings. But Mario knew that path wasn't open to him at this moment.

Slowly he backed away, retreating deep into the shadows, never taking his eyes off her.

For a while, she stayed looking up into the sky, but then she lowered her head and wrapped her arms about herself, leaning against the wall. Her demeanour suggested confusion, sadness. Mario drew in his breath sharply. He'd tried to ease those feelings in her, and had briefly thought he'd succeeded. But she was still lonely, still vulnerable, and the sight hurt him.

Once he could have reached out to console her openly, revealing everything in his heart, inviting her in, rejoicing in the unity they had seemed to share.

But that unity had been an illusion, with traps along the way, ready to bring them both down. She needed him. He felt this as he had never felt it before, and the longing to fulfil her need was taking him over, heart and soul. But her feelings for him, whatever they might be, were undermined by a caution that barred her from believing that she was his love.

'Oh, that she knew she were,' he whispered again. 'Oh, that I could convince her.'

He slipped quietly away for fear that she might see him.

Inside the hotel, he found Giorgio waiting for him in a state of agitation.

'You were right about her all along,' he said.

'Right about who?'

'Her. Natasha Bates. You suspected something troubling about her as soon as she arrived. You said you hadn't met her before but it was obvious you guessed what a suspicious character she was. And she knew that you sensed it. That's why she's so edgy when you're around.'

'What the devil are you talking about?' Mario snapped.

'We've received an email about Natasha that you must see. It's from Jenson Publications.'

'Show me.'

The email was blunt and vicious:

You should be warned about your employee, Natasha Bates. She's well known in the media business for her dishonesty and inefficiency. If you are wise you will dismiss her at once.

There was no name attached. The missive merely came from the Jenson Publications head office.

'He didn't dare put his name to it,' Mario growled. 'But this comes from Elroy Jenson, a miserable, scheming bastard who I'll strangle if I ever get my hands on him.'

'But suppose it's true,' Giorgio argued. 'You've always sensed that she was dodgy.'

'Don't you dare say that,' Mario raged. 'None of this is true and if I ever hear you say such a thing again I'll make you sorry.'

'All right, all right,' Giorgio said, hastily backing off, alarmed by the look in Mario's eyes. 'My lips are sealed.'

'Don't say it and don't even think it,' Mario snapped. 'Understand?'

'Understand,' Giorgio said. 'Sorry. It just hadn't occurred to me.'

'Yes, there are a lot of things that hadn't occurred to me either,' Mario sighed. 'But when they do occur—well, you just have to face them. This email is a pack of lies. Jenson came on to her, she rejected him and now he's out to destroy her out of spite.'

Giorgio nodded as comprehension came to him. 'So you're on her side?'

'Yes,' Mario said slowly. 'I'm on her side.'

In the past few days he'd felt a desire to care for Natasha, but those moments were nothing compared to the storm of protectiveness that invaded him now. If Jenson

had been there in person he would have throttled him
without compunction.

'Don't tell her about this,' he instructed Giorgio. 'He's
trying to scare her and I won't have it.'

'But shouldn't we warn her? She should know she's
got an enemy.'

'She already knows. But she also has us, and we're
going to take care of her. Not a word. I don't want her
upset.'

She had every reason to be upset, he realised. Elroy
Jenson might not be following her physically, but he was
after her in a far more dangerous way. Through stretching
out his tentacles of power across the world, he thought he
could still make her suffer for defying him.

But he was wrong, Mario thought angrily. Now Natasha had him to defend her and he would do so, whatever it cost him.

'She mustn't suspect anything,' he said to Giorgio.

'If you say so.' Giorgio sighed reluctantly. 'But can
we fend this man off?'

'We can and we will. She's going to be safe.' His face
became set. 'I've promised her that and I'm going to
keep my word.'

Turning back into her room from the balcony, Natasha
returned to the bed and lay down. She had a strange yet
pleasant feeling that Mario was still with her, whispering reassurances in her mind, or merely tightening his
arms protectively around her, so that she understood.

But was that what he'd meant, or was she just listening to her own hopes? She was still wondering as she
fell asleep.

She awoke feeling refreshed, eager to get up and face the day.

As soon as she swung her legs out of bed she knew something was wrong. The carpet beneath her feet was wet. Looking further, she found that the water came from the bathroom and covered most of the floor.

'Oh, heavens, I must have left a tap on!' she exclaimed in dismay.

But when exploring the bathroom she discovered not a tap but a leaking pipe, spilling water directly onto the floor.

Hastily, she called Mario and explained that she'd need a plumber. He arrived a few minutes later and swore when he saw the extent of the damage.

'This must be fixed quickly before it sinks through the floor,' he said. 'Pack your things and get out of here fast. I'll arrange another room for you.'

She was packed and finished in half an hour, glad to escape and leave the room to the plumbers who'd arrived. She found Mario waiting for her downstairs with a table laid for breakfast.

'There's a bit of a problem,' he said. 'It's high season and every room in the place is taken.'

'So I'll find a room somewhere else.'

'Certainly not. I have an apartment upstairs that you can have. I don't sleep there so the bed is free. You can relax in peace.'

'And do some work,' she said, gathering up her laptop.

His apartment was mainly a place of storage, filled with shelves and filing cabinets. She arrived to find a maid making up the bed.

'It's all yours,' Mario said. 'I'll leave you to it. Good-bye for now.'

She worked contentedly, sending her material to a dozen different sources. Then she felt the need for a short break, and crossed the room to switch on the television. But on the way her heel tangled in the carpet and she pitched forward. Reaching out, she grabbed hold of some small shelves, which promptly disgorged their contents onto the floor. With an exclamation, she dropped down and began gathering them up.

Then she stopped suddenly, as though something had grabbed her in a vice. An envelope had opened, spilling out several sheets of pale blue notepaper. On one of them she saw what was written at the bottom: *Your loving Tania.*

Her whole being was consumed by a silent howl of anguish. Tania was still communicating with Mario. After all his promises, his assurances that he had broken with her, that she meant nothing to him, the truth was that he had been in contact with her.

When she thought of how close she had come to trusting him she wanted to bang her head against the wall.

'Fool!' she murmured. 'Fool! You were so wise in the beginning. You should have listened to your suspicions.'

Was he still in touch with her? Or was it an old letter? If so, why had he kept it so long?

Because he's still involved with her, she told herself. *He's been lying all this time.*

With frenzied hands she pulled the letter open and began to read it. As she read she grew still. When she got to the end she went back and read it again. And then again, trying to believe the incredible words Tania had written.

Don't keep me at a distance. I know you told me it was over because you wanted to be with that Eng-

lish girl, but look what she did when she found out about me. She wouldn't have vanished if she'd really loved you. I thought you'd realise that and come back to me. Why won't you take my calls or answer my emails?

Don't keep rejecting me, Mario. Natasha can't possibly mean that much to you.

Your loving Tania

She read it again, murmuring the words aloud, as though in this way she could manage to convince herself that they were real.

Everything Mario had told her was true. He had broken with Tania, as he'd vowed. She had refused to accept it and kept hounding him, but it seemed that nothing would make him take her back.

'I should have believed you,' she whispered. 'Oh, my love, I should have trusted you. But why didn't you show me this? Then I would have known the truth.'

She noticed that the letter was written in English, and remembered how Tania had spoken mostly in English with the odd Italian word thrown in. Doubtless, English was her native language, and perhaps her closeness to Mario had helped his mastery of English.

Which is lucky, she thought. *If Tania had written in Italian I couldn't have understood, and I wouldn't have missed this for the world.*

A noise outside warned her that Mario was coming. Swiftly she gathered up the papers and thrust them back onto the shelf, except for the Tania letter, which she thrust into her pocket. She would want to read that again, many times.

Natasha was back in front of the computer when he came in.

'Did you manage to sort the plumbing problem?' she asked.

'Yes, it's all taken care of. It'll be a couple of days before you can move back in but, thanks to you, I was alerted in time to avoid total disaster. How are you getting on?'

'I've managed to do quite a lot of work. Now I feel like taking the evening off. I think I'll have a stroll by the river.'

'Am I allowed to come with you?'

'Why not?'

It was a joy to have his company now that she could see him in a new light. All the pain and tension of the past two years had vanished, leaving only happiness and hope.

The light was fading as they left the building and crossed the street to the river. He slipped his arm around her shoulders, and she stretched hers about his waist. Clinging together, they strolled along the bank until they reached a café by the water, and he indicated for her to sit down. Waving a waiter over, Mario spoke to him quickly in Italian and moments later the waiter returned with a bottle of wine.

'I have a reason for bringing you here,' Mario said. 'This place buys all its wine from a shop that stocks products from my vineyard.'

'The best, naturally,' she said.

'Naturally. Everyone knows about Verona's romantic reputation, but its fame as a great wine centre tends to get blocked out.'

'I've been reading a little about it recently,' she said.

'There are wine tours, aren't there? We might do a little publicity for them too.'

'Good idea. You can turn your talents on to Vinitaly. That's a wine festival that happens every year in spring.' He grinned. 'There's a lot more to Verona than you think.'

'I'm sure there is. I look forward to discovering all its secrets.'

He raised his glass to her, saying, *'Ti vol un altro goto de vin?'*

'Is that Venetian?'

'You know about Venetian?'

'Giorgio told me. The more I know, the better.'

'It means would you like some more wine?'

'Yes, please. It's delicious.'

She sipped the wine, enjoying its excellent taste and the feeling that things might be going well at last.

He watched her, wondering at the smile on her face, unwilling to ask about it. There might be more pleasure in wondering.

When at last they rose and walked on he put an arm around her shoulder, saying, 'Are you all right? Not too cold?'

'I'm all right,' she said, looking up. 'Not too cold, not too anything. Everything's perfect.'

He gave a soft chuckle. 'Does that mean I haven't offended you recently?'

She looked up at him teasingly. 'Not that I can think of.'

'You can usually think of something.'

They smiled and moved on.

She barely noticed where they were going. It was like being in a new world. Nothing was the same. His voice had a note of warmth that she had never noticed before, and his eyes held a gleam that promised much.

'It's lovely out here,' she sighed.

'Yes,' he murmured in her ear. 'It's lovely, and you're lovely.'

'You have to feel sorry for Romeo and Juliet, who could never take this kind of walk, just enjoying being together and letting the world drift by.'

'I guess we're luckier than they were.'

She turned to look up into his face. 'Yes,' she said. 'We're lucky. We were always lucky, if only we'd known it.'

His fingertips brushed her face gently. 'I always knew it,' he said. 'Now I know it even more since I had to endure life without you. I thought I'd never see you again, and the future was nothing but a terrible blank. But then you were there again and I had my life back. Suddenly, there was something to hope for.'

'Yes, for me too,' she said. 'But sometimes I can be afraid to hope.'

'Better not to hope at all, than hope and have it destroyed,' he said.

'No, I don't believe that. Wonderful things can happen when you least expect it. You have to be ready for the best as well as the worst, and then— Oh, Mario, Mario!'

She was silenced by his mouth over hers.

'Be mine,' he whispered. 'Tell me that you're mine.'

'I always was. I always will be.'

'Do you really mean that?'

'Yes—yes—'

'Say it again. Make me believe it.'

'I'm yours—all yours—yours—'

'For ever. I won't let you go. I warn you, I'm possessive.'

'You couldn't be too possessive for me,' she assured him.

His answer was another kiss which she returned with fervour.

A group of young people passed by, cheering and clapping at the sight of them.

'It's too public out here,' she said.

'Yes, let's go home.'

They slipped back into the hotel without being seen. She was glad. What was happening now was for them alone.

He came with her as far as the apartment, then stopped at the door, regarding her uncertainly.

'Don't go,' she said, holding him in a gentle but determined hug. 'Stay with me.'

'Natasha, do you mean that?'

'Yes, I mean it.'

'But don't you realise that—if I stay—no, you don't realise. I mustn't stay.'

'Yes, you must,' she whispered. 'I say you must, and I won't let you refuse me.'

It hurt her to see how tense and vulnerable he seemed. After all the hostility that had simmered between them he couldn't believe that she was really opening her arms to him; even perhaps opening her heart. It was what he wanted but something he couldn't dare believe too easily, and she longed to reach out from her heart and reassure him.

'Trust me,' she murmured. 'Things move on. Nothing stays the same for ever.'

'Are you telling me that something really has changed?' he asked.

'In a way. I've learned to be more understanding. I was always so sure I was right, but now—now I feel like a different person. I have so much still to learn.'

She took a step back through the door, holding out her hand.

'Come in,' she said. 'Come with me—stay with me.'

He still could not understand her, but he put his hand in hers and followed her in perfect trust.

'Yes,' he said. 'Take me with you. Let me stay.'

His mouth was on hers, making her rejoice with heart, mind and body equally. There was pleasure but there was also a fierce possessiveness. She wanted him and she was determined to have him. She had waited as long as she could endure and now she was determined to enjoy her conquest.

With the door safely closed against the outside world, Mario felt able to yield to his longing and take her in his arms. Yet doubts and confusion still whirled about him.

'I don't believe this is happening,' he whispered. 'I've dreamed of it so often, so hopelessly.'

'Not hopelessly,' she told him. 'I've dreamed too. Dreams can come true. Let us believe that.'

'Yes, while I have you in my arms I can believe it.'

She drew his head down, kissing him with fervour and passion, rejoicing in his response. Gradually he began to move towards the bed, easing her down onto it so that they lay together. When she felt him start to undo her clothes she was there before him, pulling open buttons, inviting him to explore her.

He accepted the invitation, tentatively at first, caressing her gently, almost uncertainly. But as his hands discovered the soft smoothness of her skin their touch became more fervent, more intense, sending tremors through her. She reached out to him, now working on his buttons so that his shirt fell open and she could explore him in her turn.

Once, long ago in Venice, she had dreamed of this. But fate had denied her dream, banishing her into a wilderness where there was no love, no hope, no Mario.

Now, at last, the moment had come and it was everything she'd wanted. His caress was tentative, almost as though he feared to touch her.

She understood. In the depths of her heart joy was warring with disbelief, scared that this might not really be true, that she would wake to find it a delusion. And it was the same with him. Instinct too deep for thought told her this was true. After so long their hearts and minds were as one, just as their bodies would soon unite.

He laid his face against her. She drew him closer, wanting this moment to last.

'Yes,' she murmured. 'Yes.'

'Yes,' he echoed. 'Natasha—are you sure?'

'I'm sure of everything—sure that I want you—'

He gave a faint smile. 'Are you sure I want you? Or shall I try to convince you?'

'I don't need convincing.' She returned his smile in full measure. 'But don't let me stop you.'

'Whatever you please, ma'am,' he murmured, intensifying his caresses.

Her pleasure rioted, but more than pleasure was the joy of knowing that they were close again. The man she had loved long ago had been stolen from her, but now she had him back. And she would never let him go again. The world might turn upside down. The heavens might fall, the seas overflow, but she would never release him from her arms and her heart. On that she was resolved.

He worked eagerly on her clothes until nothing was left. Then he removed his own garments and they were naked together. He took her into his arms, kissing her mouth, her face, her neck, then going lower to smother her breasts in kisses. She took long breaths of delight at the storm growing within her, longing for the moment when he would claim her completely. When it came, it was everything she'd hoped.

CHAPTER NINE

AS THE FIERCE excitement died they lay quietly, holding each other, coming to terms with the new world in which they found themselves. Gradually they fell into peaceful sleep, lying motionless together until the room grew lighter and the new day had come.

Mario was lying with his face hidden against her neck, but then he raised it and looked down at her.

She met his eyes, seeing in them a look of loving possessiveness that made her heart skip a beat.

'Natasha,' he murmured, almost as though trying to believe that it was really her. She knew how he felt, for she was feeling the same herself. She had told him they must believe that dreams could come true.

'I've wanted this from the first moment,' he whispered. 'But I'd given up hope. And then suddenly— beyond my wildest dreams—why?'

'The time was right,' she whispered. 'Couldn't you feel that?'

'I've often felt it, but I was always wrong before. Suddenly—everything became different between us.'

'Everything became as it should be,' she said. 'This is how it was always meant to be.'

'You really mean that? Natasha, I'm not deluding myself, am I? Things are really all right between us?'

'How can you ask me that? After the way we've spent the last night, don't you think everything is all right?'

'Oh, yes.' He gave a wry smile. 'But I didn't mean that. I meant the other things that have come between us and separated us in the past. You didn't believe what I told you about Tania, that I'd broken with her because I'd met you and you were the one I wanted. Please, please say that you believe me, that you trust me at last.'

'I trust you, my darling. I should have trusted you long ago, but I was blind. It was like being lost in a maze. Every time I thought I'd found a way out it just led to more confusion.'

She promised herself that one day soon she would tell him about Tania's letter, and the way it had confirmed everything he said. But she didn't want thoughts of Tania to intrude just now. She wanted only Mario, the warmth, beauty and contentment they could find together.

'You trust me,' he echoed as though trying to believe it. 'And you're mine.'

'I'm yours.'

'For always?'

'Always and for ever.'

'Then everything's perfect.'

'Not quite,' she said. 'Don't you have an "always and for ever" promise to make me?'

'Of course. I just didn't think you needed to hear it said. I'm so completely yours that—'

He was interrupted by the sound of his mobile phone. Sighing, he answered it, speaking in Italian. Natasha didn't understand the language, but she understood that the caller was Mario's brother, Damiano.

'*Come stai, fratello?*' Mario said cheerfully. '*Come è Sally e il bambino?*'

After listening a moment he gave Natasha a thumbs-up sign.

'They've set the christening for this weekend,' he told her. 'I'm going and they want me to take you.'

'They want me? But how—?'

'Yes or no?'

'Yes. Oh, yes.'

'Damiano—Natasha *dice di sì. Va bene!*' He hung up.

'I don't understand,' she said. 'How did they even think of inviting me?'

'You mean how did they know you were here, and we'd found each other again?' He became a little awkward. 'When I went there for the birth a while ago I may have mentioned you briefly.'

She gave him a glance of wicked humour. 'Yes, I can imagine what you said. "That pesky woman has turned up again, when I thought I'd got rid of her."'

'Something like that,' he said with a grin.

'I'd give a lot to have been a fly on the wall.'

'You'd probably have had a good laugh. I talked about you non-stop. When I told them how amazed I was when our publicist turned out to be you, Damiano roared with laughter. And Sally wanted to know everything. She thinks it's a great joke to see me conquered by a woman.'

'But I haven't tried to conquer you.'

'Of course. If you had tried I'd have fought back and we wouldn't be talking like this now. But you caught me unaware, and I was finished before I knew it.'

And before I knew it, she thought. His words struck a disturbing chord within her.

'I remember everything so vividly,' he said. 'Our first meeting—you were sitting in the restaurant of Damiano's hotel when I came in. You were so lovely I just stopped and stared at you. Suddenly you looked up and saw me. And you smiled. Such a lovely smile, as though I was the only person in the room—in the world.

'I didn't understand straight away what had happened to me. But I did know that suddenly the world was focused on you.'

'And you came and sat down at the table,' she remembered. 'You said that you worked in the hotel and were offering your services—'

'That was just an excuse to talk to you, find out all I could about you. Were you married, was a man coming to join you? I hung on your every answer as though my life depended on it. And now I realise that my life did depend on it. And then—'

'What is it?' she asked, for he suddenly seemed troubled.

'It all happened again, didn't it? When you came here I asked you the same questions the first evening.'

'You said would a man turn up to drag me home?' she remembered.

'Yes, it sounded like the practical questions of an employer, but in fact I had this terrible need to know if there was someone in your life, just like the first time. It shocked me. I couldn't believe it had happened again—'

'With a woman you hated,' she said gently.

'I didn't hate you. I told myself I did because I needed to believe it. That was my defence and I clung to it. But things change and—well—'

'I wonder how much things change,' she murmured. 'Or do they only seem to have changed because *we* have changed?'

'Maybe we've changed in some things but not in others.'

'I wonder which is which.'

'We might find that out in Venice.'

'Mmm. So Sally thinks we're a joke. Yes, it's like fate played a joke on us. Sometimes I almost fancy I can hear laughter echoing from the heavens at the way we fell for it.'

'We didn't fall for it,' he said, drawing her close. 'We won. Fate lost. When Sally sees us together she'll understand that we're having the last laugh.'

'You really want me to come to Venice with you?'

'I think it's important that we go back there together.'

She understood. By returning they would confront their memories and that would help to show them the way forward.

'Everything that happened there looks different now,' she said.

'Yes,' he agreed gladly. 'So different. So much happier. The sooner we go the better. Then we can have a few days before the christening.'

At once he called Venice again, to say they would be arriving that evening. Then he stopped, regarding Natasha uneasily.

'Sally says one room or two?' he said. 'What's your choice?'

She was suddenly struck by inspiration. 'I'd like the same room I had last time.'

'That's a single room.'

'Perhaps we should be a little discreet.'

He seemed about to protest, but then understanding dawned and he turned back to the phone. At last he hung up.

'She's fixing it.'

'Does she think I'm crazy?'

'No, she said it made a lot of sense to put the clock back. I don't need to ask what that means, do I?'

'I don't think you do.'

'Let's get packing.'

Not long after, they bid farewell to Giorgio and set off for the Verona railway station to catch the train. It was just over seventy miles, and an hour and a half passed before they found themselves on the causeway that led over the water from the mainland to Venice.

She remembered the last time she had made this journey, leaning out of the window to see the beautiful buildings grow closer. How excited she'd been during that journey, how thrilled at the thought of spending time in the magical city.

At Venice station Mario hailed a water taxi and soon they were on their way to the hotel on the Grand Canal.

'There it is,' he said, pointing forward. 'Remember?'

'Yes, I remember,' she breathed.

It was a magnificent building, a converted palace that seemed to sum up everything that was glamorous about Venice. As soon as they entered Damiano and Sally came to meet them. Damiano and Mario slapped each other on the shoulders in brotherly fashion, while Sally embraced Natasha.

'It's lovely to see you again,' she said. 'And Pietro has really looked forward to your return. He says when you were last here you used to talk to him about football.'

'That's right. And last night England played Italy.' Natasha chuckled. 'Luckily, Italy won.'

Pietro appeared. He was in his early teens, already looking strikingly like his father, and full of beans.

'Did you see the match?' he challenged at once, after which perfect communication was established between them.

'How's Toby?' she asked, meaning Pietro's spaniel, who had helped bring Damiano and Sally together.

'Here he is,' Pietro said eagerly, drawing his furry friend forward.

She greeted Toby, received his welcoming lick and looked up to find Mario watching them with a pleased smile, as though everything was working out as he'd hoped.

Then Sally took them to see the two children she'd borne her husband—little Franco, nearly three years old, whose birth had nearly cost her life, and Elena, the little girl she'd borne recently.

'Supper's in half an hour,' Sally said.

As promised, Natasha had the same room as before which, at first, gave her a slightly weird ghostly feeling. But it soon faded against the different, happier, reality of the present. Mario's room was just a few feet along the corridor, and soon he appeared to escort her downstairs to Damiano's private dining room.

It was clear to Natasha that she was being welcomed into the family. During the meal that followed she was toasted as an honoured guest.

'Wait till you see the church where we'll have the christening,' Pietro said. 'It's where Mamma and Papà got married.'

'That was quite a ceremony,' Mario recalled. 'Toby was there too, practically one of the witnesses.'

'I'm sure he performed his role perfectly,' Natasha said.

As she spoke she tickled Toby's head and was rewarded with a *woof!*

It was a happy evening. A sense of peace came over her as she realised yet again the true purpose of this trip: to put right the mistakes and misunderstandings of the past.

Only Sally's brother Charlie was missing, which Sally explained with sisterly frankness. 'Out making himself objectionable again.'

'What kind of objectionable?' Natasha asked, laughing.

'Women, gambling—you name it, he can do it. Mind you, he's not as bad as he was. Mario helped reform him a bit.'

'Me? Reform?' Mario squeaked. 'That's practically an insult.'

'Well, Damiano told me you had a "guardian angel" side, and you did keep Charlie on the straight and narrow—more or less. Time for bed, anyway.'

The party broke up. Mario announced that he and Natasha wanted to take a walk. The others nodded in perfect understanding and slipped away.

'A walk?' she queried.

'Maybe. Maybe not.'

'What was the idea—?'

'I wanted to be sure of being alone with you. Let's have a coffee. Not here—in the restaurant.'

It was almost closing time and most of the restaurant tables were empty. At once she knew why he'd brought

her here. There in the corner was the table where she'd
sat at their first meeting. He led her over, showed her to
a seat and sat beside her. A waiter brought them coffee.

'You were just here by the window,' he said. 'I watched
you for a few minutes, trying to believe my eyes, rather
like that guy over there.'

He pointed to a young man standing just inside the
door, his eyes fixed on another table just a few feet away
from them, where sat a young woman in her twenties.
She was beautiful, and she was alone.

'I can guess what he's thinking,' Mario said. 'He's
working out a good excuse to approach her.'

'You can't know what he's thinking.'

'Oh, yes, I can. When I look at him I see myself. In
fact, I see every guy trying to summon up the courage
to approach a woman he knows is going to matter more
than any other. Look, there he goes.'

As they watched, the young man approached the girl
and gestured to ask if anyone was sitting with her. She
shook her head and he took a seat.

'Does he work here?' Natasha asked.

'No, he'll have to think of another excuse. He doesn't
seem to be doing too badly.'

Amused, they watched the couple for a few minutes.
Then Mario said with a touch of unease, 'There's something I keep wanting to ask you.'

'What is it?'

He hesitated, then said, 'What happened to you after
we parted? I know you worked hard and Jenson gave you
a bad time, but was there—anything else?'

'You mean another man? But I've already told you
about that.'

'You've told me you're not married, you haven't settled down with anyone, but that's not what I meant.'

She gave a gentle chuckle. 'You mean am I secretly yearning for someone? Take a guess.'

'No, I can't see you yearning for someone who didn't return the feeling. But surely in the last two years you must have had some sort of romantic interest.'

'No. Apart from the horrible Jenson I've been alone. Which is a kind of freedom,' she added wryly.

'I know exactly how that feels.'

'Don't tell me you've been alone,' she teased. 'Every woman who passes gives you yearning looks.'

'But what matters is to be wanted by the one you yourself want,' he said. 'The others don't count.'

'That's true,' she said softly.

'So you're telling me there was no other man?'

'Hmm!' She appeared to consider this before saying gently, 'I suppose I could always say that it's none of your business. How about that?'

'It's certainly one response.' He gave her a wry smile. 'I could go and bury myself under the bedclothes because I couldn't cope with you snubbing me. Or I could get blind drunk. Or I could say that your lovers definitely are my business. And always will be. So now what?'

His eyes met hers, gleaming with a mixture of humour and intensity that struck her to the heart.

'My lovers,' she mused. 'I wonder just what you've heard.'

'Not a thing. After you vanished I tried to hunt you down for a little while, but when you never made contact with me I thought—well—' He gave a slight shrug.

'You thought, "To hell with the silly English girl! If

she wants to play it like that let her go and jump in the lake."'

'Well, maybe once or twice, but I didn't mean it,' he said, colouring.

'Oddly enough, I did end up in a lake shortly afterwards. It was a pleasure trip and the boat collapsed.'

'*What?* Were you hurt?'

'No, I just I got wet. Hey, I wonder if you made that happen. Strange to think we were in touch all that time and didn't know it.'

'Possibly. You were never off my mind.'

'Nor you off mine. And I did some cursing of my own.'

'I'm not sure I want to know about that,' he said with a grin. 'It could give me nightmares.'

'If we're asking about each other's lovers—what about yours? You must have had plenty.'

'Not lovers,' he said. 'Girlfriends, perhaps. I won't deny that I've enjoyed the company of a certain kind of woman because that way I could briefly forget the way you threw me overboard. But there wasn't anyone that I loved, even for a moment. It was always you, even when I most desperately didn't want it to be you.'

'Couldn't get rid of me, huh?' she teased.

'No matter how hard I tried.' He gave a warm laugh. 'You're a pesky woman. I told you a hundred times to get out of my heart but you just said, "Nope. Here I am and here I'm staying."'

'That sounds like me.'

He looked up suddenly. Following his gaze, she saw the other couple rise from the table and depart, hand in hand.

'I guess he got lucky,' Mario mused.

'Or maybe she did.'

'I didn't get lucky. Damiano called me to look after another customer and when I returned you'd gone. If only you could have heard me cursing.' He drained his coffee. 'Let's go.'

Upstairs, he came with her as far as her door.

'Remember last time?' he asked.

'Yes, we said goodnight at this door. I went inside and you went away.'

'I didn't really go away. I stayed out here in the corridor for ages.'

She opened the door and stretched out a hand to him.

'No need for that this time,' she said.

He took her hand at once, eagerly letting her draw him inside, then going into her arms, which she opened to him. It was she who drew them to the bed, he who followed her lead, but slowly, as though aware that they were rewriting history. Once they had wanted each other without satisfaction. Now they embraced satisfaction eagerly, joyfully.

There was physical pleasure in their caresses, but more than that was the joy of rediscovering each other. To retread the road, each seeing the other with new eyes, exploring new diversions, making wonderful discoveries; these were things they had never dared to dream of.

Afterwards, as they lay together in each other's arms, Natasha gave a sudden soft chuckle.

'What is it?' he demanded. 'What did I do that makes you laugh?'

'Don't get defensive. You could make me laugh and still be "macho".'

She laughed again and he frowned, demanding, 'So what is it?'

'It's what Sally said about you having a "guardian

angel" side. That's the last thing I'd ever have suspected about you. A rebel, a pain in the butt, a pesky clown—any of them. But a guardian angel? Or any kind of angel. I doubt it.'

His annoyance faded and he kissed her forehead. 'Thanks. I see you really understand me.'

'You don't mind being called those things?'

'Not at all. I'd have minded being called an angel. That would have been insulting. But I think "pain in the butt" rather suits me.'

'Definitely,' she said, kissing him. 'Now, I'm going to sleep. You've exhausted me for the night. Goodnight, "guardian angel".'

She snuggled against him and in a few moments she was asleep.

Guardian angel, he thought. *That's almost funny, considering how I hated you only recently. But somehow things took a different turn.*

He rested his head against her and in a few minutes he too was asleep. After several hours he awoke to find her eyes still closed and her head on his shoulder. When he ventured to move slightly her arms tightened, as though even in sleep she needed to keep him close.

He clasped her back, offering her the embrace she needed for reassurance.

Romeo's words drifted through his mind again. *It is my lady...oh, it is my love. Oh, that she knew she were.*

But she does know, he mused. *If she knows anything by now, it's that I love her.*

He kissed her gently, murmuring, 'You are my lady. You are my love.'

She sighed and nestled closer, smiling as though she'd heard him and been reassured. He leaned against her, happy and willing to sleep again, but then a noise from his phone disturbed him.

'Curses,' he muttered. 'My mobile phone. Where is it?'

Undressing hastily, he hadn't noticed it fall to the floor. Now he eased himself gently away from Natasha and leaned down to pick up the phone. Connecting, he found a text from an unknown number:

You're taking a bigger risk than you know. She's mine. Get lost.

For a moment he was simply bewildered. Who could the message be from? But then the answer came to him like a clap of thunder.

Elroy Jenson. The man who'd vindictively destroyed Natasha's career because she'd dared to defy him. The man who'd spied on her from a distance, watching where she fled to escape him. The man who still had his claws in her, and would deepen them if he could.

He was swept by such rage that his head was dizzy and the whole world seemed to turn black.

'No,' he whispered. 'She's not yours. She's mine. She's *mine*. She always was. *And she always will be.*'

Behind him, Natasha stirred, murmuring, 'Is something the matter?'

'No,' he said. 'Go back to sleep. Nothing's the matter. Nothing at all. Your guardian angel will deal with it.'

CHAPTER TEN

'How are you enjoying Verona?' Sally asked Natasha at breakfast next morning.

'I love it.'

'And Verona loves her,' Mario said. 'She's doing a great job for our hotels.'

'Perhaps she can come here later and do something for Venice hotels,' Damiano said.

'What a lovely idea,' Natasha said. 'I'll take a stroll around Venice this morning.' She glanced at Mario before saying slowly, 'Just to remind myself what it's like.'

He nodded.

After breakfast they slipped out into the narrow alley that ran by the hotel.

'You walked this way alone the first time,' he reminded her. 'But I wasn't far behind you.'

'I know.'

'You know? You mean you knew it then?'

'Yes, I told the receptionist where I was going, and you were nearby. When I came out I heard your footsteps behind me.'

'So you always knew I was following you?'

'No, but I hoped you were. I went into a shop to give you a chance to catch up. But you didn't.'

'I was tempted. When you stopped I worked out a plan to go into the shop casually and just "happen" to meet you. But I lost my nerve, so I waited a bit.'

'Lost your nerve? You?'

'You have that effect on me.'

'I'll remember that. It could be useful.'

'Be honest. You already knew that you scared me stiff.'

Laughing, they went on their way.

At last they came to the Grand Canal, the great S-shaped stream of water that wound through the city. Boats of every kind filled it. Just coming up was a *vaporetto*, one of the great water buses that transported passengers all over the city. Small water taxis were everywhere, but also the boats that everyone came to Venice to see, gondolas. Natasha looked eagerly at the slim, elegant conveyances, propelled by a man with one oar.

'You were standing here when you saw your first gondola close up,' he remembered.

'And I couldn't think how a gondola could go straight when it was only being rowed on one side,' she said. 'You told me that that side bulged more than the other, so the water took longer to slide past. I didn't understand, so you said I should take a ride in it. You hailed the gondolier—like you're doing now.'

The boat was gliding to a halt beside them. Gently, he handed her in and they settled down together. It felt wonderful, just as it had the first time.

'Aaaaaah.' Sighing with pleasure, she stretched out, looking around her at the little canal and listening to the singing coming from around the corner. 'It's lovely, but this is where I fell asleep.'

'That's right. You couldn't have made it plainer what you thought of me, Natasha—Natasha?'

She was lying back with her eyes closed. *Just like last time*, he thought.

The gondolier regarded him sympathetically. 'Some men are just unlucky, *signore*,' he said, speaking in Venetian dialect.

'True,' Mario said wryly in the same language. 'But some men are also luckier than they know. The problem is finding out which you are.'

He watched Natasha carefully for a moment, then leaned forward and kissed her. When she didn't react he repeated the kiss more forcefully.

'Hello,' Natasha said, opening her eyes.

'Hello. Sorry if I disturbed you.'

'Tell me, when I fell asleep the first time, did you kiss me then?'

'Don't you remember?'

She smiled up at him in a way he guessed was meant to drive him mad. She was certainly succeeding. Did she know that? Did she enjoy it?

'I'm not sure,' she murmured.

'Then let me remind you.'

He laid his lips gently over hers again, leaving them there for several moments.

The gondolier grinned. His job exposed him to a lot of enjoyable sights.

Natasha relaxed and put her arms about him. Although she had been asleep for their first ride, two years ago, she was sure he hadn't kissed her then because she would have remembered. Now she gave herself up to pleasure.

Afterwards, they sat leaning against each other, watching the little canals drift past. She had a mysterious sense that the journey might go on for ever, and wished that it would. But all too soon they drew up outside the hotel. Once inside, they became involved in the preparations for the christening, and for the rest of the day she barely spent a moment alone with him.

Next morning everyone set out for the church where the christening would take place. It was only a short distance away, so they went on foot.

'It's a big family occasion,' Mario said as they walked through the alley that approached the church. 'Damiano's first wife died giving birth to Pietro. One reason he married Sally was to give that kid a mother.'

'You mean it was a marriage of convenience? They seem so devoted to each other.'

'They are. They thought it was a marriage of convenience, but in fact they were really in love. They just hadn't realised it.'

She looked into her wine glass, murmuring, 'That can happen when people don't understand their own feelings.'

'So I've heard. It must be quite a stunning discovery.'

'Yes,' she said. 'It is. There's no recovering from it, or from blaming yourself for how stupid you were.'

'Would you call yourself stupid?'

'Mad, imbecile,' she said. 'Even worse than that. But a lucky fate gave me the chance to put things right.'

He raised his glass. 'Here's to fate.'

They clinked glasses.

'So did they realise they were in love?' she asked.

'It dawned on them eventually. She had a bad time when Franco was born. She might not have come through it. I thought Damiano would go out of his mind with fear and grief. He wasn't keen on Sally having another baby, but she really wanted it and he gave in.'

He gave a brief laugh. 'Few people know the real Damiano. To the outside world he's a ruthless businessman. But once that front door shuts behind him, he's a willing slave to his wife.'

'Oh, really?' She gave him a cheeky look. 'Is that how you judge a good husband? If he's her willing slave?'

'Who knows? Perhaps you'll have the chance to find out.'

There were already plenty of friends and family in place, smiling when they appeared and made their way along the aisle. Sally walked with her new baby in her arms, Damiano carried their toddler, Charlie and Mario walked together, while Pietro accompanied Natasha, holding her hand. Again she had the happy feeling of being part of the family.

It grew even better at the party that evening. Mario introduced her to everyone in the crowd, most of whom seemed to have heard of her already.

'We've all looked forward to meeting you,' said one elderly man.

'Just be a little patient,' Mario told him. 'You'll hear something soon.'

'What did that mean?' she asked as he drew her away.

'Just that people think we're a couple. Do you mind that?'

'Not at all,' she assured him. 'But what is he going to hear soon?'

'Why don't we go and talk about that?'

He drew her slowly out of the room, waving farewell to the other guests, who cheered them in a way that left no doubt that they were expecting to hear about a wedding very soon. Somehow, Mario had given that impression.

Once inside her room he kissed her before saying, 'I may have said more than I should have done without asking you first. But we so clearly belong together that people accept it.'

'And if you could have asked me first?'

'I'd have asked you to set the date for our wedding.'

'Yes, you really should have mentioned it to me.'

'Are you mad at me?'

'I'll let you know that later.' She drew him to the bed. 'For the moment I have other things on my mind.'

'So have I.' He was already working on her clothes.

We did the right thing coming here, she thought. *It's made things better, as nothing else could have done. The past is over. It didn't happen. We are free.*

Free. The word seemed to echo, casting hope over the future. As they made love she kept her eyes on his face, finding that he too was watching her, sending a silent message that she understood and returned with all her heart.

And he too understood. She recognised that from the long sigh of happiness and fulfilment he gave as they lay in each other's arms afterwards.

'If only we could have known,' he whispered.

'It was too much to hope for,' she replied. 'Even now I daren't hope. It's too good to be true. Something will happen to make things go wrong.'

'Nothing will go wrong,' he said firmly. 'I won't let it.'

'Oh, you think it's all up to you, do you, big man?'

'Right this minute I feel powerful enough to dictate everything in the world. You hear that?' he yelled up at the ceiling. 'Nothing is ever going to go wrong between us again. I insist on it. I order it.'

'Who are you giving orders to?' she chuckled.

'The little green men who try to dictate to us. From now on, I'm in charge.'

'Oh, yeah?'

'Not of you,' he said hastily. 'Just of them.'

They collapsed with laughter, rocking back and forth with delight.

Afterwards, Natasha was to remember that moment, a triumphant assertion of joy and confidence before catastrophe descended on them once more.

Next morning Mario suggested a walk through Venice.

'It was a good idea to come back,' he said as they strolled. 'The people we were then don't exist any more, and this way we've got rid of them.'

'I'm not sure I want to get rid of them,' she observed. 'There were things about you I think I'll cling to. You've always been the best-looking man for miles around. I'm not changing that.'

'Thank you, ma'am.'

He began to draw her in another direction, but she resisted.

'Why can't we stay here?' she asked.

'Because of that place,' he said, indicating an outdoor café. It was the one where they had had their quarrel.

But it need not have happened, she thought.

So many times she'd wanted to tell Mario that she knew the truth after reading Tania's letter, but somehow the moment had never been right. But perhaps this was the right time and place.

'Why don't you buy me a coffee there?' she said.

'Don't you realise what that place is?' he demanded.

'Yes, it's where we made our huge mistake and lost each other. Perhaps it's time to put it right.'

'I thought we'd already put it right.'

'Yes, but there's a little more to do. Come with me.'

She led him to the café and found that by a strange chance the same table was available.

'This is where we sat,' she said as they sipped coffee.

'Until we were interrupted, but that won't happen this time,' he said firmly. 'That woman is out of our lives for good.' He became suddenly tense. 'What's the matter? Why are you smiling like that? Don't you believe me?'

'Yes, I believe you.'

'Do you really? You believe that I was telling you the truth? You trust me? I would never deceive you. Tell me that you believe that.'

'I do. I believe everything you've told me. I know you're an honest man and you always will be.'

'You mean that? You really mean that?'

'Every word.'

He took her face between his hands and spoke softly. 'If you could imagine what it means to me to know that we're close enough for you to have learned to trust me.'

'I only want to tell you—' She stopped, silenced by a nervous feeling that she did not understand.

'You only want to tell me what? That you love me. That's it, isn't it?'

'Oh, yes, that's it.'

'Then that's all I need to hear.'

'But, Mario—'

His lips on hers silenced her. He was kissing her fiercely, powerfully, yet devotedly, longingly. She surrendered to the pleasure, knowing that this, and only this, was the whole of life.

At last he released her. She could tell that he was shaking and his breath came unevenly.

'My darling,' he whispered. 'What is it that you needed to say?'

'Nothing. It doesn't matter.'

Nothing mattered enough to break the spell of this moment. She took hold of him again, returning the kiss fervently. Around them the other diners laughed and cheered, and the waiter cleared his throat. Without looking at him, Mario pulled some money from his pocket. The waiter seized it and vanished.

'Let's go,' Mario said. 'This isn't the place for what we have to do.'

'*Have* to do?' she murmured against his lips.

'We have urgent business to attend to,' he whispered. 'Can't you feel it?'

'Yes—oh, yes.'

Seizing her hand, he rose and hurried away. She followed him joyfully. The words she'd planned to say could wait. Nothing mattered now but to be with him, in his arms, his bed, his life.

Together they ran through the streets of Venice, down alleys, over bridges, eager to get to the hotel, where they could achieve the fulfilment that awaited them, that they longed for.

At last they reached the hotel, hurrying through the entrance and across to the lift.

Sally appeared, calling, 'Ah, Mario, can I talk to you—?'

'Not now,' Mario called back.

They vanished into the lift, clinging to each other as it carried them up.

'Nearly there,' he said hoarsely.

'Yes, nearly there.'

She knew he meant they were almost at his bedroom, but to her the words meant far more. The glorious destination that had waited for them since the moment they'd met—they were nearly there.

They had reached the room. He flung open the door, drew her inside and began to undress her at once. She responded instantly, wrenching off his jacket, pulling open his buttons, tearing off his shirt.

They fell onto the bed, still working on each other's clothes until they were both naked and ready for each other.

'You're mine,' he said huskily. 'Now and for ever.'

'Yes—yes—'

She was dizzy with passion and delight, wanting him more than she had ever wanted anything in her life. Their previous lovemaking had been wonderful, but this one was pervaded by an extra sense of triumph.

She reached for him, offered herself to him, claimed him, and sensed his delight not only through his movements but by the glow in his eyes. His lovemaking was tender, emotional, and at first this was enough. But soon she wanted more. She was his, heart and body, and with every movement she demanded that he accept the gift and return it. When he claimed her finally she cried out with joy.

Afterwards, lying contentedly in his arms, feeling the warmth of his flesh and the gentle power of his embrace, she knew that she had come to the place that was always meant for her, and where she could live happily for the rest of her life.

She had meant to tell him about the letter, but things

beyond her control had swept her up. Was that an omen? she wondered. Should she try to tell him now?

'My love,' she murmured.

'My love,' he echoed, 'if you knew how wonderful it is to hear you call me that. I am your love and you are mine.' He stroked her breast. 'I was afraid this would never happen,' he whispered.

'It's not the first time we've made love,' she reminded him.

'No, but it's the first time we've made love like this, with all doubts settled, all fears gone, everything open and clear between us. When you told me that you trusted me I felt as if I'd gone to heaven.'

'Yes,' she whispered. 'I feel like that too.'

'And we must keep it that way. We lost two years, but we mustn't lose any more time. We must marry as soon as possible.'

'Marry,' she said in wonder.

'I told you yesterday that we should set the date. You didn't give me an answer. Are you trying to put me off?'

She glanced down the bed at their naked entwined figures. 'Does it look as if I'm trying to put you off?'

'I just want to be sure of you. Say yes. Say yes.'

'Oh, yes. Yes, with all my heart.'

'Now we've found each other,' he whispered, 'nothing can ever come between us.'

He kissed her again before saying, 'I've just remembered—you had something you were trying to say to me.'

'Did I?'

'Yes, it sounded urgent but I kind of distracted you.' He grinned, recalling the way he'd grasped hold of her and made her run.

'I suppose you could call this a distraction,' she agreed, smiling.

'So what were you going to say?'

Natasha's head was whirling. This was the moment she'd planned to lay bare the secret, but suddenly everything seemed different. To speak of it now would be to let Tania intrude on them again, and she was determined never to let that happen.

'Natasha?' he murmured.

'Mmm?'

'Are you awake?'

'Er...no. I—must have dozed off again. Did you say something?'

'I asked you what you'd been planning to tell me.'

'I can't remember. It's gone out of my head now, so it can't have meant much.'

'It's just that you made it sound important.'

'No, it couldn't be.' She touched his face. 'Only one thing is important now.'

'And that's us,' he agreed. 'You're right. Nothing else matters. Come here.'

She did so, taking refuge in his arms and his love, so that the rest of the world ceased to exist.

The letter didn't matter, she decided. This was how it would always be.

She opened her eyes next morning to find Mario regarding her anxiously.

'You did mean it, didn't you?' he asked. 'You really will marry me?'

'No,' she teased. 'I was just making fun of you. Oh, don't look like that. Of course I meant it. Would I have said it otherwise?'

'I can't be sure with you. You always seem to have a surprise to spring on me. I get nervous waiting for the next one.'

'Oh, really?' She regarded him with wicked humour. 'Let's see now. I could always thump you.'

'But that wouldn't be a surprise. You've already thumped me so often in different ways.'

'So maybe it's time to find another way. How about that?' She delivered a light pat on his shoulder.

'Ouch!' he cried comically. 'Now I'm in agony.'

'Good. Then I'll know how to bully you in future.'

She patted him again and they both burst into laughter.

'I don't believe this is real,' he said against her neck. 'Nobody could be as happy as I am now. It's an illusion.'

'No, we're going to teach the world what happiness looks like.'

'Mmm, that sounds nice. Can I thump you back?'

'Permission granted.'

He rolled her onto her stomach and lightly patted her behind. 'You be careful,' he said, 'or I'll do it again.'

'Is that a promise?' she chuckled.

'It's whatever you want.'

He was right, she thought, nestling contentedly against him. Nobody was allowed to be as happy as this. It must be an illusion. And she would do everything in her power to make it last.

CHAPTER ELEVEN

ENTERING THE BREAKFAST room downstairs, they found Damiano, Sally and Pietro waiting for them. They all looked up, eager for news.

'Have you got something to tell us?' Damiano asked. 'Sally seemed to think you might have.'

'You mean after she tried to talk to me yesterday and we dashed upstairs?' Mario said. 'Sorry, Sally. It was urgent.'

'Well, I gathered that,' she chuckled. 'So come on, tell us.'

'We're going to be married,' he announced. 'Natasha has decided she can put up with me.'

Pietro cried, 'Yippee!'

Sally hugged Natasha, and Damiano declared cheerfully, 'Welcome to the family, Natasha. We're all delighted that you're going to take charge of Mario and turn him into a sensible man.'

'Thanks, brother,' Mario said, grinning.

'By the time you discover your mistake it'll be too late,' Mario added. 'He'll have put the ring on your finger.'

'And I'll never let her take it off,' Mario said.

'You must marry here in Venice,' Sally said. 'After all, it's where you met. It'll be such fun to arrange.'

'That's very nice of you,' Mario said, 'but I think there's another place that would be more right for us. In Verona, we can marry at Juliet's house.' He glanced at Natasha, who nodded, smiling.

'Romeo and Juliet,' Sally mused. 'But you two can't be Romeo and Juliet. You're having a happy ending. I suppose there's still time for something to go wrong, but it won't.'

'No, it won't,' Mario said. 'We're together, and now nothing is going to go wrong. She is my Juliet, and Verona is the right place for us.'

Sally insisted on having a party for them that evening. Her warmth was a special blessing to Natasha. Her life had been lonely, with no relatives but her bitter mother. Now, suddenly, she had a brother and sister, and a cheeky nephew in Pietro.

They laughed and danced their way through the party, spent the night nestled together, and set out for Verona the following morning.

When Giorgio heard the news he roared with delight.

'Romeo and Juliet made it at last! What a story.'

'It's not exactly a story,' Mario protested.

'It is to me. You hired me as your publicity manager, and I'm going to do my job. When you've fixed the date we'll get some pictures.'

'The date will be as soon as possible,' Mario said.

'It'll have to be a Monday morning,' Giorgio told him. 'All wedding ceremonies are held then because the house has to be closed to tourists while it's happening. Then we'll have the reception here in the afternoon, and everyone in the *Comunità* will come.'

Later that day they went to the City Hall to make the booking for two weeks' time, and learned what they could about the wedding procedure. The actual ceremony would take place inside the building, with photographs taken afterwards, on the balcony.

Giorgio was in his element, planning to broadcast the information as far and wide as possible.

'This isn't just a wedding,' he said gleefully. 'It's the biggest publicity opportunity the *Comunità* has ever had. You really must make the best of it.'

'That's fine,' Mario said. 'I'm happy for everyone to know that I've secured the best bride in the world.'

But Natasha drew him aside, feeling some concern. 'Jenson will get to hear of it,' she said.

'Good!' Mario declared at once. 'I want him to know that his bullying has achieved nothing. That should stop his nonsense.'

'But suppose it doesn't?'

'Then I'll make him sorry he was born. Don't tell me you're still afraid of him. You're going to be my wife. There's nothing more he can do.' He took her in his arms. 'Trust me, darling. You have nothing more to fear from him. I told you I'd scare the living daylights out of him, and I have.'

'You scared Jenson? But how?'

'By slashing his advertising revenue. There are several media outlets I've been able to persuade to drop their adverts. Some here, some owned by friends of mine elsewhere. It should be enough to put the wind up him.'

'You did that for me?' she breathed. 'Oh, thank you—thank you.'

Blazing with happiness, she threw her arms around his neck.

'I told you I wouldn't let you be hurt,' he said. 'And I won't.'

'So you really are my guardian angel?'

'Angel? Not me. But I can put the wind up people when I want to.'

Chuckling, they embraced each other.

'It's such a weight off my mind,' she said. 'To know that he won't trouble me again.'

Now her most urgent arrangement was choosing a wedding dress. At Giorgio's orders, several gowns were delivered to the hotel for her to try on. She chose one of white satin, cut simply and elegantly.

'Perfect,' Giorgio declared when he saw it. 'It'll look great in the pictures. We must get started on them quickly.'

It seemed strange to be taking wedding pictures before the wedding, but they were to be part of Giorgio's publicity campaign to promote Verona as a wedding venue.

'The photographer will be here tomorrow morning,' Giorgio said. 'He's the same one who took the pictures of you as Romeo and Juliet. We'll put the two sets of pictures out together. Romeo and Juliet became Mario and Natasha.' He grinned. 'Or perhaps they always were.'

'Forget it,' Mario said. 'This story isn't going to end in a tomb.'

He was looking so handsome, Natasha thought as they posed together. For one picture she stood just in front of him, his hands on her shoulders as they both faced the camera. For another shot they danced together.

'Don't look so stern,' Giorgio called. 'Gaze into each other's eyes. Look romantic.'

'But why?' Natasha teased. 'We're getting married. That's not romantic; it's deadly serious.'

'Stop that,' Mario said. 'I'm quite scared enough without you scaring me more.'

She began to laugh. He joined in and Giorgio yelled with delight at the picture it produced.

'That's perfect,' he said. 'That says it all.'

As he'd predicted, the two sets of pictures worked splendidly together. When circulated to the rest of the *Comunità*, they produced a flood of excited congratulations.

There was one reaction Mario vowed to keep to himself. The text from Jenson was as spiteful as he'd expected, and he was thankful that Natasha didn't see it.

I've warned you but you didn't take any notice. Now see how sorry I can make you.

He checked the phone number of Jenson's organisation and dialled it.

'I want to speak to Elroy Jenson,' he told the receptionist.

'I'm sorry. Mr Jenson isn't accepting calls today.'

'He'll accept mine. Tell him Mario Ferrone wants to talk to him.'

A pause, some clicks, then a harsh masculine voice came on the line. 'What do you mean by calling me?'

'Ah, Mr Jenson. Good.' Mario leaned back in his chair. 'You know exactly who I am. You don't like me, and you're going to like me even less when I've finished.'

'You're wasting your time,' Jenson's voice came down the line.

'I don't think so. I think you'll find that some of my recent actions have been very significant.'

'What recent actions?' Jenson's voice contained a sneer but Mario thought he also detected a hint of nervousness.

'You'll be hearing from your Italian publications, wondering why whole batches of advertising have been suddenly cancelled.'

'Don't think you can scare me,' Jenson snapped. 'A few hotels and vineyards—'

'It'll be rather more than that. I've got friends working on this, friends you know nothing about but whose tentacles stretch great distances abroad. You'll be losing advertisements left, right and centre. And when they want to know why—I wonder what you'll tell them.'

'That's no concern of yours!' Jenson raged.

'Everything that concerns my fiancée concerns me, as you'll find out if you don't stop your nasty ways. You wrecked her career out of spite because she wasn't interested in your cheap advances and too many people got to know about it. Well, now the whole world is going to know about it.'

'What do you mean?' Jenson snarled.

'The digital age is a wonderful thing. A few texts and emails and the world will know what a pest Elroy Jenson is: a man so conceited that he felt no woman had the right to reject him, and with so little self-respect that he could never leave her alone afterwards.'

'There are laws of libel,' Jenson snarled.

'There's no question of libel. Once those texts you've sent her are revealed there would be no question everyone will know the truth.'

'Texts? I don't know what you're talking about.'

'Don't waste time trying to deny it. I've got records of every word you sent, and where they came from. I can reveal every word and prove it. The world will rock with laughter at you. And if you resorted to law you'd just keep yourself in an unpleasant spotlight longer.'

'What are you after? Money?'

'No, I just want you to leave Natasha alone. One more text or call from you and you've had it. Do you understand me?'

'You're very good at making threats,' Jenson snapped with his best effort at a sneer.

Mario grinned, feeling that he could risk a little vulgarity.

'I'm good at a lot of things,' he said. 'Which is why she chose me over you.'

'Why, you—'

'Goodbye. Go to hell!'

Mario hung up. Then he stared at the phone, trying to come to terms with his own actions. He was neither a violent nor a cruel man, but the need to conquer Jenson had brought out a side of him he'd never needed to use before.

But it was for her, and for her he would do anything. That was the effect she had on him, and now he realised that part of him had known it from the first day.

From behind him he heard a sound that made him turn in amazement. Natasha stood there, applauding.

'Well done,' she said. 'Wonderful! You've really dealt with him.' She engulfed him in an embrace.

'It was easy—just threaten to expose him as an idiot,' he said, returning her hug. 'He's far more afraid of that than losing business.'

'But I don't understand what you said about his texts. Surely you don't really have records of them?'

'Only the one he sent today. I don't have the others, but he doesn't know that and he won't take the chance.'

'No, he won't,' she breathed.

'And he won't dare send you any more because now he knows the risk he runs.'

'You're so clever.' She sighed. 'I never thought anyone could put this business right.'

'But you've got me to protect you now. And that's all I want to do for the rest of my life.'

He enfolded her in a fierce embrace.

'Three days before we're married,' he said huskily. 'I don't know if I can bear to wait that long to make you mine.'

'But I'm already yours. I always have been and I always will be.'

'No doubt about that,' he said, smiling. 'I'll never let you go.'

'That suits me just fine.'

Now things were moving fast. Two days before the wedding, Damiano, Sally and Pietro arrived and took up residence in the hotel's best suite. That evening there was a party attended by them, by Giorgio and by several members of the *Comunità*. Toasts were made to the bride and groom. Then the bride alone was toasted, leaving no doubt that she was the heroine of the hour.

As the evening wore on, Sally announced that she would retire for the night.

'I've got a bit of a headache,' she confided to Natasha.

'Me too,' she said. 'And I think Mario might enjoy chatting if he didn't have to keep breaking off to translate for me.'

Together they bid everyone goodnight and went upstairs. A warm, friendly hug and they said goodnight.

Natasha was glad to be alone for a moment for she needed to think. She must decide what to do about Tania's letter.

There had been a time when she might have told Mario

about it but events had conspired to distract her and now she knew the moment had gone. Her best course now was to destroy it so that it would be out of their lives finally and for ever.

Going quickly into her room, she went to the place where she kept it hidden.

She found the small piece of blue paper and unfolded it.

She read it again, taking in the words that had meant so much, thanking a merciful fate that had given it to her. Now she reckoned she must burn it.

'What's that?' said Mario's voice.

Startled, she looked up and saw him there. He had come in quietly, without her hearing him. Now he was standing with his eyes fixed on the blue paper that she held. With dismay, she realised that he knew what she was holding.

'What's that?' he repeated.

'It's just—'

'Give it to me.'

He wrenched it from her hand before she could protest. As he read it he seemed to grow very still.

'How did you get this?' he asked in a toneless voice.

'By accident. I came across it while I was in your apartment, after my room flooded.'

'And you kept it.'

'I needed to read it again and again. It seemed too good to be true. She says there that you'd told her it was over because you wanted to be with me. So after that I knew—'

'You knew I'd been telling you the truth,' he said slowly.

'Yes. It was so wonderful. After everything that happened, who could have thought it would be Tania who would make things right for us?'

There was a silence.

When he spoke he didn't look at her. 'Did she make things right for us?' he asked in a strange voice.

'She added the missing piece. She told me what I needed to know. After that, everything was different.'

If only he would smile and share her pleasure at the way things had turned out, but instead he was silent, frowning. It was almost as though her words troubled him.

'Tell me something,' he said at last. 'That night we took a walk by the river and when we got home you invited me into your room—had you read Tania's letter then?'

'Yes. I was so happy. Suddenly everything was all right.'

'Why? Because Tania had confirmed I was telling the truth? You knew that because *she* told you? But not because *I* told you?'

'I didn't know you as well in those days. I couldn't be sure what the truth might be. Oh, Mario, why didn't you show me the letter yourself?'

'I meant to. But I was waiting for the right moment.'

'But surely any time would have been right to show me the proof?'

'The proof?'

'The proof that what you were telling me was true. That you really had broken with her.'

A strange, tense look came over his face. 'So you could have believed me when you saw proof. But not my word alone.'

'Mario, I'm sorry about that. I see now that I should

have believed you. But does it matter now that it's been finally settled?'

'Settled.' He repeated the word softly. 'If only I could make you understand—'

'Understand what, my darling?'

'Since you came to Verona I've clung to a happy fantasy, a dream world in which we understood each other. In that world we grew close, loving each other more and more until you finally believed what I told you because you knew me well enough to know that I was true to you.'

'But I do know—'

'Yes, because you've got the evidence in that letter. But in my fantasy you didn't need evidence. You believed me because you loved me enough to trust me completely. We were so close that no doubt could ever come between us.

'That night, when you opened your arms to me, I felt I'd reached heaven. I thought our great moment had arrived at last, the moment I'd been longing for since the day we met. If only you knew how I... Well, never mind. It doesn't matter now.'

'But it does,' she cried passionately. 'Mario, don't talk like this. You sound as though everything is hopeless between us, but it isn't. We've discovered our hope at last. It's taken too long but we've finally found each other. Can't you see that?'

'I want to. If you knew how desperately I long to believe that everything can be all right now, but there's something missing and perhaps it always will be.'

She stared at him, struggling to believe what he was saying.

'Then blame me,' she said. 'I got it wrong; I took too long to understand the truth. But I understand it now.'

'Yes, because someone else told you. Not me. The closeness I thought we'd achieved doesn't exist. It was an illusion I believed because I wanted to believe it.' He gave a grim laugh. 'I remember you saying people believed what they wanted to, and boy were you right! In you I saw what I wanted to see.

'And now? Will we ever have that closeness? I doubt it. You said things were "finally settled". But when is something settled? When you finally have peace of mind?'

And now he did not have peace of mind with her. He didn't say it—but he didn't need to say it. She had thought that all was well between them, but after this would their love ever be the same?

'Do you understand the bitter irony of this?' he asked. 'The next thing is our wedding. We'll stand side by side at a site that commemorates the greatest lovers of legend. We'll vow love, loyalty, trust. *Trust!* Can you imagine that?'

'I do trust you,' she cried passionately.

'Do you? Perhaps you do, perhaps you don't. I'll never really know, will I?'

'Can't you take my word for it?'

He gave a harsh laugh. 'Are you lecturing me about accepting your word? That's the cruellest joke you ever made. I was looking forward to our wedding. Now I'm dreading it. I'm not even sure that I—'

He broke off, almost choking. His eyes, fixed on her, were full of hostility. Suddenly he turned, pulled open the door and rushed out without a backward glance.

'Mario—don't. Come back, *please.*'

But either he didn't hear or he ignored her, heading for the stairs and running down them. At the bottom he turned towards the entrance. Dashing back into the room,

Natasha went to the window and looked down, where she could see him heading down the street until he vanished.

She almost screamed in her despair. The perfect love that offered a wonderful future had descended into chaos. Now a terrifying vista opened before her. Ahead stretched a road of misery, where every hope came to nothing and only emptiness remained.

CHAPTER TWELVE

WHAT FOLLOWED WAS the worst night of Natasha's life.

It was over. Everything was over. She had lost Mario and nothing could ever matter in her life again.

Why didn't I tell him earlier? her heart cried.

But she knew the answer. However he had learned about the letter, he would have hated the fact that she'd relied on it. In his heart he no longer believed that she loved him. And now everything might be over between them. He had even hinted that he might not be there for the wedding.

For a moment she thought of chasing after him, but he'd had time to disappear and she would never find him. Her best hope was to wait for him to return.

She lay down, trying to control her wild thoughts and believe that there might still be hope. For an hour she lay there, listening for some sign of his return, but all she heard was the party breaking up.

Then there was silence and darkness, leaving her with an aching heart and terrified thoughts.

Why didn't he return?

Would he ever return?

She slept for a while and awoke in the early hours. There was no sign of Mario, but perhaps he'd gone to his own room. She slipped out into the corridor and went to his door, where she stood listening for a moment. But there was no sound from within.

Tentatively, she opened the door and slipped inside. The bed was empty. He had not returned.

'Come back,' she whispered. 'Don't let it end like this. Come back to me.'

But another two hours passed with no sign of him.

A terrible sense of irony pervaded her. Suddenly it felt as though she was Juliet again, a star-crossed lover facing the final destruction of her joy.

There was nothing to prepare her for what happened next.

A shrill from her mobile phone made her look to find a text. Incredibly, it was from Jenson.

You think you're clever, setting your lover on me. Take a look at this.

Below it was the address of a website. Studying it, Natasha realised that it was an English provincial newspaper, doubtless belonging to Jenson.

He'd said he knew something about her, implying that he could smear her in print. But she couldn't think of anything she would be reluctant to have known.

She got to work on her laptop, typing in the web address. There on the screen was a printed page with a photograph. A cry broke from her as she recognised her father.

Forcing herself under control, she looked closely at the text. It was dated eight years ago and named the man as Charles Bates. It seemed to be part of a series about people who had been brought down by misfortune. Charles

Bates had turned to crime and gone to prison following a tragic crisis in his life.

He had given the interview two days after being released. As she read what he'd had to say, Natasha felt her blood run cold.

'I blame my wife. I loved her and the girl I thought was my daughter. But then I discovered she wasn't mine. It broke my heart. I ran away as fast as I could go.'

So her mother had betrayed her husband and she, Natasha, was not his child. She struggled to deny it, but lurking in her memory was a quarrel she had overheard between them. Her father had shouted, 'Who was he? Tell me!' And he'd called her mother some terrible names. The next day he had gone.

Another memory returned—Jenson walking into the room as she was telling this story to a fellow employee. How sympathetic he had been, encouraging her to talk. How kind she had thought him, while all the time he was softening her up so that he could pounce on her, while storing the information in case it could be a useful weapon. That was his way. He liked to have weapons against everyone.

Checking back, he'd found that one little item and made a note of it. Mario's action over the advertisements had convinced him he had nothing left to gain, and still he'd lashed out to hurt her for revenge.

Now she saw that years of being warned not to trust men went back to this point. Her mistrust had made her wary of Mario, but it was based on a lie. And that lie threatened the love they shared.

Unless she could find a way to solve the problem.

Suddenly she found words whispering through her head. *I have a faint cold fear thrills through my veins, That almost freezes up the heat of life.*

Juliet had spoken those words, faced with the decision that would change everything. And now Natasha felt the cold fear running through her. She must do something to make Mario return. But what?

'*She* will know,' she said. 'I'll go and ask her.'

Hurriedly, she flung on some clothes and rushed out of the room and downstairs.

Damiano was just crossing the hall. 'Just on my way to breakfast,' he said. 'No Mario?'

'He'll…be a while,' she stammered.

Damiano chuckled. 'Ah, still asleep, is he? I guess you must have exhausted him.'

She managed a smile. 'Something like that. I have to hurry away for a while.'

She quickly went out, seeing the hotel driver just outside. She approached him.

'Please take me to the Via Capello.'

In a moment they were away. She didn't notice Giorgio standing in the doorway with a puzzled frown.

For the whole journey she sat tense, watching Verona glide past her, wondering what the city would mean to her in future. The place where she and her Romeo had achieved their happy ending? Or the place where the star-crossed lovers had been forced to accept that their love was never meant to be?

At last they drew up outside the Casa di Giulietta and she got out.

'Shall I wait for you?' the driver asked.

'No. I don't know how long I'll be. Thank you, but go back.'

He drove off, leaving her standing there. Then she went to the house, which had just opened for the day. A doorman greeted her, recognising her as a bride who was booked in a couple of days ahead.

'You'll find everything just as you're hoping for,' he called cheerfully.

'I'm sure I will,' she called back politely.

But would her wedding be as she was hoping for? Would anything in her life be right again?

As always, Juliet was standing in the courtyard. Natasha headed for the statue, glad that for the moment they were alone.

'I never asked your advice before,' she said. 'I believed you were just a fantasy. But now my whole world is upside down, and maybe you're the one person who can help me.

'What can I do? I made a silly mistake but I was confused. I didn't want to hurt Mario. I just couldn't understand what it would mean to him. Now he thinks I don't really love him, but I do. How can I make him believe that?'

Silence.

'Oh, please, you must help me. You know more about love than anyone. Tell me what I can do.'

She pressed her hand against her chest.

'You understand that, don't you?' she said to Juliet, who also had a hand on her breast. 'You know what it's like to press your hand over the pain, hoping to make it go away. But it doesn't go, and you become frantic trying to think of something that will help. I can't think of anything. What can I do?'

She took a step closer to Juliet, seeking to look her in the eye. She told herself not to be fanciful, otherwise she might have imagined Juliet's soft voice saying, *He's as troubled and unsure as you are.*

I know. He's suffering terribly and it's my fault. I thought the worst of every man because of my father, but now I realise that I shouldn't have done.

Discovering that you'd read the letter hurt him. He hasn't completely recovered.

Nor have I.

You're coping better than he is.

Truly? What can I do now?

Be kind to him. He is confused.

But what is it that confuses him?

You. You always have, although he would never admit it.

Does our love really have a future?

Who can tell? You can only hope.

And hope might come to nothing. That fact had to be faced. She would return to the hotel and find him not there because he no longer wanted her. It was over. He would never return.

Tears filled her eyes, blurring her vision so that the street around her seemed to become a swirling mass. She groped her way forward, missed the edge of the pavement and crashed to the ground. She was intensely aware of pain going through her head before she blacked out.

The first person Mario met on his return was Damiano.

'So there you are!' his brother exclaimed. 'I thought you were still upstairs, sleeping it off while Natasha was away.'

'Away?'

'She came downstairs a few hours ago. She went off somewhere in a hurry.'

'Went somewhere? You mean she's gone? Where?'

'She didn't say where she was going. Just walked out and didn't come back. You don't mean there's something wrong, surely? The two of you are getting married tomorrow. She's probably making last-minute preparations for the wedding.'

'Yes, of course,' Mario said in a voice that was deliberately blank to hide the storm of alarm that was rising within him.

'I expect she's preparing a special surprise for you.'

Yes, Mario thought desperately. Natasha was preparing a surprise for him, and he had a dreadful feeling that he knew what the surprise was.

'Oh, no!' he breathed. 'How could she do this to me?'

'What do you mean?' Damiano demanded.

'She's done it again.'

'Done what again?'

'What she did before—leaving without a goodbye, when I wasn't there to see. Disappearing into thin air like she'd never existed.'

'I'm sure you're wrong about that,' Damiano protested.

Mario tore his hair. 'You have no idea,' he raged. 'She vanished and I spent weeks looking for her before I realised that I'd never find her because she'd shut me out of her life.' His voice rose in anguish. *'Now she's done it again.'*

Nobody had noticed Giorgio entering the hall. He stood watching Mario with a puzzled frown.

'What's happened?' he asked at last.

'Have you seen Natasha today?' Mario demanded.

'Yes, I saw her get into the car with the chauffeur a few hours ago. He was only gone half an hour.'

'Fetch him,' Mario said.

Giorgio went out and returned with the chauffeur.

'Where did you take her?' Mario demanded.

'To the Via Capello.'

'And you brought her back?'

'No, she told me not to wait for her.'

'So she's gone,' Mario muttered. 'She's gone.'

He turned away so that they shouldn't see his face, which he knew must betray his pain, greater than any he'd known in his life before. He'd wanted so much to believe in her. Since their quarrel the night before he'd brooded over what lay before him. A life with her, always worried about the strength of her love? Or a life without her?

He'd paced the dark streets for hours, trying to understand his own heart. By the time he'd arrived home he knew that Natasha mattered more than anything in the world. However hard it was for him, he would do what he had to for their love to succeed; the thought of losing her was unbearable.

And he had arrived to find her gone.

He wanted to howl with rage, but even more with misery. She had betrayed his love, abandoned him, while knowing what it would do to him.

'Why don't you look in her room?' Damiano said. 'If she's really gone she'll have taken everything with her.'

'All right,' Mario said heavily.

What was the point? he thought. He would find her room deserted and the brutal truth underlined. Moving mechanically, he went up to her room and opened the door. Then he grew still.

The wardrobe was open, and inside it he could see her clothes. Pulling open drawers, he found more clothing.

'She hasn't gone for good,' Damiano said, coming in behind him. 'Or she would never have left all this behind.'

'But where did she go?' Mario asked hoarsely.

'The chauffeur said he took her to the Via Capello,' Giorgio said. 'Surely she went to Juliet's house.'

'Yes,' Mario said at once. 'I understand that now.'

Everything was becoming clear to him. Natasha had gone to consult Juliet, and now she would know how the two of them could put things right.

One thing was clear. He must join her as soon as possible. He headed for the front door.

'Hey, Mario,' Giorgio called. 'Where are you going?'

Mario paused and looked back at him. 'I'm going to find my lady,' he said.

As he drove himself to the Via Capello the words haunted him, as they had many times before. *It is my lady. Oh, it is my love.*

'"Oh, that she knew she were,"' he murmured.

At last Juliet's house came in sight. He parked and ran down the street to the alley that led to the courtyard. There was no sign of Natasha. All he could see was Juliet, staring ahead, coolly indifferent to her surroundings. He placed himself in front of her.

'Was she here?' he demanded. 'Did she come to you and ask your help? Did you help her?'

No response. Nor had he expected one. Nobody else could help them now.

He wandered through the house, seeking her without success. In one room he stood looking around him, reflecting that this was where their wedding was supposed to take place, and wondering what the future held.

Once more he returned to Juliet. A small group of tourists had gathered in front of her, pleading for her attention.

'It's very tempting to talk to her, isn't it?' a woman said to Mario. 'We came here earlier and there was a lovely young woman talking to her as if it really mattered. But I don't think she had any luck because as soon as she left she got hurt.'

'Hurt? How?'

'I'm not sure what happened. She just seemed to lose her balance. She went down hard and hit her head on the pavement. The last I saw, she was being taken to the hospital.'

Barely able to speak, he forced himself to say, 'You said she was a young woman. What did she look like?'

'Pretty, blue eyes, blonde hair.'

'And how did she seem?'

'Not sure, really. She wasn't moving. I suppose she might actually have been dead.'

He swallowed. 'Thank you for telling me,' he said hoarsely.

It took him ten minutes to get to the nearest hospital. There, he tore inside and up to the desk.

'A young woman was brought in this morning,' he gasped. 'She had a fall in the Via Capello. I must see her.'

The receptionist made a phone call and a nurse appeared.

He followed her into a small side ward and held his breath at the sight of Natasha lying on the bed. Her eyes were closed and it seemed to him that she was frighteningly still.

'Is this the person you are looking for?' the nurse asked.

'Yes, this is the person I was looking for.'

'Please tell me who she is.'

'Her name is Natasha Bates.'

'And who is her next of kin?'

'I am. I'm her husband. At least, I will be in a few days. If she lives.'

He had to force himself to say the last few words, but the fear was more than he could endure.

'We don't yet know how seriously she's hurt,' the nurse said. 'She's still unconscious, but hopefully she'll soon come round.'

He moved to the bed, looking down at Natasha lying there. She seemed different to the strong, determined young woman he remembered: smaller, more frail and vulnerable.

A sudden fearsome echo haunted him: Romeo coming to Juliet in the tomb, seeing her lying there, silent and motionless, believing her dead. He tried to fight the thought away but he had a terrified feeling that she would leave him unless he could prevent her.

'Natasha,' he said, taking a chair beside the bed. 'It's me, darling. Can you hear me?'

She neither moved nor spoke.

'Are you there?' he begged. 'Please tell me that you're there.'

His heart sank. Her breathing told him that she was still alive, but in another sense she wasn't there. She was living in another universe, one where she might be trapped for ever.

'You went away from me once,' he whispered. 'I thought I would go mad at your rejection, but you came back and we found each other. Then today I thought you'd abandoned me again, and losing you was even worse than before.

'What happened was my fault. I couldn't bear discovering that I'd been living in a fantasy, that you loved me less than I'd thought. But if that's true—' he hesitated '—if the love is mainly on my side, then…then I'll live with that as long as I can have you. Do you understand? I'll accept any conditions as long as I don't lose you again. Even if—' he shuddered '—even if you never really wake up, but stay like this always, I won't leave you. I'll care for you and love you for years and years, until the day we can be finally together for ever.'

He leaned closer to murmur into her ear, 'Don't leave me. I'm yours in every way and I always will be. Natasha? Can you hear me?'

'Yes,' she whispered.

'I followed you all the way to Juliet's house. You went to ask her help, didn't you?'

'Yes.' She whispered the word so softly that he wasn't sure he'd heard properly.

'What?' he asked eagerly, leaning closer.

'She was very kind to me.'

He was suddenly sure that they understood each other. He must seize this moment, lest there should never be another.

'I tried too,' he said. 'But she stayed silent. I reckon she was telling me to see the truth for myself.' Inspiration came to him. 'And the truth we have to understand is that we love each other more than we can say in mere words. We've always known that, but we've never managed to face it before. But now the time has come and if I do nothing else in the world I have to make sure that you know.'

He kissed her again softly before murmuring, 'You are my lady. You are my love. Oh, that you knew you are.'

'Am I?' she whispered. 'Am I truly?'

'You know you are. And you will always know that you are.'

'How can I believe it? It's too good to be true.'

'Then I'll have to spend my life convincing you. I was so afraid you wouldn't wake up.'

'I was in such a strange place. I couldn't tell which way to turn, but suddenly you were there, beckoning me.'

'I always will be. I'll never let you go.'

The nurse appeared. She checked Natasha's pulse, read the machines and smiled at the result.

'This is what we hoped for,' she said. 'It's not serious. A few days' rest and you'll be back on your feet.'

When she had left they hugged, looking deep into each other's eyes, reading the depths for the first time. But now no words were spoken. No words were needed. Soon Natasha's eyes closed and Mario held her while she slept, thinking blissfully of the years ahead when he would hold her many times in his arms and always in his heart.

The wedding had to be delayed for two weeks, but at last the time came when they entered Juliet's house and made the vows of lifelong love and fidelity. Once, many years before, another couple had vowed the same, only to see their happiness cut short. But Natasha and Mario had no fear.

After the ceremony they went out onto the balcony, where Giorgio had arranged for a photographer to be clicking his camera madly. But the bride and groom were barely aware of him. They saw only each other.

'Just us,' he said as they held each other later that night.

'Not quite just us,' she murmured. 'There were two other people there. Couldn't you sense them?'

'Yes, they were there, watching over us as they've always done. And perhaps they always will.'

'No need,' she said. 'From now on we'll watch over each other.'

'Do you really think we can?'

'Yes, we can.' She turned in the bed, taking him in a fervent embrace.

'Come here,' she said. 'Come here *now*.'

* * * * *

MEET THE ~~FORTUNES~~ MENDOZAS!

Mendoza of the Month: Matteo Mendoza

Age: 28

Vital statistics: Brown bedroom eyes and a quiet soulfulness that could melt a lady's heart.

Claim to fame: So far, the Miami-born pilot has been flying under the radar. But not for long!

Romantic prospects: They'd be a lot better if his flirtatious brother Cisco wasn't around. The two of them always seem to be in competition— especially for the heart of gorgeous and elusive Rachel Robinson.

"To my brother, love is just a game. But for me, the stakes are much higher. I will fight for Rachel if I have to. She's the one I've been waiting for. So far, she's been holding back. Why? Could my radar be that far off? Is she really interested in Cisco? Or is there something else she could be hiding?"

The Fortunes of Texas: Cowboy Country
Lassoing hearts from across the pond

MENDOZA'S
SECRET FORTUNE

BY
MARIE FERRARELLA

Published in Great Britain 2015
by Mills & Boon, an imprint of Harlequin (UK) Limited,
Eton House, 18-24 Paradise Road, Richmond, Surrey, TW9 1SR

© 2015 Harlequin Books S.A.

Special thanks and acknowledgment to Marie Ferrarella for her contribution to The Fortunes of Texas: Cowboy Country continuity.

ISBN: 978-0-263-25117-3

23-0315

Harlequin (UK) Limited's policy is to use papers that are natural, renewable and recyclable products and made from wood grown in sustainable forests. The logging and manufacturing processes conform to the legal environmental regulations of the country of origin.

Printed and bound in Spain
by CPI, Barcelona

USA TODAY bestselling and RITA® Award-winning author **Marie Ferrarella** has written more than two hundred books for Mills & Boon, some under the name Marie Nicole. Her romances are beloved by fans worldwide. Visit her website, www.marieferrarella.com.

To Marcia Book Adirim, whose mind works
on many more levels than mine does

Chapter One

"Hey, Rach. Nice to see you again!" the regular lunch customer at The Hollows Cantina called out as he walked into the dining area with several friends.

With a compliant smile, the hostess drew several menus into her hands and led the rather vocal men to table number four, listening to them as they swapped stories and laughed.

She was getting pretty good at this, Rachel Robinson silently congratulated herself, especially since nothing in her previous life could have prepared her for doing something like this. Back then, she'd been accustomed to being the one who was served, not the one doing the serving.

Poor little rich girl.

That was the title, Rachel thought, that probably would have best described her as little as five years ago, but not anymore. She had taken great pains to hide any hint of her past life. No one in this tiny, one-horse town nestled approximately four hundred miles away from Austin had any idea that she was one of Gerald Robinson's daughters. They had no clue that her father was a wealthy computer genius who had more than left his giant mark on the tech world.

Her father had left his mark in other places as well, places she'd learned about only when she had accidentally stumbled across the truth five years ago. Her discovery had prompted her sudden exodus to Horseback Hollow, a place she had found by closing her eyes and then jabbing her index finger at a map of Texas.

A place where she was hoping to get a completely new start and be herself rather than Gerald Robinson's daughter.

It seemed rather ironic to her to be here at this point in her life. She had already reinvented herself once. Her childhood had been spent mostly on the outside looking in.

Odd girl out, that was her.

She was always the tallest girl in her class, at times taller than all the boys, as well. Tall and thin as a rail, which made her an easy target for other girls who felt their own stock was enhanced if they could bring hers down by several notches.

So they did.

Though she had thought of herself as an outcast, her father, in one of his rare times at home rather than at work, insisted that she was "special." To that end, he saw to it that she was enrolled in a number of different classes—dance, tennis, piano, whatever it took—and Rachel discovered that she was good at all of them.

That discovery fueled her confidence, and Mother Nature stepped in to take care of the gawky, awkward issue. Thinking she was doomed to go through life all knobby knees and elbows, Rachel was delighted to find herself transforming from a plain duckling to a lovely swan.

It was a transformation that did *not* go unnoticed by the local males. Suddenly the center of attention, she continued to be so through her college years. She was flying high when her entire world came into question at the end of her senior year, courtesy of a former friend turned jealous rival. A rival who chose the dance floor at the senior-week dance to humiliate her by making certain allegations and so-called secret facts about her father public.

That was when Rachel's world came crashing down around her. A short time later, she arrived in Horseback Hollow.

Though done in haste, it had turned out not to be such a bad move after all. She didn't mind hard work. It brought her a sense of satisfaction. And here she wasn't anyone's daughter or sibling. She was just Rachel Robinson, hardworking restaurant hostess.

And she liked it that way, Rachel thought as she deposited the menus on the table, presenting each of the three men with the daily-special cards.

As she distributed them, she became acutely aware that one of the men was sizing her up closely. He leered at her. Rachel quickly looked away.

"Your server will be right with you, and let me know if there'll be anything else you need," she said, addressing the trio.

"Maybe you could get us some extra napkins for

these two to use when they stop drooling," the oldest man at the table suggested.

Rachel flashed an automatic smile and told him, "I'll see what I can do, sir."

She was about to head back to the hostess station up front when the one who had been eyeing her so closely said, "Don't rush off so fast." He caught her by the wrist. "Where have you been all my life, darlin'?"

The inner feistiness that she always tried to keep under wraps broke through. She heard herself answering, "Well, for the first half of it, I wasn't even born."

Rather than being put off because his friends laughed at her response, the man, still holding her wrist, said, "Lively. I like that in a woman."

With a hard tug, Rachel pulled her wrist free. "Pushy. I don't like that in a man," she replied sweetly.

The man who had asked for extra napkins laughed and said, "She sure got your number, Walt."

She certainly did, Rachel thought. And that number was a big zero.

Matteo Mendoza was running late. There were few things he hated more, but sometimes—like today—it just couldn't be helped. Still, he knew that his older brother, Cisco, would have some sort of asinine remark to toss his way. He braced himself for the onslaught.

Preoccupied, he passed by the table with the boisterous cowboys and heard the whole exchange play out. The young woman was certainly far too beautiful for the job she was doing, but that didn't mean she deserved to be treated with anything but respect.

Rather than look for his father's table, he approached this one first.

"Problem here?" Matteo asked, coming up behind the attractive hostess.

"Just havin' a little fun. Nothing serious," the man called Walt said, raising his hands to indicate that it was hands-off from now on as far as he was concerned.

"Thank you," Rachel said to the tall, dark and handsome knight in shining armor who had ridden up to defend her honor. She moved away from the rowdy cowboys' table. "But that wasn't really necessary. I can take care of myself."

Matteo inclined his head, as if to agree with the young woman. "Nobody said you couldn't," he replied.

With that, he moved farther into the dining area, scanning it to find where his father and brother were seated.

For the most part, when he joined his brother, Cisco, and his father for lunch at The Hollows Cantina, Matteo was thinking about going home. Home in both his and Cisco's case was Miami. Being here, in this little town with the improbable name of Horseback Hollow, was nothing short of an overwhelming culture shock.

Initially, he and Cisco had come to this slow-as-molasses, underdeveloped Texas town because their baby sister, Gabriella, had inexplicably fallen in love in Horseback Hollow.

Specifically, he and Cisco had come out here for Gabi's wedding to Jude Fortune Jones.

But the wedding had come and gone, and much to

Matteo's chagrin, he and Cisco were still here. Their father had prevailed upon them to stay a little longer— as a personal favor to him.

Orlando Mendoza had been the first of their immediate family to come out here from Miami. It wasn't a sense of wanderlust that had prompted the patriarch's relocation, but rather a feeling of urgency, a search for a purpose. Orlando was desperately trying to find a way to go on with his life after losing the love of his life, his wife, Luz.

A former air force pilot who had retired to care for his ailing spouse, Orlando found new purpose in his life when he came to Horseback Hollow. He joined Sawyer and Laurel Fortune in their fledgling venture, the Redmond Flight School, and also used his expertise to help operate the occasional charter service they ran.

It was while he was flying one of the planes—a plane, as it turned out, that had been intentionally tampered with—that he suffered a plane crash and had gotten seriously injured. The moment she got the news, Gabi had been quick to fly in from Miami in order to nurse him back to health.

As luck would have it, Gabi wound up nursing herself right into a love affair. Marriage turned out to be a by-product of that affair.

It was obvious to Matteo that Gabi, as well as his father, really liked this town and preferred it to Miami. His father had already tried subtly to talk Cisco as well as him into relocating to Horseback Hollow. Orlando made no secret of the fact that he wanted nothing more than to have his entire family living somewhere in proximity.

Although he loved and respected his father, Matteo couldn't see himself staying here indefinitely, much less living here.

"No offense, Dad, but this place is just too small, too mundane and too rural for my tastes." Snagging another tortilla chip, he popped it into his mouth and then continued, "It's like everything moves in slow motion around here. They even roll up the sidewalks at ten o'clock." He nursed his tall, cold glass of beer.

"Now, Matteo, you know you are exaggerating," Orlando chided him.

"There's no nightlife here," Matteo countered, "not to mention that there's just no excitement whatsoever in this town." He leaned over the table to get closer to his father. "I'm not like you, Dad. I'm young. I need excitement."

Orlando laughed the way a man might when he saw himself in his son's words. Everyone needed to take risks and behave foolishly, getting it out of their system when they were still young. He fully understood that. But he also had a father's desire to have his children learn from his mistakes so that they wouldn't repeat them.

"Oh, there's excitement here in this town, *hijo,*" he assured Matteo. "Trust me, there is excitement. It's just of a different nature."

Matteo smiled just before he tilted back his glass again. Obviously he and his father had *very* different definitions of "excitement," and he could understand that. At sixty-one, his father had earned the right to kick back and take it easy, while he, a pilot like his father and twenty-eight to boot, wanted nothing less than to take on anything that life might want to throw at him. Doing so got his adrenaline going and made him feel alive. He'd always had a competitive streak, especially when it came to his brother. He and Cisco had been competing against one another for as long as either one of them could remember.

"Give this place a chance," Cisco said with the thousand-watt smile that all the women within a ten-mile radius always found to be nothing short of spellbinding. "I know I am."

Matteo looked at his jet-setting older brother in disbelief. He'd been right. Cisco *had* decided to stay on for a while. He couldn't help wondering why. Cisco loved the pace in Miami as much as he did.

"You're staying?" he asked. There had to be an angle that Cisco was playing, but what?

Cisco lifted his glass in a mock toast to his brother, then drained it before answering, "That's what I just said."

Cisco liked to party more than he did. His choosing to stay here didn't make an iota of sense. "Why?" Matteo asked.

Cisco raised his broad shoulders and let them fall again in a vague, careless shrug. "Dad and Gabi seem sold on Horseback Hollow. That means there's got to be some merit to this town, right? I intend to stick around awhile and find out if I see it for myself. Might be some good real-estate investments going begging here." And then Cisco all but lit up. "Speaking of merit," he said, his attention directed toward something—or someone—he saw over his brother's head.

Curious, Matteo turned around in his chair, looking behind him. Which was when he saw her. The hostess he had verbally defended against the clowns at the other table a few minutes ago. She was heading their way. Matteo caught himself sitting up a little straighter.

When he had come to her assistance, he'd noted her height and the color of her long hair. He had of course observed that she was very attractive, but hadn't gone out of his way to really take in each aspect of her beauty. Besides, her looks had nothing to do with his coming to her defense, and his attention had been focused more on the men annoying her, anyway.

He could see her head-on now. Suddenly everything that had previously been on his mind evaporated from his brain. Matteo forgot all about missing Miami or being stuck in what he'd thought of as a one-horse town.

Forgot about everything except what was right there in front of him and coming closer.

Heaven in an apron.

He could almost feel the electrical charge this beautiful young woman seemed to radiate with every step she took.

Matteo had to remind himself to continue breathing. Air kept getting stuck in his lungs. And if his mouth were any dryer, dust would have come spilling out the second he tried to talk.

He wasn't the only one who was mesmerized by this vision. Out of the corner of his eye, Matteo saw that Cisco suddenly sat up, snapping to attention, his laid-back attitude becoming not quite so laid-back the second the hostess came into his line of vision.

As if on cue, the hostess stopped at their table, smiled and introduced herself to the trio.

"Hello, my name is Rachel, and I'll be your server

this afternoon. One of our regulars called in sick, and I'm covering for her." She glanced from Orlando to his two sons. Recognizing the one on the older man's right as the man who had come to her defense just a few minutes earlier, her smile grew wider in acknowledgment—chivalry should always be applauded. "Have you gentlemen decided yet?"

Matteo knew what he would have liked to order. *Her.* He kept that response to himself.

After his father and Cisco had placed their orders with the dark-haired, blue-eyed beauty, Matteo knew that he had ordered something, but for the life of him, he couldn't remember what less than three seconds after the words had left his mouth.

He had been fixated on the way her lips moved as she spoke and the way his entire system reacted to the melodic sound of her voice.

"Are you all right, Matteo?" his father asked once Rachel had retreated to the kitchen.

Cisco smirked. Annoyance flared in Matteo's veins. Now what?

"Yeah, sure. I'm fine, Dad." He turned to look at his father, puzzled. "Why would you ask that?"

"Well, I have known you for your whole life, and in all those years, I do not remember a single time when I saw you eating a salad as your main course. I believe you referred to salads as—"

"Cow food," Cisco interjected, unable to remain silent any longer. His laugh was full-bodied and hearty. And, right now, very annoying to Matteo. "I think my little brother was mesmerized by the lovely Rachel and didn't know what he was ordering, Dad."

"I wasn't mesmerized," Matteo protested with indignation, giving his brother a dirty look.

Matteo loved his older brother, but he hated being teased by Cisco. Cisco could be relentless, picking at him for days on end about a single thing if the spirit so moved him.

Now he grinned that wicked grin of his. "Hey, brother, I thought that she was a really hot little number, too."

Orlando could see that this had the makings of another family fight. Matteo sounded as if he was taking offense for the young woman—who surely hadn't a clue that she was the subject of this discussion, the older man surmised. As for Cisco, Orlando knew that the older boy loved to get Matteo riled up.

"We are all agreed that she is a very attractive young lady, Cisco. There is no reason for a dispute— or for you to give your brother a hard time," Orlando chided his older son.

Matteo frowned. He knew his father meant well, but he didn't need him coming to his aid this way. He wasn't ten years old and unable to hold his own against Cisco. Even at ten, he hadn't welcomed the interference.

"It's okay, Dad," Matteo said evenly, shifting his eyes to his brother. "Cisco didn't mean anything by that."

"Actually, I did," Cisco contradicted him. "Are you declaring dibs on Rachel? 'Cause if you are, it looks like maybe you've found that reason to hang around Horseback Hollow for a while—until she rebuffs you in favor of someone else, of course." Matteo's brother chuckled to himself as he continued eating the triangular chips from the bowl in the center of the table.

"You mean you?" The question came spontaneously to Matteo's lips, without any real thought necessary on his part.

Cisco's grin spread wider, annoying Matteo almost beyond words. "Just possibly."

"Matteo, Cisco," Orlando chided them sharply. "You're not children anymore, bent on competing until one of you collapses in exhaustion," he said. "It is time for you to behave like men."

"Men compete, Dad," Cisco reminded his father in all sincerity. "You know that."

For a moment, Orlando was catapulted back in time. He remembered his late wife, vividly remembered what he had gone through in order to win her hand in marriage. Remembered, too, what it had ultimately personally cost him.

"Sometimes men compete," Orlando admitted, then added, "but not my sons." He made the four words sound like an edict. "They do *not* compete against one another."

"Don't worry, Dad," Cisco assured him with a well-intentioned smile on his face. "It's not really a contest, is it, Matteo?" It wasn't so much a question as it was, in Cisco's opinion, a statement of fact. He raised his eyes to his brother's, waiting for a response. Or more accurately, waiting for his agreement.

Matteo knew just what his brother was inferring. That Matteo didn't stand a chance at winning over the striking young hostess, because Cisco had always been the lucky one when it came to all of their bets. More important, the one who always got the girl because he was so outgoing, charming and downright irresistible.

But Cisco was also the one whose relationships did not last, not even as long as the life cycle of a rose.

Terminating those relationships was always of his brother's own choosing, but that didn't change the fact that when all was said and done, Cisco wound up standing alone.

"She's a person, not property," Matteo pointed out tersely.

Cisco remained undaunted. "I completely agree," he replied in an even tone. He leaned forward just a touch. "So, tell the truth, brother. Does the lovely Rachel make you rethink leaving this tiny town?"

"She makes me rethink having you for a brother," Matteo informed him in as level a voice as he could manage. He was fighting the urge to cut Cisco down to size, but he had a feeling Cisco was looking forward to just that—so he refrained from playing into his brother's hands.

"Boys, *bastante*," Orlando declared, calling an end to the discussion before it got completely out of hand. "No fighting," he emphasized. "I asked you both here for a nice, peaceful lunch. I thought this restaurant might remind you a little of the ones you liked to go to back ho—back in Miami."

At the last moment, Orlando corrected himself. Referring to Miami as "home" was counterproductive to what he was currently attempting to promote—a sense that this place, Horseback Hollow, with its peaceful surroundings and room for growth, held a great deal of potential. Potential he felt that someone like Matteo—more so than Cisco—could tap into.

His youngest son was a pilot, like he was, but while he had been a risk-taker in his youth, Matteo admittedly was turning out to be far steadier at this point in his life than Orlando had been when *he* was twenty-eight.

Losing Luz just reinforced for Orlando that life was fleeting. However many years—or months—he had left, he wanted to spend them with his children. But at the same time, he knew that strong-arming them was not the way to proceed successfully.

Cisco—for the time being—was a done deal. He was staying in Horseback Hollow—he had even rented a small ranch house just outside of town. And of course, Gabi had already settled in here. Matteo, however, was going to require some major—and just possibly underhanded—convincing in order to get him to stick around. When they had come to eat at this restaurant, Orlando had thought his dilemma of winning his youngest son over was all but insurmountable.

Now, however, he finally had some hope. Many a man had done some unpredictable things in order to impress a young woman, and from what he could see, Matteo seemed to be pretty taken with that attractive hostess.

Orlando kept the conversation flowing, talking up the merits of Horseback Hollow, the closeness of its local citizens and how living here made a man focus on what was really important in life: his family and his health.

In recent months, the patriarch had regained the latter and was in the process of reinstituting the former.

With just a little luck and a healthy dose of his persuasion, Orlando felt he would succeed here, as well.

When the hostess returned shortly with their orders, Orlando carefully observed his younger son's reaction to her. That made him feel this indeed was the right path for him to concentrate on. His youngest son all but lit up like the proverbial Christmas tree when the woman approached.

Orlando noted that his older son seemed to come to life a little more, as well.

This had all the earmarks of an intense rivalry, Orlando observed. He had always tried to discourage that sort of thing, thinking that brothers should support one another, not attempt to best each other at every turn—especially when Cisco usually triumphed over Matteo. The last thing he wanted was for the latter to suffer another loss at the hands of his brother, but at this point, he couldn't think of another way to get Matteo to consider remaining in Horseback Hollow for a little while longer—and ideally, permanently—than bringing his son together with this hostess.

His secret hope was that if Matteo—and Cisco— did remain here for a number of weeks, both would be won over by the town's charm, and they would come to see that the merits of living in a small town trumped living in a large, indifferent metropolis where people lived next door to one another and remained strangers.

"Senorita, please, another round of cervezas for all of us," Orlando said once their server had emptied the tray she had carried to their table.

"Coming right up. And I'll bring back another bowl

of tortilla chips, as well," Rachel promised, picking up the empty woven basket and placing it on her tray. "Anything else?" she asked, her eyes sweeping over the three men.

"Maybe later," Cisco replied.

Rachel smiled as she inclined her head. "Later, then," she agreed cheerfully. "Anything else for you gentlemen?" she wanted to know, glancing at the other two men at the table.

Matteo stared down at what was to be his lunch. He honestly couldn't remember asking for the salad. In any event, that was *not* going to satisfy his appetite. "Yes. I'd like a cheeseburger, please," he said.

"Is something wrong with your salad?" she asked.

"No, I just thought that the cheeseburger would be more filling," Matteo explained, feeling as if he was tripping over his own tongue. He had never had Cisco's glib ability to spout clever rhetoric at the drop of a hat.

"Then you'd like me to take the salad back?" she asked.

"Not if it gets you into trouble." Now, why had he said something so stupid? Matteo upbraided himself. He should have just said yes and left it at that.

But to his relief, she smiled. "That's very considerate of you, but no, it won't." Picking up the salad, she placed it on her tray. "One cheeseburger, another round of cervezas and a bowl of chips coming up," she told him.

Captivated, Matteo watched her hips sway ever so slightly as she walked away from their table.

He could have sworn his body temperature went up a full five degrees.

Maybe more.

Chapter Two

Orlando looked at his youngest son and chuckled knowingly. "Well, I'm guessing there's at least one thing the Cantina has to offer that will have you coming back here again."

"Don't count on it." Cisco cavalierly waved away his father's words to his brother. "Matteo doesn't know a good thing when he sees it. I, on the other hand, can spot a good thing a mile away." Cisco leaned back in his chair, tilting it on its rear legs in order to get a better view of Rachel as she rounded a corner and disappeared into the kitchen.

"She's not a 'thing.' She's a woman," Matteo snapped at his brother. He didn't care for the way that Cisco had reduced the woman to the level of a mere object rather than giving her the proper due as a person.

"She certainly is that," Cisco agreed with a wide, appreciative and yet very devilish grin.

"No," Orlando announced firmly, instantly commanding his sons' attention.

"No, what?" Cisco asked as he looked at his father. They hadn't said anything that required a yes-or-no decision.

Orlando frowned, turning his affable face into a stern, somber mask. "No, you two are not going to butt heads and who knows what else while competing for the same woman."

Among Cisco's many talents was the ability to look completely innocent even when he was completely guilty. He assumed that look now as he turned his gaze on his father.

"What makes you think that Matteo and I are going to compete for the same woman, Dad?"

An exasperated look flashed across the patriarch's face. He was not about to be hoodwinked—or buried beneath his silver-tongued son's rhetoric.

"Is the Pope Catholic?" Orlando asked.

"Last time I checked," Cisco replied. His tone was respectful. The gleam in his eye, however, gave him away.

Orlando shook his head firmly. "And there you have your answer," he told Cisco. "I never said very much when you boys were growing up and insisted on turning everything into an emotional tug-of-war. I even thought—God forgive me—that it might help you two to build your character—"

"Matteo's a character all right," Cisco joked. "However, as far as I'm concerned—" He got no further.

Orlando looked as if his patience was wearing thin

and might even be in danger of giving way entirely. "But above all, I want you two to remember that you are brothers. No prize is worth sacrificing that relationship. Not even a woman you might think you love."

But he, Orlando added silently, was the exception that proved the rule. However, that wasn't something he was about to share with his sons. It went against the point he was trying to make.

"Don't worry, Dad. There isn't going to be any competition," Cisco assured his father as he slanted a quick glance at his brother.

Orlando nodded his silver head. "That's good to hear."

"By the way she looked at me, I've already won," Cisco concluded with that smile that always managed to get right under Matteo's skin.

And his brother knew it, Matteo thought, unable to do anything about it without getting on his father's bad side.

But he had to say *something*, however innocuous. So he did. "In your dreams," Matteo retorted.

"I agree with you there, Mattie. That little lady certainly is the stuff that dreams are made of," Cisco told his brother. "Besides, what difference does it make to you? Aren't you the one dying to leave this place in the dust and take off for good ol' Miami?"

Although when push came to shove—and under duress—Matteo would admit that he did love his brother, there were times when he would have liked nothing better than to strangle his irritating sibling with his bare hands.

Cisco had a way of getting to him like nobody

else could. So much so that if Cisco said "black," it instantly made him want to shout "white!"

Because of that feeling, it came as not much of a surprise to him when Matteo heard himself say, "Maybe I've changed my mind. Maybe I've decided to stick around Horseback Hollow for a little while longer."

Delighted and confident that given enough time here, he would be able to convince Matteo of the merits of living in this wonderful small town, Orlando leaned over and clapped his youngest son on the back. "That is wonderful news, my boy. Wonderful."

Matteo almost felt guilty about his father's reaction. He wasn't staying here because of his father. He was going to be hanging around a few extra days or so to see if he could win over the hostess before she succumbed to his sweet-talking brother.

"Yes, well, someone has to protect Horseback Hollow's unsuspecting women from the likes of him," Matteo told his father, nodding at his brother.

"And you've elected yourself that protector?" Cisco hooted, amusement highlighting his face at his brother's declaration. "That's one mighty tall order, little brother."

"Don't call me that, Cisco. I'm not your little brother," Matteo told him.

Cisco's amusement only grew. "Well, you're certainly not my big brother, now, are you, Mattie? I *am* the older one."

Matteo scowled. "Two years isn't all that much," he reminded his brother. And not even a full two years at that, Matteo thought.

"Oh, but it can amount to a lifetime under the right

set of circumstances," Cisco countered with a very mysterious grin that *really* annoyed Matteo.

Orlando sighed. He had had just about enough. Listening to this back-and-forth banter and bickering required something stronger to drink than just beer, but it was still too early in the day to contemplate downing any hard liquor.

"Might I remind you two boys that you no longer *are* boys. You are men," Orlando told his sons. "It is time to take on that responsibility and act accordingly—or do I have to drag you both into a back alley and use my belt on you?"

The truth of it was that their father had never used his belt on either of them in a back alley, or any other area for that matter. But a reply to that declaration was temporarily tabled because Rachel had returned, bringing with her three freshly opened individual bottles of dark beer as well as Matteo's cheeseburger and the new bowl of chips.

Setting down Matteo's meal in front of him and placing the bowl of chips in the center of the table, Rachel proceeded to refill the men's empty beer glasses, beginning with Orlando's.

"Will there be anything else?" she asked with a gregarious smile as she made the rounds between the three men.

Cisco spoke up unexpectedly. "You could settle an argument for us," he said.

Instinct had Matteo shoot his brother a silencing look, but it was already too late.

"What kind of an argument?" Rachel wanted to know, filling Cisco's glass.

"If you had to go out with one of us, which would you choose?" Cisco asked her innocently.

The question seemed to catch her completely off guard, but Rachel managed to recover gracefully without missing a beat.

"That all depends," she responded, going on to Matteo's glass.

"On what?" Cisco asked her before Matteo had a chance to.

Her eyes met Matteo's for one brief and surprisingly intense moment before she looked back at his brother. "On who would ask me first."

"All right," Cisco said quickly, making sure that he got the jump on his brother. "Rachel, would you go out with me tonight?"

It all happened so fast that Matteo felt as if he had just been torpedoed—and sunk—by an enemy sub.

"My shift doesn't end until eight," Rachel replied, still not giving him a definite answer.

It was her way of stalling. It wasn't that she wasn't flattered, because she was—the man who had asked her out just now was every bit as good-looking as his brother—and it wasn't that she was trying to play hard to get, because she wasn't. The reason she was stalling was because she was hoping that the one who had *really* caught her attention, the cute younger brother, who had come to her defense earlier at the other table, would put in his two cents and ask her out, as well. Then she knew who she'd pick.

But from what she could see, the one she had heard referred to as "Matteo" seemed to fold up his tent and just withdraw, allowing his brother to have total access to the entire playing field.

In this case, that meant her, Rachel thought.

"Perfect," Cisco was saying, referring to when her shift ended. "I'll be waiting out front."

Ever since she'd left her home in Austin five years ago, Rachel had been somewhat leery when it came to dating. She'd already gone through her ugly-duckling period and her swan period, during which time she had preened and posed, absorbing each and every flattering word that was sent her way, and viewing it as gospel.

But in time she had learned that those compliments were just empty, meaningless words, easily spoken and even more easily forgotten. She had more important things on her agenda than dating these days. She was busy not just finding herself, but also finding her place in the scheme of things.

Her place in the world.

She was working here as a hostess, but she had recently won an internship at the new Horseback Hollow office of the Fortune Foundation, which had opened its doors several weeks ago. As of yet, the office was still not fully up and running, but she intended to be there right from the start, learning everything she could from the ground up.

Her plan was to make something of herself.

To that end, she was going to continue with both positions, amassing as much money as she could. Her father had offered to support her when she'd left home, as he well could, but she had refused his money. She wanted to make it on her own so that no one else could take the credit—or the blame—for what she had become. It would be all on her, one way or another.

She might not appear so to the patrons seated here

at the Cantina, but she was fiercely dedicated, not to mention full of pride.

Ordinarily, this sort of a work agenda would leave a person with no room for anything else, but she knew that having some sort of a social life was important. She supposed this "date" tonight qualified as just that.

She would have preferred being asked out by the younger hunk, but the one who *did* ask her out wasn't exactly shabby, either. Who knew? Maybe she would wind up having a better time with him than Mr. Cheeseburger, she mused.

So Rachel nodded and gave the man who had just asked her out a smile.

"All right, if we're going to go out, I'm going to need to know your name," she told him.

Cisco inclined his head in a polite, surprisingly formal bow as he said, "Francisco Mendoza at your service." Raising his eyes to hers, he added, "Everybody calls me Cisco."

"Then I guess I'll just have to join the crowd," she told him. With that, she looked at the other two occupants of the table. "Since I'm taking names, you are—" she asked Matteo.

"A day late and a dollar short," Cisco supplied before Matteo could answer her.

If looks could kill, the one that Matteo slanted at him would have completely vaporized Cisco in under ten seconds. The scowl abated somewhat as he turned to look at the hostess and told her, "Matteo Mendoza."

"And I am Orlando Mendoza," Orlando told her. In typical old-fashioned, courtly manner, Orlando rose slightly in his chair and bent forward so that he could take her hand in his. He brought her hand to his lips and kissed it as per the custom of his ancestors.

Rather than appear amused, Rachel looked touched and just slightly in awe.

"Mendoza," Rachel repeated, then asked, "Brothers?" as her eyes swept over all three men.

"You are only partially right." Orlando laughed, fully aware that the young woman had asked the question tongue-in-cheek. "And partially a flatterer." He glanced at Cisco and told his son, "This one can hold her own against you."

Cisco's eyes were filled with humor as well as a healthy measure of appreciation as they met hers. "I'm sure she can."

Realizing that she had already spent way too much time at one table, Rachel flashed another quick smile at the trio and began to withdraw, saying, "I'd love to talk some more, but I've got another order up," before she turned on her heel and left.

"And that, little brother," Cisco said as soon as he felt that the hostess was out of earshot, "is how it's done."

Matteo looked at his older sibling, more than a little annoyed at the latter's presumption. "I don't need pointers. And even if I did, it wouldn't be from you."

"Touchy, touchy," Cisco observed with a pitying shake of his head. "You might not be aware of it, little brother, but you definitely are in need of something." He dug into the chicken enchiladas before him. "I just beat you to the punch with Rachel—and the worst part of it is, you let me."

"Beat me to the punch," Matteo repeated incredulously. "Is that what all this is to you? A game? Just a game?"

Cisco refused to get embroiled in an argument, especially one that didn't look as if it could have a clear winner—at least not verbally. He took another bite before saying anything in reply.

"What it is, is invigorating," Cisco told him. "And I intend to have a really good time with the fair Rachel."

Matteo's scowl grew deeper. "If you know what's good for you, you'd better treat her like a lady," he warned Cisco.

"Or what?" Cisco asked, curious as to just where this conversation was going. "You'll beat me up?" Orlando felt that he had sat by in silence long enough. The last thing he wanted was to see this escalate beyond a few hot words traded. Even that was too much.

"Stop it, you two. You are brothers. Remember that," Orlando ordered. "And Cisco, you had better behave like a gentleman with this girl. I will not stand for anything less," he warned his older son.

Cisco didn't want to provoke his father, but the whole thing had made him curious. His father must have sown a few wild oats in his day. There was still a hint of a wicked twinkle left in his eye.

"Don't you remember being young once, Dad?" Cisco asked him.

Orlando made no effort to deny it. "Yes, I do, which is exactly why I am saying this to you now." And then he turned his attention to Matteo. "And you, you have no business telling your brother what to do after you neglected to act according to your own feelings."

Matteo just looked at him, mystified.

"She was waiting for you to say something," he told Matteo. "And you let her slip through your fingers."

Matteo had no idea she was anywhere *near* his fingers to begin with. He had just been working up his courage to engage her in a conversation when Cisco all but pounced on the hostess.

"If you ask me, the better man won," Cisco commented to his father with just a hint of a smirk directed at Matteo.

To be honest—and he was, in the depths of his own heart—he had only asked the hostess out because he saw that Matteo was exhibiting interest in her. Beating him to the punch was, he thought, a good way to light a fire under his brother and get him moving so that the next time, Matteo would be the one who was first to ask her out.

"No one asked you," Matteo snapped.

Orlando looked from one son to the other and wearily shook his head. "You know, perhaps I was too hasty to try to convince you boys to move out here to live. The peace and quiet I had for all those months made me forget how you two were always going at one another when you were growing up. Apparently you haven't outgrown that trait."

Cisco laughed. "I see right through you, Dad. You can talk and complain all you want, but admit it. You missed having us around, competition and all—not that it was ever much of a competition once I decided to throw my hat into the ring." He gave Matteo a smug, superior look that he knew would bother the younger man.

"You're delusional," Matteo told him.

"And you have no memory of things at all. Otherwise, you'd know I was right. If I set my sights on something or someone, the game is already over because, for all intents and purposes, I have won it. All that remains is to collect my winnings," Cisco concluded. He secretly watched Matteo from beneath hooded eyes to see if his words had succeeded in pushing his brother into action. In his opinion, there were times when his little brother was too laid-back. Goading him this way was for his own good. And if not, well, it was Matteo's loss, right?

"Enough," Orlando warned. "I invited you two here to have a nice family meal—so eat!" He looked from one son to the other. After a beat, both complied with his command.

Orlando found the silence gratifying and refreshing. At least now he could hear himself think.

And what he was thinking about was how nice the silence was.

Chapter Three

Rachel closed the door to her apartment behind her and walked into the kitchen. A minute later, she did a U-turn and crossed back to the door. Not to open it again in hopes of catching the man who had just dropped her off because she'd had second thoughts about not asking him in for a drink, but to flip the top lock into place to ensure her safety. The original lock that came with the door was rather flimsy at best.

Five years and security was still an afterthought for her, Rachel thought with a shake of her head.

That was because five years ago, she was living with her seven siblings in a palatial home in Austin. The servants who took care of the house were the ones who made sure doors were locked and everything was always secured. The entire house and grounds were wired with a state-of-the-art security system.

It had been a whole other world then. As one of Gerald Robinson's daughters, her every need had been anticipated and met. Had she wanted merely to float through life, doing nothing more strenuous than enjoying herself and contributing nothing to the world around her, that option had been there for her to take.

But she had always been the stubborn one who wanted to make her own way, earn her own money, *be* her own person. And never more than now—for herself as well as to atone for her father's indiscretions.

Maybe, Rachel mused as she stepped out of her high heels on the way to her tiny bedroom and more comfortable clothes, that earlier way of life had jaded her somewhat, spoiling her for the actual realities of life.

What other reason could there be for her feeling like this after the evening she had just had?

Cisco Mendoza had been as good as his word, waiting for her outside the Cantina when she'd walked out at a few minutes after eight o'clock tonight.

Any other woman would have felt like Cinderella, being whisked off not in a coach that had formerly been a pumpkin but in a shiny, fully loaded black luxury SUV. When she'd asked him where they were going, he'd given her a sexy wink and said in an equally sexy voice that it was a surprise.

She had to admit to herself that *that* had made her a little nervous. Growing up in Austin as the child of a very rich man, her mother and the family housekeeper had made her and her siblings acutely aware of being on their guard against possible kidnappers. Having money did not come without a certain downside.

She was fairly certain that Cisco Mendoza didn't

know about her real background—although she
couldn't be 100 percent sure—but then again, there
were other reasons for women to go missing.

Cisco must have noticed her tension, because several minutes into their road trip, he laughed and told her
where they were going. He was taking her to Vicker's
Corners, a town that was roughly twenty miles away
and had once been as quaint as Horseback Hollow. But
the citizens of Vicker's Corners had chosen to embrace
progress, and the town was now well on its way to becoming far more urban than rural.

"I'm taking you to The Garden," he'd added. And
then, just in case she wasn't aware what that was—she
was, but she pretended she wasn't because he seemed
to delight in surprising her—he went on to tell her,
"It's a trendy little bistro. I thought you might like to
have a little change of pace. It's different from The
Hollows Cantina," he promised.

She knew he meant it was more romantic than the
upscale restaurant where she worked. Apparently
Cisco Mendoza was pulling out all the stops.

She wished her heart was in it—but it wasn't, no
matter how hard she tried.

She'd told him that she appreciated his thought-
fulness, then felt the need to point one little fact out,
careful to keep it generalized so that he didn't know
she was well-informed about the restaurant in question.

"If it's so trendy, wouldn't getting a reservation on
the spur of the moment be really difficult? They're
probably booked way in advance." She made it sound
as if she was guessing, but the truth was that she *knew*
for a fact The Garden was booked solid.

Cisco's grin had gotten wider at that point—and, if possible, sexier.

Another wink only intensified that impression, especially when he said, "Leave that part to me. I've got a few strings I can pull. That should be able to get us in."

She was surprised that he was being secretive about that connection of his. She knew better than to pry and try to find out anything beyond what was being volunteered. She was just rather stunned that Cisco wasn't trying to impress her with his mysterious connection.

But that wasn't the real problem as she saw it. The bistro had indeed turned out to be trendy as well as really captivating. It had stained-glass windows, copper ceiling tiles and a vintage art-nouveau crystal chandelier in the entryway.

Moreover, the food was perfect, the conversation was interesting and Cisco was charming, funny and a complete gentleman from start to finish. The date didn't end abruptly or last too long. In the words of Goldilocks, Rachel thought, changing into a pair of jeans and a baggy sweatshirt, it was "just right."

So why had she left Cisco at the door, hotfooting it inside and *not* inviting him in, not making herself available to be kissed good-night?

As she went in, Cisco had acted as if there was nothing out of the ordinary going on, but she could tell that she had surprised him—and disappointed the man, as well.

Rachel walked back out into her living room and flopped down on the sofa. Picking up her remote control, she turned on the TV and automatically began flipping through channels.

She was searching for something—*anything*—to distract her.

Rachel frowned, wondering if there was something wrong with her.

It had been a perfectly nice date, and she had had a perfectly nice time. Granted, there hadn't been a magical spark of chemistry blowing her away, but hey, that was lightning in a bottle, right? Finding something like that was exceptionally rare.

Especially since her mind kept drifting off, envisioning that *other* Mendoza at her side instead of his equally handsome, equally intelligent older brother.

Right up to the end, as she waited on their table earlier today, she kept hoping that Matteo would be the one who would ask her out or, barring that, the one who ultimately showed up in Cisco's place, murmuring vague apologies for his brother and saying something about Cisco being unavoidably detained.

She had found out fairly early in their time together tonight that Cisco was a real-estate investor. So being detained by an important deal was perfectly plausible.

But Cisco hadn't been unavoidably detained, and Matteo hadn't come to take his brother's place. Cisco had been the one waiting for her, the one who followed her home so that she could leave her car there and then ride in his as they went out.

On paper, the man was perfect—and very easy on the eyes, as well. But she heard no bells ringing and no banjos playing when they were alone together. And she really didn't want to settle for anything less than bells and banjos. More than anything else, she wanted a magical relationship—or nothing at all.

It was just as well that it had been Cisco tonight and not Matteo, she told herself, still flipping channels and looking for something numbing and mindless to help her unwind. Cisco had told her that his younger brother was a pilot "like our father." She felt that flying was somewhat risky, and flying for a living just increased that risk.

The last thing she needed was to lose her heart to someone who had a dangerous occupation and might not be there in a week or a month.

This way, there were no unnecessary complications for her to deal with. Just a nice date. End of story, she told herself.

"Face it, Rach. This is *not* the time for you to get involved with anyone." First, she had to get her life in gear and on track—find out where she was going with this Foundation internship she'd taken on. Once that was settled, *then* she could think about getting romantically involved with someone and falling in love, she thought, giving herself a mental pep talk since she had no one to turn to for any sort of support. "Don't go putting the cart before the horse. Remember, you've got a plan and order is everything."

It made for a good argument, she thought, watching channels as they whizzed by.

But deep down in her soul, she wasn't completely convinced.

Just as she had anticipated, Rachel didn't sleep all that well following her date. Every time she managed to doze off, her brain would conjure up fragments of dreams.

For the most part, they had to do with her evening out. But oddly enough, instead of the charismatic and confident Cisco, she saw Matteo at her side.

The dreams seemed so vivid that she felt they were actually happening—until she would wake up and find herself in her bed.

Sweating profusely—and very much alone.

After she'd gone through three such cycles, Rachel gave up all attempts at getting any sort of decent rest.

Besides, she reasoned, it was actually already too late for that. Her alarm was set to go off at seven-thirty. That was in less than another hour. She was going to work at the Fortune Foundation this morning, and she wanted to get there early, before her workday actually started. She wanted to absorb everything she could about the company.

Rachel already knew that the Foundation had been founded in the memory of Fortune patriarch Ryan Fortune, a man who had been a firm believer in paying it forward. He had lived his life that way, personally doing just that at every opportunity.

She'd learned that from the people who had been chosen to run the Horseback Hollow branch of the Fortune Foundation: Christopher Fortune Jones and his new wife, Kinsley.

The couple were returning from their honeymoon today, and Rachel wanted to be right there when they came in—not just to welcome them back, but to be able to listen to everything Christopher had to say.

She sympathized with Christopher and the way he had initially felt about the Fortunes when he had discovered that he and his siblings were actually directly related to the wealthy family. He had learned about this unexpected connection not all that long ago, and it had turned his entire life upside down until he finally made peace with the information.

That had taken a bit of doing on his part, as had adjusting to the fact that his mother, Jeanne Marie, was actually one third of a set of triplets. She and her sister had been given up for adoption. Her brother, James Michael, had grown up not knowing a thing about his two sisters, with only the vaguest memory that they existed.

It was through his relentless efforts to find them that his two sisters were told of their true identities. Both women took it a lot better than their families did at first.

Amazing how being part of that family created such drama for some people, Rachel couldn't help thinking.

The next moment, she pushed the thought aside.

She couldn't just sit around, contemplating life's little tricks and secrets. She had a job waiting for her. A job that *wouldn't* be waiting long if she started coming in late—or calling in sick.

Now, where had that last thought come from? Rachel upbraided herself. It certainly hadn't been on her mind a moment ago.

This was what happened when she broke with her routine, she chided herself. Last night had been an aberration from her normal course of operations, and now she was paying the price by feeling just a little bit better than death warmed over.

Or maybe just as bad.

Knowing she needed a boost, Rachel stopped in the kitchen to pour herself a cup of coffee. Her coffee-maker was ready for her, as she'd set the timer to brew at the ungodly hour of four-thirty in the morning.

Closing her eyes as she took her first sips, Rachel gave herself a moment to allow the jet-black hot liquid to go slowly coursing through her veins, bringing everything in its path to attention.

How did people live before coffee was invented? she idly wondered.

"Better," she pronounced after a few more moments had gone by. She felt almost human now.

Fortified, Rachel set the cup down on the counter and hurried off to take a quick shower.

It was only belatedly, several moments later, that she realized a face had flashed through her mind's eye when she'd closed her eyes to savor her coffee.

The face belonged to Matteo Mendoza.

This time she didn't bother trying to deny it or to talk herself out of her obvious attraction to the man. Instead, she just found herself wondering if she was going to see Matteo again.

And if so, when.

Rachel made it to the Fortune Foundation office at ten to nine, approximately fifteen minutes before the newlyweds arrived.

Their attempt to slip in quietly was quickly thwarted. Several of the other people who worked in the office saw them the moment they walked in and greeted them with hearty words of welcome.

Rachel added her voice to theirs, genuinely delighted to see the happy couple.

"Welcome back, you two," Rachel cried, speaking up to be heard above the rest. "We missed you."

Christopher laughed as he looked in her direction and replied, "No offense, but we didn't miss you."

Chris looked back at his wife, and Rachel knew exactly what he'd meant with his last remark. That Kinsley filled up his whole world and there was no space left over for anyone else, so no one else could possibly be missed.

Rachel felt envy pricking her. The love Christopher and Kinsley had for one another was almost visible.

She caught herself wondering if she was *ever* going to find someone who loved her like that—someone whom *she* could love like that, she silently added.

If the way she'd felt yesterday evening after her date was any indication, the answer to that was a depressing but resounding no.

Pushing that daunting thought aside—and knowing that the couple undoubtedly was on cloud nine and not quite ready to descend and start working just yet—Rachel came over to them.

"So, how did the big family reunion go?" Rachel asked him. When Christopher looked at her, clearly puzzled, she clarified her question. "At the wedding. That was the first time you actually met some of the other members of the Fortune family—your family," she corrected herself. "Right?"

Christopher nodded, the look on his face telling her that he was partially reliving the scene in his mind. "Right."

"And?" Rachel prompted him eagerly.

"And," Christopher continued after taking in a deep breath, "it was kind of rocky at first. I wasn't

sure how they'd all react to all of us, or to me," he
said glibly. He spared no words criticizing his own behavior. "I mean, I hadn't exactly welcomed the news
with open arms initially myself. To tell you the truth,
I was pretty surprised that they even showed up at
the wedding."

"But your mother invited them," Rachel pointed
out.

"That made no difference." And then he smiled.
The smile was equal parts humor and relief. "But just
as when I first met most of them in Red Rock last
year, they turned out to be a lot more understanding
than I expected. I can truthfully say that they are a
very nice bunch of people as a group *and* individually," he added. "To be honest, if I had to pick my own
family, I couldn't have done a better job than picking the Fortunes. They're charitable and decent, and
they don't behave as if they feel they're privileged or
something particularly special."

Christopher abruptly stopped talking. "You've got
a strange look on your face, Rachel. Is there something on your mind you'd like to talk about?"

*Yes, there is. But you didn't come back to work to
be burdened by my problems.*

"No," she said out loud. "I was just curious."

But maybe now wasn't the time to satisfy her curiosity. After all, there was the matter of that little
gold band on his left hand. That undoubtedly would
take him a bit of time to get used to, too—even *after*
the honeymoon.

For now, Rachel decided, she was just going to
keep a low profile and do her job—or jobs, she cor-

rected herself, since, just for a moment, she had forgotten about her job at the Cantina.

The second she thought of the Cantina, an image of Matteo flashed through her mind. Something else she couldn't think about right now, she silently chided.

With effort, she focused on what she had to do right this moment, at the Foundation—but it wasn't easy. Thoughts of Matteo continued to tease her brain.

Chapter Four

It took a few more minutes before things settled back down and the office returned to its former rhythm, with everyone focusing on preparing for next month.

Rachel hardly had a chance to sit at her desk again when there was a slight commotion at the outer door. Since the Foundation wasn't scheduled to open until April 1, they were still closed to the general public.

As far as she knew, everyone who was supposed to be here *was* here.

So who were these two people, a man and a woman, walking into the second-floor office?

Looking at them more closely, Rachel was struck that although the woman was a blue-eyed blonde and the man had dark hair and dark eyes, both bore a striking resemblance to Christopher. Were they part of his family? she wondered.

The way he greeted the duo the next minute answered her question for her.

"Hey, look what the cat dragged in." Christopher laughed, crossing the room to them with his wife.

"I told you we were ready to come do whatever it is that you're doing here," the man reminded him, looking around the room as if to get properly oriented.

Christopher had an inch on the other man, and his dirty-blond hair was more like the woman's. He looked genuinely pleased to see both of them.

"You're not fooling me," Christopher told the man. "You just think you can hide out here, away from our crazy matchmaking relatives. I can tell you now, it won't do either one of you any good. They'll find you."

Having said that, Christopher glanced around at the other people in the office, all of whom were looking at the two latest arrivals, clearly wondering who they were. Their curiosity was short-lived, thanks to Christopher.

"Hey, everybody, I'd like you all to meet my big brother, Galen, and my little sister, Delaney. Study them carefully. They're the last of their kind," he declared with no small amount of amusement.

Delaney frowned. "You make us sound like we're about to go extinct."

"Well, aren't you?" Christopher asked with a straight face. "Hey, don't blame me," he pretended to protest. "You two started it by calling yourself 'the last remaining singles.'"

"Well, what would you call us?" Delaney wanted to know. "Now that you and our other three siblings have gone to the other side and joined the ranks of the happily married, everybody thinks Galen and I should follow suit and hurry up and get married—like, yesterday." She tossed her head, sending her blond hair flying over her shoulder in one swift, graceful movement.

"Neither one of us is in any hurry to tie the knot—certainly not just to please the rest of the family," she informed Christopher—*not* for the first time. "I, for one, intend to enjoy my freedom for as long as I possibly can. I *like* being my own boss and coming and going as I please."

He'd been of a like mind once, Christopher thought. But that was before he'd fallen in love with the most beautiful woman in the world.

"You make marriage sound like a prison sentence," Christopher told her.

Delaney looked across the room and saw her new sister-in-law talking to one of the workers. "No offense to your lovely wife, but…" Delaney deliberately allowed her voice to trail off.

"How about you?" she asked, moving closer to Rachel. "Don't you agree that it's really great to be single?"

There were times, especially when she saw how happy some couples were, that Rachel longed to be in a committed relationship. Before they had locked horns, vying for the same position—the one that she now currently held—she and Shannon Singleton had been friends. Shannon had been the very first friend she'd made in Horseback Hollow. Now her friend was engaged to one of the British Fortune relations, Oliver Fortune Hayes.

Another thing she couldn't help thinking was that

she missed having a friend, missed the intimate ca-maraderie of having someone to share secrets with, or just to talk to for hours on end about nothing in particular.

Oh, she was friendly when their paths crossed, but that was rare these days. Shannon was much too busy with her new relationship and her new life. For the most part, it didn't bother her too much. But there were times, when she was home, that she would have given *anything* to have a real friend to talk to.

Someone like Christopher's baby sister, she thought suddenly.

There was something about the young woman that made Rachel take an instant liking to her the moment Delaney had opened her mouth.

There weren't many people she felt an immediate and strong connection to, Rachel realized, but Delaney was someone who could definitely qualify if she was interested in reciprocating the feeling.

"Being single has its moments," Rachel finally said in response to Delaney's question.

"Not exactly a ringing endorsement," Delaney allowed philosophically, "but I'll take it." The younger woman gave her a wide, infectious grin. "You obviously know my name—Chris's voice is kind of hard to block out—but I don't know yours," she told Rachel as she raised one expressive eyebrow, waiting.

"Rachel," Rachel answered. Belatedly, she put out her hand. "Rachel Robinson."

"Well, Rachel Robinson, I'm very pleased to meet you," Delaney said, warmly shaking her hand. "Maybe you can give me a clearer idea of what it is that we do here, other than look noble while we're doing it," she added with a somewhat bemused smile.

"What we're doing is getting ready. We're not open yet," Christopher informed his sister, cutting in before Rachel had a chance to make any sort of a reply. "Our official opening is set for next month. April," he added for complete clarity. "So right now, we're just running around, scrambling to get all systems up and running."

Delaney nodded, as if something had just clicked into place in her head. "Is that why you said you didn't care how casual I dressed and that jeans and boots would even be a good idea?"

"Did it take you that long to figure out?" Galen asked with a laugh. "I knew Chris was after cheap labor right from the get-go."

"What do you mean, 'cheap'?" Christopher asked. "The word is *free*. At least for now," he added before either one of his siblings could comment or pretend to protest. Turning toward Galen, Christopher deadpanned, "You still have that strong back?"

Rather than instantly answer in the affirmative, Galen's response was a guarded one. "That all depends on what you want done."

Fair enough, Christopher thought. "I've got some desks that are going to need moving."

Galen shook his head. "Then the answer is no. I threw my back out herding cattle," he told his brother.

Christopher's eyes narrowed as he studied Galen's face. He could always tell if his brother was bluffing. "You did not."

For a moment, the expression on Galen's face made the immediate future unclear. And then the oldest of the Fortune Jones clan shrugged, surrendering. "It was worth a shot."

Before they discovered that they were all directly related to the Fortune family thanks to their mother, they had been the Jones family, ranchers who made a living but could never boast that they thought of themselves as being even remotely well-off. Their lives consisted of hard work. Unexpectedly finding out that they were Fortunes with the kind of inheritance that befit someone from that family changed nothing, other than the fact that they now knew they would never be in a hand-to-mouth situation again.

The discovery certainly didn't alter their work ethic, didn't suddenly change them into a family of squanderers. But now, instead of working to keep body and soul together, they worked because ranching was what they enjoyed.

Galen pretended to sigh and acted put-upon. "So when do you want me to get started breaking my back?"

Christopher was about to answer when there was another commotion at the office door. His attention was instantly focused there.

"Could be the furniture arriving now," he told Galen cheerfully.

He was just yanking his older brother's chain. Christopher had no intentions of relying exclusively on his brother to shift around and arrange the furniture. It would be arriving with a crew of moving men in attendance. He just enjoyed giving Galen a hard time while he still could.

But when the doors into the office opened, it wasn't to admit a team of movers bringing the rest of the furniture for this office—or any of the other Foundation offices in the newly constructed two-story building.

Instead of moving men, Orlando and Matteo Mendoza came walking in.

Rachel felt her heart reacting the second she looked up and saw Matteo. It took her almost a full minute for her to regain her composure.

What was he doing here?

By the look on Delaney's face, she'd noted the sudden change in Rachel. But mercifully, she made no comment, which only further cemented the budding friendship in Rachel's mind. To her, friends knew things about friends without asking outright.

Almost automatically, Rachel rose to her feet and found herself slowly moving closer to the front door and the two men who had entered.

If she was surprised to see Matteo, he looked twice as surprised to see her.

Perhaps, Rachel thought, he looked a little *too* surprised.

Had he somehow known she'd be here today?

She tried to remember if she had said anything to Cisco last night about having to work here at the Foundation's office today.

But even if she had, the little voice in her head that came equipped with a large dose of common sense maintained, why would Cisco have shared that information with his younger brother? From the interaction she had witnessed yesterday, the two had an ongoing rivalry, competing with one another over just about *everything*.

But if that was the case, then what was Matteo doing here?

It didn't make any sense to her.

"What can I do for you?" Christopher was asking the two men as he crossed the office to get to them.

"It's what we're here to do for you," Orlando corrected him. The older man nodded his head toward Matteo. "My stubborn mule of a son and I are here to deliver a shipment of supplies for your office from your Red Rock headquarters."

Not willing to be mischaracterized, Matteo chimed in, "My more stubborn father suffered a bad injury last year and really should still be taking it easy instead of making these cargo flights," Matteo explained. "I came along in order to ensure that he wasn't taking on too much too soon. I'm also a pilot," he added, wanting Rachel to know that he wasn't just ineptly tagging along after his father but had a true purpose as well as a true vocation.

Orlando snorted like a parent who was trying patiently to endure the know-it-all attitude of his well-meaning children. "This one thinks I'll have a heart attack and he'll have to grab the controls and heroically land the plane." Orlando puffed up his chest ever so slightly and added, "Apparently he doesn't realize his father is as strong as an ox."

"Yeah and just as stubborn as one," Matteo interjected. He turned toward Christopher. "If you just tell me where you keep your dolly, I'll load it up and bring the supplies up for you."

"I'd appreciate that," he said to Matteo. Turning toward Rachel, he recruited her help. "Rachel, would you show Orlando where we keep the dolly? Then bring him back to the storeroom when he's ready so he can stack the supplies there." He glanced at Orlando.

He had forgotten just how much he had ordered. "Is it a large shipment?"

Orlando nodded. "I would say so, yes."

The smile on Christopher's lips was spontaneous as well as wide.

"It's all coming together," he announced, partly to the people in the office, partly to himself.

While ranching had initially been a way of life for him, running a branch of his newly discovered family's charitable foundation seemed like a very noble endeavor to him. And the more involved he became, the more committed to the cause he felt.

"We keep the dolly in the storeroom," Rachel told Matteo. "Come on, follow me. I'll show you where it is."

Matteo fell into step with her as she walked quickly to the end of the floor and the storeroom.

"So, you work here, too?" he asked her, sounding somewhat puzzled.

That Matteo asked the question disappointed her a little. It meant that this meeting really was just an accident rather than something he had deliberately orchestrated.

What was she thinking, assuming that Matteo had gone through complex machinations just to get a glimpse of her again? Sometimes a chance meeting was a chance meeting and nothing more, she told herself.

But the fact that it was obviously true in this case stung her a little. The scenario she had put together in her head had been far more romantic.

Grow up, she chided herself.

Looking at Matteo, she realized that he was waiting for some sort of an answer.

"I just started working here," she replied. "The Foundation doesn't officially open to the public until next month."

Matteo was still trying to piece things together. He knew so little about the woman who had captivated him with no effort whatsoever. He had deliberately been avoiding Cisco this morning because he didn't want to take a chance on hearing his brother brag about what had gone on last night.

"So, yesterday was your last day at the Cantina?" he asked.

That was a shame, he thought. He'd given serious consideration to dropping in there tomorrow, supposedly for lunch but actually just to see her again. Now it looked as if that plan wasn't destined to make it off the ground.

Opening the door to the storeroom, Rachel gestured toward the dolly—located right in front—and stepped out of Matteo's way.

"No, actually, it wasn't. My job at the Cantina is really part-time, and I'm keeping both jobs, at least for a while," she told him. Just saying it made her feel tired. But this wasn't about getting her beauty rest. It was about her future and getting ahead. "I want to see where this is going before I make any major decisions about my life."

Pushing the dolly out of the room, he followed Rachel toward the elevator. "Have you always been this ambitious?" he asked her.

She had to admit that this was an entirely new direction for her. When she'd moved out here, she

hadn't a clue on how to start rebuilding herself—or
even how to earn a living. All she knew was that she
wasn't running toward something—at least, not at
first—but *from* something.

"No, I wasn't," she told him, pressing the down
arrow beside the elevator. "You should have seen me
five years ago." She recalled all the empty partying,
the meaningless kisses and even more meaningless
words that had been exchanged. "I was a slug," she
confessed with a self-deprecating laugh.

Matteo didn't believe it for a moment. He considered himself a fair to middling judge of character, and
Rachel Robinson was a woman with a purpose. He
would lay odds that she always had been.

"I sincerely doubt that," he told her, dismissing her
words. "But I would have liked to have seen you five
years ago," he admitted.

Rachel couldn't think of a reason why he would
have wanted to do that. "To compare then and now?"
she guessed.

"No. If I *had* seen you five years ago, that means I
would have known you for five years." And he would
have been able to get her attention before Cisco had
a chance to move in on her. "But I guess since you
live here and I grew up in Miami, that wouldn't have
exactly been possible," he concluded.

"No," she agreed, "it wouldn't have." But that
didn't mean that she wouldn't have wanted it to be
possible, she added silently.

As Matteo stepped into the elevator, pushing the
dolly before him, he was surprised to see Rachel get
on with him. He'd just assumed that she would wait

for him to return to the storeroom with the supplies. "You're coming with me?"

"If you don't mind."

His smile was very wide as he told her, "No, I don't mind. I don't mind at all."

Chapter Five

"What happened?" Rachel asked Matteo as they stepped out of the elevator with the dolly on the ground floor.

Since the question seemed to come out of the blue, Matteo looked at her, puzzled. He wasn't sure what Rachel was asking him. In all honesty, he might have been so captivated by her proximity that he'd completely zoned out for a moment, thereby missing a possibly vital part of the conversation.

He would have attempted to bluff his way out of it, but that could have been successful only if he'd had an iota of a clue what she was referring to. And he really didn't.

When in doubt, his father had taught all of them, honesty was the best policy.

"I'm afraid I don't know what you mean," he told

Rachel, feeling more than a little awkward about the admission and hoping that she didn't think he was a complete idiot.

She flashed a smile that corkscrewed its way directly into his gut, tightening it.

"I'm sorry," she said. "I have a tendency to start questions in my head, leaving vital parts out when I engage my mouth. You told my boss that you came along with your father because you were afraid he hadn't sufficiently recovered from his injury. I was just curious about what kind of an injury it was."

Before I engage my mouth. The words she'd used echoed in his brain as he looked at that very same mouth now. He would have liked to engage that mouth in his own way, he couldn't help thinking.

With effort, he made himself focus on the question she had asked and not on the woman herself.

"It's a long story," he told her as they got off the elevator and headed past the reception area, toward the front doors. "The short version is that his plane malfunctioned and he crashed. The doctors thought his recovery was amazing. I just didn't want him to overdo things. He doesn't like owning up to a weakness, especially a physical one. But he *is* human, so things can happen that are beyond his control."

They approached a silver midsize van parked several feet from the building's entrance.

"I'm stunned that your father actually got into a plane and flew again after that," Rachel said.

Matteo smiled to himself. She caught herself thinking that he had a really gorgeous smile. It was the kind that lit up the immediate area around him—and her.

"My father is probably the most bullheaded man

who ever walked the earth," Matteo told her. "He does *not* like backing away from any sort of a challenge— and he's been a pilot for most of his life. Flying is second nature to him, like breathing."

Rachel nodded intently, as if absorbing every word. "I see. Well, good for him," she declared with feeling. "Sometimes being stubborn like that is all we have to see us through."

Matteo wondered if she was talking about herself rather than his father. Something in her voice made him think she at least related to the experience.

Rachel paused on the sidewalk while he unlocked the back of his father's van.

Climbing inside, he moved the supplies his father had flown in, dragging them closer to the bumper. Then he jumped down again. Box by box, he loaded a third of the supplies onto the dolly. A third was all that it would hold at one time.

"Okay, let's go," he told her.

Rachel looked at the back of the van as he pushed the doors closed. "What about the rest of it?" she wanted to know.

Positioning himself behind it, he began to push the loaded dolly toward the front entrance. "I'm going to have to come back. There's no way I can get the supplies into the storeroom all in one trip."

"Oh," she murmured. Rachel saw it as an opportunity to spend a little more time with Matteo than she'd initially anticipated. Not that he actually needed her help, but since Christopher hadn't specifically told her to show Matteo the storeroom and then come right back, she gave herself a little leeway in the matter. After all, Matteo might have a question for her regarding the supplies.

Orlando, still talking with Christopher, glanced in their direction as they got off the elevator and made their way toward the storeroom.

"If you have an extra dolly," Orlando said, speaking up and addressing the words to Christopher, "we can get the supplies up here twice as fast."

But Christopher shook his head. "Sorry, we've got only the one. But there's no reason to hurry," he assured Orlando. "I figure once we're open, things are really going to start hopping. Until then, we can take life at a bit of a slower pace."

Orlando nodded, as if in agreement, but he didn't fool his son. Matteo knew his father was just going along with what Christopher Fortune Jones had said to come across as agreeable. In reality, his father didn't know how to take life at a slower pace.

That wasn't his father's style. The man had worked from the time he had been a nine-year-old boy, growing up on the streets of Juarez in Mexico, looking for a way to help support his family. When his parents had moved the family to Miami the year he turned ten, things hadn't changed for Orlando. The locale might have been different, but his work ethic had stayed the same: work as hard and as much as you could today because tomorrow was an uncertainty.

As they approached the storeroom, Rachel moved slightly ahead of Matteo in order to open the door for him. She quickly ducked inside to give him room to come in with the dolly.

Following her into the storeroom, Matteo righted the dolly and parked it in order move the supplies off and place them on the shelves, which were only half-stocked at this point.

He had a feeling that this trip to the Foundation might just be the first of many. Suddenly the future was beginning to show promise. Thoughts of returning to Miami took a backseat for the time being.

When he finished taking the first load off the dolly, stacking each container on top of others with the same dimensions, he started to leave. Rachel, he noted, was right behind him.

Was she coming with him? Had he said something to make her feel obligated to do that? Matteo felt bad, as if he was putting her out. Guilt began to nibble away at him like a determined chipmunk.

"You know," he told her, "you don't have to come back to the van with me."

"Sure I do," she contradicted him innocently. Then, with a smile that seemed to seal itself immediately to the inside of his heart, she added, "If I stay behind, who's going to press the elevator button for you?"

He laughed at the absurdity of the question, a little of the tension leaving his shoulders. They no longer felt as if they resembled a landing pad.

It almost felt intimate, sharing the moment—and a joke—with her.

"You're right," Matteo responded. "What was I thinking?"

Had she asked *him* that, he would have had to have answered, *I was thinking about you.*

By the time they made the third and final round trip to the sidewalk and back, the van had been com-

pletely emptied and this particular storeroom—Matteo
learned there were others—filled to capacity.

So much so that there was precious little room in
which to maneuver.

Rachel found that out the hard way.

Moving back to get out of Matteo's way, she found
that her back was blocked by a huge floor-to-ceiling
stack of boxed printer paper. A wall of ink cartridges
were right next to the boxes of paper.

Matteo, unaware that she had nowhere to go, attempted to move past her and wound up brushing up
against her.

The moment of contact did *not* go unnoticed.

By either of them.

He was acutely aware of brushing against the
sweetly supple, heart-melting brunette as every part
of him—not just the parts that had made actual contact, but *all* of him—felt as if it was experiencing an
electrical surge that seemed to fill every single space
in his body.

Had he looked down instead of directly into her
beautiful blue eyes, Matteo was certain that he would
have seen sparks flying between their bodies.

As it was, she took his very breath away so completely he felt he was in danger of asphyxiating right
then and there.

Breathe, idiot, breathe! Matteo silently ordered
himself.

He felt his head spinning around for a moment.
This tall, willowy young woman had that sort of an
effect on him.

Kiss me, Matteo, Rachel silently begged as her
body came alive, tingling intensely from the fleet-

ing and all-too-real contact between their two bodies. *Please kiss me.*

Rachel held her breath, hoping.

Praying.

Refusing to budge a fraction of an inch, hoping that
would encourage Matteo to make a move.

Her eyes held his. If mental telepathy was an actual thing rather than a myth, Rachel couldn't help
thinking, Matteo Mendoza would have already swept
her into his arms, held on to her tightly and kissed
her soundly. If nothing else, the way she was looking
at him would have hypnotized him into making that
first move. She could definitely take it from there.

What was *wrong* with him? Matteo silently upbraided himself.

If he were more like Cisco, this would already have
been a done deal. He would have pulled this woman
whose mere glance set him on fire into his arms like
some soap-opera hero, said a few well-articulated
words that would have swept her off her feet and then
kissed her the way she had never been kissed before.

Matteo continued to berate himself. If he were
more like Cisco, he wouldn't be thinking about it.
He would be *acting* on it. It would have already been
done.

Or perhaps even be ongoing.

So what was to stop him from doing just that?
From acting instead of just thinking? Matteo silently
demanded of himself.

*Come on, Matteo, do it. Go with your instincts and
kiss her already.*

Making up his mind, Matteo squared his shoulders
and then he began to lean into her.

The very air stood still around her.

It's going to happen. He's going to kiss me. Finally!
The thought telegraphed itself through her brain as
the rest of her grew excited in anticipation.

Every nerve in her body felt like applauding and
cheering wildly. She was afraid to move or even
breathe.

His mouth was almost on hers, his breath tantaliz-
ing her as she felt it on her face.

Do it, Matteo. Do it, Rachel prayed.

Contact seemed totally inevitable.

And then it wasn't.

"So there you are. I was beginning to think you
and that dolly had disappeared."

Orlando's voice seemed to almost boom as it rang
out through the storeroom. The elder Mendoza was
right there, standing in the entrance, larger-than-life
and twice as loud.

"How long does it take you to unload a simple shipment?" Orlando wanted to know before he suddenly
stopped dead in his tracks, taking in the scenario and
what he belatedly realized were the intense vibrations
throbbing all around him.

So near and yet so far, Rachel thought, deeply disappointed and struggling not to show it to either of
the men within the crammed room.

Matteo's spirits came crashing down, almost op-
pressing him. "Just finishing up with the last of it,
Dad," he responded, doing his best not to snap at
his father.

Damn it, Dad, talk about having awful timing,
Matteo thought. He caught himself at the last minute, keeping the words from escaping his mouth.

His insides felt as if they were all revved up and humming with absolutely no release in sight.

Matteo thought of following Rachel back to her cubicle to explore further the intense magnetism he felt palpitating between them. If it was any stronger, he was convinced it would have been a visible, solid entity.

His sense of disappointment in the way things had turned out was beyond measure.

She had to admit that she was very surprised a plume of smoke wasn't trailing in her wake. The way Matteo looked at her—never mind that their bodies had brushed against one another—he'd certainly made her feel as if she was not just hot, but that an out-of-control five-alarm fire was raging within her.

And that Matteo was the additional fuel.

Glancing in the glass door as she approached her office, she saw Matteo's reflection. He was following her. And judging by his expression, he was rather determined to have his way.

Oh, please, let it be what I think it might be.

She sent up a silent prayer to the saint of hopeless cases, St. Jude, bartering then and there and promising to send a sizable donation to a charity that bore his name if only her dream scenario became a reality.

It didn't even have to be a long kiss, she bargained. It was possible to contain and lock passion into a small container. Doing so didn't diminish its strength by any means.

She was debating just thrusting herself in Matteo's path so that he had no choice but to grab her to move her out of the way. She wanted to give him an excuse to make contact again. If they remained alone, who knew where this might go?

But before anything promising could happen, her cell phone rang.

The sound, usually a pleasant one to her, was simply jarring this time around, causing her more than a degree of discomfort.

Her intuition told her that the ringing wasn't about to go away. Rachel had a feeling that whoever was on the other end of the call would just keep calling until they got her on the phone, rather than leaving a message on her voice mail. Served her right for turning her phone on. She should have left it off.

"Hello, this is Rachel." The words came to her tongue automatically. She didn't even stop to think about them before speaking.

And then she stiffened as she recognized the voice on the other end. Of all the phone calls for her to get while standing less than three feet away from the object of her budding affection, this was the last one she would have expected—or wanted.

"So your cell phone does work," the male voice said, amused. "You are a very hard lady to reach." The chuckle was deep and throaty, fading into the atmosphere before the man continued. "This is Cisco Mendoza."

"Yes, I realize that," Rachel acknowledged, her voice still sounding a bit stiff.

Matteo caught her intonation and instantly looked at her in utter amazement. A gut feeling told him that she was taking a call from Cisco. The same gut feeling that had urged him to kiss her. That he'd failed to follow the first instinct would be something he feared he was going to regret for the rest of his life. At least.

Speaking again, Cisco's voice carried, despite the fact that she had the cell closer to her and it wasn't on Speaker.

"I had a really great time with you last night," Cisco was saying to her. "I was wondering if you'd like to do it again."

"Do it again?" she echoed. Out of the corner of her eye, she could see Matteo suddenly look her way. Her last words had obviously caught his attention.

Listening.

"Yes. I was hoping that you would be able to go out with me again tonight," Cisco told her. "See if we can recapture that feeling we had last night."

"Um, I'm not sure that I can make it," Rachel said, uncharacteristically stumbling over her own tongue.

She was *not* usually this socially awkward. After all, Cisco was a perfectly nice person who had been a complete gentleman last night. But he didn't make her toes curl or her blood rush. She didn't want to encourage Cisco since there had been no sparks, especially not the kind that she had just felt with Matteo.

But she didn't like being cruel, either. There had to be a painless way to ease out of this situation without hurting the man's ego.

Watching Rachel, Matteo saw the distressed, uncomfortable look on her face. Filling in the blanks and going on what little information he had picked up about her, he realized that Rachel was trying to find a way out of starting a relationship with Cisco without bruising his brother's feelings.

Another reason to really like the woman, he thought.

His brother, Matteo knew, had a skin as thick as a rhino. He doubted there was anything anyone could say to Cisco that would even mildly upset him.

And if, perchance, he was wrong, and getting turned down by Rachel would crush his brother's cavalier spirit, well, those were just the hazards of love and war. These things happened.

He surprised her by putting his hand over hers on the cell. When she looked at him quizzically, he mouthed, *May I?*

Unable to think of a reason why she wouldn't want him to talk to his brother, she nodded and released the cell phone to him. Matteo smiled at her before addressing the person he assumed was on the other end.

"Cisco?"

There was a bewildered pause before Cisco finally responded. He sounded a bit confused when he did. "Is that you, Matteo?"

"Yes, it's me. Rachel can't see you tonight because she's already going out with someone."

"Who?" Cisco challenged him, surprised.

"Me," Matteo told him.

Rachel's mouth dropped open. Had there been a feather available in the immediate area at that very moment, it could have knocked her over.

Easily.

Chapter Six

The silence on the other end of the line stretched out to almost half a minute. Matteo was beginning to think that Cisco had either hung up on him or lost the connection.

He was about to hand the cell back to Rachel when he heard his brother say, "I'm impressed, little brother. You've gotten quicker."

Pulling the phone closer again, Matteo responded, "Yeah, well, sometimes you just have to be."

Out of the corner of his eye, he saw the way Rachel was looking at him. She seemed to be completely stunned. He supposed that announcing to his brother that she was going out with him might have rattled her a little.

Had he scared her off by his assertive behavior? God, he hoped not. This was what he got for acting impulsively, like Cisco.

"You want to talk to Rachel again?" he asked his brother.

"Sure, why not?" Cisco said gamely. As far as Matteo could tell, Cisco sounded amused. What he couldn't fathom was why.

Matteo held out the cell phone to her. "Here," he murmured. "He wants to talk to you again."

Rachel took her phone back, not really knowing what to make of the entire exchange she'd just heard. She definitely wanted to go out with Matteo instead of Cisco, but she didn't like the idea that she—and any input that she might have had on the subject—had been completely usurped in this whole process. Matteo hadn't even asked her to go out. He just seemed to have assumed that she would agree.

That wasn't like him.

Not like him? What are you, lifelong friends? You just met him. How much do you really know about the man? a small voice in her head asked.

The answer to that was a painful "not much." She was going strictly on gut instincts alone. There were times, she knew, when that wasn't nearly enough. This could be one of those times.

"Hello," Rachel said uncertainly as she brought the cell phone closer to her ear.

"Just wanted to wish you luck with my little brother tonight," Cisco told her cheerfully. "Maybe we can go out some other time." He sounded rather confident that they would.

She, however, was of a different opinion. "Maybe," she replied without any indication of how she really felt about that.

"I'll hold you to that." He laughed, then said, "'Bye," and ended the call.

Belatedly, Rachel followed suit.

The second she tucked her phone away in her pocket, Matteo started talking. He sounded somewhat uncomfortable. "Listen, I'm sorry about that." He nodded toward the pocket that contained her cell phone.

"Sorry?" Rachel echoed. She hadn't the slightest idea what Matteo was actually referring to or apologizing for. Was he sorry about taking the phone from her, or was he apologizing for jumping the gun and saying they were going out?

"I know how pushy Cisco can be, and I just wanted to help you out if, for some reason, you didn't want to go out with him." He had to admit that the sound of his brother's voice had been like waving the proverbial red flag in front of a bull. It just set him off, and he had acted rashly. "You don't have to go out with me, either, if you don't want to."

Now she *really* felt confused. Exactly what was he saying?

"So, you're *not* asking me out?" She wanted to pin this Mendoza down. "That wasn't just an oversight on your part? That little step you forgot to take?"

It was his turn to be confused. "What step?" Matteo asked.

"The step where you actually *ask* me out," she responded.

Damn, but she had him all tied up in knots. Just looking at her was scrambling his brain, Matteo thought. He couldn't think straight. He knew he should just let this go and back away, but his need to know got the best of him.

"If I did ask you out," he said slowly, watching her carefully, "what would you say?"

"I don't know," Rachel answered. Granted, it was a lie, because she knew *exactly* what her answer would have been, but she felt he deserved to twist a little in the wind over this. "I never know how I'll react to something until it happens. I guess you'll actually have to ask me out to find out my answer," she informed Matteo glibly.

Talk about putting himself out there, he thought. "You're kidding."

A Mona Lisa smile gently curved her mouth. She was *not* about to back down. "No, I'm not."

"Okay." Taking a moment, Matteo centered himself, focusing on his words and the woman he was saying them to. He asked, "Rachel Robinson, would you do me the honor of allowing me to have the pleasure of your company this evening?"

He sounded so formal. The only thing that was missing was the clank of armor as he took her hand in his just before he asked her out.

Tickled, Rachel smiled broadly at him. These Mendoza men were a complicated lot, she couldn't help thinking. And then she quickly set his mind at ease. "I thought you'd never ask!"

"Just so I'm sure, is that a yes?"

"Well, it's not a no," she deadpanned, then laughed as she confirmed, "Yes, that's a yes."

Matteo's face lit up. "Great," he said enthusiastically. "What time do you get off from here?"

"Five," she answered. She knew that once the

Foundation was open, her hours might be more structured. But for now, it was a nine-to-five job.

Matteo nodded, as if that was what he'd expected
to hear. "Why don't you give me your address and I'll
pick you up at six? Unless that's not enough time to
get ready," he quickly interjected.

Now, that was certainly thoughtful, she thought,
impressed. "That's enough time even if I was going
to rebuild myself from top to bottom," she assured
him. Rattling off her address to him, she then asked,
"What should I wear?"

"Clothes would be good, but it's up to you." Okay,
maybe he was channeling *too* much of his brother
now, Matteo lectured himself silently.

He noticed with relief that Rachel appeared to be
amused more than anything else.

"I've got that part down already. What *kind* of
clothes?" she wanted to know. His brother had taken
her to a fancy, romantic restaurant in Vicker's Corners, but she had a feeling that unless Matteo was
planning to compete with his brother on every level,
he wasn't the structured, romantic-restaurant type.

"Casual," Matteo replied. Then, in case that wasn't
enough information, he specified, "Boots-and-jeans
casual."

Since those were the clothes she tended to favor,
Rachel was more than happy to go along with his
suggestion.

"Boots and jeans it is."

It was amazing how many different tops a person
could try on and discard within the space of fifty-
three minutes, Rachel thought, looking at the disar-

rayed piles on her bed. She'd had no problem with the bottom half of her outfit. Picking out which jeans she was wearing was a snap—the boot-cut ones that hugged her curves.

And she didn't own a large selection of boots—there were only two pairs on the floor of her closet.

But tops, well, that was another story. She had a couple dozen of those—if not more—and every one had something wrong with it.

Or so it seemed when she pulled each one out of her closet and critically looked it over.

Running out of time, Rachel knew she finally had to make her choice, picking the last top she'd pulled on, mainly by default. It was either that one or nothing—and Matteo was at her door right now, ringing the doorbell.

Her heart seemed to be doing a little Irish jig in her chest. Nonetheless, she gave herself a quick once-over in the mirror, murmured, "Here goes nothing," and hurried to open the door.

Matteo had been preparing his opening lines all the way from his father's house to her apartment. He changed a word here, substituted a word there.

When Rachel opened her door to admit him, he promptly forgot every single one of those words. Looking at her had knocked every one of them out of his head like so many dried grains of rice raining down on a harsh terrain. All he could say was "Wow."

As it turned out, he couldn't have come up with a better word to use. Hearing the single word, rendered as an assessment, brought a huge smile to her lips.

He liked the way her eyes lit up when she smiled.

"Thank you. That's the nicest thing anyone has ever said to me."

Matteo caught himself thinking of his brother. Cisco seemed to possess a silver tongue, charming his way into—as well as out of—many a situation. He was fairly certain Cisco had laid it on thick last night.

"I doubt that," he responded, taking a single step just inside her apartment.

"Where are we going?" she wanted to know, grabbing her jacket and her purse before heading back to him and out the door.

"How do you feel about horseback riding?" Matteo asked her, paying close attention to the expression on her face more than the words that would be coming out of her mouth. He didn't want her just going along with something because he suggested it. He wanted her to be enthusiastic about the evening.

Taking out her key, Rachel locked her door. His question brought visions of home instantly to her mind. Among the other lessons her parents had paid for, she had taken horseback riding. She'd become very proficient at it, but then, it was easy being good at something she enjoyed.

Turning toward Matteo, she told him, "I love horseback riding."

He saw that she meant it. "Good, because we're going on a trail ride."

"Sounds great," she responded with enthusiasm.

What Matteo was proposing was miles away from the kind of date she'd had with Cisco. That evening had been formal, yet flashy. She had no doubt that it cost a pretty penny to dine at that restaurant. But maybe because of how she'd grown up and what she had found out about her father five years ago, flashy made no impression on her whatsoever—except perhaps in a negative way.

So she was relieved and delighted when Matteo brought his car to a stop near a stable and told her that he'd reserved a couple of stallions for them. The horses were both saddled and ready to go.

One had what appeared to be a large wicker basket attached to the saddle horn.

"What's that?" she asked, nodding at the basket.

"That," he told her, "is a surprise. You need any help getting on your horse?" he asked before mounting his.

"Not on your life." She laughed.

As he watched, she mounted her horse in one fluid, graceful movement.

It was like watching poetry in motion, he thought. The line had never meant anything to him before now.

Getting on his horse, Matteo indicated the direction they were about to take. Twilight was still a little more than a hint away.

"Let's go," he told her.

"Does it have anything to do with food?" she teased him, nodding at the basket.

It took him a second to realize what she was referring to. He was far too busy just drinking her in to have room in his thoughts for anything else.

"It might," he finally said. "Play your cards right and you could find out."

In the waning light, she seemed to glow. If he hadn't been half-taken with her already, he would have been now.

Rachel laughed again, the sound wrapping itself around him like a warm embrace. "You're on."

She lost track of time.

They rode their horses along a well-cleared road. It was framed by tall trees on both sides. The sense of peacefulness was irresistible, and she felt both enthusiastic and contented at the same time.

Before she realized it, the sun had completely receded, calling it a day and allowing the full moon to take over.

"Okay, I think it's time to show you that surprise," he said, reining in his horse and dismounting.

She'd almost forgotten about that. "I'm game if you are," she told him, getting off her horse.

Matteo tied his horse's reins to a low-hanging branch on a nearby tree, then took the reins from her horse and did the same.

Rachel wiped her hands on her back pockets and asked, "Need any help?"

He did, Matteo thought, but it wasn't anything that she could help him with. His pulse was just going to have to stop racing on its own.

"No, but thanks for offering," he replied, setting the basket on the ground. He flipped back the top and took out the classic red-checked tablecloth. Two small but bright battery-powered lanterns followed.

As Rachel stood to one side, watching, he went on to get what she thought was a rather impressive picnic dinner for them: fried chicken, biscuits with butter and two servings of fresh fruit. "Dinner is served," he told her.

She didn't sit down at first. Instead, she took it all

in. This, she thought, had taken a lot of effort. When had he had the time to throw it all together? She'd agreed to go out with him only a couple of hours ago.

"Very impressive," she told him. "Where did you fly the chicken in from?" She assumed that was what he'd done since he was a pilot like his father, and making cargo drops appeared to be his main source of income.

You're assuming things again, that little voice in her head chided her.

What he said in response to her question confirmed she was wrong. "I didn't."

"You bought the fried chicken locally," she concluded.

"No," he told her, giving her a coated paper dinner plate that looked prettier than some of the real plates she had seen. "I fried it locally."

Rachel wasn't sure she was following him. "Come again?"

He said it as simply as he could. "I made the chicken."

She looked from the tempting pile of fried chicken pieces to Matteo and then back again. She furrowed her brow in disbelief. "Did you make the biscuits, too?"

His eyes crinkled as he smiled. "Biscuits, too," he repeated.

Her eyes swept over everything one more time. It all looked too perfect. Most men were not this detail-oriented—unless they were professional chefs, and this man was *not* a professional chef.

"You're kidding," she breathed.

Matteo slowly shook his head, then replied, "Not

that I'm aware of." Pausing, he took in her expression. "You look surprised."

"I am," she admitted. "I didn't think that bachelors knew how to cook. Especially city bachelors." Which was what he was, coming from Miami and all, she thought. "It's far too easy to pick up the phone and order takeout than to stand over a hot stove, fooling around with measuring spoons."

"Easy," Matteo agreed. "But doing it that way— calling for takeout—lacks a certain feeling of accomplishment. Although, to be completely honest, I have to admit that I'm a big fan of eating out. They have some truly *amazing* restaurants back in Miami." Temporarily warming to his subject—and recalling favorite meals—he told her with enthusiasm, "Any kind of food you can name, there's a restaurant that specializes in making it.

"I also got to sample my fair share of different kinds of cuisines in some of the cities around the world while I was an airline pilot," he told her, putting a couple of drumsticks on his plate.

She'd thought he just flew cargo. Working for the airlines broadened his base. "Oh, like your Dad."

"Yeah."

Rachel could hear the pride in his voice when he acknowledged that.

"If you like eating out so much," she said, "how did you learn how to cook?" It sounded as if he'd had a busy life. When would he have had the time to take cooking lessons?

"By watching my mom." A fond look slipped over his face. It completely captivated Rachel. "She was an absolutely amazing cook. And she never followed any recipes. She just did everything purely by instinct."

Rachel liked that. Liked the fact that Matteo wasn't embarrassed to learn how to cook or to credit his mother for it. He had no way of knowing that he had just gone up several notches in her book. But he had.

"Is your mother still in Miami?" she asked casually, wondering what the woman was like.

Matteo's face darkened just for an instant before he answered her question. "No. My mother died a few years ago."

She heard the pain in his voice, even though he didn't say anything more on the subject.

"Oh, I'm so sorry, Matteo." Rachel placed her hand over his in a sign of sympathy and comfort. "That must have been so terrible for you and your family."

Taking a deep breath, Matteo shrugged, trying to shed both the feeling and what he assumed was her pity. He didn't want to dwell on the subject any longer.

"Yeah, well, that's all part of life, I guess." And then, just like that, he changed the subject. "I took a chance with the chicken," he admitted. When she looked at him, puzzled, he explained, "Not everybody likes fried chicken."

He had to be hanging around different circles than she did, Rachel thought.

"Well, I never met anyone who didn't like fried chicken. Speaking of which, this has to be just about the very *best* fried chicken I've ever had." It was crisp and golden, light and definitely not greasy—and there was a certain flavor to it that she couldn't put her finger on, but it was very different than the standard fried chicken. She'd bet on it. "What did you use?" she wanted to know.

"I make my own bread crumbs," he admitted.

She stared at him. "God, but you're enterprising." Her bread crumbs came out of a container labeled Seasoned Bread Crumbs.

"It's a secret recipe," he told her, his dark eyes dancing. "But I guess I can trust you. I grind up seasoned garlic croutons, soda crackers and some almonds. Then I mix them all together. Each piece of chicken gets a few drops of extra-virgin olive oil to coat it. Then I dip both sides of the piece in the bread crumbs. After that, the only thing left is the frying." Matteo smiled. "No big deal."

"Well, it tastes like a big deal once it gets to your tongue," she told him. "Your mother would be very proud of you."

The words had no sooner left her mouth than she realized that perhaps he didn't want the conversation to go back in that direction. He had all but closed up a minute ago, right after he had mentioned his mother's passing.

Raising her eyes to his, Rachel glanced at him rather hesitantly. To her relief, rather than looking extremely sad again, Matteo had a small smile on his face. Granted, it was etched with sorrow, but it still qualified as a smile.

"Thanks," he told her. "It means a lot to me to hear that."

Even though he knew Rachel had no idea what his mother would have thought, the idea that his mother would have been proud of him for something so simple as cooking a meal bolstered him.

It occurred to Matteo, as he looked into Rachel's face, that his mother would have liked this woman.

Perhaps even as much as he did.

Chapter Seven

In general, Matteo wasn't a man who was given to impulsive behavior. That was more Cisco's department. For his part, Matteo was a man who thought things out, who weighed things very carefully before making any sort of decision. If Cisco was the fast-moving hare of the famed Aesop's fable, Matteo was the tortoise. Slow and steady, always with his eye on the distant prize.

But just this once, Matteo allowed impulse to rule him. Just this once, he put himself in Cisco's shoes and asked himself what his brother would do in a case like this—*feeling* like this.

Maybe he needed to take a page out of Cisco's book. After all, Cisco was the one who had the girls all clamoring for his attention as far back as Matteo could remember. Cisco was the one who never, *ever* lacked for female companionship.

And Cisco didn't sit around waiting for things to happen. He *made* things happen.

Maybe it was time that he did the same, Matteo thought as desire continued to swirl through him, growing larger and more intense.

With that last thought uppermost in his mind, Matteo cupped Rachel's chin in his hand ever so lightly, tilted her head back and brushed his lips against hers without so much as a whispered preamble or a hint of a warning.

One second they were talking. The next he was seizing the moment and kissing her.

Her lips were incredibly sweet, tasting of the strawberry she had just consumed and her very own unique and tempting flavor. Matteo felt awe and excitement at the same time.

Her scent filled his head, and her taste filled his soul, tempting him. Making him long for things he knew he shouldn't be longing for, not at this point.

It was too soon.

Unlike Cisco, he wasn't the love-'em-and-leave-'em type. That, to him, was the very definition of irresponsibility. To Matteo, family was everything. And he would not accidentally create any new members until after the proper steps had been taken. Caution, he silently argued, could only be thrown to the wind so far before a man's moral fiber wound up being sacrificed.

That wasn't him.

And yet...

And yet she made him ache so badly. Made him want to do and be things that he normally wasn't.

Rachel had to remind herself to breathe.

This was not as good as she thought it might be—it was better.

Miles better.

So much better that she thought perhaps this was what some people referred to when they talked about having an out-of-body experience, because heaven knew, her consciousness had definitely gone *somewhere* these past few minutes.

Without thinking, she wrapped her arms around Matteo's neck, cleaving the upper part of her body to his, her heart racing so madly she thought it might very well burst.

And when it was over, when Matteo pulled his lips from hers, she almost cried out. Part of her wanted to stop him from moving back. She wanted to keep the moment going indefinitely so that she could lose herself in his kiss until both their boundaries were blurred and she didn't know where hers ended and his began.

She felt as if she was free-falling through space.

It wasn't realistic and she knew it, but just for this small interlude of time, she had parted company with reality.

Happily-ever-after fairy tales were more her speed right now.

When he drew his head back, there was an apology automatically hovering on Matteo's lips. But one look at Rachel's face and something told him that it wasn't necessary to apologize. The exact opposite was true. That if he apologized, he would be in effect ruining something perfect.

Something they both treasured in their own unique way.

With effort, Matteo reined in both his thoughts and his growing desires. He told himself he needed to know more about her as a person. This magnetic pull he was experiencing had to have more than just physicality at its core. He wanted to have feelings for the total person, not just the sexy intern/hostess whose presence ignited his soul.

"Does your family live here in Horseback Hollow?" he asked her. Maybe it was a lame question, but it was a start.

The question, coming out of the blue, caught her off guard. Why was he asking that now?

"No, they're back in—someplace else," she ended, deciding at the last moment that it served no purpose to give away too much information.

It wasn't that she didn't trust Matteo or wanted to project the image of some sort of woman of mystery. She just didn't want him to get it in his head to look up her family on one of his piloting jaunts. Who she had been back in Austin was *not* who she was here in Horseback Hollow. She wanted to be judged on her own merits, not on whose daughter she was.

"Why do you ask?" she wanted to know.

His shrug was casual. "Just being curious," he replied. "I have a big family, and we're pretty close. Always makes me wonder what everyone else's family is like."

"My family's big," Rachel acknowledged. "But we're not close," she said flatly, "so it really doesn't count all that much *how* big we are. There were times when we were just ten individuals under the same roof, nothing more."

"Ten, huh?" Matteo whistled at the number. "Well, you've got me beat. I've got only five siblings in mine. But we're all pretty close," he added, wondering if she would take that as a criticism about her family. He certainly didn't mean it that way. "Gabi's the youngest—

and the only girl. When my dad was hurt in that plane crash, Gabi dropped everything and came right out to take care of him. While she was here, she wound up meeting and falling in love with Jude Fortune Jones. After my dad recovered, Gabi got married.

"That's why Cisco and I are out here," he explained. "We came for her wedding."

She liked that about him, liked his family loyalty. She'd been at the wedding, too, but their paths had never crossed. She'd never even caught a glimpse of him. She would have remembered if she had. "She made a beautiful bride, didn't she?"

Matteo nodded. "Yes."

His little sister *had* made a beautiful bride. He couldn't recall ever seeing her glow like that. He was very happy for her. At the same time, he wondered if he was ever going to have that sort of a connection with someone, the kind of connection that felt as if the other person completed him. And he couldn't help but wonder how he and Rachel had spent the night at the same affair without meeting. Without sharing a look or a dance.

Rachel pointed out the obvious. "And you're still here." It gave her an inkling of hope that perhaps he intended to stay around for a while—perhaps even permanently.

Matteo shrugged again, lifting one shoulder carelessly, then letting it drop. "I'm not sure about Cisco's reasons, but as for me, I thought I'd stick around for a little bit just to please the old man. Dad wants all of us to relocate here." He smiled, recalling the blatant hints his father had dropped since he'd arrived in town. It surprised him that Cisco was actually on board with the idea of staying for a while. His brother's primary real-estate market was back in Miami. He would have thought that Cisco would have already been on a plane headed back home. "Dad likes having family close by."

Rachel saw through the layers of rhetoric. "But you want to go back to Miami."

"That was the plan," he admitted, looking up at the sky with its network of stars. If he looked at her, he knew he would be sorely tempted to kiss her again— and this time it might not stop there. So he looked at the sky for both their sakes.

Was. He'd said that "was" the plan, Rachel thought, seizing on the word. Did that mean that there was a new plan in place? Or was she just indulging in a great deal of wishful thinking?

She wasn't sure, and she didn't want to ask Matteo to clarify that for her. He might take her question the wrong way or misunderstand why she was asking.

At this point, even *she* wasn't exactly sure what she meant with all this wavering back and forth she was doing, especially while it was going on with these strange, intense feelings she was having that served as a backdrop for what might or might not be going on between them.

All she knew was that she had never felt so confused before: excited and frightened all at the same time. And it was centered on this man sitting inches away from her.

Rachel pretended to compare the lure of Miami with what Horseback Hollow had to offer. "We don't have the kinds of restaurants or nightlife that Miami boasts," she readily agreed. "But you certainly can't find a more peaceful place than this town." And right now, that was a very high priority for her.

"Assuming I'm looking for peaceful," Matteo pointed out.

"Everyone looks for peaceful once in a while," she told him. And then, thinking it over, she amended her own assessment. "Well, maybe not everyone," she allowed. "Your brother doesn't seem like the type who values peaceful. He seems more like someone who's drawn to nightlife."

He couldn't tell if she was just making an assessment of Cisco—or comparing his brother to him and finding him lacking. Finding him, in a word, dull.

He'd taken second place to his brother more times than he could remember, and while it had only mildly irritated him when he was a boy, this time around, the thought really bothered him.

Matteo began to gather up the dishes and what was left of the picnic, depositing everything rather haphazardly into the basket.

"It's getting late," he announced. "I think I'd better take you home."

She could have sworn she'd seen something flash across his face a moment ago, a thought that didn't sit well with him or some sort of an epiphany that had made him feel less than comfortable.

Whatever it was, it had been abrupt, and she could feel that the mood changed instantly.

Was it something she had unwittingly said? Or done? She didn't have a clue, and it bothered her.

For a moment, Rachel debated just coming out and asking him what was wrong. But that could make things even worse. In the end, she pretended nothing had happened and this was just the natural ending to a moonlight picnic.

As he put away all the plates and utensils, she folded up the tablecloth and handed it to him. She placed the lanterns side by side in the wicker basket.

"Thanks," he murmured, avoiding her eyes.

"Least I can do," she responded. "I really did have a very nice time." She thought perhaps that needed to be reinforced in light of the way their evening had abruptly ended.

For a moment, Matteo stopped moving and packing and looked at her. Was she just being polite while secretly regretting that he wasn't his brother?

Damn it, was he ever going to be rid of this constant feeling of competition, of being measured and rated against his brother—and found lacking? He had his own career, his own way of doing things, his own identity. Why, then, was there always this feeling that he was forever struggling to get out from beneath his brother's long shadow?

"Yeah, me, too," he told her.

His brief acknowledgment coaxed a small smile from her.

It went a long way in warming him up.

Matteo brought her to her apartment door. He wasn't the type just to deposit a woman on her doorstep while he kept his car engine running, ready to make a quick getaway.

He was, however, planning on turning on his heel and leaving as soon as she was safely inside with her door locked.

At least, that had been his initial plan, formed while driving Rachel back.

But as he walked beside her to her door, he felt an

overwhelming desire to linger with her, to say something, *anything*, that didn't brand them as two strangers who happened to have shared an evening meal together, accompanied by an assortment of insects.

He watched as she put her key into the lock and turned it. *Talk now, or forever hold your peace*, he told himself sternly.

Almost to his surprise, he heard himself saying, "Would you mind if I called you sometime? I mean, while I'm still here in Horseback Hollow?"

"You mean you wouldn't fly in from Miami just to see me?" she deadpanned. The next second, she saw the look on his face and realized that he thought she was serious. "I'm kidding," she assured him quickly. "I'm kidding. And no, I wouldn't mind." If ever a man needed a fire lit under him, it was Matteo. "I'd rather like that."

She had surprised him. Matteo was aware of the fact that he hadn't exactly put his best foot forward in the last part of their date. That she was still willing to see him again despite that had him smiling broadly at her. "You would?"

"Uh-huh. Of course, you might have to ply me with more of your fried chicken," she told him.

He looked at her a little uncertainly, as if trying to ascertain whether or not she was pulling his leg.

The man had a lot of good qualities, she thought, but he definitely needed to work on his sense of humor. Someone had forgotten to issue him one.

"Everyone's got a price," she told him, smiling. "Fried chicken is mine. *Your* fried chicken," she emphasized with what was now a wide grin.

Her smile managed to coax a similar one from him. "That can be arranged."

"Good," she said. Had there not been a glimmer in her eyes, he would have been tempted to think that she was serious. Nonetheless, the fact that she had mentioned the main course he'd made for her pleased him.

He knew that he should be leaving. But then, he argued with himself, if for some reason this was the last time they were to be together, it made no sense for him to beat a hasty retreat, especially since she wasn't the one who was trying to get him to leave.

Searching for something to say, he fell back on work. That was always a reliable topic, and right now, it was probably also a necessary one.

"You, um, might want to tell your boss to clear some more space in one of the smaller rooms in your building. Dad told me that there're going to be several more deliveries made to your branch of the Fortune Foundation this month. We're going to be flying between Red Rock and Horseback Hollow at least three more times."

She couldn't begin to imagine what they would be flying out on three more trips—even as she was doing a little happy dance in her head. Three more trips meant seeing Matteo at least three more times— at the very least.

She knew it took a lot of supplies to start up a large office and run it efficiently. There were still offices that were essentially empty within the two-story building. She imagined that Matteo and his father might even be flying in the furniture for those offices, among other things.

"I guess that means we'll be getting more than

just printer paper and ink cartridges delivered," Rachel said.

Matteo laughed. He'd seen the pages upon pages of inventory regarding the cargo being shipped to the Horseback Hollow branch office.

"Way more," he agreed.

"Are you going to be the one delivering those deliveries? Does your dad agree to having you pilot the cargo plane instead of him?" she asked.

Having opened the door to her apartment, she now leaned against the door frame, reluctant to cross the threshold and thereby officially call an end to their date.

"Delivering those deliveries," he echoed, then grinned. "Say that three times, fast."

Rachel felt her heart flutter. She could so easily get lost in that appealing grin of his.

"My tongue doesn't tangle, if that's what you're indirectly asking about." Then, to prove it, she repeated the sentence three times, enunciating each word quickly and clearly. "Anything else you'd like to hear me recite?" she asked.

He could have sworn there was mischief in her eyes. This was a woman who everyone thought was relatively quiet, but who, in reality, was a live wire who seemed capable of doing anything on a whim, then resuming looking angelic.

He wasn't sure which one attracted him more, the angel or the devil.

Most likely, he thought, it was a mixture of both. But he didn't want to waste whatever precious moments there were left before she retreated into her apartment and he drove back to his father's house.

He had his suspicions that dreams of Miami weren't going to be nearly as strong and alluring tonight as they had been of late.

"I just wanted to tell you one more time that I had a very nice time tonight," he said.

She surprised him—and herself—by saying, "Show me."

Matteo looked at her, confused. "What?"

"Show me," Rachel repeated.

"How?" he asked, not exactly sure he understood what she was getting at.

Her mouth curved, underscoring the amusement that was already evident in her eyes.

"Oh, I think you can figure it out, Mendoza," she told him. Then she sighed loudly, took hold of the two sides of his button-down shirt and abruptly pulled him to her.

Matteo was more than a little surprised at this display of proactive behavior on her part. She really was a firecracker, he thought.

The next moment, there was no room for looks of surprise or any other expressions, for that matter. It was hard to make out a woman's features if her face was flush against another face the way Rachel's was against his.

She lost no time in putting a piece of her soul into the kiss. If the first kiss between them during the picnic was sweet, this kiss was nothing if not flaming hot. So much so that Matteo was almost certain he was going to go up in smoke any second now.

The thing of it was, he didn't care. As long as it happened while he was kissing Rachel, nothing else mattered.

Chapter Eight

"I'd better leave now, while I still can," Matteo told her a full two minutes later, separating himself from her.

He knew he had to pull back, and it had to be *now*. He had a very strong feeling that, despite any noble sentiments to the contrary, if he waited even a single moment longer, he would be completely lost. A man could resist only so much temptation before he gave in, and in all honesty, he wasn't altogether sure that things were happening for the right reasons.

Did this woman make his blood surge because he was so attracted to her, or was it because somewhere, deep down, he felt his brother was interested in Rachel, and he was trying to best Cisco at his own game?

If it was the latter, then going any further tonight would be a complete disservice to her, not to mention wrong.

And she deserved better than that. Better than to be the object of a tug-of-war between two brothers.

Rachel looked somewhat dazed and sounded a bit breathless when she said, "You're being a gentleman."

Matteo wasn't sure if she was making an assessment or asking him a question. In either case, the answer was the same. He was taking no credit for something that was not a done deal.

"I'm trying."

Rachel smiled up into his eyes, both disappointed and absolutely thrilled and touched.

"I appreciate that," she whispered.

And even though she truly wanted to make love with him, she had to admire his restrained behavior. Not every man was like that, holding back until they had spent more time together.

"Then, like I said, I'd better leave now." Matteo took a step back, away from her door. His eyes never left her face. "I'll see you soon," he promised.

She had no doubt that she would see him again. But in what capacity? "Professionally or privately?" Rachel asked.

Matteo merely smiled enigmatically at her and said, "Yes."

Turning from Rachel, he began to walk away. As he left, he heard her cell phone begin to ring. In his gut, he knew who it was.

Cisco.

Stiffening, he slowed his pace, wanting to see if he was right. He had no idea how he knew who was calling her. He just did.

Confirmation came as he listened to her end of the

conversation. He could feel his gut twisting. Maybe he *should* have let things progress naturally.

Every word she uttered pierced his skin like tiny blades.

"Oh, it's you. No, just surprised, that's all. Yes, I just got in. Very nice, thank you."

Matteo resisted the temptation of pulling the cell out of her hand and telling his brother where he could go. Gritting his teeth, he kept walking.

By the time he got to his car, Matteo had sufficiently worked himself up. Looking down at his sides, Matteo realized that both his hands were clenched.

Had Cisco been standing in front of him right now, he wouldn't have been standing upright for long.

The following morning found him sitting across from Cisco, having breakfast at a cafe in Vicker's Corners. The arrangements to meet had been made a week ago, to discuss their father's situation without having their father present. But at the moment, the subject of their father was the furthest thing from either of their minds.

Cisco was consuming his breakfast as if he didn't have a care in the world. No such laid-back attitude resided on Matteo's side of the table. Matteo had come because he had given his word, but he was not happy about having to be in such proximity to his brother, who was, for the most part, acting even more cocky than usual, in his estimation.

Cisco seemed to be scrutinizing him. Why? What was going on in his brother's head? Matteo couldn't help wondering.

"I hear your date went well last night," Cisco told

him, nodding his head in approval. "A moonlight picnic. You're improving, little brother. There's hope for you yet."

Matteo didn't like Cisco's blatantly high-handed attitude, nor did he like the fact that his brother was prying into his personal life as if he had every right to. He saw it as nothing less than an invasion of privacy.

"What business is any of this of yours?" Matteo wanted to know. He angrily swished his fork through the eggs on his plate. If they hadn't been scrambled already, they would have been now.

Scrambled, but not touched.

That was not the case with Cisco's order. His breakfast was disappearing quickly. "Why, you wound me, Mattie." He pressed his hand dramatically against his chest, in the general vicinity of his heart. "Everything about you is my business. If I don't look after you, who will?" he asked loftily.

Matteo narrowed his eyes. "I don't need looking after," he snapped.

"That is a matter of opinion," Cisco replied, amused. Pausing, holding his fork aloft, he asked, "Have you asked her out again?"

Matteo's eyes narrowed. "Asked who out again?"

Cisco shook his head. He made it obvious that this kind of a response was definitely beneath his brother. "Oh, don't play dumb, Mattie. We both know you're not dumb. You might lack energy and drive, and God knows you're slow to pick up on signals—"

Matteo was trying to ignore his brother, but Cisco was making it next to impossible. "*What* signals?" he demanded.

Cisco used his fork as if it was an extension of

his hand, waving it at his brother as he spoke. "See, that's my point exactly. You don't even know there *are* any signals. Since I'm your older brother and I believe in leading by example, if you don't take advantage of what's right there in front of you, then I'm going to have to step in and do it for you—for your own good, of course."

Now, what was *that* supposed to mean?

A waitress approached their table at that moment, a coffeepot in her hand. She topped off Cisco's coffee with more than half a cup.

There was hardly room for a drop more in Matteo's cup. It was obvious that he hadn't touched any of his breakfast.

"Is everything all right with your meal, sir?" the young woman asked.

"My *meal* is fine," he told her. His eyes never left his brother.

The waitress, looking somewhat confused, withdrew.

The moment she did, Matteo asked his brother incredulously, "You're putting me on notice?"

"I suppose that's one way of saying it," Cisco allowed. "Bottom line is that we can't have Rachel thinking all the Mendoza men are slow to act just because you are."

He could see that Cisco was enjoying this exchange. He, on the other hand, definitely was not.

"Stay away from her," Matteo warned his brother, his voice low, foreboding.

Everything about Cisco's body language told Matteo that his older brother was not about to follow instructions.

"I'm afraid I can't do that," Cisco said. "This is a free country, little brother, and the last time I looked, there weren't any 'taken' signs on Rachel."

If they hadn't been sitting in a public place, Matteo would have been sorely tempted to wipe the smirk off his brother's all-too-handsome face. "Then use your imagination," he growled.

"Oh, I am," Cisco assured him with a hearty laugh. "I am."

At this point, goaded this way, it took every last drop of restraint that Matteo possessed to keep him from jumping up from the table and making his brother eat his words.

Maybe he wouldn't have succeeded—Cisco wasn't exactly a ninety-pound weakling; he was a man who believed in exercising to keep physically fit—but Matteo would have gotten a great deal of satisfaction out of trying and landing at least a couple of well-placed punches.

But he refrained from any sort of physical action because he knew that if word got back to his father—and it would—that he and Cisco were publicly brawling, it would really upset the old man. Not because it happened in public, but that it happened at all.

His father was very big on family unity. Trying to beat each other up didn't exactly strike a blow for family unity. It just struck a blow.

But if he couldn't vent his anger via his method of choice, at least he didn't have to remain here, listening to Cisco talk as if he was the leading authority on women and relationships.

Standing up, Matteo threw a couple of bills on the table.

"Where are you going?" Cisco asked innocently. He indicated Matteo's plate. "You haven't finished your breakfast yet."

"Oh, I'm finished with it, all right," Matteo retorted. "Besides, I suddenly lost my appetite."

Cisco nodded as if he had been expecting to hear that. "Unresolved love issues can do that to a man."

Didn't Cisco ever stop pontificating? Or, at the very least, get sick of the sound of his own voice?

"I don't have time to listen to you babble. I've got work to do," Matteo said, turning on his heel and walking away.

Cisco leaned back in his chair, tilting it slightly so he could get a better view of his brother as he left the restaurant.

"If that means making deliveries to a certain charitable foundation, say hi to her for me," Cisco called after him.

Matteo bit his tongue. Answering his brother would only lead to yet another round of exchanges that went nowhere. Cisco was not one to surrender his right to get in the last word—*each time*. Matteo had no doubt that his brother would probably go on talking from the grave if it seemed as if someone got in the last word after him.

Besides, the truth of it was, he really did have to hustle. His father *was* making another round-trip run today to the Fortune Foundation's headquarters in Red Rock and back again.

He knew for a fact that his father would take off without him if he wasn't there on time. While Orlando Mendoza made it known that he enjoyed all his children's company, he also made it known that it irked him no end to have anyone think he needed a keeper or someone watching over him, ready to step in at the first sign of any sort of weakness.

Matteo supposed, as the comparison snuck up on him, that his father felt the same way about his being around for the flights as he himself felt hearing Cisco tell him that he was willing to lead by example.

"But it's different," he said out loud, as if he was making the argument to his father instead of just talking to himself as he drove to the airfield. "If something goes wrong or I don't act fast enough, I'm not going to crash and burn."

And neither was his father. Not if he had anything to say about it.

Which was why he needed to get to the airfield right now. He wanted to check out the plane himself despite the fact that the Redmond Flight School and Charter Service kept a very reliable mechanic on its payroll.

"I was just about to leave without you," Orlando told him as Matteo raced onto the field, having parked his vehicle as close as was allowed. "I thought perhaps your date with that cute girl went well, so you weren't going to be my shadow anymore now that you found something better to do with your time."

"Nothing's better than working with you, Dad," Matteo told him, forcing a cheerful smile onto his face. "Was your plane checked out?"

"Yes, *hijo*," Orlando said patiently, rolling his eyes heavenward as if he resented being treated like a man who had been born without common sense, "my plane has been checked out. Why aren't you with that girl?

The one from the Foundation—Rachel?" he wanted to know. "Didn't the two of you go out last night?"

Did *everyone* know his business? Matteo wondered. "How did you know about that?" he asked, doing his best not to show that having his personal life viewed as something on public record was extremely irritating to him.

"I'm a father," Orlando told him matter-of-factly. Matteo knew that he was not above doing a little snooping or information swapping to keep an eye on his sons. "Fathers know these things." And then he asked, concerned, "Didn't it go well?"

Since they were flying an empty plane, there was no reason for any further delay once they were on board. "Yes, Dad, it went well."

"Then what are you doing here?" his father wanted to know as he got on the plane. "Why aren't you having breakfast or whatever with her?"

Matteo followed his father onto the plane, entering the cockpit right after he did. "Because she's working at the Foundation this morning, and I'm working here with you. And, according to the timetable you showed me, we're falling behind," he pointed out. "So let's get going."

Orlando, strapping himself into his seat, paused for a moment to look sharply at his youngest son. "Has anyone ever told you that you nag?"

Matteo grinned cheerfully. "Not lately, Dad."

Orlando snorted. Putting on the glasses that he was too vain to wear in public, he looked over his manifest. "Well, you do."

"Must run in the family," Matteo said, staring at his father pointedly.

Orlando ignored him.

"Hey, Dad?"

Orlando glanced in his direction. "Now what?"

"How do you know if a woman's right for you? If she's 'the one'?"

"She tells you," Orlando said as he went over his controls.

"No, really. I'm serious."

"So was I." But because he saw that his son was actually waiting for him to say something, Orlando told him the only thing he could. "Something in your soul connects with hers, perhaps just for a second, and that feeling is so wonderful you just *know* you were meant to be together."

"Was it like that for you and Mom?" Matteo wanted to know.

After a moment, Orlando replied quietly, "Yes."

Matteo knew better than to take the discussion any further.

She was too old for this, Rachel thought a little more than two weeks later as she sat in her cubicle at the Foundation.

Too old to be behaving like a schoolgirl.

Yet no matter where she was, whether working her part-time job at the Cantina or her full-time job here at the Foundation, every time she heard an outer door open or glimpsed someone coming in out of the corner of her eye, before she could make out who it was, her heart was already skipping a beat in hopeful anticipation.

She would have thought, after having gone out with Matteo several times now, to the movies in Vicker's

Corners, for another picnic and to the fancy restaurant where Cisco had initially brought her—which seemed so much more special with Matteo—that she would have gotten a little calmer about the whole thing. Instead, the exact opposite seemed to be true. Each time they went out, she grew more excited about seeing him. It didn't matter what they were doing; it just mattered that she was doing it with him.

Rachel thought back to the last date they'd had and she smiled, reliving it.

"That was really good," she recalled commenting as they left the restaurant in Vicker's Corners. "Not as good as the fried chicken *you* made, of course," she'd amended, a smile playing on her lips, "but still good."

"Yeah, yeah." Matteo had laughed and taken her hand in his. "Feel like going for a little walk before we drive back to Horseback Hollow?"

She'd inclined her head, pretending to think it over, then said, "I'm game." And she was. Game for anything that allowed her to have a little more time with the man she was developing deep feelings for.

"That's one of the things I like about you," he'd told her. "You're game, but you don't play games. Other women think that keeping secrets and being hard to read makes them more desirable to a guy. But with you, I know that what I see is what I get. No games, no mysteries, just total honesty." He'd squeezed her hand affectionately. "That's a rare trait."

She'd frozen then, although she'd tried not to. But the very thing that he'd professed to like best about her wasn't true. She wasn't being up-front and honest with him. In that case, she was being the exact opposite.

She'd felt like a liar—and yet, she couldn't tell him

about her father, about her. Not yet. Not until she felt confident enough about their relationship, about him, to trust him with her story. This wasn't some tiny, inconsequential thing. To her this was a major secret.

She'd stopped walking. "You know, it's getting late. Maybe I should be getting back."

He'd looked at her, undoubtedly surprised by the sudden change in her demeanor. What he'd said next confirmed it for her.

"Did I say something wrong, Rachel?"

"No, no," she'd adamantly denied. "I just forgot that I promised Christopher I'd look into something for him before tomorrow morning. Sorry. I did have a lovely time," she had emphasized.

For a second, he'd looked uncertain—and then he'd grinned. "Come on, Cinderella," he teased. "I'll get you home before you turn into a pumpkin."

"It's the coach that turned into a pumpkin." She laughed, relieved that he wasn't making a big deal out of her sudden reversal.

"Whatever," he'd said good-naturedly.

And that was that. Or so she fervently hoped—although she had caught him looking at her a couple of times as if he knew she was holding something back.

But then again, that could have just been her guilty conscience and her imagination.

It still didn't change anything about the way she felt about him. If anything, since he didn't grill her, it just made her more attracted to him.

And anticipate his appearance each time anyone came into the office or the Cantina. And most of the time, she was disappointed. It was only someone else coming in.

But then again, there was that handful of times when she wasn't disappointed.

That handful of times she and her skipping heartbeat were right.

Those were the times Matteo and his father came walking in, a clipboard in Matteo's hand with a receipt for her to sign in acknowledgment of that day's incoming shipment.

Those were the times that all was right with the world—and her heart.

Thanks to Matteo and his father, the Foundation's offices were taking shape, becoming close to fully operational.

And, also thanks to Matteo, so was their relationship.

Oh, it wasn't progressing by leaps and bounds by any means. Theirs was more of a work in progress, moving along by inches, not feet. But every inch gained was a strong inch, an inch that wouldn't give way or break under its own weight.

Anything worthwhile took time to build. Wasn't that something her father had once said to her back when she thought that the sun rose and set around the man?

Just because everything she had known about her father had turned out to be a lie didn't mean that everything he'd said had been a lie, as well.

There had been *some* truthful things that had come out of his mouth. She had to try to remember that, Rachel told herself.

As she sat at her desk this bright, sunny March day, her mind wandering rather than focusing on the work she had pulled up on her computer monitor, Rachel couldn't help wondering what her father would have thought of Matteo Mendoza.

The very next moment, as if coming to, she abruptly shut that thought away.

It didn't matter to her what her father thought about anything, she upbraided herself. Especially not about the man who had so easily found his way into her heart.

Her father had had a place in her heart, and he'd just thrown that away because of all of his lies.

Because of who—and what—he had finally admitted to being. As far as she knew, she was the *only* one who knew about his secret, but that didn't make her feel privileged.

It made her feel ill.

What would Matteo say if he knew her father was a philanderer, a liar?

Rachel looked up at the clock on the wall. It was getting close to two o'clock.

She could feel her spirits beginning to sink lower. If Matteo and his father had been coming in today, they would have already been here by now, she thought. She'd made a mental note each time the two men came in with a shipment of supplies. The times varied, but they'd never arrived this late.

Apparently, today wasn't a day that they would be dropping off anything at the Foundation, she concluded.

Rachel did her best not to show her disappointment.

"You haven't been to lunch yet," Christopher said as he stopped by her cubicle on his way to his own office.

She was surprised that her boss had noticed. She thought of him as being too busy to notice minor details like that.

"I'm not very hungry," she confessed, then added, "Too much coffee, I guess," in case he was going to comment on the possible reason behind her loss of appetite. The last thing she wanted was to have anyone here speculating about Matteo and her.

"Well, take a break at least. I don't want people thinking I'm working my interns to death," Christopher said. He was smiling, but she could tell that he was serious.

Just then, they heard a commotion in the hall. Though she tried to disguise her reaction, she felt her face light up instantly. She was more than familiar with that particular noise by now. The Foundation's dolly had one squeaky wheel.

Apparently it wasn't as late as she had thought. Matteo and his father had arrived with their latest shipment of goods for the Foundation.

She sat up at attention, ready to be of assistance. It didn't go unnoticed.

"Appetite suddenly reappear?" Christopher asked her, amusement highlighting his handsome features.

"I think that maybe I could eat something after all," Rachel answered evasively.

Although she had a feeling that there really was no point in pretending indifference to Matteo's arrival. It seemed as if everyone on staff here was aware of her feelings for Matteo Mendoza.

Everyone, that was, but Matteo himself. He seemed to be rather oblivious to it. But some men, she knew, took a while to come around, and that was fine with her. She was in no particular hurry.

The next minute, Matteo came into the office, pushing the dolly before him, a very low recurring squeak accompanying his route. The dolly was loaded down with all manner of supplies, including a good month's worth of coffee, the kind that needed to be brewed.

Apparently Christopher knew how to treat his people, Rachel thought absently. The bulk of her attention was otherwise focused.

The moment she made eye contact with Matteo, she automatically began to smile broadly.

Matteo's expression, however, was far more in keeping with being grim.

The next minute she saw why.

His father, being the pilot of record, had of course made the round-trip from here to Red Rock and back with him. But there was also someone else who had come in with them.

Cisco.

Chapter Nine

Circumventing both his father and his younger brother, Cisco headed straight for Rachel the second he walked into the room.

"Hello." Greeting her warmly, he took her hands between his and held them for what seemed to Matteo to be an overly long period. "I see you're looking just as lovely as ever." He spared Matteo the most fleeting of glances before turning his attention back to Rachel. "I guess my brother's efforts to show you a good time have been at least moderately successful."

As gracefully as possible, she extracted her hands from Cisco's. To say that his appearance here surprised her would have been a huge understatement. It also made her somewhat uncomfortable. She had thought that the notion of the two brothers engaged in a competition was a thing of the past. Now she wasn't really all that sure that it was.

"Cisco, I didn't expect to see you here."

The smile Cisco flashed at her widened. "I came to lend my father and little brother a hand—and, of course, to see you again," he told her with what sounded like sincerity.

He moved to take her hands in his again, but she outmaneuvered him, picking up a clipboard from her desk and holding on to it with both hands.

"It hasn't been that long since we saw each other," she pointed out. Her smile felt tense around the edges. She slanted a quick glance in Matteo's direction to see how he was dealing with all this, but his expression was unreadable—and stoic.

"Well, it certainly feels that way to me," Cisco confided. Once again, he glanced over his shoulder toward his brother. "But I didn't want to intrude or steal my brother's thunder, such as it is."

She could feel a blush coming on. It was a direct result of her embarrassment and the flustered feeling that was growing more intense by the second. She had no idea why Cisco was paying this amount of attention to her—they had had a nice date that one time, but it couldn't have been considered spectacular by any means. And the important thing was that Cisco hadn't followed up on it—other than that first time when Matteo had grabbed her cell phone from her and said that he was her date that night.

On the other hand, she and Matteo had had several dates now, and in her opinion, the two of them seemed to be getting closer.

Until today.

If she were to go only by the expression on Matteo's face, she would have said that they did *not* have *any* sort of a relationship at all. He looked distant and removed.

Feeling somewhat frustrated, Rachel turned toward Orlando, hoping to uncover a bit of sanity there. The senior Mendoza had behaved as if he liked her, and she gravitated toward that now.

"What are you delivering today, Mr. Mendoza?" she asked, moving closer to the older man and completely ignoring the other two men for the moment.

"The tables and chairs for the main break room," he told her. "As well as some small appliances. Besides this mini refrigerator, there are a couple of microwaves in the truck." He nodded at Cisco. "Cisco volunteered to help get them off the truck and bring them up in the elevator, putting them where they belonged."

"We're bringing in a couple of vending machines, too," Cisco told her. "Can't have my father and my little brother straining their backs with all this heavy lifting."

Pivoting the dolly so that they could bring it and what was on it to the proper place, Matteo snapped between clenched teeth, "Stop calling me that."

Cisco positioned himself on the dolly's other side. Industrial-size bungee cords were in place to keep the mini refrigerator from moving around in transit, but it seemed that they still needed someone or something to stabilize the appliance's weight. That was Cisco's part in all this.

"Calling you what?" Cisco asked his brother in an innocent voice.

Matteo blew out a breath. Cisco knew exactly what

he was referring to. Why was he pretending not to? "Your little brother."

Cisco's innocent expression never wavered. "Well, you are, aren't you?"

Not knowing how else to deal with this tense situation—and afraid it might get worse any second—Rachel decided to make light of it, desperately hoping to change the mood for the better.

She turned toward their father and asked, "Were they always like this?"

"No," Orlando replied in all seriousness. "They were much worse." Rachel didn't know if she quite believed that was possible. "I think," Orlando went on, "they're on their good behavior because of you."

As if to reinforce his father's statement, Cisco offered her a wide, wide smile. It was obviously forced, yet somehow still rather appealing.

Only Matteo remained silent, applying himself instead to bringing the mini refrigerator they had on the dolly to the appropriate place.

Unaware of the location of the official break room that they were charged with setting up, Matteo looked at Rachel and, nodding at the dolly, asked, "Where do you want this?"

"You mean she has to direct you around the office?" Cisco marveled, chuckling to himself. He looked at Rachel. "I've got to say, Rachel, not every woman would be so patient."

Matteo had had just about all he could take. Ordinarily, what Cisco said when he got on this leader-of-the-pack kick went in one ear and out the other. But this time it was different. This time there was more at stake than just his ego.

"You want to step outside?" Matteo challenged his brother.

"Later," Cisco replied calmly, as if they were having an actual discussion, "to get the next load after we put this one wherever it's supposed to go."

Matteo's eyes narrowed. "That's not what I meant," he said under his breath, only loud enough for his brother to hear.

"But that's what you should have meant," Cisco answered cheerfully, as if he were the soul of reason and hadn't a clue what was bothering Matteo. "You coming?" he asked as he nodded toward the break room. "Or are you saving your back for a rainy day?"

At that precise moment, Matteo could have strangled him—but there were far too many witnesses around. Instead, he pushed the dolly down the hall, his biceps straining and displaying an impressive network of definition.

The view wasn't lost on Rachel.

It went like that for most of the delivery. Barbs between the brothers were exchanged, fast and furiously at every available opportunity. It continued even though Orlando had upbraided both his sons, taking advantage of Rachel stepping out of the room.

He knew that Matteo would take Cisco's ribbing only so long and then he'd come back giving as good—or better—than he got. He didn't want this growing conflict to get out of hand—and he didn't care for the fact that it was on display where someone outside the family could be privy to it.

Especially the woman who was apparently at the center of the reason for this conflict.

"What has gotten into you?" Orlando demanded of Cisco, drawing him over to one side.

"Just making sure that little brother makes the most of his opportunities."

Confused, Orlando stared at his older son. "Really? Well, from here it looks like you are doing your best to undermine Matteo and run him into the ground right in front of that young woman."

"You are right, Dad," Cisco agreed, stunning his father with what seemed like an admission. "It looks that way. But it's not."

Walking into the break room, Cisco frowned at the mini refrigerator that he and Matteo had brought up earlier. He turned to his father and said, "Someone's going to have to call a plumber to hook this baby up if they want it up and running when they finally open their doors to the public in April."

Matteo paused to look at the connections and the capped-off copper tubing. "They don't need a plumber," he told his father. "I can hook this up. I've got a toolbox in your truck." Passing his father, he promised, "Be right back."

"You are a handy little guy to have around, aren't you?" Cisco proclaimed with a laugh.

Matteo stopped for a second right next to his brother. "You call me little one more time and it's not my handy side that you'll be seeing."

Cisco looked amused to have riled his younger brother to this point. "Tempting as that might be to witness, I will do my best to curb my desire to refer to you as little," Cisco told him.

Matteo made no reply as he left the room and took

the stairs to the ground floor. He apparently needed to blow off some steam.

Neither brother realized that they were being watched and that Rachel had heard the entire exchange between them.

Because the physical preparation of the Foundation's offices were part of her duties, Rachel made herself accessible the entire time the Mendozas were at the Foundation. It didn't matter whether they were unloading the truck or bringing up the various pieces of furniture and appliances. She made sure that she was right there, ready to help in any way that was necessary.

Unlike the previous occasions when Matteo and his father made deliveries, with Cisco present, Matteo didn't do much talking. Because Rachel didn't want to get in the middle of whatever was going on between the two brothers, she found herself doing a great deal of talking to their father.

The senior Mendoza was a strikingly handsome man who was every bit as charming as Cisco and just as warm and genuine as Matteo. As she spoke to the man, discussing work and his family, she delicately inquired how he was getting along on his own after having been married for so long.

Orlando took a moment to frame his reply.

"I am not surprised that you know," he told her. "You strike me as a very intelligent young lady who makes a point of looking into people's backgrounds if you are going to be dealing with them on any sort of a long-term basis."

He had her pegged, she thought. At least, he had

the old Rachel pegged. The one who had yet to be blown out of the water by her own father. Reconstructing a life wasn't easy after discovering that the person you thought you knew was a complete and total stranger to you—like her father was to her.

The worst part of it, she thought now, was that she *hadn't* actually been able to confront her father about her discovery. She had found it easier to leave home, spouting some nonsense about finding herself.

But for right now, she was focusing on Orlando. "You didn't answer my question," she pointed out gently.

"No, I didn't," Orlando agreed. Then, because he knew she meant well and wasn't being nosy, he told her, "I'm getting along as well as possible, seeing as how she was the light of my soul and she was taken from me much too early." With a vague little shrug, Orlando went on to say, "I miss her every day. I suspect I will until the day I die."

"You should try going out," Rachel suggested sympathetically.

He looked at her as if she had suggested that he run naked through traffic at twilight.

"From what you told me, your wife sounds like she was a lovely lady who wouldn't have wanted you to go on grieving for her endlessly. She'd want you to go out, to have a good time and to meet other people."

The idea of putting himself out there after all these years was not an appealing one. "No, I think that, at least for now, I should remain on the sidelines. I have plenty to keep me occupied," he added quickly, building up his excuses so that this young woman would refrain from the idea of playing matchmaker

in case that was her inclination. "There is my job, flying cargo to various places, not to mention playing
referee between my two sons. Although, I must say,
I can see why they would be butting heads over you."

She could feel her cheeks reddening again. "Now,
don't you start," Rachel warned him, half kidding.
He was, after all, a Mendoza, and his sons had to get
their flirtatious personas from somewhere. Orlando
raised his hands as if in surrender. "I only made an
observation. After all, I am not blind, and even I can
see how very lovely you are."

Laughing, she shook her head. "I can see that Cisco
inherited his silver tongue from you."

Orlando dramatically placed his hand over his
heart. "Please, senorita, you make me blush."

"Not hardly, Senor Mendoza," she responded,
looking at him knowingly. "Not hardly."

Matteo and Cisco worked hard to set up the break
room. Even so, Cisco made sure that he had time to
interact with Rachel several times during the length
of their workday—and always in full view of Matteo. The latter seemed determined to continue working nonstop—especially when Rachel tried to talk to
him. She made three attempts at having a conversation with Matteo, but each time, he made it clear that
he was busy with some other part of the shipment,
unable—and possibly unwilling—to take the time to
stop and talk with her.

By the time the three men were ready to leave, she
was more than willing to see them go. At least when
it came to Matteo. His deliberate inattention toward
her had stung.

Picking up on the tension that was humming between the duo, Cisco leaned in and told her—quite audibly—"Don't worry. He'll get over it."

Whatever "it" was, she thought.

"I'm not worried and I really don't care," she informed Cisco with a toss of her head. She made a point of completely ignoring Matteo, acting as if he wasn't even there. After all, a woman had her pride, Rachel thought. Without it, she was nothing, and she for one was determined never to feel that way, not even for five minutes.

"See you around, beautiful," Cisco said cheerfully by way of parting.

"See you around," she echoed, holding on to the receipt that Orlando had given her for that day's deliveries.

Orlando hung behind and gave her a courtly bow. "Thank you for everything—and I do apologize for my sons," he emphasized again.

"You have only one to apologize for," Rachel pointed out. "The other one—Cisco—" she added in case there was any doubt "—was very charming."

It was obvious that Orlando had another opinion on the matter, but he didn't contradict her. Instead, he said, "Perhaps that is why I need to apologize— for the other one," he emphasized. "Do not write him off too quickly, please."

Maybe there was a misunderstanding about all this, she thought. "I'm not looking for anything right now, Senor Mendoza."

Orlando gave her another small, courtly bow. "Understood," he told her.

He withdrew from the room and then from the

building. Both of his sons were waiting in the truck. He intended to give one of them hell, but not necessarily the one that Rachel had assumed would be on the receiving end.

"Idiot!"

The word echoed around her apartment—not for the first time.

Rachel called herself a fool for caring about Matteo. She knew she should consider herself lucky that she had been made privy to his sullen side before things had really heated up between them.

It would have been so much worse if she had fallen in love with him, she thought, roaming around her ground-floor apartment like a caged tiger, unable to find a place for herself. Everywhere she sat down felt all wrong. *She* felt all wrong.

She'd never felt this restless before.

And he had done that to her, she thought angrily. Matteo Mendoza had taken her goodwill and her affections and made mincemeat out of them, treating her like less than a stranger just because his brother had flirted with her. She certainly hadn't done anything to encourage Cisco.

Was Matteo afraid she would become enamored with the flirtatious words his brother was spouting? Did he really think so little of her that he assumed she'd just fall all over herself if his brother flashed a sexy smile at her and acted as if he was interested?

And why was she wasting time sulking about Matteo when she should be purging all thoughts of him out of her head? She hadn't done anything wrong and Matteo had barely talked to her today.

As a matter of fact, he *hadn't* talked to her. He'd just grunted and uttered single-word sentences. Well, that wasn't going to fly, not where she was concerned.

Rachel looked around her apartment. Suddenly it felt too small to her. She felt trapped, as if she needed to get out.

But where and with whom?

She hadn't made too many close friends here aside from Shannon—who was now occupied with her new family-to-be—and that was her own fault. She'd been leery of getting hurt again. Her father, she thought not for the first time, had done some number on her.

What she needed to do was swear off any contact with men whatsoever, young *or* old.

Right now, that didn't seem like a hard thing to do.

When the doorbell rang, it caught her completely by surprise. She wasn't expecting anyone, and she didn't know anyone who was prone to paying visits at the drop of a hat.

When the doorbell rang again, she came to the conclusion that whoever was on the other side of the door was not about to go home until she gave the order. And right now, she was angry enough to do exactly that.

Swinging the door open, she shouted, "Go away!" just as she came face-to-face with her uninvited guest.

And found herself looking at Matteo.

Chapter Ten

For a second, she could only stare at him.

"Matteo, what are you doing here?" Rachel finally managed to ask. He was the very *last* person she would have expected to turn up on her doorstep tonight.

Or, considering today's display at the Foundation, ever.

All the way over to her apartment, Matteo tried to talk himself out of coming to see her. At each corner, he told himself to turn the car around and go back. If he went through with this, he was only setting himself up for a fall. Rachel was going to break his heart. He was sure of it.

Coming here tonight, feeling the way he did, was *not* a good idea, he muttered to himself as he drove.

Yet somehow he couldn't get himself to turn

around, couldn't make himself pull over and rethink his next move.

Carefully.

It was as if he was on automatic pilot and had no real say or control over what he was about to do.

Though he was afraid of what he would see, Matteo looked over Rachel's shoulder into her apartment—or what he could see of it.

"Am I interrupting anything?" he asked her, his voice low, bordering on an accusation.

"Yes, you're interrupting something," she informed him, her hands on her hips and her eyebrows furrowing. "You're interrupting my efforts to secure some peace and quiet, which, after the kind of day I just had, would be desperately appreciated."

"You're sure that's all I'm interrupting?" Matteo asked pointedly.

Granted, he hadn't seen Cisco's car when he'd driven up, but that didn't mean it wasn't parked somewhere on the other side of the small apartment complex. And it certainly didn't mean that his brother wasn't here, perhaps even in her bedroom, waiting for him to leave.

Matteo looked at her, his sensitive face dark, his eyes pinning her in place. "I'm not interrupting your date?"

"What date?" she demanded. She was getting really angry at his attitude, and she was more than a little insulted.

He'd gone this far. He might as well spit out the rest of it, even though something within him wanted him to retreat. "With Cisco."

Rachel tossed her head, struggling to contain her anger.

"I *have* no date with Cisco," she informed Matteo coldly. "If I did, I wouldn't try to hide it. But I don't. So now you have your answer, and you can go back to wherever it was you came from."

Angry, hurt, insulted, Rachel started to slam the door on him, but Matteo put his hand up against it. He was a great deal stronger than she was, and he kept the door exactly where it was.

Exasperated, Rachel cried, "What do you want from me?"

Had he cared about her less, he would have behaved more rationally. But this was brand-new territory for him, and he was having trouble finding his way.

No more games, he told himself. *Just the truth.* "I came to ask you a question."

She could see that she wasn't going to be rid of Matteo until he got this—whatever *this* was—off his chest. She resigned herself to hearing him out.

"All right, ask your question. The sooner you ask, the sooner you can go away," she retorted.

He was putting himself out on a limb, hanging fifty feet above the ground, vulnerable and stark naked. But it had to be done. He needed to know. So he asked her, "Which brother are you interested in?"

Whatever she was expecting him to ask, it wasn't this.

Rachel blinked. "What?"

Was she deliberately making this even harder than it already was for him? "It's a simple enough question," he told Rachel, his voice devoid of any emotion. "Which Mendoza brother are you interested in?"

Half a dozen answers sprang to her lips, jockeying for first place. But they all faded back. Rising out of her hurt feelings, none of her possible responses were honest. And she had learned to treasure honesty above all else—even though, right now, she was sorely tempted to shout *Neither of them!*

"I should just throw you out on your ear," she told him. "But if you must have an answer, I'll give you one. It's you. It's been you all along, and I really should have my head examined, because the first man I lose my heart to in five years turns out to be a crazy person." Her hand was back on the doorknob, and she was all set to close the door. All she needed him to do was to take a step back. "All right, you have your answer. Now go."

It had taken a moment for her initial words to sink in.

Him.

She'd picked him.

And that changed everything.

Instantly.

"I have feelings for you, too," he told her quietly, the edge gone from his voice.

As if she really believed that, Rachel thought angrily. "They tell me that's not fatal," she said sarcastically. "You'll get over it."

Suddenly he realized all he stood to lose right at this moment, because he had acted like an idiot. He knew he had to make her understand why he'd come here tonight—and why he'd acted so bullheaded this afternoon.

"I'm serious, Rachel. I don't *want* to get over it. I know I behaved a little strangely today—"

She laughed shortly, interrupting him. "I see you're given to understatement. I had no idea," she told him tersely.

Matteo didn't have a single clue how to start making amends for his behavior or pleading his case, other than to apologize sincerely—as many times as he needed to until the apology finally took.

"Rachel, I'm sorry. I really am," he told her. "It's just that Cisco was acting as if you and he had something going on between you—and I just lost it."

"If that's what you thought, you could have come out and asked me instead of skulking around like some angry, jealous admirer," she told him.

She was right, and he didn't have a leg to stand on if he wanted to mount an argument for his side. His best recourse was to throw himself at her mercy.

"I know," he agreed. "And I behaved like a jackass today."

It was hard to remain angry at a man who was beating himself up for his behavior far better than she could have done.

"Keep going. You're on the right track," Rachel told him.

Matteo instantly noticed that the edge was gone from her voice. It gave him hope that maybe, just maybe, he hadn't completely blown his chances with her. And then, a moment later, Rachel stepped back, opening her door wider, her invitation clear.

"Do you want to come in or keep apologizing until a crowd gathers?" she asked, keeping a completely straight face.

"If that's what it takes to get you to forgive me, then I'll do it."

She was a sucker for sincerity, and he *did* sound sincere.

"You're in luck," she told him. "I'm feeling generous today. I'll take an IOU, though, to be tendered at my discretion."

He could have sworn she sounded serious. Even if she was, he figured maybe he owed it to her.

"You got it." Once inside with the door closed behind him, he took her hands in his, his eyes holding hers. The look in his was repentant and contrite. "I'm really, really sorry, Rachel. It's just that, all my life, Cisco has made a game out of going after anything that mattered to me. He's always liked showing me up and beating me, no matter what the stakes or the prize."

Apart from her father's actions, she always tried to find the positive side of everything. This was no different. "Maybe Cisco's just trying to get you to rise to the challenge, be the best you can be."

He hadn't attributed that sort of noble sentiment to Cisco. His brother had always seemed to be about nothing more serious than having a good time.

However, maybe there was something to what Rachel was saying. But now wasn't the time to delve into the matter. Now was the time to make amends.

"I think you're giving him too much credit," he told her quietly. "In any case, I shouldn't have acted the way I did toward you." Matteo paused, weighing his words carefully. He wanted her to know what had motivated him to behave so badly. "But you have to understand, I thought that he was making a play for you."

"And if he was?" she asked, her tone telling him that it didn't matter what his brother had attempted. He wouldn't have been successful in his endeavor.

"All my life, I've watched women flock to Cisco. All he ever had to do was show up, and if he wanted a girlfriend for the night or the month, he just had to put out his elbow. There'd be a girl hanging off it in no time flat."

"What does that have to do with me?" Rachel wanted to know. "It sounds like you're describing some empty-headed, vapid Valley girl type, not a real, red-blooded American woman." And by that, she made it clear that she meant herself.

Matteo regretted his behavior. "You're right. I should have had more faith in you. It's just that there are times Cisco makes me so angry, I can't see straight."

"But you have so much to offer. Why does what Cisco does—or doesn't do—bother you so much?" she asked. Since he looked so unconvinced, she began to enumerate his good qualities. "You're trustworthy, helpful—"

"Kind, don't forget kind," he interjected. "That's part of the Boy Scout Law, too."

Was he insulted to have those qualities attached to him? "There's nothing wrong with being a Boy Scout," she told him.

She was kidding, right? "Most women aren't attracted to Boy Scouts."

"That depends on who the Boy Scout is," she countered in all seriousness.

Okay, he'd bite, Matteo thought. "And if it's me?" he asked.

"I can foresee tons of women being attracted to those qualities—and to you," she told him, then repeated, "Tons," in a lower, far sexier voice.

That was when Matteo finally gave in to what was going on inside him. Gave in to the passions that were making such urgent demands on him.

Framing Rachel's face with his hands, he leaned in to kiss her.

For just a moment, his heart stopped pounding.

It was supposed to be only a simple make-up kiss, full of contrition, apology and a great deal of relief. Matteo should have known that those three ingredients created a far more volatile reaction when they were combined.

It was as if he'd just had an infusion of molten lava into his veins, shooting all through him, igniting every part of him, especially his desire.

His heart slammed against his chest and then began to pound.

Hard.

He'd thought he had it all under control, but he underestimated the power of his passions when combined with hers. Suddenly, nothing else meant anything. Not time, nor place, nor all those rules he'd always held rigidly in force. The rules all broke apart.

Matteo told himself he was still in control. That he would just allow this momentary aberration to continue for a few more glorious seconds, and then he'd put a stop to it. As painful as it might be to him, he'd pull back. After all, he'd done it before.

But, he quickly discovered, that was then and this

was now. It seemed as if a whole incredibly long lifetime had occurred in between.

In place of common sense and control, there was an insatiable insanity that was running riot through him, eagerly savoring every nuance of every kiss, every caress he delivered, every wondrous, silky inch of her that he touched.

Rachel wasn't sure just how it happened. Maybe it had to do with the complete reversal she experienced, going from the depths of an inky sadness to the utter dizzying heights of supreme joy.

Truthfully, she didn't know, couldn't even begin to reasonably speculate. All she knew was that there was this wild squadron of feelings, comprised of peaks and valleys that approximated the giddiness of riding a roller coaster going at top speed.

The only thing she could do was give herself permission to enjoy the sensations as they swept over her one by one while she held on by her fingertips.

Rachel and the man she had lost her heart to went from standing at her door to her sofa. There they assumed various positions while in the throes of the all-consuming passion that had seized them in its viselike grip.

From there they went onto other surfaces—the sofa, the floor—only half-conscious of doing so. Making the halting trip surrounded by a frenzy of heat as they tugged off each other's clothing, desperate for the sensation of bare skin against bare skin.

And all the while, Matteo's strong, full lips were branding her, bringing the ache that was within her up to a full, near-deafening crescendo.

She'd had no idea that a touch so gentle could still

be so provocative, so possessive. Though she kept it to herself, there was no question in her mind that at this very moment, on this page of history, Matteo *owned*—her. She was his from the moment his fingers skimmed along her flesh, no question, no doubt about it.

Rachel kept on kissing him, feeling as if she was never going to get enough of Matteo, never tire of trailing her lips along his skin. And when he returned the favor, she was certain that she was slowly becoming delirious.

She embraced the state, as long as he was there with her.

She was sunshine in a bottle—without the bottle, Matteo thought, unable to believe that what he was experiencing was real. That joy this pure actually existed.

He had never known lovemaking could be like this, had never known that he could *feel* like this. Because he seriously felt as if he could fly and touch the sky— but only as long as she was with him.

If he'd believed in magic, she, here like this with him, would have been the perfect example of it.

The exquisite tension was building up within his body, and he was aware that he couldn't hold back any longer. What it quickly came down to was that it was now—or never.

He chose now.

Matteo pressed her lightly back onto the sofa, then came to her, eager with still a drop of restraint left to him.

His gaze taking hers prisoner, Matteo whispered her name as if he were saying a prayer.

And then he made them one.

The subsequent rhythm that took hold of him captured her as well, and they rode the wave, dancing the eternal dance until they found their way to the very top of the summit.

The gratifying explosion quickly occurred. Fireworks covered them like a sparkling blanket with more than a small amount of euphoria in its weave.

He held on to the feeling for as long as was humanly possible.

Held on to her.

But eventually, the sensation faded back into the shadows, leaving them on the sofa, their bodies and souls entwined, their energy spent.

When he finally found his voice, Matteo quietly said, "I'm sorry."

Her eyes were shut, and she was in a half-dreamlike state. At the sound of his apology, her eyes flew open. She stared at him incredulously. Hurt formed just under her skin.

"For?" she asked, her voice hoarse as she prayed he could find a way out, a way not to shatter this feeling of happiness that was so new to her.

"For earlier. For this afternoon when I first opened the door." And then he summarized it and wrapped it all up with a big baby-blue bow. "For acting like an absolute jerk."

Rachel was extremely relieved. For a moment there, she had thought Matteo was apologizing for making love with her. For her part, she didn't think her heart could have taken that, his apologizing for making love with her.

"You're forgiven," she told him. And then she smiled. "I'd say that, on the whole, everything turned out pretty well, wouldn't you?" she asked teasingly.

"More than well," he agreed, nodding. "I'd even venture to use the word *excellent*."

Rachel considered the word. "Yes, it was," she agreed, then sighed contentedly. "It was excellent."

Matteo propped himself up on one elbow, looking down into her face. He enjoyed the view.

"If I wasn't as exhausted as I am, I'd be tempted to see if I could up the ante," he told her.

"Up the ante?" she repeated, not quite sure what he meant by the gambling term. "How would you go about doing that?"

"You know, see if I can beat my own personal best."

"Where I come from, we don't mess with a perfect thing," she warned him teasingly.

"Are you trying to tell me that I can't mess with you, then?" Matteo asked. There was a twinkle in his eye as he regarded her.

"I wouldn't dream of telling you that," she said, just as she turned her body into his.

"Oh, good," he said, brushing his lips along her shoulder ever so slowly. "Because, as it happens, I'm already dressed for the experience."

She laughed then, and the sound felt good as it echoed through her.

She felt good.

Rachel wasn't sure what the future held, but she

prayed that Matteo Mendoza was in hers and that she was in his.

That, she thought, would make for a totally perfect world in her estimation.

All she could do was hope.

Chapter Eleven

It took Rachel several moments to orient herself as she slowly emerged into a wakeful state. She didn't open her eyes immediately.

The events of the night before seemed to come racing back to her the second she was fully conscious, bringing a rosy glow along with them that filtered all through her. It had been a wondrous night, full of revelations, both about herself and the man she had been so strongly attracted to.

She wanted to wrap her arms around the sensation and hug it to her.

Wanted to hug Matteo.

Rachel turned toward him.

He wasn't there.

Sitting up in her bed, where last night's revelry had eventually brought them, Rachel pulled her knees up to her chest, hugging them instead. She just wanted to allow herself to savor the sensations that were sweeping through her like the tail end of a hurricane.

For the life of her, she'd had no idea that she could react as strongly as she had, nor feel this wild abandonment that had taken possession of her last night. She had been a completely different person with Matteo.

Slowly her smile began to fade as reality, dragging jagged-edged uncertainty behind it, began to wedge its way sharply into her consciousness.

Yes, last night had been wonderful in her estimation, but if it had been wonderful for him as well, why wasn't Matteo still here?

The place beside her where he had lain was cold to her touch. That meant that he had gotten up a while ago.

There were a lot of reasons for him to have left. She got that. And she would have even been fine with that if he had just told her he was going.

If he had just said goodbye.

But he hadn't.

And she couldn't think of a single reason for Matteo to go without either first waking her up or, barring that, leaving her some sort of a note, saying he had to leave. She didn't think she was being too unreasonable, asking for that. She didn't need pages of effusive writing. A couple of lines on a Post-it saying he had to go but he'd call her at the first opportunity he got would have been enough.

It certainly would have made her happy instead of fostering this empty feeling that was beginning to take hold of her very soul.

Suddenly entertaining a shred of hope, Rachel pulled back the covers and lifted Matteo's pillow, hoping that perhaps the note he'd written had gotten lost in the bedding. But it hadn't.

Getting up, she checked under the bed. She found the left sandal she'd lost almost a month ago and a pen she'd been looking for, but no note.

Neither was there one to be found on her bureau.

Or anywhere else in the room.

"Face it, Rach," she murmured under her breath to herself. "He didn't leave you any note."

And any hope that Matteo might still be on the premises, maybe making coffee or even breakfast for the two of them, was quickly yanked away from her when she stopped to listen for the sound of distant movement. A cabinet being closed, a chair scraping along the kitchen floor, *anything.*

There was nothing.

No telltale sounds, no noises to indicate that she wasn't alone in the apartment.

Because she was very much alone.

With a sigh, Rachel sat back down on the bed, feeling dejected, trying very hard to reconcile this disappearing act with the man she'd been with last night. The man who'd disappeared and the man she'd been with last night weren't even close to the same person.

Last night, Matteo had been kind, sensitive, passionate, loving and just about sweetest man who had ever walked the earth. He had been far more than anything she could have hoped for in a lover.

Today, with his disappearing act, he was none of those things.

Maybe he never had been any of those other things,

Rachel suddenly thought. Maybe it had *all* been just an act for him, a means to an end. Maybe what she had actually been for him was a feather in his cap, a trophy he could brag about because he had slept with the woman his brother had indicated that *he* wanted. And Matteo had slept with her when Cisco had not.

That was it, wasn't it? Rachel asked herself, feeling angry tears stinging the inside corners of her eyes. She was the prize at the end of the tug-of-war Matteo's father had told her that Matteo was forever waging with Cisco.

That had to be it.

Why else would he just disappear without a trace like this the morning after they'd made love? The only thing that made sense was that he felt he'd gotten what he came for. Once he had, he left. It was as simple as that.

And that made *her* a prize-winning fool, Rachel thought, feeling both ashamed and madder than hell.

What was *wrong* with her? she silently demanded as she went into her bathroom to take a quick shower. She was supposed to be smart enough not to be utterly blinded like that by someone like Matteo.

Good looks only went so far. Integrity and dedication were the real turn-on in her life, and apparently Matteo Mendoza had neither integrity nor any sort of loyalty to speak of. When she'd been at the top of her game, she would have seen through Matteo in a heartbeat. Instead, her heartbeat wound up blinding her to his flaws.

And now it was obviously time to pay for it, she thought bitterly.

Squaring her shoulders as she stepped into the

shower, Rachel attempted to give herself a pep talk. After all, she had already endured a great deal in her short life, uprooting herself and leaving everyone she knew—or *thought* she knew—behind. This was just another bump along the way.

"This, too, shall pass," she murmured under her breath, trying to think herself past the hurt she was feeling, even as the water from the shower head mingled with the tears that wouldn't stop flowing.

Although Matteo hated to admit it—even if it was only to himself—fear had made him leave Rachel's bed in the middle of the night.

Fear of what he might see in her eyes when she looked at him in the morning.

If he saw regret there—or even just a glimmer of regret—it would tear him apart. Better not to have been with Rachel at all than to see the regret that the deed had created and brought forth there in her eyes.

Doubts and uncertainty about what had transpired between them had crept in the moment the last of the breathtaking euphoria had finally receded, slipping away from him.

They had made love twice last night, and as impossible as it seemed, the second time had been even better than the first. The second time, he'd known what to expect, yet somehow it had still wound up being a joyous surprise because of the intensity that had woven itself in and through the familiarity that was there beneath the top layer.

But as with all good things, eventually that had faded into the shadows, leaving darkness in its place. Darkness and the specter of mind-numbing disappointment, the silent passenger who had ridden in during the night, ready to undermine every single thing that had happened the moment morning's first light seeped into Rachel's small, cozy bedroom.

Matteo knew only one thing for certain. That he had never felt like this before—fearful—because he'd never experienced this sort of a surging high before, one that grasped hold of him and just made everything a hundredfold better.

Lovemaking, when it occurred in his life, had always been, for the most part, an enjoyable activity. But it never bore any consequences, and the pleasure it brought would disappear into the past for him practically the moment it happened. Certainly within a few hours.

But from the first moment he had taken Rachel into his arms, he knew that this was going to be different.

And it was.

Because *she* mattered.

He'd thought he'd lost her before anything ever began because Cisco seemed so interested in her and because his brother had deliberately asked her out, moving quickly right in front of him. It was as if Cisco was rubbing Matteo's nose in the fact that if he wanted someone, all he had to do was snap his fingers and she was his.

Had Cisco asked her out like that because he was as taken with Rachel as he was? Or was it because Cisco saw how taken *he* was with Rachel and that was enough of a reason for his brother to try to steal her away?

He had no answer for that.

It was all so complicated.

Making love with Rachel should have settled things for him. Instead, it just confused them even further. Matteo felt perplexed, vulnerable and at a total loss as to his next step—if one was to even be taken.

He would have felt better about his course of action if he'd known for certain that Rachel would remain with him, that last night had not been a onetime thing but the beginning of a long relationship.

Matteo knew that he was in it for the long haul, but what if she wasn't? What if she had made love with him last night to get back at Cisco for taking her for granted?

Or maybe she made love with him because she felt sorry for him. That would have hurt worst of all, he thought.

All these thoughts and self-doubts had been assaulting him as he slipped out of her bed and gathered up his scattered clothing from the floor. Carrying them into the living room, Matteo quickly hurried into his jeans and shirt.

Then, carrying his shoes, he tiptoed out of the apartment and pulled the door closed behind him.

The click of the lock told him that he had taken an irreversible step. Even if he changed his mind about this and wanted to slip back into her bed, he couldn't.

The matter had been settled for him.

He had to move on.

Rachel desperately wanted to call Matteo, to yell at him; to ask him calmly why he had left her apartment so abruptly, without a note or anything; to tell him that she never wanted to see him again.

A hundred different conversations materialized in

her head, each one with a different approach, each eventually being shot down.

The only thing they had in common with each other was that the hundred different conversations all included the word *why?* in them.

She desperately wanted to know why.

By the time she had gotten ready and was driving to work, Rachel had managed to semi-convince herself that what had happened was really for the best. Not the night of lovemaking, but specifically her waking up to find him gone.

If, as she was now beginning to suspect, Matteo had just been there to get what he could from her and, once that was accomplished, he was just intent on moving on, then at least she was spared the agonizing decision she might have been faced with down the line. Namely, having to tell Matteo about her father. If they had remained together, she would have to explain her past to him, a past she was trying to divorce herself from.

She would have to tell him that she had left home because she had discovered her father had been living a lie, a lie he'd had his whole family believing in since the day she had been born. A lie he had perpetuated for her entire life.

Most likely the entire lives of all her siblings. None of them had ever acted as if they had discovered this massive cover-up her father had engineered to erase his tracks.

"This massive *lie*. Call a spade a spade, Rach," she lectured herself.

She felt that her father's secret shouldn't continue to be covered up any longer, but she didn't want to hurt her siblings or her mother. Every day that went by without his confession was another day he spent living a lie.

All those late nights her father had claimed to be at the office, working—they had been late nights, all right, but late nights spent perpetuating the legend of his life and indulging his appetites.

She was willing to bet on it.

It wasn't something she intended to make public, but in all honesty, eventually she would have to tell the person she was seriously involved with about this.

For now, of course, that was nobody, Rachel thought. Her heart felt heavy over the admission, especially when she tried to excise the very image of Matteo from her mind.

So far, that was *not* working.

She was relieved that at least for today, her workday began and ended in The Hollows Cantina. She sincerely doubted she would see any of the Mendoza men here. After all, Orlando lived in Horseback Hollow, so it was only to be expected that he would eat most of his meals at home. And now that his two sons were visiting him here, all three would undoubtedly eat at his house.

She was safe, Rachel told herself. She repeated that to herself probably a dozen times in the space of a few hours.

Even so, every time the front door opened, her heart would leap up to her throat and then take a while to settle down into place again.

At this rate, Rachel was fairly convinced that she was going to be a wreck by the dinner shift, if not before.

"So how is it going?"

The question, catching her off guard, came from Wendy Fortune Mendoza, who circled around until she faced her. Wendy, along with her husband, Marcos, owned the Cantina. It was their first real business venture together, opened after their changes to the Mendoza family's first restaurant in Red Rock, Red, proved to be such a huge success.

Wendy was checking on the Cantina's operations to make sure everything was running smoothly and no adjustments needed to be made. The Cantina was her and Marcos's baby, and as it had only been open for a few months, it was still in its infancy. She wanted to do whatever it took to make this restaurant a success.

Rachel looked at the woman, startled by her question. It sounded harmless on the surface, but was it? Wendy was a Fortune by birth. Did she suspect Rachel's secret? Was that the reason for her question?

Or was she asking about Matteo, about how it was going between them?

That seemed the more likely question. Wendy was probably asking because of her husband, who was also a Mendoza.

Rachel tried to be as vague as possible about what was—or wasn't—happening between her and Matteo without being rude.

"I really don't know," she told Wendy. "All right, I guess. It's too soon to tell. I don't know if there's going to be another one," she said, referring to a date, since that was what she assumed Wendy was asking about.

Wendy looked at her. "Another one? I doubt it. At least, not so soon."

She was right. Rachel's heart sank. "Then he's talked to you?"

"No, but he doesn't have to," Wendy replied. "Some things you just know. Maybe in a year or so, but not now."

"A year?" Rachel echoed, now thoroughly confused. "He expects me to wait a year?" Talk about being overly confident—

"Wait, what?" Wendy cried, staring at Rachel. "Who expects you to wait a year?"

"Matteo," Rachel said, more confused than ever. "Aren't we talking about your husband's cousin?"

"I thought we were talking about my husband's decisions about the restaurant." Wendy began to laugh at the obvious error that almost seemed to have a life of its own for a few go-rounds. "Perhaps we should start from the beginning," she suggested once she stopped laughing.

Rachel blew out a breath. A wave of unexpected relief washed over her. She really hadn't wanted to discuss—or even think about—Matteo right now. She smiled at Wendy. "Perhaps we should."

Chapter Twelve

Wendy tried again, this time being more articulate and specific in her questioning.

"What I was trying to ask you was how you think things are going *here* at the Cantina. In other words, do the customers appear to be satisfied? Do you think there's something that can be improved upon, or brought in, or eliminated from the menu that would make dining here a much more pleasurable experience for the customers?" Wendy paused for half a second, allowing her question to sink in before continuing, "I also want to know if you have any personal complaints about the working conditions here."

"Personal complaints?" Rachel echoed. While she could understand why the woman was interested in keeping the customer happy, she was more than a little surprised by Wendy's second question regarding her feelings about the state of the working conditions.

"Yes. Personal complaints," Wendy repeated with emphasis. "Do you find the work atmosphere here too stressful, too difficult to put up with on a regular basis?" She became even more specific by asking, "Is the assistant manager too demanding?"

"Julia?" Rachel asked incredulously.

Julia Tierney, the former grocery store manager, had lobbied strongly for Marcos and Wendy Mendoza to select Horseback Hollow as the site for their second restaurant. Her hard work had eventually paid off, changing many people's minds as well as making the case for this location to Marcos and Wendy. Julia was at least *half* the reason that the restaurant was built in Horseback Hollow and not somewhere else.

To show both their gratitude and their loyalty to someone who had been so instrumental in helping them, the couple had installed the former grocery store manager as their assistant manager at the Cantina.

Julia loved running the restaurant. Everyone who worked for her knew that.

"What can I say?" Rachel asked. "Julia's a great boss. If one of the girls calls in sick, Julia pitches in and takes her place. I've never seen her try to lord it over anyone. And no, I definitely have no personal complaints.

"As to your first question," Rachel continued, "from everything I can see, the customers seem very happy with the service and the actual meals themselves."

When the Cantina had opened up in June last

year, it had been regarded by some as too upscale for
their taste—a real "rich folks" restaurant—but after
a while, the detractors had come around. The atmosphere here was warm and friendly.

"I'd say that the customers think the food was excellent, the prices reasonable and the service—" here
she grinned broadly, lumping herself in with the rest
of the group "—exceedingly friendly and outgoing."

Rachel knew that there were still going to be those
few who would complain, but those were just hard-
ened malcontents who were never really happy unless
they could find fault with something. As far as she
was concerned, those people were to be disregarded.

"Thank you for being so honest with me and letting me pick your brain for a minute," Wendy told her.
The next moment, the co-owner drew a little closer
to her so that she wouldn't be accidentally overheard
by any of the other servers. In a lower tone of voice,
Wendy asked her, "Now, would you like to tell me
what the problem is with Matteo?"

The moment the man's name was mentioned, Rachel's nerves began jumping and doing somersaults
inside her.

"Problem?" Rachel repeated, trying her best to
look puzzled. "What makes you think there's a problem?"

Wendy's eyes met hers, as if to say *Oh, puh-leazze*.
But she allowed the young woman her dignity and
addressed the question seriously. "Because he was
the first thing you thought of when I asked you how
it was going. Has he done something to upset you?"

Rachel pressed her lips together, uncomfortable

with the topic. "I'd really rather not talk about it, Mrs. Mendoza."

"No need to be so formal, Rachel," Wendy told her. "You can call me Wendy. And as for the rest of it, I understand totally." She leaned her head a little closer before saying, "The Mendoza men can be utterly infuriating, and the worst part of it is that they don't even realize it.

"But they are worth the trouble if you have the patience to wait them out until they finally come around. I vividly remember what it was like, being your age and unsure of almost every move I made. Not only that, but my own family regarded me as a black sheep, never managing to see things through, bringing them only heartache and grief. It took a lot for me to turn things around. I just want you to know that nothing is beyond your reach if you want it badly enough." Wendy closed the topic for now, adding only, "I am available if you find you need to vent." With that, Wendy patted the hostess on her shoulder just before she began to walk away.

And then she abruptly stopped. Swinging back around to look at Rachel, she announced, "Incoming. Ten o'clock sharp."

For a second, Rachel had no idea what the Cantina's co-owner was saying to her. And then she realized Wendy was alerting her to the fact that someone was coming in, pushing open the front door.

Not just someone but *that* someone.

Matteo.

Rachel instantly stiffened.

Wendy's protective, mothering instincts rose to the

surface instantly. "Want me to stick around, be your wing lady?" she offered Rachel.

Rachel shook her head. "No, I'm fine, but thank you for offering."

She had left the old Rachel behind five years ago, when she'd left home and forced herself to become independent of her family *and* their money. She was not about to hide behind anyone for any reason, especially not because she was facing an uncomfortable situation. Dealing with that sort of thing was all just part of being an adult, and Rachel was determined not to slide backward.

Matteo hadn't wanted to come here this morning. But he knew that the longer he put this off, the harder it was going to be and the larger the specter of what was between Rachel and him would grow.

He needed to have this one-on-one with Rachel before his nerves became too great to handle.

Walking in, Matteo looked around the Cantina to see if he could spot her.

"Table for one?" the hostess at the front desk asked him cheerfully.

"Two," the deep male voice coming from behind him corrected the hostess. "Table for two."

Managing to hide the fact that he had been caught by surprise, Matteo swung around to look accusingly at his brother.

"What are you doing here?" he demanded. Cisco hadn't been there a minute ago. Nor had he seen his brother's car when he'd parked his own close to the restaurant a couple of minutes ago.

Cisco's grin was wide and charming—at least to

everyone but Matteo. "I thought you might like some company."

Matteo narrowed his eyes. "You thought wrong." He didn't want to cause a scene, but neither did he want his brother here with him. He couldn't say what he had come to say if Cisco was anywhere within hearing range.

"Nobody comes to a restaurant to be alone, little brother," Cisco told him. "That's what drive-throughs are for. Tell you what," Cisco proposed magnanimously, "my treat."

Matteo had no intentions of accepting his brother's money or being bought off with a plate of enchiladas. "I don't need you paying for me," Matteo retorted.

Cisco changed directions faster than a sidewinder making his way across the sand. "Okay, your treat. I promise not to order the most expensive thing on the menu."

While Matteo was trying to rid himself of his brother, the woman at the reception desk had beckoned over the closest waitress.

"I'll do that," Rachel told the waitress. She wasn't officially on duty yet and she wanted an excuse to see just what was going on between the brothers.

"Sure," the waitress said, stepping back.

Taking in a breath, Rachel made her way over to the reception desk. She picked up two menus along her route.

"Ah, we meet again," Cisco declared, his broad grin never wavering. "It must be fate, don't you think so, Matteo?" he asked glibly, turning toward his brother. When the latter made no reply, Cisco looked from him to the young woman, who then turned on her heel and began to lead them to their table. Stony silence accompanied them.

"Is it just me," Cisco asked, "or has the temperature suddenly drastically dropped? It's like there's an artic breeze blowing through here," he noted, still being annoyingly cheerful.

"It's you," Matteo bit off between clenched teeth.

This was like a nightmare. He'd come here to try to explain himself to Rachel as best he could. He didn't really expect her to believe him, but he wanted her to know that his leaving her bed before she was awake had nothing to do with her—at least not the way she probably thought it did.

But he couldn't say any of that if Cisco was right there, listening to every word he uttered.

Turning to Cisco as Rachel brought them to their table, he told his older brother, "I want you to get lost."

"Can't," Cisco replied glibly. "I know my way around too well."

Matteo should have known that there would be no cooperation coming from Cisco. "Then go somewhere else," he said.

Cisco made himself comfortable, sitting down first. "But this is the best restaurant in town, Mattie," he teased, "and I'm hungry."

Matteo had a solution for that. He struggled to hold on to his temper. He couldn't have a meltdown in public. That would make him look unstable in Rachel's eyes—and that was the *last* thing he wanted.

Looking at Rachel, he told her, "Whatever he orders—" he jerked a thumb in his brother's direction "—make it to go."

Cisco laughed drily. "Boy, you certainly don't make a brother feel welcome."

"There's a reason for that—you're not," Matteo told him point-blank.

Yes, at bottom they were brothers, and if called upon, Matteo would come to Cisco's aid and do a great deal for his brother, but right now all he wanted was to have his brother get up and go away.

"Lucky for you I'm not thin-skinned," Cisco informed him.

"Right, lucky. Order," Matteo instructed him, pointing at the lunch selections.

Cisco ordered, but he took his time about it, reading every description of every one of the different lunch entrees and specials the Cantina offered out loud. Only then did he make his choice: beef and bean enchiladas as well as a tostada salad.

"Is that your lunch," Matteo asked Cisco, "or the meal you intend to consume before you go into hibernation?"

"Just lunch," Cisco replied brightly. "I'm hungry— especially since my little brother's paying for it."

It was getting more and more difficult to hold on to his temper, Matteo thought. "What did I say about calling me that?"

Cisco's eyes crinkled as he grinned in amusement. It really was too easy, he thought, getting his brother's dander up. "Are you going to beat me up right here, in front of witnesses?"

Their eyes met and held for a long moment. Matteo did his best to get himself under control, refusing to allow Cisco to win the round. "Why do you do it?" Matteo wanted to know.

"Do what?" Cisco asked as if he really had no idea what his brother was talking about.

Matteo chose his words carefully, determined not to make himself look like a hothead—or an idiot. "Tear me down all the time."

Cisco regarded him in silence for a moment, then said something that Matteo hadn't been prepared for. "To get you to build yourself back up again. Every time you do, you're a little bit stronger, a little bit feistier, a little bit more confident than the version that came just before."

"You're crazy," Matteo accused him.

Cisco had just made that up on the spur of the moment, Matteo thought. His brother was a playboy. He always had been. To him, it had always been about winning the girl of the moment, the one he set his sights on. If Cisco thought Matteo was interested in her as well, all the better because the stakes went up. There was nothing noble about it.

"Like a fox," Cisco countered.

It never ceased to amaze Matteo how his brother always manipulated things to make himself come out on top. "That's not how I see it."

"And you're entitled to your opinion," Cisco said. "Doesn't make you right, but you're still entitled to your opinion."

And then Cisco easily slipped into his ultra-charming mode as he watched Rachel return to their table. The tray she was carrying had Matteo's order on it as well as Cisco's, which was bundled in a large, sturdy paper bag with the Cantina logo stamped on both sides.

"You have your breakfast," Matteo said the moment Rachel had once again left their table. "Now leave."

Cisco shook his head like a teacher whose lesson had fallen on deaf ears. "You really have to work on your social graces, Mattie."

Matteo looked his brother in the eye. "You have no idea how hard I'm working on them right this minute."

Cisco laughed, appearing genuinely to enjoy this exchange between them. "I get the message. Two's company and all that."

Matteo's eyes darkened. "Get out of here now," he ordered in a barely audible voice.

"Needs a little more work," Cisco pronounced, obviously still pretending to assess the effects of his handiwork on his brother, "but pretty good." With that, he took the supersize doggie bag and rose from the table. "See you around, Matteo."

It seemed rather inevitable that they *would* see each other around at some point, given all the Mendozas in town, but Matteo for one was going to work as hard as he could to keep their paths from crossing with any sort of frequency.

Because his trust for Cisco had eroded to nearly nothing by now, Matteo made a point of watching his brother not just walk away from the table, but leave the restaurant entirely.

Only when his brother was truly good and gone did he turn his attention to the reason he had come here in the first place.

Rachel.

She was all the way across the room, seating another table. He watched patiently, waiting until she finally looked in his direction in an unguarded moment.

The second she did, he raised his hand, calling her over.

Reluctantly, concerned about what he might say now that his brother was gone, she made her way over to Matteo's table.

"Is there something wrong with your meal, sir?" Rachel asked in the most detached, distant voice she could summon.

How did they get here after last night? The question nagged at him. Could there be this amount of animosity because he had left without a word? Apparently the answer to that was yes, he thought as he tried to surface above the guilt.

"No, there's nothing wrong with the meal. It's fine. What's not fine is the problem between us," he told her. "I came here to talk to you."

Rachel glanced over her shoulder to see if either Wendy or Julia was anywhere in the vicinity, watching her. They weren't.

"I'm sorry," she told him crisply. "I can't have any long conversations with the customers while I'm working," she lied. "It's against restaurant policy."

That seemed simple enough to circumvent. "Then go on your break."

As if she could just snap her fingers and have it happen. "I—"

"Please?" he added with such sincerity, it got through all the protective layers of indifference she'd been busy wrapping around herself ever since she'd woken that morning.

Rachel suppressed a deep sigh. She had every right to be angry at this man and just cut him dead every time their paths crossed from here on in.

So why did all her fine resolutions, all the promises that she had made to herself, just dissolve like so many soap bubbles dancing in the wind when he looked at her with those big, brown, contrite eyes of his?

Why couldn't she stand firm instead of melting like a scoop of ice cream that had fallen onto the concrete in the dead of summer?

"Wait here. I'll see what I can do," she told him, her voice strained. With that, she left his table and disappeared behind the rear of the reception desk. She was looking for Julia, who made up their weekly and daily schedules.

Rachel was gone for several minutes.

Long enough for him to think that perhaps she had said whatever she needed to in order to make an exit, and once she had, she had chosen to give him the slip. For all he knew, she might have told her boss that she felt sick and was, even now, on her way home, leaving him here with his food getting cold.

So now what?

Was he just going to sit here until doomsday, waiting for a woman who wasn't about to return? Just how many times did he have to be hit by a two-by-four before he moved out of range?

Taking out his wallet, he removed several bills and was about to leave them on the table to pay for both Cisco's meal and his own when he heard her voice. Rachel was talking to someone close by, a redhead who looked vaguely familiar. He'd probably met her at some family function or other, Matteo thought.

The next moment, he realized that Rachel was getting permission to take her break earlier than scheduled.

And she had done it because he'd asked her to.

It was a promising start, he thought.

Now, as she sat down and joined him, it was up to him to keep the promising start going so that it turned into something that bore fruit.

He crossed his fingers.

Chapter Thirteen

"All right, I don't have that much time," Rachel said.

She folded her hands in front of her on the table like someone who had resigned herself to getting something distasteful but inevitable over with, ideally as quickly as possible.

"You wanted to talk," she told him coldly, "so talk."

He had just the one chance to have this come out right, Matteo thought. One chance to try to make her understand why he had left her bed so abruptly last night. At the same time, he needed to word his reason in a way that wouldn't place him in too negative a light.

Some negativity was inevitable. He knew that. But he also knew that a balance had to be struck. If it wasn't, how could he expect her to consider having a relationship with someone who behaved more like an adolescent than a man?

No matter what was said to the contrary, most women wanted to be with bad boys and heroes. Wishy-washy and indecisive were not part of the description when women went looking for the man they would regard as their other half.

All he could be, Matteo thought, was honest with her and hope for the best.

"Last night," he began, his eyes meeting hers, "was without a doubt the singularly most fantastic night of my life."

Rachel wanted so *badly* to believe him. "If that's true," she said skeptically, "what happened to you? Were you kidnapped by aliens who refused to give you any time to leave a note, some kind of an explanation as to why you suddenly had to dash off into the night?

"Who *does* that kind of thing?" she demanded. "I'll tell you who. Men who don't give a damn about anyone's feelings but their own. Who are only interested in their own satisfaction—and don't care who they hurt as long as they get what they want."

Her eyes were blazing as she spoke, but there was still a tiny glimmer within her, maybe even less than tiny, that hoped he'd come up with something she could believe. Something that would make her want to forgive him.

She didn't want to feel this way about him—but what choice did she have?

"Are you finished?" Matteo asked quietly after a beat had gone by.

"Very," she retorted. She was a fool for thinking he could explain his actions away to her satisfaction, she thought in disgust.

She began to rise from her chair, but Matteo put

his hand on hers, silently pleading with her to remain where she was.

"Would it help to say I was very, very sorry?" he asked.

"No," she responded firmly. But then, because last night had turned her entire world upside down, Rachel willed herself to give him just a little more time to plead his case. "But it's a start," she said more magnanimously. "Go on."

He gave it to her straight. "I've told you I'm not very confident when it comes to women, Rachel. I wish I were, but I'm not. I'm not Cisco," he emphasized.

Why would he think that she wanted him to be more like his brother? "I didn't pick Cisco. I picked *you*," she reminded him.

Maybe he'd just won by default, Matteo thought. "But you did go out with him."

Was he going to hold *that* against her? Seriously? "Only one time, Matteo. Because he asked, and at the time, I had no reason to turn him down."

She had a point, and if the subject wasn't such a sensitive one for him, he would have backed her sentiments all the way.

Still, he needed to have something settled in his own mind before he put all this to rest. "So there's nothing between you and Cisco?" he asked.

Part of Rachel wanted to just get up and walk away without saying a word, making Matteo stew about the situation the way he had made her agonize over finding herself alone this morning, causing a stampede of self-doubt to come storming through her as she tried to figure out what she could possibly have done to cause him to leave like that.

But it was specifically *because* she had gone through all that herself that she couldn't make another human being go through the haunting uncertainty that she'd been dealing with these past few hours. So she *didn't* just get up and walk away.

Revenge was not part of her makeup. It never had been. She was better than that.

"No," she answered Matteo, "not in the way you mean." She saw the question in his eyes. So there would be no further misunderstanding, she elaborated. "Cisco is a charming *acquaintance*. Maybe someday he'll even become a friend, but that's it. Nothing more," she emphasized. With that, she glanced at her watch, as if she was running out of her allotted minutes. "Anything else?"

He had a feeling that he still hadn't managed to make her understand what it was like, living in his brother's shadow.

He tried again. "All my life, I've felt…well, out-shined, I guess, by Cisco." The shrug was partially hapless. "I think I might even have unconsciously used that as an excuse." He could see that she still didn't understand, not that he blamed her. He was having trouble coming to terms with this self-analysis himself. "Whenever I didn't get what I had set out to get, I blamed it on him rather than myself for not trying hard enough. It was easier that way, I guess, having a built-in excuse. Saying that Cisco was faster, better, smarter, handsomer." He blew out a breath, forcing himself to continue, "I used that as an excuse to avoid moving forward."

Rachel's eyes never left his. "You know that's not right, don't you?"

"What's not right?" he asked, confused. "Moving forward?"

"No, the part where you said Cisco was smarter, better, handsomer." Someone else might have said those things fishing for a compliment, but not Matteo. That much she knew about him. He was not full of himself in any sense of the word. And he obviously didn't realize his own self-worth. "None of that's true. You're all those things when you want to be."

It was on the tip of his tongue to discount her words, saying something to the effect that she probably felt obligated to compliment him for the sake of being polite.

But there was something about the way Rachel said it, the way she sounded, that made him pause. "You mean that?" he asked.

"I wouldn't say it if I didn't." A small, private smile curved the corners of her mouth and filtered into her eyes as she thought of the way they'd been last night. The way *he'd* been last night. Gentle, caring and then wildly passionate, bringing every fiber of her being to life. "I was there, remember?"

"I remember," he replied in a low voice that was overflowing with emotion. "I remember every single magical moment of it."

Reaching across the small table, Matteo took her hands in his. Looking into her eyes, he did something he wouldn't normally do. He went out on that very shaky limb, leaving himself totally exposed. He knew there might be a chance she would begin to have doubts the moment she walked away—unless he did this. "I need to tell you something."

"Talk quickly," she urged him, looking at her watch again. "My break's almost over."

Matteo shook his head. "This isn't something that I can say quickly." Granted, it was only one sentence, but he needed time to work up to it. What he had to tell her demanded that it have time before as well as after so the words, the sentiment, could be given the respect they both deserved and commanded. "Could I pick you up after your shift?" he asked.

Rachel had driven her car here, and there were logistics to take into consideration, but the bottom line was that he was asking her out, she thought. Asking her out so that he could get this—whatever *this* was— off his chest. She'd already made up her mind to give him another chance.

"Sure," Rachel replied. "I get off at six today."

"Six it is," he told her.

And then she hurried away.

Matteo whistled as he paid his tab and left the restaurant, a smile on his face.

"Judging by your smile," Wendy commented as Rachel passed the co-owner on her way to wait on a new table, "I see that my cousin has managed to redeem himself."

"He's working on it," Rachel replied.

The smile on her lips told her boss that she strongly suspected Matteo would manage to accomplish exactly what he set out to do.

"What's that?" Matteo asked, nodding at the very large paper bag Rachel was carrying when he met her in front of the Cantina six hours later.

"Your cousin's wife insisted I take this for you,"

Rachel told him, keeping a very straight face. "She said she thought you'd be hungry after having nothing but humble pie to eat this morning."

"Humble pie?" he repeated, not quite certain what the other woman had meant. Assuming that it was heavy, he took the bag with its carefully packed collection of small containers from her. He was right. The bag was heavier than it looked.

Rachel nodded. "It's a figure of speech, referring to—"

Matteo held up his hand. "I know what it is," he told her, cutting her explanation short. "What I'm wondering about is how she would even know anything about our situation."

He personally had less than a nodding acquaintance with the pretty brunette his cousin had married. For that matter, he knew only Marcos by sight. He doubted if he and the other man had ever exchanged more than a couple of words at any one time.

Had Rachel been talking to the woman, unloading—and perhaps even complaining—as some women were prone to doing?

"That's easy enough," Rachel told him. "Wendy saw you—and Cisco—at the Cantina this morning, remember?"

Matteo felt contrite. He should have known that Rachel wouldn't do anything to either compromise his integrity or embarrass the hell out of him in any way.

Mentally he apologized to her, silently promising to make amends.

"Now I do," he admitted. "I have to confess that when I'm around you, I have a tendency to forget a lot of other details—like how to breathe," he said, lowering his voice just for a moment.

She was not about to allow herself to get carried away with that imagery. It would be all too easy to do that, and she had to remain grounded, she reminded herself. After all, she wasn't exactly the best judge of character, now, was she? She'd thought the world of her father—and look how wrong she'd been about *that*.

So she made light of what Matteo had just told her. "You could try writing that in a dark, indelible marker on the inside of your wrist. That way you won't ever forget—and accidentally wind up asphyxiating."

He glanced at his wrist, as if momentarily considering her suggestion and envisioning something being written there.

"Indelible marker, huh? I think I'll just take my chances with my memory," Matteo said.

There was amusement in her eyes. "Just trying to help. You said you had something you wanted to talk to me about," she reminded him.

"We can get to it after dinner," he told her, nodding at the bag he had taken from her.

Rachel looked at him knowingly—and somewhat amused, as well. "You know you're just stalling, right?"

Matteo made no attempt to deny it. "Yes, but in the best possible way," he said glibly.

Mentally he crossed his fingers and hoped that she would understand and agree with his assessment once she knew what he wanted to tell her.

Rachel sighed with a touch of drama. "Wendy was right."

Maybe he *should* get to know Wendy better, at least while he was still in Horseback Hollow. She seemed to have considerable influence with Rachel. "Right about what?"

"She said that Mendoza men require a lot of patience." Taking the large bag back, she put it on the floor of the passenger side in her vehicle, then turned toward Matteo. "We'll each drive our own cars. You can follow me."

She told him that just in case he'd forgotten how to get to her apartment. She knew how easily bruised male egos became when asking for directions. Some would rather wander around endlessly than admit they needed help.

"To the ends of the earth," Matteo told her willingly.

"To guest parking at my complex will be good enough," she quipped, grinning as she thought over his words.

"Consider it done," Matteo told her.

His car was parked two rows behind hers. Moving quickly, he hurried over to it now and started it immediately, pumping the accelerator to give it extra gas. The car all but roared in response, ready to tear out of the parking lot like the proverbial bat out of hell.

That made two of them, Matteo thought.

He couldn't stop smiling all the way over to her place.

"Looks like Wendy had the chef pack a little bit of everything that was on tonight's menu," Rachel told Matteo, peeking into the bag once they were inside her apartment. She smiled as she looked up at him.

"I guess she thinks maybe you're in need of some fattening up."

He laughed shortly, helping Rachel unpack the various small containers and placing them on her kitchen counter for the time being.

"That makes it sound like I'm a Thanksgiving turkey that needs to gain some weight in order to make an acceptable meal."

"Not to worry," she told him, patting his face before moving to open the cupboard. "Nobody's going to be pulling on your drumstick."

"Well, there go all my plans for the evening," Matteo said, snapping his fingers.

"Those were all your plans?" she asked, amusement tugging at the corners of her mouth.

He looked at her significantly. He could feel his temperature rising just looking at her. "Well, most of them, at any rate," he joked.

They were both skirting around the real reason for his being here. She grew serious. "So what was it that you had to tell me?"

"Eating first, remember?" Matteo reminded her, taking down some of her dishes so they could empty the different containers and place them all on her table for a sit-down meal.

"Boy, you certainly know how to draw something out, don't you?" Rachel marveled, although she made no effort to get him to say whatever it was he wanted to tell her now. If it turned out to be something she didn't want to hear, she could definitely wait to have it out in the open.

"Think of it as a cliff-hanger," Matteo suggested, getting out her utensils. "Except people aren't hanging onto a ledge by their fingertips," he said when she looked at him quizzically. "It's more of an emotional cliffhanger."

"If you say so," Rachel murmured. Looking around, she checked to make sure she hadn't forgotten to put out anything Wendy had sent home with her.

Now who's stalling? she silently asked herself.

Satisfied that everything was out, she gestured for Matteo to take a seat. "Everything looks so good," she observed, still standing next to the table, "I honestly don't know where to start."

"I do," he told her.

"Where?" she asked, curious as to what out of the entire spread appealed to him most. She turned to look at him.

That was when he kissed her, softly brushing his lips against hers, sending her heart racing wildly.

"Does that answer your question?" he asked in a low tone.

His words seemed to dance along her skin.

Rachel didn't say a word, didn't trust her voice not to crack. Instead, she just nodded her head, her hastily gathered-up ponytail swishing to and fro to some inner rhythmic tune that only she was privy to.

When she could finally speak again, she uttered only a single word: "Yes." It was another couple of minutes before she could give voice to what she was thinking. "But when we finish eating dinner, you have to tell me what it is you wanted to tell me back in the restaurant. Do we have a deal?" she asked, putting out her hand to Matteo.

He enveloped it in his and shook it. "We have a deal," he agreed.

* * *

It seemed to Rachel that he was taking an inordinate amount of time finishing his meal.

Maybe it was her imagination, but Matteo seemed to be chewing far slower than a man of his age and energy should be able to.

"It's because of what you have to tell me, isn't it?" she finally asked. All through the meal, she'd ignored the elephant in the room, but now it was time to do something with the animal.

"What is?" he asked innocently.

"The way you're eating your dinner," she said, gesturing at his plate. "You're practically chewing in slow motion."

"Chewing too quickly results in people choking on their food." He was teasing her now—and maybe stalling just a little. If she took what he had to say badly, then it was all over. This was for all the marbles—or nothing at all.

"No chance of that happening," she assured him. And then, after giving the matter another few moments, she told him, "It's okay."

Now he actually *was* confused. "What is?"

"You don't have to tell me what you wanted to say earlier today."

He opened his mouth to speak, but she held her hand up, wanting him to hear her out completely before making up his mind or saying anything.

"If you've decided that you'd rather keep whatever it was to yourself, that's okay. I understand. I wouldn't want you to—"

"I love you."

Chapter Fourteen

Her eyes widened as she stared at Matteo across the table in utter disbelief. She was positive that she had imagined the whole thing, or at the very least, mis-heard him. Both sounded far more plausible to her than the words she'd heard coming from him.

Still, she had to ask, had to be sure. "What did you say?"

Matteo enunciated each word clearly as he re-peated, "I love you."

The three words shimmered in the air between them like carefully cut prisms in the morning sun. Matteo held his breath, watching her face, waiting to see her reaction.

Praying.

He had just risked absolutely everything. Had he made a complete fool of himself—or had he just won the biggest prize of his life?

Stunned, for a moment, Rachel couldn't think, couldn't speak. And then, afraid to allow herself to be swept up in what could turn out to be an impossible fantasy, she protested, "How can you love me? You don't even know me."

They had a difference of opinion on that, Matteo thought. "I know all I need to know."

"No, you don't," she told him in a voice so quiet it unsettled him.

"All right," he said, bracing himself. "Then tell me." He sincerely doubted that *anything* she had to say would change how he felt about her.

But she shook her head. Her father was still a very raw spot for her. Maybe someday it wouldn't be, but that day wasn't now.

"I don't want to talk about it."

Rachel was really making this difficult, he thought. Once or twice during their conversations within the past week or so, he'd gotten the feeling that she was hiding something. But given the woman he had come to know, he'd decided to shrug it off. After all, just how bad could it be?

However, the look on her face now gave him pause. He might as well get a couple of things cleared up and out of the way.

"Did you kill someone?" he asked Rachel out of the blue.

The question caught her completely off guard. "No, of course not."

"Then it can't be that bad," he concluded. The look in her eyes told him he was wrong in his assessment. He took into account who he was dealing with. Rachel had a tendency to magnify her own flaws. "Look, we've all done things we're not proud of, things we wouldn't exactly want to become public knowledge.

"But the important thing is that we get beyond it. That we learn from whatever we did in the past and become better people *because* of it. You're working as an intern at the Foundation—you're doing good work. *That's* the part that counts."

She wasn't convinced. He could see it. "Okay, what did you do that was so bad?" he coaxed her. "Steal someone's boyfriend? Cheat on your college entrance exams? Drive a getaway car? Come on, Rachel, you have to get it off your chest so that you can start healing."

Rachel's head jerked up at the mention of the getaway car, stunned and a little indignant.

"No, I didn't drive a getaway car," she cried, horrified that he could even think something like that about her.

"See, that's my point exactly. You're not so bad," he told her, lightly caressing her face.

That was a matter of opinion, she thought. Looking back, she definitely didn't like the younger version of herself, the woman she had been five years ago.

"I was self-centered and petty and shallow," she told him.

He was *not* taken aback. "It's called being an adolescent," he told her.

"And that doesn't bother you, knowing that I was like that?"

Matteo laughed, thinking that she was adorable— and that, more likely than not, she was going to save him from becoming cynical and withdrawn.

"Nope. The only important thing is that you're none of those things now," he answered.

They had gone out on only a handful of dates. How could he possibly think he knew her well enough to say something so flattering about her character?

"How do you know that? What you just said, how do you *know* that I'm none of those things?" She wanted so badly for him to say something to convince her.

"I just do," he assured her. "I gave you a lot of excuses about why I wasn't there this morning when you woke up, why I ran. Everything I told you was true, but the main reason I pulled that vanishing act was because I was—" and this was still difficult for him to admit out loud, but it *was* the truth, so he had to tell her "—well, scared."

"Scared?" she repeated. She couldn't see Matteo Mendoza being afraid of anything. It just didn't seem to fit. "Of what?"

His mouth curved just a little. "Of you."

"Me?" She stared at Matteo as if he'd lost his mind. "Why would you possibly be scared of me?" For all he knew, she was a simple hostess, a fledgling intern, while he belonged to a big, loving family that backed him in any endeavor he set his mind to.

He'd started this, so it was up to him to see it through and tell her the truth. "Because of the way you made me feel. Because I knew that I loved you. That gave you power over me," he pointed out, "and I didn't want you to have that power."

"Power?" she repeated as if it was a foreign word. "What would I want with power over you?" He had to be pulling her leg, she thought. "You're not making any sense."

"What didn't make any sense was my running out on you this morning, and I'm really, really sorry about that. You're the best thing that ever happened to me." He anticipated her protest and headed it off by saying, "And I'm not just saying it because Cisco was interested in you. You knocked me for a total loop the first moment I saw you—and that was *before* Cisco had ever made a play for you."

Rachel regarded him skeptically. It went without saying that she was extremely attracted to him, really *felt* something for him—which was why she knew it would hurt once he returned to Miami or moved on to wherever he was going.

The possibility of his remaining with her never even crossed her mind. She was certain that when this interlude between them was over, she would be left behind. The very thought of Matteo going away without her once she'd opened her heart to him made her ache fiercely inside.

"I think you should know that I don't plan to give up," Matteo informed her. "I'm going to keep after you until I wear you down." There was a hint of mischief in his smile. "I just wanted to give you fair warning." His eyes were practically dancing as he added, "How does that old saying go? All's fair in love and war, right?"

He knew very well what that old saying was, she thought. He knew far too much for *her* own good.

"You're going to regret this," she warned him so solemnly, it gave him pause and had him wondering all over again about the nature of the deep, dark secret that was eating away at her.

But Rachel would tell him when she was ready. He was confident of that. In the meantime, he was going to avail himself of her company and focus on the positive aspects rather than search for the negative ones, the way he always used to do.

She had improved him already, Matteo realized with a smile. And she didn't even know it.

"The only thing I'm going to regret," he told her, "is if you suddenly take off and vanish from my life without a trace."

She looked at him, startled. He'd practically described to a T what she had done to her family five years ago. It had taken her a while to make herself get in touch with her mother. Even then, their contact had been short and abrupt. She'd let her mother know that she was fine and that she was trying to find herself without relying on the aid of family money.

It wasn't really the truth, at least not entirely. But this way, her mother didn't worry that she had been kidnapped or was lying dead at the bottom of some ditch. Her behavior could be written off as typically rebellious rather than something worse. In her case, a reaction to discovering that everything she had once thought to be true was really a lie. A lie perpetuated by the father she had once worshipped and adored.

"What?" Matteo asked in response to the look on her face. "Was that what you were planning?" he wanted to know, thinking he'd accidentally hit the nail on the head. "To vanish? It's not nearly as easy as it sounds—and I'd look for you," he told her. "I'd go to the ends of the earth to find you if I had to."

She was about to laugh that off, but something in his eyes kept her from doing that.

Rachel looked at him for a long moment. Amid the lighter banter was a solid vein of truth. "You mean that, don't you?" she asked. "You'd really come and look for me if I suddenly took off."

Matteo nodded. "Now you're getting the picture," he told her.

She was silent for a moment, thinking over what he'd just said and carefully examining how that made her feel. She would have expected it to make her feel hemmed in, maybe even trapped.

But it didn't.

It had a completely different effect. Matteo made her feel as if she mattered. As if he wanted to keep her safe and protected. It had been a long time since she had felt that way. It was a comforting feeling, knowing that there was someone who cared that much about her.

She supposed she owed him something for that, for making her feel as if she was part of something, part of some*one*.

So she gave him just a sliver of information.

"My father's estranged from his family."

She'd learned that much, at least, during her research into her father's true background. For some mysterious reason, it seemed that he had turned his back on his parents and siblings and on who he really was. That was when "Gerald Robinson" was born.

"That's too bad," Matteo told her, sounding as if he genuinely meant it. "According to my dad, one of his brothers is like that, won't talk to the rest of the family for some reason, most likely because of an imagined slight he thought he'd suffered. Nobody can even remember what it was about or how it all started.

"I have a whole bunch of cousins I've never gotten to know. It feels kind of strange, knowing there's a number of people who are my family, yet I wouldn't recognize them even if I tripped over them on the street," Matteo told her. There was genuine regret in his voice.

Rachel said nothing, offering neither a comment nor any sort of condolences. He knew that was his cue to leave the subject alone.

So he did.

For now, he was focused on making her feel safe with him. Feeling safe involved knowing that she could relax around him and not worry about being unexpectedly interrogated about something she had no desire to talk about.

Matteo changed the subject. "That was a great dinner," he told her.

The fact that he was saying it to her like a compliment made her laugh. After all, she hadn't had a hand in preparing it. She'd just put it into her car and carried it into her apartment.

"I unpacked it all with my own little hands," she quipped.

"Hey, unpacking is important. It has to be done just right," he deadpanned.

She broke down, laughing. It felt wonderful as the tension slipped away from her. "You're crazy, you know that, right?"

Matteo surprised her by stealing one small kiss, then saying, "Sure I'm crazy. Crazy about you." He nodded at the squadron of empty plates all over the kitchen table. "Let me help you with the dishes."

The last thing she had on her mind right now was dishes that needed washing. He'd just brushed his lips against hers, behaving exactly as if they were a couple, comfortable with one another and having done things like that—casually stealing kisses—for years now.

If only that could be a reality...

Would you still want to steal kisses from me if you knew who I was? Whose daughter I was? And that I'm keeping all that from you because I don't want to drive you away?

She didn't want to think about the answer.

Matteo ran the tips of his fingers along her forehead, lightly—but firmly—smoothing it out. She looked at him quizzically.

"You're doing too much thinking," he told her. "Your forehead is furrowing again. You're forcing me to take action."

"What sort of action?"

"To keep you smiling, of course," he told her as if it was the only logical course of action.

"And just how do you intend to do that?" Rachel asked.

In order to keep her hands busy—and off him— she had turned her attention to arranging the dishes behind one another in the dishwasher.

Matteo took the rest of the dishes out of her hands before she had a chance to line them up. He put them back on the counter, his attention completely focused on her.

"Oh, I think I can come up with something," he

told her just before he took her into his arms. And then he kissed her again.

She had every intention of resisting, of blocking out the sensations that she knew would jump to the fore the second she let her guard down.

But it was already too late.

The very moment his lips touched hers, they also touched off a series of explosions within her, explosions that broke apart all the walls she had fooled herself into believing she could resurrect and retain against the onslaught of passions and sensations that Matteo seemed to draw out of her just with his very presence.

She was melting in the very spot where she was standing.

Her arms went around his neck, holding him closer, melding her body against his so that she could feel every delicious eruption at its conception as well as following it to its ultimate release.

Suddenly, the hours between last night and now, with all their insecurities and recriminations, completely disappeared as if they had never even existed, burned away in the fire that was being created by the two of them as they came together.

All there was, was now and the glorious endeavor of lovemaking.

Rachel abandoned herself to it, living in the moment and loving it.

As well as loving him.

For once, just for now, all her excuses vanished, and all that remained was the truth.

Whether it was going to set her free or imprison her remained to be seen.

Chapter Fifteen

"So, have you given any more thought to returning to Miami, Matteo?" Orlando asked his son.

They were flying in another shipment to the Fortune Foundation's new office. This would be the last one before this branch's official grand opening.

The surrounding sky was a perfect blue, the kind that could make a man forget his mundane, day-to-day annoyances and problems and lose himself in the majesty of the heavens as he soared, unencumbered.

Flying in this sort of a setting also made a man look at the bigger picture. It always had for him, Orlando thought.

Orlando glanced now at his son in the copilot seat. Who would have ever thought that small, sensitive young boy would have grown into the man he now saw sitting next to him?

The years were going by much too quickly, Orlando thought. He needed to make the most of them while he was still able.

"You trying to get rid of me, Dad?" Matteo asked, obviously amused at his father's phrasing.

"You know better than that," Orlando told him. "I would like nothing better than to have you all stay right here in Horseback Hollow. Yes, I know it doesn't have the kind of nightlife Miami has, but as you get older, you realize that there are far more important things in life than partying until dawn."

"I know," Matteo replied quietly.

Considering how imperative Matteo had made nightlife sound only a few weeks ago, his simple affirmation now surprised Orlando.

"You do?"

"Yeah, I do," Matteo said. "I've been thinking that it's time I decided what I wanted to do with the rest of my life."

This was beginning to sound very hopeful, Orlando thought. "And what did you decide?"

Matteo turned in his seat, looking at his father. "Dad, how would you like a partner?"

By nature, Orlando had always been a cautious man who didn't count his chickens until he'd watched all of them hatch. He needed more input before he declared this to be a victory.

"What sort of a partner?" he wanted to know.

"At the Redmond Flight School and Charter Service—specifically at the Charter Service branch of it." Matteo supposed he was taking a lot for granted. Just because he'd been hovering around his father, elbowing his way onto every supply run his father had made back and forth between Red Rock and Horse-back Hollow, didn't mean his father would be willing to accept his presence on a permanent basis.

"I'd like that fine, Matteo," Orlando told him, a smile covering his distinguished, handsome face. "Just let me run it by Sawyer and Laurel," he said, referring to the owners of the business. "Though I'm sure they'll be happy to have you."

"Good, because working with you will help me pay the mortgage on that ranch house I just put a deposit down on," Matteo deadpanned.

Orlando's mouth dropped open. "A ranch hou— When were you planning on telling me this?" he cried, stunned as well as delighted.

Matteo grinned broadly. "I just did."

"But I had to ask," Orlando pointed out.

"I just did it yesterday, Dad. I'm still getting used to the idea myself," Matteo told him. He nodded toward the controls. "If you're tired, I can take over, you know."

Orlando laughed, shaking his head. "Yes, I know, and I am not tired. You should know by now that flying makes me feel alive. It's good to have a passion," he pronounced with feeling. He slanted another glance toward his son. "Speaking of that, have you and that pretty girl with the two jobs resolved your problems yet?"

Rachel was the underlying reason why Matteo had decided to risk everything and change his entire life around. Considering that they hadn't even remotely discussed the future beyond one-week periods, he knew he was taking a huge chance.

No risk, no gain, right? he told himself.

Even though he's just shared some of his plans with his father, he wasn't altogether sure he wanted to discuss the romance aspect of his life just yet—beyond getting the older man to use her name rather than to refer to her as "girl."

"Rachel, Dad. Her name is Rachel."

Orlando nodded. "That's right, I forget. All right," he tried again, "have you and Rachel resolved your problems?"

Matteo still didn't feel he was up to discussing anything of such a personal nature just yet, at least not until he had some positive feedback from Rachel to work with.

"I really don't know what you're talking about, Dad."

On a roll, his father apparently couldn't be put off. "Of course you do. I did not raise any stupid children. Anyone can see that you care about this Rachel, and she certainly seems to light up whenever you are around. You want my opinion," he went on as if Matteo had just said yes.

"I think it's time for you to stop dragging your feet and do something about the way you feel." Orlando paused, then went a layer deeper. Who knew when another opportunity for a heart-to-heart with his youngest son would present itself? "This thing between you and your brother, it has to stop, you know."

Matteo *definitely* didn't want to talk about this. "Tell him, not me."

His father caught him off guard by saying, "I have. Cisco claims that he was only doing it for your own good."

"Jumping the gun and asking Rachel out before I

got the chance was for my own good?" That was a load of horse manure, and both his father and brother knew it, Matteo thought.

"According to Cisco, he feels that it was his behaving that way that finally got you to make a move. Otherwise," Orlando continued, "Cisco believes you would still be standing at the starting gate, hesitating to take even a single step forward."

Matteo resented being second-guessed, even by family—and especially by someone he thought of as being far too smug. "Oh, he did, did he?"

"Yes, he did. And to be perfectly honest, son, I believed him when he said he did that for you," Orlando confided. "I know that Cisco is perhaps a little unorthodox—"

"A *little*?" Matteo echoed in disbelief. "He's the poster boy for unorthodox, Dad," he insisted.

Orlando frowned. His son had just given him good news, but it was all for nothing if members of the family were feuding or not talking to one another at all. He needed to have this feud nipped in the bud, before it became too big to handle.

"Matteo, I want you to settle things with Cisco," he said seriously.

Matteo was honest with his father. "I don't know if I want to be bothered, Dad."

For a moment there was silence, and Matteo thought that his father had dropped the subject, at least for now. He should have known better.

"If you don't," Orlando said quietly, "if you allow this, this *thing* between you to grow and fester, you will wind up regretting it for the rest of your life."

He gave his younger son a penetrating look. "Trust me, I know."

The level of emotion in his father's voice surprised him. Matteo looked at his father, wanting to ask questions, to find out just what was behind those words, but he instinctively knew that this was a subject that couldn't be touched upon, at least not yet.

Not until his father was ready.

His father, he could tell, was also waiting for an affirmative response from him. For the sake of family peace, Matteo surrendered.

"I'll talk to him," Matteo promised, even though it cost him to do so.

"Good boy," Orlando responded with a broad smile.

Matteo had promised his father to make amends, and he had never intentionally broken his word to anyone, but this time, he was sorely tempted to do just that.

No matter how confident he felt, whatever strides he'd taken, the moment he was in Cisco's presence, all that progress seemed to vanish. He suddenly became the awkward kid brother standing in his older, more sophisticated brother's shadow.

But a promise was a promise. He knew he at least had to try.

So once he and his father had landed the small aircraft and unloaded it, putting the supplies onto Orlando's waiting truck, Matteo forced himself to make a side trip to Cisco's real-estate investment office. His brother had surprised all of them by making arrangements to set up the storefront office temporarily.

He'd told his father that he wanted to test the waters in Horseback Hollow before deciding to make the move permanent. Matteo had a feeling that Cisco had other reasons for setting up the office, but that was his brother's business, and he wasn't going to pry.

Right now, Matteo wanted to get this so-called peace talk over with as soon as possible. This was something he definitely did not want looming over his head. He was well aware that the disagreement would only grow into unmanageable proportions if he allowed any amount of time to pass.

Even so, Matteo stood outside his brother's door for a moment, looking in and wondering if it was too late to turn on his heel and go.

And then Cisco looked up from his desk and saw Matteo through the bay window. The door on his opportunity to escape slammed shut.

Resigned, Matteo walked in. "I guess you've decided to settle in Horseback Hollow," he said, gesturing around at the office.

"Never miss out on what could be an opportunity," Cisco responded, then asked, "So, to what do I owe this unexpected pleasure?"

Having Matteo appear on his doorstep had caught him totally off guard, but he was accustomed to recovering quickly. In less than half a minute, he had gotten himself together and acted as if this was a regular occurrence between them.

Because of the way Matteo viewed their relationship, every word out of Cisco's mouth always sounded as if it was dripping with sarcasm to him.

But he was here, so he might as well give this a decent shot. "Dad thinks we should call a truce."

"A truce?" Cisco repeated. "Is there a war going on between us?" he asked innocently. He gestured toward the chair next to his desk. "Why don't you have a seat?"

Matteo would have preferred to stand, but for the sake of appearing genial and moving this along, he sat down in the only other chair in the room besides Cisco's. He sat on the edge as if ready to take flight at less than a moment's notice.

"You know there's a war," Matteo said pointedly.

Still maintaining an innocent expression, Cisco looked at him and asked in the same tone, "Are you at war with me, Matteo?"

Did he really think he could use this act to his advantage? "Actually, it's more like the other way around," he told Cisco. "You're the one who's at war with me."

"No, I'm not," Cisco told him. "I think I'd know it if I were."

Why was Cisco denying it? They both knew what Matteo said was true. "What do you call undermining me at every turn?"

"I call it lighting a fire under you—and it's not at every turn, just the ones I think are important," Cisco corrected his brother.

Did Cisco expect Matteo to be grateful for this? His brother had just admitted to manipulating him like some mindless marionette.

"So now you're a master puppeteer who's pulling the strings? And I'm what, your puppet?" Matteo demanded. The very thought of that was an insult to him.

The next moment, he told himself that meeting

Cisco like this to hash it out had been a bad idea. Better to let sleeping dogs lie indefinitely than to poke them with a stick.

For his part, Cisco appeared to take offense at what was being said, as well.

"No, you're my thick-headed little—excuse me—younger brother," he corrected himself, "who moves around like he's got glue in his veins and uses me as an excuse *not* to act on his feelings. All I did was goad you a little. Hell, Mattie, you and Rachel belong together. If I could see it, so could you. I figured if I acted as if I were interested in her, you'd wake up and snap to it instead of letting that girl slip through your fingers."

Matteo's head was spinning. Right about now, black was white and down was up. "So you're not interested in her?"

Cisco leaned back in his chair. "I'm interested in *every* woman, but not in a permanent way. If this one has caught your fancy, then you have my blessings. Enjoy." Cisco grinned knowingly. "If my instincts serve me correctly, you already have enjoyed her, haven't you?"

He held up his hand before Matteo could say something sarcastic in response.

"That was a rhetorical question. That wasn't poking around for an answer or any details," he assured Matteo. Pausing, he grew serious and asked, "It *is* serious between you two, isn't it?"

Matteo shrugged his broad shoulders. He still had to work a few kinks out. "I'm not sure."

Cisco shook his head. His brother was making this

way more complicated than it actually was. "You either care about the lady, or you don't," Cisco told him.

That was the only part Matteo was sure of. "Oh, I care about her, all right. I care about Rachel a great deal."

Cisco spread his hands, confounded. "So what's the problem?"

Matteo sighed, looking off into space. "It's complicated."

Cisco was not buying that. His brother was just using another excuse. "Only as complicated as you make it," Cisco told him.

Because this actually was beginning to have the makings of a truce, Matteo leveled with his brother. "I've got some misgivings."

"About her?" Cisco asked.

"In a way—yes, about her," Matteo said, changing his mind midsentence about just how far he wanted to take this.

Cisco looked genuinely interested. Ordinarily, he would have thought it was an act, but now he wasn't sure. "What kind of misgivings?" he asked.

Matteo told him what had been eating away at him almost from the start, when he'd asked Rachel about her family. "I don't think she's being entirely honest with me."

"About what?" Cisco prodded him.

"There's something about her family that she's not being entirely honest about."

That, to Cisco, was small potatoes. Definitely *not* something to cause a breakup in a promising relationship. And from what he'd picked up, Matteo and Rachel had all the makings of a promising relationship.

"Hey, little brother, Rachel's human. Everyone is entitled to have *some* secrets. Secrets keep you on your toes and make a person more interesting, if you ask me." He smiled as he said, "Oh, ye who are without secrets, cast the first stone."

Matteo frowned. "I don't want to cast the first stone—or any stone. I just want to feel that she trusts me and knows she can confide in me."

"Time, buddy," Cisco advised him. "That kind of thing takes time. But you and the lady will get there—just take it one step at a time. Show her that she can count on you not just when you want to be there but when she *needs* you to be there, as well."

It suddenly hit Matteo that Cisco was giving him some very solid, sage pieces of advice. "Where are you coming up with all this?"

"On-the-job training, Mattie. On-the-job training. Now, go and make me proud," Cisco urged him with a fond wink. "Oh, and I get dibs on being best man once you and she get around to tying the knot."

Matteo formed a fist and knocked on his brother's desk twice, as if to counteract a jinx. "If we ever finally do get to that point," he told Cisco, "the job's yours."

Cisco laughed. "I'll hold you to that."

Matteo had absolutely no doubt that his brother would do just that. And when it came right down to it, if this *did* turn out the way he hoped it would, then he definitely *wanted* Cisco as his best man.

But first Rachel had to say yes.

Rachel didn't know why she should have these butterflies crashing into one another inside her stomach.

After all, she wasn't going to be called upon to speak. Her boss, Christopher Fortune Jones, was. Her only function here was to be one of the well-wishers and enjoy the ribbon-cutting ceremony.

A substantial number of people had responded to the invitation to attend the ceremony. They gathered in front of the brand-new building that housed the latest branch of the Fortune Foundation.

In addition to all the people who would be working at the Foundation, the ceremony was being attended by some of the more important members of the Fortune family. There was Emmett Jamison, the former FBI agent who ran the Foundation these days, Lily Fortune, still a stunning, exotic-looking woman at sixty-nine, and James Marshall Fortune. James was the sixty-three-year-old family member who, Rachel had heard, had gone through such great pains to find his two sisters—he was one of a set of triplets and the only member of the family to have been kept as a Fortune, while the other two had been given up for adoption.

It was because of James's relentless efforts that Christopher's mother finally found out about her true identity.

Rachel looked at the faces around her, faces that belonged to members of the Fortune family.

Look at them all, she thought.

She didn't know why she felt such butterflies dive-bombing inside her. Was it anxiety causing this reaction?

Or something else?

A hush fell over the crowd as Christopher stepped forward. Wielding a giant set of scissors, the newly minted member of the Fortune family cut the ribbon in front of the building, signaling the official opening of the Fortune Foundation.

Once both sides of the wide red ribbon had gently floated to the ground, cries of "Speech" echoed throughout the crowd. Resigned, Christopher put down the scissors and reluctantly gave the onlookers what they asked for.

"I don't really have a speech," he confessed. "I'm not much good at talking to more than a couple of people at a time. But I just wanted to say that I still wake up in the morning and think that all this was just a dream. That James Marshall Fortune did not come into my life and the lives of my siblings and mother, and he didn't tell us that we were all part of the Fortune family—long-lost members he had finally tracked down.

"As you all probably know, I resisted at first, as did some other members of my immediate family, because we had the misconception that the Fortune family was made up of snobs who thought of themselves as being privileged. Boy, was I wrong."

Laughter met his statement, and he waited until it died down before continuing.

"I can't tell you exactly what it means to find out that you're a Fortune—I'm still learning about that part every day. But I can tell you that it comes with a warm feeling, knowing there's a network of people who have your back. A network of people you can always turn to if there's a problem.

"Being a Fortune means never, ever being alone, even if you think you are. I had to learn that the hard way because I resisted taking on the name, resisted the idea that I was part of them and they were part of me. But I'm not always bright about things. I do know, thanks to them, that you can never have too much family. Until my dying day, I will always be grateful that Uncle James has embraced all the Fortunes of Horseback Hollow. You have no idea what that means to all of us, Uncle James."

He addressed these last words to the man who had brought about this vast change in his life.

James nodded in response, a smile gracing his thin lips.

A wave of applause went up.

Rachel had tried, really tried, to stand there and smile as her boss talked about this rare gift that had been bestowed on him and on the members of his family. She'd almost made it through the entire speech intact, her eyes dry, her body almost rigid. She was determined that no one around her would guess the secret that she had been living with for the past five years.

But when Christopher continued to go on about what it meant to be a Fortune, and then turned toward James Marshall Fortune to sincerely thank him for embracing *all* the Fortunes—while she was standing out here in the cold, unrecognized and certainly not part of the actual inner circle, something within Rachel just gave way.

The dam broke. Before she could stop herself, she was crying. Tears were sliding down her cheeks. At any second, one of the Foundation's guests would notice and could very well start asking all manner of questions.

Questions she didn't trust herself to answer coherently right now. Feeling like an outcast, she was far too emotional to deal with something like that properly.

Rachel bolted, blindly running from the area and praying that she would be able to find someplace to hide until she could cry this out of her system.

Barring that, she'd just go home. She had made a grave mistake coming to the ceremony.

She didn't belong here.

Rachel was beginning to feel that she didn't really belong anywhere.

Chapter Sixteen

At the last minute, Matteo had come, along with his father, his sister, Gabi, and her new husband, Jude Fortune Jones, to take part in the dedication ceremony. Truthfully, he was paying far less attention than he should have to what Christopher was saying. Instead, he was busy searching the crowd for Rachel.

Which was why he saw her when she ran from the gathering. Surprised, he was quick to follow.

Within moments, it became obvious to him that Rachel's long legs were not just for show. She covered an impressive amount of ground in a short time.

He was really having trouble catching up to her. She zigzagged through the crowd, making a beeline for the perimeter. He had no idea where she was heading after that.

All he knew was that he had to catch her before

she disappeared on him. He'd caught a glimpse of her face from a distance and saw that she was crying.

He couldn't even begin to guess why.

But something was very wrong. He needed to get to the bottom of this, to make it right no matter what it took.

For the first time since they had initially gotten together, he realized that Rachel had the makings of a prize-winning runner.

If he was going to catch her, Matteo told himself, he was going to have to dig deep and really pour it on.

So he did.

Rachel didn't realize that anyone was running after her until she was more than half a block away from the Fortune Foundation building. The sound of rhythmic footfalls directly behind her registered in her brain. The sound was getting closer.

And then someone was catching her arm and pulling her around to face him.

Her heart thudded against her rib cage.

Matteo.

"Rachel, what's wrong?" Matteo asked, almost undone by the sight of tears. Every protective fiber of his being went on red alert. "You're shaking. And you're crying," he said needlessly. "Why are you crying?"

She didn't want to talk about it. She couldn't. He'd think she was being an idiot. But that still didn't take the pain away. "Dedication speeches always make me sad."

"Okay, you got that out of your system," he said, pushing the quip aside. "Now tell me the truth." He put a hand on each of her shoulders, just in case she was thinking of darting away again. "What happened back there to make you cry? What's wrong?"

But Rachel just shrugged, wishing he would drop the subject. "It's complicated."

He hadn't thought it was going to be a simple matter. "That's all right. I have all afternoon. And if that's not enough time, I can clear the rest of the evening, as well." He had no intention of leaving her side until she told him everything. She was in no condition to be left alone.

Rachel waved him away. "You won't understand," she told him.

But Matteo remained steadfast. His place was here, with her, even if she didn't know it yet. "Then *make* me understand," he told her. "Why are you crying?" he repeated patiently.

Matteo was not going to leave until she told him. She could see that in the set of his chin, the look in his eyes. He had a very sensitive, sensual face, but it could also be an exceedingly stubborn face, as well.

So she proceeded to tell him—and braced herself for either ridicule or annoyed dismissal.

"Because Christopher was going on about how James Fortune was embracing the missing branch of the family he'd discovered in Horseback Hollow and how wonderful everything was going to be."

Matteo still didn't see a reason for her to burst into tears. "What about that—other than being maybe a little bit syrupy?"

She avoided his eyes and looked at the ground as she said, "It's not true."

Matteo was doing his best to understand what

she was telling him and why she was so upset, but it wasn't easy. She was giving him middle pieces of the jigsaw puzzle without allowing him to see any of the defining corners.

"Then he's not embracing them?" Matteo asked, using the word she had repeated, since it seemed somehow important to the underlying matter.

"No, not all of them," Rachel told him, still avoiding his eyes.

Matteo hadn't heard anything about the patriarch turning his back on anyone, as she seemed to be telling him, but he refrained from saying as much to Rachel.

Instead, he asked, "Who's James rejecting?" When she finally raised her face to look at him, there was something there in her eyes, something she'd been hiding. A glimmer that suddenly flashed the answer to him. "You?" he asked her uncertainly.

The moment he asked, he knew.

It *was* her.

But how was that possible? She'd said her last name was Robinson. As far as he knew, that wasn't a surname associated with the Fortunes.

Had Rachel been lying to him all along? Was her last name really Fortune? But what reason would she have to hide that?

Try as he might, he just couldn't see her doing that. He would have bet any amount of money that Rachel *couldn't* lie. Lying just wasn't part of her makeup.

There was no point in hiding it anymore, Rachel thought. The other Fortunes, new or otherwise, wouldn't accept her as one of them, so making herself publicly known as a Fortune served no purpose there.

But it did here, between Matteo and her. She wasn't about to lie to him, the man she loved, even if part of her was afraid he'd turn his back on her because she'd kept this from him until now.

"Yes," she told him stoically, "I'm a Fortune—at least, I think so."

He had to admit, this nearly knocked him for a loop. "How do you know that?" he asked. "Wait, start from the beginning."

Taking her hand, he led her even farther away from the Fortune Foundation building. He was playing a hunch that if she went on a walk with him, talking might come more easily for her.

"The beginning," she repeated, as if to orient herself where that would be. "Okay. I grew up thinking that my father, Gerald Robinson, was this computer genius who started up his own company and made a ton of money while he was at it. He wasn't around all that much, and I thought it was his work that kept him away. Other kids' fathers were workaholics, so it was okay that mine was, too.

"Dad tried to make up for his absences by giving my brothers and sisters—and me—everything we could possibly have wanted. Private lessons in everything imaginable, expensive clothes." She paused for a moment as the irony of what she was about to say next got to her. "Whatever we wanted, we got. I realize now that he did that to make up for his guilty conscience—not because he was away from us, working, but because he was away from us…indulging in other things," she finally said as delicately as possible.

"Other things?" Matteo repeated. He wasn't sure he understood what she meant.

It took her a second to make peace with what she was about to share—and then she told him.

"Women. I think he was trying to fill some inner void. My dad was—and most likely still is—estranged from his family. I don't know why or how it started, but I got the feeling that they were the ones who turned their backs on him—although maybe it was the other way around. I don't know for sure. All I do know is that I feel like I've been living a lie all of my life."

"You're not the one who's lived a lie, Rachel. Your father's the one who did. He's the one who lied to you, not the other way around." Matteo could understand why she felt so disoriented, so rejected, and he didn't want her going through this alone. He was there with her all the way, starting from this moment on. "And you think that your father's really a Fortune?"

She nodded. "Just before I finally left home, I looked through some of his things—he was away again, as usual, and my mother was gone with some of her friends for the weekend. I found some correspondence addressed to a Jerome Fortune and a very old driver's license for the same name. The picture on it belonged to a much younger version of my father." She remembered that her heart had stopped when she saw the picture. At that moment, it was as if her life had literally turned on its head. "He's either got a dead ringer wandering around somewhere with his face—or my father is one of the Fortunes."

He still didn't see the problem. It could be so easily resolved, in his estimation. "If that's what you think, why haven't you said something to one of them? You see Christopher several times a week. You could have told him your suspicions. He might have helped you find out the truth one way or another."

She shook her head. The fewer people in on this secret, the better. "If I'm right, they didn't want my father. Why would they want me?"

"Are you kidding?" Matteo cried, stunned by her question. He stopped walking and turned to look at her. "I can't imagine anyone *not* wanting you." He gently pushed aside a few stray hairs from her face, lightly caressing her cheek. "I want you every minute of every day. I want you so badly, I can *taste* it."

Rachel found that she was having trouble swallowing. "You're just saying that," she whispered hoarsely, her eyes never leaving his.

"I'm *just saying* that because it's true," he told her. "I meant what I said the other day, Rachel. I'm in love with you, and I want to be with you. Forever. If you'll have me," he qualified. He didn't want her feeling that she had no choice in the matter—although it would kill him if she didn't want to be with him.

"Stop talking like that," she warned him. "Or you'll make me say yes."

"That's the whole idea," he pointed out.

There was a time when she'd bought into happily-ever-after, but now she wouldn't dare. There were too many obstacles in the way. She didn't want to believe him and then go on to have all her hopes dashed because he had come to his senses.

"You don't know what you're saying," she told him. "Besides, you're going back to Miami soon."

Once again, he surprised her by telling her, "No, I'm not."

Then he was staying here? With her? "Don't do

this, Matteo. Don't tease me like this." She didn't want to deal with more disappointment. She'd had enough to last a lifetime.

"If I was planning to go back to Miami, why did I put money down on a ranch house right here in Horseback Hollow?" he asked her innocently.

This was the first she'd heard of it. He hadn't even mentioned that he was *thinking* about buying a ranch house.

"You did what?" she asked, stunned.

"I bought a house." But he had more news than that to share with her. "And I'm going to be working with my dad at the Redmond Flight School and Charter Service." He grinned. He and his father had had a few rocky moments as well as differences of opinion on some matters, but now everything was stabilizing, and he had every reason to think things would continue on this even keel. "We've worked out the details."

"But what about the nightlife in Miami?" she asked, remembering that he had told her there was nothing like it and that he couldn't wait to get back to it. "You said you missed it."

"Not half as much as I'd miss you if I left," he told her with all sincerity.

He knew without asking that this was where she wanted to be. He might convince her to come with him to Miami, but she wouldn't be happy there. Besides, Horseback Hollow was growing on him, God help him.

"Miami nightlife will have to go on without me." He smiled at her. "I found something much better to do with my time—convincing you to be my wife. If you'll have me."

"Matteo—" she began.

He couldn't read her expression, which meant that he didn't know what she was going to say.

What he was afraid of was that she was going to turn him down, saying no to his proposal. Right now, he couldn't face hearing that hurtful word, so he began to talk quickly, hoping to steer Rachel's conversation in a slightly different direction.

"I want you to know I'm not going to pressure you," he told her solemnly. "You can take as long as you like to make up your mind."

Rachel tried again. "Matteo—"

And again he headed her off. "You don't have to give me an answer anytime soon, Rachel. Really. I'm good. I can wait as long as I have to in order to hear you give me the right answer."

"Matteo—" There was just a little bit of an edge to her voice this time.

"I'm serious," he continued, talking right over her. "You don't have to say anything now. We can go back to the ceremony like nothing's happened and—"

"Matteo!" Frustrated at not being able to squeeze in a single word, even edgewise, Rachel finally raised her voice to almost a shout so that it would be heard over his voice.

"What?" Matteo asked, fearing that defeat was tottering just an inch away.

He knew that she certainly hadn't had enough time to think this through yet. He needed time to convince her about this.

"Yes!" Rachel finally declared the second there was an iota of silence between them.

For a second, the word didn't register with Matteo, shimmering instead just on the outskirts of his comprehension. And then it hit him what she was saying yes to.

Or at least what he fervently *hoped* she was saying yes to.

"Yes?" he asked, almost hesitantly, watching her face intently.

This time Rachel nodded as well, her smile so wide, he thought he could just fall into it and stay basking in the wattage for a couple of lifetimes, all his needs met and answered.

"Yes," she assured him.

He had to be sure, crystal clear sure. "Do you mean yes, you'll marry me?"

"Of course I mean yes, I'll marry you—if you're absolutely sure you want me." Rachel still felt she had to qualify her words—just in case.

For his part, Matteo looked almost serene when he answered, "I have never been so sure of anything in my life."

"Then what are you waiting for?" she asked, clearly expecting something. "Aren't proposals usually sealed with a kiss?"

"You're right," he said solemnly. He was able to maintain that look for a total of five seconds before the smile came out. "What was I thinking?"

"That you want to kiss me, I hope," Rachel told him in a low, sultry voice that was meant for moments just like this.

He left nothing more up in the air, or to chance. Neither did he allow another second to go by without kissing the woman who had simultaneously conquered him and crowned him emperor of his world, of *their* world, all with the same breath.

"I have no idea what I did," he said, enfolding her in his arms, "to deserve this. To deserve you."

"Santa said you were a very, very good boy this year," she teased him.

"Remind me to give Santa a discount shipping rate for his annual run this year," he told her.

"Consider it done," she murmured just a second before her lips found his. "No more talking," she told him. "Just doing."

"No more talking," he agreed.

And, as always, Matteo Mendoza was a man of his word.

Epilogue

Battling the sweetest kind of exhaustion that a man could ever wish for, Matteo fell back on the king-size hotel bed in the throes of waning euphoria. With his last bit of strength, he threaded his arm around the woman who had so quickly become the center of his universe and drew her even closer to him.

"Wow," he gasped when he could finally suck in enough air to form words. "You've completely worn me out, woman. You keep that up and I'm not going to live long enough to make it to the wedding."

Grinning, Rachel turned her body into his, glorying in his sensual warmth.

"I'm afraid you brought that on yourself by being such a stud. But if you're having trouble keeping up, we could always postpone the wedding. That way, you can build up your strength."

"Postpone the wedding?" he echoed. "And risk you changing your mind? Not on your life." Running the back of his hand along her cheek, Matteo grew a little more serious. "How did I get to be so lucky?" he asked in a whisper.

Rachel's eyes crinkled. "Funny, I was just thinking the same thing."

"Now all I need is an unlimited supply of vitamins to keep up with you, and I'm all set." He tightened his arm around Rachel just a little more. "Tell me, what do you think about the summer?" he wanted to know.

Rachel pretended to think over his question seriously. "It's usually a little hotter, but in general, it's a nice season."

He laughed and shook his head. She was one of a kind, and he adored her. "I meant for the wedding, wise guy."

"Spring, summer, fall, today, tomorrow night, whenever you want to do it is fine with me." The important thing was that he loved her. Everything else was a distant second.

"We're going to need some time to get everything ready," he pointed out, nibbling a little on her shoulder. The woman had the sexiest limbs he'd ever come across. Everything about her just drove him wild.

"I'm ready at any time," she responded.

Any time did not leave time for all the trappings that went with a wedding. "The words *wedding gown, wedding cake, wedding invitations, reception hall* mean anything to you?" he wanted to know.

"Yes, headaches. They mean headaches," she underscored. "I don't need all that as long as I have you." And she meant that from the bottom of her heart. He was all she required for her happily-ever-after.

Matteo looked at her in amazed disbelief. "I thought it was always the woman who wanted something big and fancy."

She spread one hand, indicating herself. "You got the exception."

"So did you, I'm afraid," he countered. He liked the idea of a big wedding, of showing Rachel off to the entire universe. "My father is very traditional. He likes to see his kids get married with all the trimmings." Matteo paused for a moment, studying her expression. And then it came to him. "You're worried about inviting your family, aren't you?"

Rachel shrugged one shoulder in halfhearted semi denial. "Not worried, exactly, but it's been five years since I've seen any of them." What if they all turned down the invitation? She tried to tell herself it wouldn't matter—but it would.

"Don't you think it's about time to put that all behind you, start fresh?" Matteo suggested. "Clean slate and all that stuff?"

"Is that why you insisted on bringing me here to Austin?" She'd wondered about that ever since he'd told her that he'd booked a suite at the Hilton Hotel right outside Austin. Wondered and worried, as well.

"I brought you here because this is the best hotel I know of. The fact that it's located in Austin is just a coincidence. Not that I mind. Coming here lets me see the city that's responsible for raising a beauty like you." He felt as if her eyes were boring straight into him. "Why are you staring at me like that?"

"I'm waiting for your nose to grow," Rachel said with a perfectly straight face.

His expression, on the other hand, was seductively wicked. "I'm lying here naked next to you," he pointed out. "That's not the part of me that's being affected."

She laughed and kissed him, then raised herself up on her elbow so she could get a better look at his face. "I'm being serious."

"So am I," he said, cupping the back of her head and bringing her mouth down to his.

"I can't say no to you when you do that," she told him, her words escaping on a breathless sigh.

"Lucky me," he murmured just before he began making love with her again.

Bemused, so in love she could hardly stand it, Rachel feigned being asleep and watched her fiancé head to the shower through barely opened eyes.

Matteo hadn't bothered putting anything on as he left the bed. For the hundredth time, she thought to herself that he had a truly magnificent body, the kind that created goose bumps in its wake.

She was very, very happy and luckier than she'd ever thought possible.

The bathroom door closed. She heard the sound of water being turned on. She was tempted to get up and surprise Matteo by joining him in the shower.

But first she had something else to do.

Though he hadn't said it in so many words, she knew that Matteo had brought her back to the city where she had grown up for a reason. He wanted her to make peace with her father, to reconcile their differences because he felt that she wouldn't have any peace until she did.

He knew her so well, Rachel thought now, smiling as she pulled the blanket over her.

Drawing the hotel phone over to her on the bed, she pressed a series of keys on the keypad. She surprised herself as her father's cell-phone number came back to her so easily.

The pit of her stomach quivered a little as she heard the phone on the other end ring. It tightened into a complete knot when she heard the deep male voice say "Hello?"

"Daddy? Daddy, it's Rachel," she said. "I'm here in Austin. Can I come by the house? I need to talk to you." Rachel paused for a second, then added, "It's about the Fortunes."

* * * * *

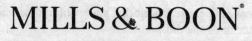
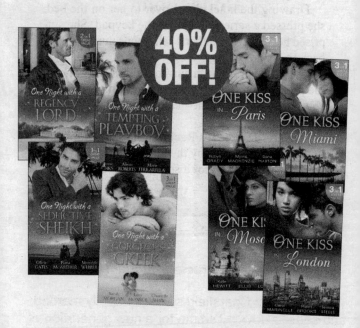

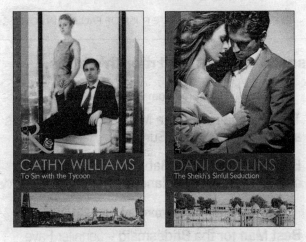

MILLS & BOON®

Cherish™

EXPERIENCE THE ULTIMATE RUSH OF FALLING IN LOVE

A sneak peek at next month's titles...

In stores from 20th March 2015:

- **The Millionaire and the Maid** – Michelle Douglas
  and **The CEO's Baby Surprise** – Helen Lacey

- **Expecting the Earl's Baby** – Jessica Gilmore
  and **The Taming of Delaney Fortune** – Michelle Major

In stores from 3rd April 2015:

- **Best Man for the Bridesmaid** – Jennifer Faye
  and **The Cowboy's Homecoming** – Donna Alward

- **It Started at a Wedding...** – Kate Hardy
  and **A Decent Proposal** – Teresa Southwick

Available at WHSmith, Tesco, Asda, Eason, Amazon and Apple

Just can't wait?
Buy our books online a month before they hit the shops!
visit www.millsandboon.co.uk

These books are also available in eBook format!

0315/23

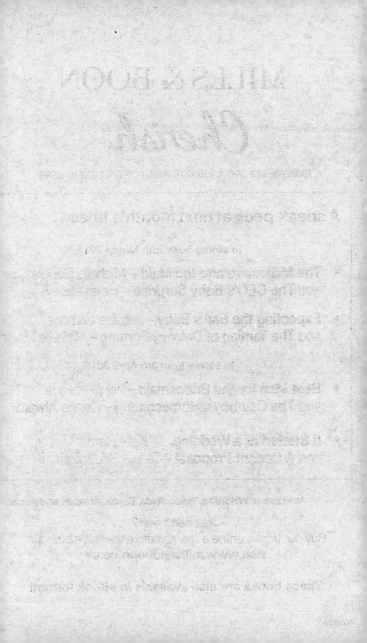